# The Bartered Bride

# Mary Jo Putney

# The Bartered Bride

BOOKSPAN LARGE PRINT EDITION

BALLANTINE BOOKS • NEW YORK

This Large Print Edition, prepared especially for Bookspan, contains the complete, unabridged text of the original Publisher's Edition.

A Ballantine Book
Published by The Ballantine Publishing Group
Copyright © 2002 by Mary Jo Putney

All rights reserved under International and Pan-American Copyright Conventions. Published in the United States by The Ballantine Publishing Group, a division of Random House, Inc., New York, and simultaneously in Canada by Random House of Canada Limited, Toronto.

Ballantine and colophon are registered trademarks of Random House, Inc.

ISBN 0-7394-2604-4

Manufactured in the United States of America

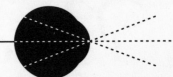

This Large Print Book carries the
Seal of Approval of N.A.V.H.

*To Tehila, Daphne, and Maytal—*
*Welcome to the clan!*

# Acknowledgments

For help with the Indonesian section of the book, my thanks go to Mandy L. M. Lee and her friend Rodney M. W. Lai.

Laurel Watson, Esq. and Susan Broadwater Chen lent their expertise to help me sort out the alarming complexities of the nineteenth-century British legal system.

Also, many thanks to my mayhem consultant, Laura Leone Resnick, for her explanations of the art of *pentjak silat.*

# END GAME

*The Tower of London,*
*Autumn 1835*

The stones of the Tower radiated anguish and despair. How many prisoners had paced these rooms, praying for escape?

As a nearby church bell tolled seven times, Gavin Elliott lay on his narrow bed, eyes closed. Soon he must rise and prepare for the trial that would begin today, but he preferred to hang on to the rags of a pleasant dream as long as possible. Transparent aquamarine water, white sand, Alexandra laughing with the vitality that made all other women pale by comparison.

Alex. The dream splintered and fell away. Wearily he sat up and swung his legs from the bed. The stone floor had the chill of death. Two warders were always posted in the room with him, ubiquitous as the stony chamber's cold drafts. He'd lived shoulder to shoulder with other men when he first went to sea as a common sailor, but he'd spent too many years as the captain, the owner, the taipan, to enjoy this return to constant scrutiny.

The door opened, closed again. "Your breakfast has arrived, sir." The warders were scrupulously polite. Not their fault the tea was prepared so far away that it was tepid by the time it reached the prisoner in the Bloody Tower.

Moving to the washstand, Gavin splashed cold water on his face to clear his mind, then shaved with extra care. It wouldn't do to look like a murderous villain today. The face in the mirror didn't inspire him with confidence, though. Grief, strain, and weeks of imprisonment shadowed his eyes, and years of sun and sea had left him with a weathered, tan complexion that Britons considered ungentlemanly.

The coat and trousers he donned were black for mourning. He wondered if his judges would consider that hypocritical.

The door opened again. The taller of the

warders, Ridley, mumbled a protest. The reply was much clearer. "I have permission."

Recognizing the voice, Gavin turned to greet the Earl of Wrexham. They'd come a long way since that first meeting in India seven years before. Kyle Renbourne had been Lord Maxwell then, a restless heir running away from his staid English life. Gavin had been in dire straits, a string of disasters having driven his trading company, Elliott House, to the brink of collapse.

After a night of talking and drinking they struck a deal on a handshake, and became friends as well as partners. That bond held even now that Kyle had inherited his father's honors, while Gavin was the scandal of London.

Kyle crossed the room, his long coat darkened with rain. "I thought I'd accompany you to your trial."

And in doing so, he'd make a public display of support. "Good of you," Gavin said gruffly, "but there's no point in tarnishing your reputation."

His friend gave a faint smile. "An advantage of being a lord is that it doesn't much matter what people think about me."

"It matters when one is assumed to be a murderer."

With a gesture, Kyle cleared the room of warders. When they were alone, he said, "The investigator has a couple of leads that might prove who tried to make you look guilty. Pierce or your damned cousin are capable of doing it."

Gavin shrugged into his coat. "It's easier to believe that I'm a murderer than that I'm the target of a vast, complicated conspiracy."

"You're no murderer."

"I didn't kill Alex, but there are other lives on my conscience. Maybe divine justice is catching up with me."

"Defending your life and protecting others isn't murder. The so-called evidence that you were responsible for Alexandra's death is absurd."

"It's strong enough to hang an upstart Scottish-American merchant." Especially a merchant who had angered powerful men. "Given the circumstances, it's not hard to build a case for me wanting to rid myself of an inconvenient wife."

"No one who saw you look at Alex would believe that."

Gavin's throat tightened. His friend was perceptive. "Even if I'm acquitted, it won't bring her back."

"Don't give up on me, damn it!" Kyle snapped. "There's no point in hanging for a crime you didn't commit."

The door opened and the warders returned, accompanied by four guards who'd come to take the prisoner to his place of trial. Surrounded, Gavin descended the tower stairs and walked out in the rain to reach a waiting carriage. Kyle stayed with him, his silent presence a comfort. In a world gone mad, at least one man believed in Gavin's innocence.

As the carriage left the Tower precincts, a group of onlookers shouted, "Wife killer!" and "Hang the bluidy bastard!" Stones rattled off the sides of the vehicle.

Gavin's gaze was caught by a group of three men, better dressed than the rest of the mob. The three who most wanted him dead. Barton Pierce, face weathered and expression like granite, who'd nursed his hatred for years. Philip Elliott, who had the most to gain if Gavin was hanged. Major Mark Colwell, who'd felt that only a soldier deserved Alexandra. Did any of them have triumph in their eyes? Impossible to tell in the rain—but all would dance on his grave when the time came.

He turned away from the window, expression grim. His life had begun spinning out of control the day he met Alexandra. Who could have guessed that his desire to help a woman in distress might lead him to the gallows?

# BOOK 1

# The Price of a Woman's Life

# CHAPTER 1

*The East Indies, Spring 1834*

The silence woke her. No screaming wind, no groaning timbers, no pounding waves trying to crush the ribs of the ship.

Scarcely able to believe the *Amstel* had survived the storm, Alexandra Warren carefully detached herself from her sleeping eight-year-old daughter, untied the ropes she'd used to secure them in the bunk, and stood. Every inch of her body felt bruised from the battering they'd endured. She had stayed awake for two days and a night, but finally fallen into exhausted sleep, cradling Katie protectively in her arms.

The porthole over the narrow bunk showed a lightening sky. Dawn must be close. The ship appeared to be anchored in a large, quiet bay surrounded by rugged hills. Eagerly she opened the porthole so fresh air could dispel the cabin's staleness.

The warm, spice-scented breeze caressed her face like a blessing. Alex gave a prayer of thanksgiving for their survival. Though she'd hidden her fear from Katie, she'd believed the *Amstel* was doomed, and that she'd never see England again.

At twenty, she'd been eager to accept Major Edmund Warren's proposal. Her father, stepfather, and grandfather had all been army officers, and as a child she'd followed the drum through the Peninsular Wars under the watchful eye of her mother. What could be more natural than to marry Edmund, both for himself and for the adventures she'd find as his wife?

Though Edmund had been a decent husband, the raw new land of Australia had offered more suffocating snobbery than adventures, and Alex had missed her home and family far more than she'd expected. Having a child had intensified that, for it saddened her that Katie had never met her grandparents, uncles, aunts, or cousins.

"Mama?"

Alex glanced down and saw a dark yawn open in the pale oval of her daughter's face. "I'm here, Katybird."

"The storm is over?"

"Yes. Would you like to look outside?"

Katie scrambled out from under the covers and stood on the bunk so she could see out the porthole. "Where are we?"

"I'm not sure. We were about two days southeast of Batavia when the typhoon hit." She smoothed her daughter's tangled blond hair, which had escaped from her braid as she slept. "There are thousands and thousands of islands in the East Indies—more than the stars in the sky. Some are civilized, some are filled with savages, some have never been visited by a European. But Captain Verhoeven will know where we are. He's a fine sailor to have brought us through the storm without crashing into an island."

At least, she *hoped* the captain would know where they were. He seemed a capable man. When the numbness from Edmund's death from fever began to wear off, Alex had been so impatient to go home that she'd booked passage on the Dutch *Amstel* rather than wait indefinitely for a British vessel. The merchant ship was bound for Calcutta via Batavia and Singapore. In India it would be easy to find passage home to England. Though the crew was much smaller than the navy ship that had taken her and Edmund to New South Wales, Alex and Katie had been treated well and the journey had been pleasant, at least until the typhoon hit.

"I'm hungry," Katie said wistfully. "Can we eat now?"

Alex was hungry, too. The galley fire had been extinguished as too hazardous during the storm. Even if food had been available, they had felt too queasy to eat. "I'll see what I can find in the galley. The cook may already be up and preparing breakfast."

Since Alex had slept in her clothing, she had only to slip on shoes before leaving the cabin. The ship was still, except for the constant creak of wood and rattle of lines. The captain must have decided to give his hard-pressed crew the rest of the night off before assessing the damage.

The island was becoming clearer, though the surface of the water was obscured by patches of low-lying mist. Near the helm she saw the dark silhouette of the officer of the watch. From his height and thinness, she guessed it was the young Dutch second mate. She raised one hand in salute and received a respectful bow in return.

As Alex headed to the galley, a muffled splash sounded not far from the ship. She frowned. A leaping fish?

The sound came again. She scrutinized the mist, catching her breath when shadows slowly became recognizable as two praus—the long, narrow boats used by natives of the islands. Several times praus had been paddled out to the *Amstel* when the ship sailed near an island, eager to offer fruit and fish and poultry to crew and passengers. Alex had bought a doll for Katie from one woman.

But she knew these were no friendly traders. Not this early, and taking such pains to be quiet. Knowing the islands were infested with pirates, she raced to the mate, praying that she was wrong. "Look!"

His gaze followed her pointing arm, and he uttered a guttural curse. Bellowing a warning, he galloped toward the main hatchway to raise the rest of the crew. In the lead prau, a hulking Malay reared up and hurled a spear. It streaked across the water to bury itself in the young mate's throat. Alex gasped, paralyzed by the swiftness with which peace had turned into horror.

Abandoning secrecy, the praus leaped forward under maximum rowing power, accompanied by the deep, terrifying boom of war gongs. As they neared the ship, they separated to box the *Amstel* in on both sides. Within a minute of Alex's first sighting, heavy hulls banged against the merchant ship, grappling hooks flew over the railings, and pirates began swarming aboard. She estimated that there were forty or fifty men in each prau—far more than the crew of the *Amstel.*

Aroused by the mate's shouts and the war gongs, sailors armed with cutlasses, pikes, and guns boiled up from the hatchway to defend the ship. The broad, powerful figure of Captain Verhoeven ran by Alex, pistols in each hand. "Below, now!" he roared in his heavily accented English. Without slowing, he fired one pistol. A tattooed pirate in a loincloth screamed and fell back over the railing.

Paralysis gone, Alex darted belowdecks. Halfway down the passage, Katie stood in the cabin doorway, her eyes enormous. "What's happening, Mama?"

"A pirate attack, but the sailors are fighting back. The captain says to stay here until it's safe to come out." Praying the attack could be beaten off, Alex ushered her daughter into the cabin and bolted the door. Then, hands shaking, she pulled her trunk from under the bunk and felt under the clothing until she found the box containing Edmund's pistol. Thank God she'd learned how to shoot as a girl. After loading the pistol, she perched on the edge of the bunk and put an arm around her daughter.

"What will happen to us?" Katie struggled to control a quaver in her voice.

There was no point to offering easy lies. "I don't know, darling. We must be prepared for . . . anything."

Menacing shots and screams sounded overhead, then a heavy splash. Alex stood to look out the porthole. One of the *Amstel*'s boats had been launched and crew members were frantically rowing toward the island. As she watched, another sailor dove into the water and began swimming clumsily toward the boat.

Appalled, she realized that the battle was

lost. More interested in plunder than murder, the pirates probably wouldn't bother pursuing the crewmen. But she and Katie were trapped in a cabin with a port-hole too small for escape. The best they could hope for was to be taken captive and ransomed back to their own people. The worst—she glanced at Katie and shuddered—was unthinkable.

She sat by her daughter again. "Have I ever told you how lovely it is to walk through green British hills on a magical, misty morning?"

"Tell me again, Mama," Katie whispered.

Alex recounted favorite memories until an impatient hand rattled the door, followed by a gruff Malay curse at the discovery that it was locked. More voices, then an improvised battering ram slammed into the door. As the planks shuddered under repeated blows, Alex cocked the pistol, aimed at the door, and tried to steady her breathing. "No matter what happens, Katybird, remember how much I love you."

"I love you, too, Mama." Katie pressed so close Alex could feel the child's beating heart.

The door shattered, jagged pieces flying into the cabin. Ducking his turbaned head, a huge, half-naked Malay with a wild black beard stepped inside. He carried a wicked, wavy-bladed kris dagger, and elaborate tattoos covered most of his visible skin. From his bearing and the richness of his ornaments, she guessed he was the pirate chief.

"Keep away," she ordered, trying to project authority.

"Drop gun," he said in a thick, barely intelligible accent.

Despairingly she acknowledged her helplessness, for one bullet wasn't enough to save them.

The chief advanced a step, his men crowding in behind him. She raised the pistol, the barrel level with his heart. At this range, she couldn't miss. "One more step and I'll kill you."

He smiled, revealing betel nut–stained teeth that had been filed to points. "Surrender—live. Shoot—both die."

Alex's pistol wavered. Her single bullet could be used to save Katie from assault or slavery. But dear God in heaven, she couldn't kill her own child!

Taking advantage of her hesitation, the pirate wrenched the pistol away. Uncocking it with the ease of familiarity, he thrust it into the waistband of his sarong. His eyes narrowed as he studied his captives. He was a barbarian, but his dark eyes were shrewd. His gaze judged Alex's face and figure like a farmer judging livestock.

She flinched back when one coarse hand caressed her cheek. While there was life, there was hope. She would demand they be ransomed. Her family was well connected, so she and Katie were far more valuable as hostages than as slaves.

The chieftain's hand moved to Katie's hair, golden in the early morning light. "Pretty." He reached to lift the girl from the bunk.

"No!" Clutching her daughter with both arms, Alex kicked at her captor.

Swearing, he dodged and her foot struck only his thigh. A hand motion brought two men forward to pin Alex roughly to the bunk while the chieftain swept Katie from her mother's arms. Panicky, Katie struck at him with her fists. "Mama! *Mama!*"

"Katie!" Frantically Alex tried to fight her way to her daughter. With contemptuous ease, the chieftain reversed his kris and struck her head with the hilt.

She was unconscious even before her screaming daughter was carried away.

# CHAPTER 2

*Maduri Harbor, East Indies,*
*Autumn 1834*

The island of Maduri was protected by dangerous shoals and forbidding volcanic cliffs, making the one good harbor even more welcoming. As the schooner *Helena* dropped anchor, Gavin Elliott's young first mate said, "It's a handsome city, Captain. I'd have thought Maduri would look more wicked."

Gavin grinned. Benjamin Long was a fine Yankee sailor with plenty of experience, but this was his first voyage to the East Indies. "The Islands are dangerous in their variety. There's no more beautiful place on God's earth, and none more treacherous. Some of the finest people you'll ever meet live here, and some of the most brutal. The islands that look civilized, like Maduri, are where you need to be most wary because it's easy to think the men who live here are like us. They're not."

Benjamin shaded his eyes to study the gleaming white palace that crowned the highest of Maduri's rugged hills. "The men are a little uneasy about coming here. The Portuguese carpenter claims that Sultan Kasan is an eater of souls."

"More likely a torturer of flesh, but he's a shrewd ruler who values trade. I've never heard of a Western ship being troubled here." Maduri was safe because anyone who broke the sultan's law risked being skinned alive, very slowly, or maybe roasted over a fire, but Gavin didn't mention that. Sailors were a superstitious lot. No point in disturbing them unnecessarily.

"There might've been no trouble in the past, but I don't mind admitting this place makes me uneasy, too." Benjamin's sober gaze followed a large, elaborately decorated prau rowing smartly toward them across the sun-splashed harbor. It was an official vessel, probably the local harbormaster and customs agents.

"We'll be here only a day or two. Just long enough to drop off our cargo and take on more provisions." Since Gavin had never visited Maduri, he'd been pleased when a shipping agent in Manila asked him to transport several small boxes consigned personally to Sultan Kasan. Given the shipping fee, they must be very valuable indeed, and the stop would take him only a few days off his planned route.

The remote island was a near legend in the East. Rich, powerful, and secretive, the sultans of Maduri refused to accept Dutch claims to rule the East Indies, and the Dutch were wise enough not to press the issue. Wild tales circulated about the people, the island, and most of all, the sultan. The stories were enhanced by the fact that foreigners were not allowed beyond a narrow strip of wharves and taverns. Like the Chinese, Maduri sultans did not want their people corrupted by Western ideas of education and free trade and justice for the common man.

Personally, Gavin liked subversive Western ideals. His gaze went to the American flag snapping high above. The *Helena*, named for the girl he'd married and lost too soon, was the fastest and loveliest ship in his fleet. The design was an enlarged version of the sleek Baltimore clippers, and well suited to the China trade. Good cargo space joined with speed and seaworthiness to form a vessel that could outrun pirates or ride out the worst typhoon. It also carried sizable guns, for only a fool sailed these seas unarmed.

He'd miss being master of the *Helena.* Though he'd started as a sailor, as his business grew he'd come to spend more and more time on land. When they left Maduri, he'd set his sails for England, where Benjamin would take over the *Helena* while Gavin established a London branch of Elliott House.

His operations in Macao and Canton were in strong, honest hands, as was his home office in Boston. London was the last great challenge, the mercantile capital of Europe, and the goal he'd set his sights on decades earlier. He would settle there and be a brash, upstart American who'd beat the London merchants at their own game, and settle some private scores as well. There would never be another Helena, but perhaps he'd meet another gentle lady he could love. And if anyone remembered his father or that Gavin Elliott had been born and bred in Britain before being taken to America, that would make his triumph all the sweeter.

It would be years, if ever, before he returned to the East, so this voyage was his private farewell. Though Britain and America were in his bones, he'd miss the brilliance of the Indies, the islands scattered across the bluest seas on earth like jewels tossed carelessly from a giant's hand. He'd miss China, too, where he'd spent much of his time in the last years, in his airy villa in Macao or the cramped foreign settlement in Canton, the source of much of his wealth.

His reverie was interrupted when the second mate came up to him. "Captain, the Maduris wish to give you a personal message."

Guessing they knew he carried a special shipment for the sultan, he approached the three men who'd boarded from the prau. Two looked like regular port officials, but the third was Chinese, not Malay. His dark hair streaked with silver and his clothing all of silk, he was clearly a man of authority.

Gavin inclined his head respectfully.

"Welcome to the *Helena,* gentlemen," he said, speaking the simple bazaar Malay which was in common use throughout the islands. "Your presence honors my humble ship."

To his surprise, the Chinese official replied in good English. "The honor is ours, Captain Elliott. I am Sheng Yu, chief minister of Maduri, and I come bearing an invitation from His Gracious Highness, Sultan Kasan."

Long experience enabled Gavin to conceal his surprise. How did Sheng know his name when he and his ship had never visited this port? And how did an American sea captain rate an invitation from a sultan? Granted, Gavin was also a successful merchant, a taipan, as the head of a trading house was called. But this invitation didn't fit what he knew about local customs. Maybe the sultan was just anxious about his precious boxes. "I shall be delighted to personally escort the sultan's cargo to the palace."

"That is unnecessary—I shall take charge of the cargo. His Highness's desire is for you to accompany me to the White Palace to dine and spend the night as the sultan's guest."

What the devil was going on? Clearly this invitation couldn't be refused unless Gavin was ready to sail away immediately. Well, he sensed no threat and he'd always had too much curiosity. "I am overwhelmed that such honor is shown to a humble captain. Pray take some refreshments while I prepare to go with you."

Gavin turned the Maduris over to Benjamin for hospitality and went to change into his dress clothes. This part of the world set great store by a rich appearance, so he'd had a Macanese tailor augment a basic naval uniform with blinding quantities of gold braid and flamboyant medals. The flat bicorn hat even had feathers. He had trouble wearing the outfit with a straight face, but it never failed to impress.

Before dressing he rang for Suryo Indarto, a Malay whose duties defied easy classification, though for convenience's sake he was called a steward. Suryo had been with Gavin for over a dozen years as a source of priceless information about the East, a teacher of the arts of Indies hand-to-hand fighting, and most of all, as a friend.

Soft-footed as a cat, the Malay entered the cabin. At sea he usually wore the sarong of the Islands, but in port he wore a dignified tunic and trousers of white cotton. "Captain?"

"I've been invited to spend the night at the White Palace and I want you to come, too," Gavin explained. "What should I know about Sultan Kasan?"

Suryo frowned. "Be careful, Captain. Kasan would not ask unless he wants something from you. He is called 'the Leopard of Maduri', and enjoys playing with people as a cat torments a mouse."

"What might I have that he could possibly want?"

"Perhaps he wants the ship. There is none other so fine in these waters."

Gavin belted on his ceremonial sword, which combined a chased and bejeweled hilt with an extremely functional blade. "The *Helena* isn't for sale."

"It is not easy to deny a sultan."

"Do you think that accepting his invitation is dangerous?"

Suryo considered. "No, killing a foreign

captain would be bad for Kasan's trade. But make no bargains with him. A leopard is a treacherous partner."

"Understood." Gavin unlocked a cabinet containing a dozen expensive European art objects suitable for gifts in circumstances like this. He decided on an exquisitely crafted music box that played Mozart while the enameled figures of an eighteenth-century man and woman revolved in a mock minuet. "Pack this and bring it along with a change of clothing."

One didn't go empty-handed to interviews with sultans.

By the time Gavin reached Sultan Kasan's huge, airy audience chamber, he'd observed abundant evidence of Maduri's wealth. He hadn't seen so much shining marble and gilded statuary since a visit to the Maharajah of Mysore in India. The rooms he'd been assigned were worthy of a prince. Cynically he decided the sultan must want something big.

A gong was struck, silencing the soft voices of several dozen courtiers who clustered along the walls of the audience chamber. In the hush Sheng Yu announced,

"Highness, allow me to present Captain Gavin Elliott, Taipan of Elliott House, master of the ship *Helena.*"

"Welcome to Maduri, Captain Elliott." Like Sheng, Sultan Kasan spoke excellent English. A tall, powerfully built man in his early forties, he glittered with silk and jewels. His massive throne was designed like a peacock-feather fan, and set with a king's ransom of dazzling blue, green, and purple gemstones.

Tearing his gaze from the throne, Gavin replied, "Thank you, Your Highness. I have heard many tales of the wonders of Maduri, but never thought I'd be fortunate enough to see them in person." He beckoned to Suryo who came forward with the polished walnut case that held his gift. "Please accept this trifle as a mark of my gratitude for the honor you do me."

Suryo removed the music box from its case and gave it to a servant who climbed the steps to the throne and knelt to offer the gift to the sultan. Kasan took the music box and studied it with approval. Gavin was about to demonstrate the key that wound the mechanism when the sultan figured it out for himself.

The delicately sculpted lord and lady began to dance as bright notes of Mozart spilled into the noon sunshine. The courtiers clustered along the walls of the chamber watched raptly, and even the sultan smiled. "A handsome gift, Captain. Thank you."

He wound the key twice more and let the mechanism play itself out before returning the music box to the servant who still knelt by his feet. Somehow the box slipped from the servant's hands and crashed to the marble floor. There was a gasp from the courtiers as the dancing figures broke off and skittered away.

Scowling, Sultan Kasan drew a short riding whip from his golden sash and struck the servant savagely across the face. The servant cried out, then bent his head in submission as blood welled from the gash in his left cheek. An inch higher and the whip would have destroyed his eye.

Unnerved by the casual brutality, Gavin realized the palace must be staffed by slaves, not servants. No man who worked for wages would accept such treatment from his master.

Tucking the whip back into his sash,

Kasan rose from his throne and descended the steps to where Gavin stood. This close, his dark eyes had the menacing glitter of a snake. "Join me outside, Captain."

Gavin followed Kasan through one of the arches that led to a broad patio where benches were shaded by clustered palms and flowers. Looking at the stunning view of the city and harbor, he said, "You speak English flawlessly, Your Highness."

"I speak Dutch and French equally well. My father brought tutors from Europe so I would learn the languages and ways of our enemies."

"Do you regard me as your enemy, Your Highness?"

"You are American, not English. Your people have fought two wars with England. The enemy of my enemy is my friend." At the right end of the veranda a spyglass was mounted on a post and swivel so it could be turned in any direction. The sultan stepped up to the eyepiece and trained the instrument on the harbor. After adjusting it, he gestured for Gavin to look through. "Your ship is a handsome vessel."

The image of the *Helena* sprang into Gavin's sight, so clear he could see Benjamin Long on the quarterdeck and a seaman in the rigging. He could even see the carved waves of golden hair on the figurehead, a soaring, angelic lady inspired by the real Helena. Suspecting Suryo's guess was correct, Gavin turned from the spyglass. "Thank you, Your Highness. The *Helena* is the jewel of my fleet." He hoped that conveyed that the ship was not for sale.

Apparently hearing what was unspoken, Kasan said with dry amusement, "You're a man who prefers directness, Captain. Why not say outright what is on your mind?"

"Very well, Your Highness. Why am I here, where few if any Westerners have been invited? Surely not for mere social pleasantries."

"You are correct. I don't want your *Helena,* Captain Elliott." The sultan gave a slow, feral smile. "I want your entire fleet."

# CHAPTER 3

Wondering if the sultan could possibly be serious, Gavin said, "My business is not for sale."

"I do not seek to buy, but rather to develop a partnership that will benefit us both. You have a reputation for great competence and impeccable honesty. Maduri is a rich island, and I wish to develop my trade with the world in a manner that will not damage my domain. That means I must employ an agent I can trust absolutely. A Western trading company that is not European."

"So you want me because I know Western markets and customs, but won't open the door to English or Dutch control."

"Exactly so, Captain. Are you interested?"

Gavin hesitated. There could be great profit in an exclusive trading agreement with Maduri, but he remembered Suryo's warning: *A leopard is a treacherous partner.* If Gavin agreed to Kasan's proposal, every one of his ships and sailors who came to Maduri would be a potential hostage to the sultan's erratic temper. "Your suggestion is intriguing, but I'm about to move to London to establish a new office. You need someone based in the East to watch over your shipping interests."

"You would need to spend much time on Maduri, but I do not think you would find that unpleasant." The dark gaze was compelling. "You are successful now, but I can make you a prince of the East, with wealth and power beyond your imagination."

Gavin had dedicated his life to building wealth and power, and yet . . . *a leopard is a treacherous partner.* "You have given me much to think about, Your Highness. I will need time to consider."

The sultan smiled charmingly. "That is why I have invited you to spend the night.

Let me show you the splendors of my city. Perhaps that will influence you."

A brisk walk through the sprawling palace brought them to a pair of waiting sedan chairs, which were better suited to the city's steep streets than a carriage. A company of smartly dressed palace guardsmen accompanied them on their tour. Gavin didn't see a single beggar, which was unheard of in any other city he'd ever visited. He wondered what was done with them, and hoped it didn't involve whipping or the severing of limbs.

The tour concentrated on the area around the harbor where the sultan owned all the warehouses, leasing space to merchants. Scents of sandalwood and tea and spices permeated the steamy heat along with the waterfront aroma of salt and dead fish. Less peaceful were batteries of large, modern cannon positioned to rake the harbor with their fire. If the British or Dutch tried to invade, they'd be blown out of the water.

The city had the potential to be one of the great trading centers of the East, but the more Gavin saw, the more uneasy he became. Kasan insisted on absolute control in his kingdom, and that would include any man who worked for him. In fact, Gavin suspected, the sultan was the sort who would revel in breaking a strong, independent man to his service. That price was too high no matter how much could be earned shipping and marketing the island's products.

After a visit to the shipyards, the sultan ordered the sedan chair bearers to return to the palace. Their route ran through a wide market square where a crowd churned around an open-sided pavilion. Gavin asked, "Is this an auction site?"

"Yes, and one of my most profitable enterprises. Come and observe."

The bearers lowered the chairs so the occupants could step out. As the Maduris recognized their ruler, a path opened through the crowd to reveal a platform where two men stood. The silence was absolute until Kasan gestured for the auction to continue.

Gavin's mouth tightened when he saw that the center of attention was a young Malay dressed only in a loincloth and chains. He stared above the crowd stonily as the auctioneer circled around, chattering in the local dialect as he squeezed the young man's biceps and clapped a hand on one muscular thigh.

"This is the largest slave market outside of Sulu in the Philippines." The sultan studied Gavin's expression. "You disapprove? Slavery is part of life. Though the British have outlawed it, your nation has not."

"It is a subject on which people disagree." Once in Boston Gavin had been discreetly asked about the possibility of carrying slaves illegally to the Caribbean. He'd thrown the enquirer from his office, and doubled his annual contribution to the anti-slavery efforts of the Quakers.

"Then we shall not linger." The sultan's words were polite, but his eyes showed amusement at his guest's discomfort.

The young man's sale was completed after brisk bidding, and he was led to a table where money and bills of sale changed hands. Sickened, Gavin turned away and saw the next "lot" being brought from a shed behind the pavilion—a tall woman with tangled dark hair, downcast eyes, and a crude gag bound over her mouth. A tattered sarong and shirt revealed filth and bruises, while chains rubbed raw patches on her wrists and ankles.

Seeing the direction of Gavin's gaze, the sultan said, "She's a handsome wench under the dirt, but the gag means she has a vicious tongue. Probably wild as well, or she wouldn't be sold at public auction like a kitchen slave."

For a man who had been raised to honor all women, it was unbearable to see a female humiliated like this. Feeling it would be cowardly to look away, Gavin forced himself to watch as she was led to the platform.

At the foot of the stairs a guard made a jeering remark and ripped the shirt half off the woman's torso, exposing a breast much whiter than her tanned face. Swift as a serpent, she grabbed hold of her wrist chains and swung them like a weapon, smashing the iron links across the face of her tormentor. The guard shrieked and fell back, his crushed nose spewing blood.

The woman's momentum whirled her around toward Gavin, revealing a gaunt face and raging aqua eyes. Dear God, she was European!

Recognition blazed in the woman's eyes. Dragging down her gag, she bolted toward Gavin. "Help me, *please!*"

Her cry was cut off when three guards

wrestled her to the ground. She fought ferociously, until a guard stunned her with a blow and the gag was yanked back in place.

As Gavin instinctively moved to intervene, the sultan's cool voice said, "The slave interests you?"

Reminded of the circumstances, Gavin halted, fists clenching. "Yes. How do I go about buying her?"

"I thought you didn't approve of slavery."

"I don't. I wish to set her free."

He realized his error when he saw the calculation in Kasan's face. By showing interest, he'd given the other man a dangerous advantage.

The sultan snapped out a series of orders in the local dialect. The guards bobbed their heads, then dragged the woman back to the shed where the slaves were kept until sale. She cast a despairing glance at Gavin before she vanished from sight.

Making his expression casual, Gavin asked, "May I speak to the seller? A wild woman must be of no great value, so we should be able to reach an agreement."

"It is forbidden to sell slaves to Christians," Kasan said. "But perhaps something can be worked out. Come. It is time to return to the palace."

Wondering if Kasan had just invented the law about not selling to Christians, Gavin silently returned to his sedan chair. He must bide his time until the sultan was ready to discuss the woman. But as the bearers labored to carry him up the steep hill, he couldn't stop wondering what her story was.

The banquet that night must have included half the nobility of Maduri, and it seemed endless. Gavin sat at the sultan's right hand, with Sheng Yu on his other side. The Chinese minister spoke pleasantly, but Gavin wondered how the man felt about the sultan showing such favor to a foreigner. He suspected that below Kasan's iron hand seethed a scorpion's nest of rival factions fighting for royal favor.

He drank the rice wine and ate the exotically spiced food sparingly as Kasan tested his knowledge and discussed how Elliott House might serve Maduri's needs. The sultan was extremely well informed and asked shrewd questions. Despite Gavin's doubts, he was intrigued by the thought of developing worldwide markets for the island. The challenges would be great, the risks and rewards even greater.

During a break in the endless courses of food, nine female dancers entered, lithe and elegant as young fawns. An island gamelan orchestra of mostly percussion instruments had been playing softly in the background, and now it shifted to a new, compelling rhythm. The women began to dance in slow unison. The sinuous movements and subtle hand motions were very different from Western dance, but any man could enjoy the grace and beauty of the performers.

Kasan asked, "Would you like a dancer to come to you tonight?"

Despite his years in the East, Gavin's Presbyterian conscience had never become inured to this kind of casual pandering. "Thank you, but no. I have much to think about, and will do it better without distraction."

"Your thoughts turn to the slave woman?" The sultan smiled lazily. He'd drunk a good deal of wine for a man who was nominally Muslim. While his speech remained clear, his edges became sharper as the evening advanced.

Glad the subject had been broached, Gavin replied, "As I said earlier, I'd like to buy her, but not as a bedmate. She didn't interest me that way." Uneasily he recognized that wasn't true. Even shabby and abused, she had been a striking woman. The kind who would always attract second and third looks from men.

"You are—what is the English word?—something of a Puritan, Captain."

"Perhaps," Gavin said, "but you seek honesty and hard work, and those are Puritan virtues."

"Touché." Kasan snapped his fingers, and the slave behind him gave his master a pair of twelve-sided objects about two inches square. Kasan rolled them in his hand. Carved of ivory, they had symbols etched in gold on each pentagonal facet. "Maduri has a unique form of dice. Do you care to test your luck?"

"We Puritans are not fond of gambling," Gavin said dryly. "Especially when we don't know the rules."

"The twelve-sided dice are very ancient. As a pair, they are used for gambling or divination. A single one is used in what we call *Singa Mainam.* The Lion Game."

Kasan tossed a die across the table. When it skittered to a stop, he said, "When a warrior wished to challenge his chief for leadership, he threw five times. Each symbol tests the strength, wisdom, or courage that a good leader must have. Swords or chess. Swimming or marksmanship. Diving or fighting the dragon. This symbol means unarmed combat. The hands of the gods determine what the challenger faced."

He gave another lazy smile. "You understand that this was long before Islam came to the Islands and we became civilized. But the Lion Game is still part of us."

Intrigued, Gavin said, "Maduri is surely unique among the Islands."

"And it will continue so. We will not become meat for European weapons." Kasan's voice was soft and deadly.

Thinking the man was both admirable and alarming, Gavin lifted his glass of rice wine in a toast. "May your land always be safe from European invasion, Your Highness."

Kasan smiled and lifted his glass in response, and the conversation became more casual. Nonetheless, it was a relief when the banquet finally ended. Wearily Gavin followed his guide through the corridors of the sprawling palace. He wondered if the guide was another slave. Probably. Why should the sultan pay wages when slaves were so readily available?

The subject turned his thoughts to the European slave woman again. Was she lying in some dank cell, praying that he might be able to help her? Or was she beaten and bloody and beyond hope? He hoped that Suryo might have learned something about her—Gavin had sent his friend to socialize with the palace serving staff and learn about real life in Maduri.

Gavin entered his rooms, and stopped in astonishment. A huge, hexagonal cage made of heavy gilded bars had been erected in the center of the suite's drawing room. And huddled in one corner was the slave woman.

# CHAPTER 4

Alex had finally dozed off in a corner of the cage, but she jerked upright at the sound of footsteps. Slavery had taught her that changes were seldom for the better, and she'd been frightened ever since guards brought her to the palace to confine her in this triple-locked cage in a strange, luxurious chamber.

At first, the dim light of the single lamp showed only the arrival of a tall, intimidating male. Then she recognized the European who'd visited the slave market. She'd begun to wonder if he was a hallucination, but he was real enough—a tall, powerful man with an air of command. Those gray eyes and the fair hair sun bleached to gold had to be European. She rose and crossed the cage, pressing against the bars as she studied him hungrily. The gaudy uniform wasn't British—perhaps German or Scandinavian.

She clamped down on her longing by reminding herself that being European didn't mean he'd help her. Though she had instinctively pleaded for his aid at the market, now that they were face to face she reminded herself that Westerners who frequented the far corners of the world were adventurers and renegades. Perhaps this one had asked the sultan for the use of the European slave woman.

No matter. Even if his motives were vile, he was her best chance for freedom, and she'd do whatever necessary to ingratiate herself so he'd help her.

The man halted with shock when he saw her. Glad that he probably wasn't responsible for her presence, she asked, "Do you speak English? *Parlez vous Francais?*"

"Both," he replied in English. "How did you come to be in my rooms?"

"I have no idea." Unable to repress her

bitterness, she added, "Slaves aren't usually told why things happen to them."

His expression tightened. "I'm sorry—that was a foolish question."

Though she'd repaired her battered cotton shirt as best she could, she was uncomfortably aware of how her breasts strained against the thin, worn fabric. She was larger than most Island women, and there had been no *kebaya* her size.

When his gaze reached her breasts, he looked away in embarrassment. She found that reassuring—a man with a sense of the decencies might be more likely to help her.

He stepped into the bedroom and returned with a neatly folded shirt. "Would you like this?"

"Oh, *please.*" He passed his shirt through the bars and she immediately pulled it over her head. The garment fell almost to her knees. Before rolling up the sleeves, she rubbed her face in the crisp white fabric. "This smells so good. So *clean.*"

He glanced around the cage, which contained nothing but her and a brass chamber pot. "Do you need anything else? Food or drink?"

She moistened her lips. Not having eaten

or drunk since early that morning, she'd spent her first hour in the cage staring longingly across the room at a bowl of fruit on a low table. "Water, please. And then . . . could I have some fruit?"

"Of course." He set the fruit bowl on the floor so she could reach through the bars to help herself.

While she peeled and ate a juicy local orange called a *jeruk manis,* the man collected pillows from a bench and pushed them through the bars. Gratefully she sank onto one. The last months had made her appreciate even the smallest of comforts.

"No water, only rice wine, I'm afraid." He settled on another pillow outside the cage, holding a bottle and two glasses. "Drink with caution. This is quite potent."

"Thank you." The rice wine went rather well with the banana that she chose, and she welcomed the spreading warmth that unknotted her tight muscles. She closed her eyes for a moment, reveling in the company of her own kind. "I'm sorry, I've forgotten proper behavior. My name is Alexandra Warren, and I'm English."

"I'm Gavin Elliott out of Boston, and master of a merchant ship." He noted her gaze.

"Ignore the uniform—it was designed only to dazzle."

An American? Not quite as good as a fellow Briton, but close enough. "Why were you at the slave auction?"

"Pure chance. Sultan Kasan wants my trading company to become his exclusive shipping agent, so he showed me his city."

She smiled cynically. "Did he also show you his pirate fleet? Probably not—I think it's on the other side of the island."

He stared at her. "The sultan owns pirate ships?"

"I'm not sure whether he is their chief, or merely allows them to use his island as a base in return for a percentage of their loot. In either case, dozens of pirate praus call Maduri home."

Elliott's expression turned forbidding. "I know that in this part of the world piracy is considered just another family trade, but I don't share that point of view. You were captured by pirates?"

"My husband was in the army, stationed in Sydney. About six months ago, after his death, we were returning to England when pirates attacked after a storm." She shivered. "It might have been better if we'd sunk. I tried to persuade our captors that we could be profitably ransomed, but they paid no attention."

"We?"

She clenched the bars separating them, knuckles whitening. "My daughter Katie was taken from me as soon as we were captured."

He caught his breath. "I'm sorry. How old is she?"

"Eight. Almost nine now." Alex thought of Katie as she'd last seen her. How much had her daughter grown? Where was she now?

"Eight," he said softly. "So young."

Seeing the compassion in his face, she pleaded, "Can you help me, Captain Elliott? If you will buy my freedom, I swear you'll be repaid twice over."

He frowned. "This afternoon I asked the sultan if I could do that, but he said that it was impossible."

So he had already tried, and failed. Bitterly disappointed, she asked, "Why won't the sultan allow me to be sold? I'm worthless. That's been beaten into me every day since I was captured."

"Sultan Kasan has a . . . a complicated mind. Since I haven't accepted his offer, he might want to use you as a means of persuasion."

"That's absurd. I am nothing to you." She reached through the bars for another piece of fruit. "Why should my fate make a difference in whether or not you agree to ship his goods?"

"It was obvious to him that I hated seeing a woman of my own people enslaved." Elliott's expression became thoughtful. "That must be why he had you placed in this room. If I was concerned with the fate of a woman I didn't know, I'll be even more concerned once we've become acquainted."

He rose in one lithe motion and circled the cage, testing the gilded bars. "This is bolted to both floor and ceiling and the door locks are formidable. With time and the right tools you could be freed, but there's no way it could be done tonight so I could spirit you off to my ship. All we can do is talk. Become friends rather than strangers." He shook his head with reluctant admiration. "Kasan is diabolically clever."

"So now I'm not only a slave, but a pawn." She wanted to weep with frustration at being utterly dependent on the goodwill of a stranger. Elliott seemed to be a decent fellow, but there would be limits to how far he would go to help someone he'd just met. She buried her face in her hands, close to despair. "To think that when I was young, I wanted to be a boy so I could have adventures! I should have stayed in England."

"Because of your daughter?" He sat again and replenished their wine glasses.

She nodded, fighting for control. "Katie is so bright and blond and beautiful. She was the happiest baby I've ever known. Now when I try to sleep, I hear her screams as that horrible pirate carried her away. I wonder all the time where she is. How she's being treated. How to get her back. If I ever escape this damnable place, I'll go to Singapore. Perhaps some army men will help because her father was a fellow officer."

"I'm sure they'll want to do whatever they can."

Hearing the reservation in Elliott's voice, Alex said tightly, "You must think I'm fooling myself to believe I'll ever see my daughter again. She's probably hidden in a rich man's harem, impossible to find. She . . . she might even be dead."

"It's far more likely that she's being treated well," he said comfortingly. "The people of the Islands are friendly and kind to children, and she's young enough to be adaptable. Though she was probably sold as a slave, surely she'll be cherished, both for herself and because a beautiful, blond girl-child is rare and valuable."

But Elliott didn't say that he thought Alex might see her daughter again. "I pray that you're right. Can . . . can you imagine what it's like to lose your child?"

After a long silence, he said, "A little. My wife died in childbirth, and our daughter a day later. We had named her Anna. She'd be about eight now."

Alex caught her breath, shocked out of her own grief. She'd been looking at Captain Elliott only in terms of how he might affect her plight. Now she saw him for himself. He was a few years older than she, somewhere in his mid-thirties, she guessed. Though his tanned face was forceful, there was also humor and intelligence, and the hard-earned wisdom of a man who'd lived a wide, full life.

He was also, she realized, strikingly handsome. It was a measure of her frayed mental state that she hadn't even noticed. "I'm so sorry about your loss, Captain."

He shrugged. "One learns to endure."

But the pain never went completely away—she could see it in him still. "You humble me," she said quietly. "I hope I don't have to learn such strength."

"You already have. You've survived six months as a slave, and are unbroken." He sipped his rice wine. "Have you been awaiting sale all these months?"

"This was my third sale." She rested her head against the gilded bars. "I'm not a very good slave. Two different men bought me for their harems because I was an exotic foreigner, then decided I was too unruly and rebellious to keep around. The second time my price was lower than the first, and as you saw, this time I was gagged to still my wicked tongue and consigned to a public market."

He gave a low whistle. "You're an indomitable woman, Mrs. Warren."

"Not indomitable. Desperate," she said flatly. "I fought so I could go after Katie. If not for her, I might have surrendered. It would have been so much easier." And safer. She would bear the scars of her intransigence for as long as she lived.

"Is Katie in Maduri?"

"A woman in the first harem, Amnah, asked some questions on my behalf, and was told that Katie was taken to a different island, but she didn't know which one. Katie could be anywhere." Alex paused to send a silent blessing to Amnah, who had been kind to a foreigner who was half-mad with grief. "But I will find her if I have to spend the rest of my life searching."

"No one should bear such a burden alone." Expression taut, Elliott reached through the bars toward her hand, then withdrew without touching her when she instinctively flinched back. "I swear that you will be free, Mrs. Warren. And I'll do my best to help you find your daughter."

She gasped, amazed that a near stranger would make such a sweeping promise when he scarcely knew her. But he meant every word—she could see that in his eyes. With swift insight, she recognized that losing his wife and infant daughter gave him a powerful need to save her and Katie. Though he hadn't been able to save his own family, aiding her might assuage some of the guilt and grief that haunted him.

Slavery had stripped her down to ruthless pragmatism. She wasn't proud of the fact that she would do anything to get Katie back, even use a good man's pain, but no matter. Pride had been one of the first things to go. "I'll keep you to that, Captain Elliott," she said unsteadily. "And God bless you for your help."

"How could I not help a woman in your situation?" Not even aware that he had just done something extraordinary, he rose to prowl the room, scanning the sumptuous furnishings. "I presume you're here for the night, so we must make you comfortable. This screen will give you some privacy."

He folded the carved sandalwood screen and slid it between the narrowly spaced bars. The spicy scent of the wood tickled Alex's nostrils as she pulled the screen inside, then positioned it to shield a corner of the cage from the view of the main door and Elliott's bedroom. "This is perfect. I can't tell you how much I've longed to have some privacy." Tonight she'd sleep behind the screen, and also use it to mask the humiliatingly public chamber pot. Modesty was another quality she'd had to surrender. "Thank you."

"What else do you need?"

"Is there a blanket or coverlet? It's getting rather cool."

He disappeared into the bedroom and returned with a folded square of *ikat* fabric richly woven in scarlet and brown. Gratefully she wrapped it around herself, appreciating its beauty and its warmth. "I'm going to spend the night in luxury. Thank you, Captain."

"Gavin." One side of his mouth quirked up. "Since we're sharing quarters, we might as well be less formal."

In normal society such a request would seem forward, but they were strangers alone together in a world far from home, and that created a rare kind of intimacy between them. "I'm called Alex by those who know me well."

He sat opposite her again. "Alex. It suits you."

"Actually, as a child I was called Amy. At fifteen I decided I wasn't an Amy anymore." She smiled as she reflected on simpler, happier times. "My middle name is Alexandra, which sounded so much more grand and grown-up. So I stopped answering to Amy, and soon everyone was calling me Alexandra or Alex."

His face lit with amusement. "You must have been a proper handful as a girl."

"I was. The result of wanting to be a boy, I suppose." Her amusement faded as she thought about the decisions that had brought her to such a dreadful situation. "Being around my mother wasn't always easy. I suppose that was one of my reasons for marrying a man who would take me away from England."

"Your mother is difficult?"

Alex thought of Catherine Kenyon, missing her so much she wanted to weep. The wine was weakening the defenses she'd built for survival. "Only because she's so . . . so perfect. The most beautiful woman in England, a wonderful mother, and so good and kind she was called St. Catherine when we followed the drum through Portugal and Spain. She made our life seem like a grand adventure."

"You grew up with Wellington's army? No wonder you found normal life tame."

"Since I didn't know anything different, I loved our life. It's only looking back that I realized how difficult it must have been for my mother. She was responsible for me and two servants, often without enough money or supplies, and my father going off with his troops for weeks at a time." There had also been her father's endless infidelities, but that was a topic that was never, ever referred to, even after Alex had become a married woman herself. "Once she and I were almost captured by bandits. She drove them off with a pistol. She did everything right, while I"—her voice broke—"I couldn't even protect my own daughter."

"You can't blame yourself for that, Alex," he said sharply. "When pirates attack a small, unprepared merchant ship, passengers are lucky to survive."

Again she swallowed back threatening tears. "You've been attacked by pirates?"

"Four times." He absently touched a faint, almost invisible scar high on his left cheekbone. "The first time I was just a boy. That's when I learned that a well-run vessel can never drop its vigilance. Later attacks, when I was chief mate and then master, didn't do much damage. I only hire captains who share my views on setting a good watch, and my ships are better armed than most merchant vessels. Though extra guns reduce cargo capacity, I've never lost a ship, and my fleet sails some of the most dangerous waters on earth."

So he wasn't only a captain, but owner of a substantial trading company. It was clear why Sultan Kasan wanted Gavin Elliott's services. "Were your parents Scots? Your accent is becoming steadily more Scottish."

"It must be the wine." Idly he swirled his glass. "My mother was from Aberdeen, the daughter of a Scottish vicar. I was born there. We lived in Scotland and England before my parents emigrated to America when I was ten."

"So you're British," she said, pleased that he'd been born in her own country. "A London lawyer told me 'once a Briton, always a Briton'."

"There's some truth to that. I've never forgotten my childhood home," he said slowly. "But America formed my mind and ideas. We have our problems, but the country isn't crippled by a class of arrogant, parasitic noblemen, as the nations of Europe are. A man can create himself in ways that are impossible in England."

She made a mental note not to tell him that she was closely related to several noblemen, some of whom had their share of arrogance. "Have you created yourself as a new man, Gavin?"

He smiled with a touch of humor. "I've done my best."

She divided the last of the wine between their glasses. "A good thing there's no more, or I'd be in danger of drinking too much. I'm surprised there's any wine at all, actually, since the Indies are Muslim."

"My Malay steward, Suryo, is my expert on the Islands. He says while Maduri is nominally Muslim, there is still a Hindu influence, as well as older, traditional beliefs. In other words, the Maduris worship Allah but like to drink." Covering a yawn, the captain got to his feet. "It's late, and we both need rest. There is much to be done tomorrow."

"Good night," she said, feeling safe for the first time in months. "And thank you."

He smiled again, this time with a warmth that reached across the room and eased her heart. His expression said that she was no longer alone. Gavin Elliott was not only kind, but perceptive. What a remarkable man.

As he withdrew to his bedroom, she stepped behind the screen and stripped off her sarong and *kebaya* before donning the shirt again. Lord, what luxury to have a clean garment to sleep in! If—when—she was free, she'd never take such things for granted again.

Drowsily she rolled up in the *ikat* and rested her head on a pillow, hoping her fatigue would allow her to sleep despite her excitement. Tomorrow, God willing, she would become a free woman. And all because of a stranger who, in one short hour, had become her hero.

# CHAPTER 5

Gavin awoke early, his fuzzy head making him wonder if he'd dreamed the previous night's encounter. No, it had been real—he could never have imagined a woman like Alexandra Warren.

He rose, shaving and dressing in his normal subdued style rather than the gaudy faux uniform. Since he would give the sultan his decision, he'd do it as himself.

Quietly he entered the main room. The gilded cage glowed in the dawn light, the sinuous patterns at top and bottom improbably pretty for a slave cage. Not seeing Alex, he circled the enclosure to make sure she was there. It wasn't impossible that the sultan could have had her removed during the night. But she was safely curled up behind the screen, her finely cut features relaxed in sleep.

Her strength amazed him. She'd spent the previous six months like a caged bird beating frantically against the bars of slavery, desperate to escape and find her daughter. Knowing how the loss of his own daughter haunted him, he could only begin to imagine how much worse it would be to lose an eight-year-old. He hoped to God that Alex would someday be reunited with her Katie, but the odds weren't good.

She sighed and rolled onto her back. The coverlet fell away, revealing that she wore only his shirt, which covered her only to mid-thigh. The sight of her bare, shapely legs was piercingly erotic, and struck him with the impact of a swinging spar.

After a dozen heartbeats, he wrenched his gaze away and retreated to the bedroom, shamed by his desire for a woman who was so vulnerable. Beautiful female slaves were not bought to be scullery maids, and Alexandra Warren had surely endured abuse and rape from her owners before being discarded as insufficiently docile. A lesser woman would be hysterical or paralyzed. Alex had been honed to pure steel. Though he couldn't undo the humiliations she'd suffered, he could honor her tacit desire not to discuss what had happened, and treat her with the respect she deserved.

He rustled through his belongings, deliberately making noise, before returning to the main room. "Alex?"

"Just a moment," she called.

He saw shadowy movements behind the screen and heard the sound of tearing fabric. Then she emerged with the bright sarong swishing gracefully around her ankles, and his voluminous shirt converted into a tunic. With her battered shirt refashioned into a sash that emphasized her slim waist, and one ripped sleeve tying back her unkempt hair, she actually looked rather dashing, if one overlooked the raw flesh that circled her wrists.

Keeping his gaze from following the deep V of the shirt's neckline, he offered his comb. "Sorry I didn't think of this last night."

"A *comb*." She took it reverently. "You are a saint."

"Hardly." He'd merely learned a few things during his years of marriage. "My steward, Suryo, should be here soon. He'll find you breakfast and anything else you need. He's a master forager. By this time he'll have made friends with the chief cook, the head groom, and the captain of the guard." And he would discover half the secrets of the palace in the process.

She untied her hair and began combing the tangled ends. The thick waves were brown, not black, with auburn and golden highlights that marked her as a European. "What happens next, Gavin?"

"I'm to join Sultan Kasan for his morning meal. I'll ask him again about allowing me to buy your freedom."

Quiet as a cat, Suryo entered the room, a basket in one hand. He showed no surprise at the sight of the giant cage or its occupant. After Gavin introduced the two to each other, Suryo bowed. "I had heard you were here, puan." *Puan* meant lady, as *tuan* meant lord. He opened the basket to reveal bread, rice, fruit, and a jug of hot tea. "Would you care to breakfast?"

"Efficient as always." Gavin poured some

light, sweet tea into a small cup and passed it through the bars to Alex.

She sipped the drink with a sigh of pleasure. "I suppose that everyone in the palace knows that a foreign woman is caged here like a wild beast."

"The kitchens of a king know all that happens in the palace," the Malay agreed.

Though the room offered no concealment for eavesdroppers and there could be few people in Maduri fluent in English, Gavin dropped his voice when he asked, "What do the sultan's people think about Kasan?"

"He is a good ruler, though perhaps not a good man," Suryo said slowly. "He can be cruel, and toys with people like a tiger toys with its prey. In his mind, he and Maduri are one, and he will be ruthless for his nation's sake. Though he is a great sportsman and gambler who loves to win, he respects those who have the skill and courage to defeat him. A dangerous man, Captain, perhaps a tyrant, but not a vicious madman."

That confirmed Gavin's own impressions, and offered guidance for dealing with the sultan. "If I refuse to work for him, will he strike me dead on the spot?"

"I do not think so," Suryo said seriously.

Gavin found that less than reassuring, but before he could ask more, one of the sultan's slaves appeared in the door and bowed deeply. "Captain Elliott," he said in bazaar Malay. "His Highness awaits."

Gavin glanced at Alex. Sounding as if she was trying to convince herself, she said, "There is no reason for him to keep me a slave."

Gavin hoped she was right. But his sailor's instinct for trouble told him it wouldn't be that simple.

A leisurely repast in a palace in paradise should have been relaxing, particularly with balmy tropical breezes wafting through airy rooms decorated with gilded statues and silk rugs that would be worth a fortune in the West. Nonetheless, Gavin was knotted tighter than a sailor's rope. Though neither he nor Suryo thought the sultan was the sort to kill a man for disagreeing, that didn't mean it couldn't happen if the sultan was feeling bloodthirsty today.

As the last course of fruit dishes was removed, Gavin watched a jewel-bright songbird swoop inside to steal a tidbit, then land on the head of a gilded statue. An ancient goddess of fortune, perhaps, since her outstretched palm held a pair of the twelve-sided Maduri dice.

He hoped the goddess would favor him today, since he'd need all the luck he could get. The lengthy private meal had confirmed that Kasan wanted Gavin not only as an honest trader, but a window to the West—an ambassador to represent Maduri's interests when dealing with Europe and America. He'd also discussed how much Elliott House would earn from the partnership. If Gavin accepted, within a decade he'd be rich beyond the dreams of avarice.

Kasan rose and beckoned for Gavin to walk through the graceful arches onto the terrace, which had a stunning view of the western end of the island. Gavin said, "This is a sight for a sultan, or perhaps the great legendary *garuda* bird of the Islands."

"Become my chief agent, and your villa will also be on this mountain."

His comment signaled that it was time for business. Mentally crossing his fingers, Gavin said, "I am deeply honored, Your Highness. But I cannot accept."

The atmosphere chilled noticeably. "Why

not?" the sultan asked. "Would your profit be insufficient?"

"You are generous beyond imagination," Gavin said truthfully. "But my mind and ambitions lie elsewhere."

"What ambition could be greater than to be a prince of Maduri?"

"Going to London is not merely an ambition. It is a matter of . . . settling scores that have haunted me for a lifetime."

Settling scores was something Kasan understood. "Settle them and return."

Changing his tack, Gavin asked, "Why are you so determined to have Elliott House as your agent? You have spent years studying Western trading companies, and surely there are others that will suit your needs."

"None so well as you." The sultan's eyes glinted with dark humor. "Your honesty and stubbornness are known throughout the East. I have considered other captains—the English Barton Pierce, the Dutch Nicolas Vandervelt, the French Foucault, among others. Good men all, but you are the best. Your allegiance is not given lightly, but if you pledge your loyalty I will be able to trust you absolutely."

Gavin's face blanked when he heard

Pierce's name. The weak link in an otherwise sound list of merchants. "There are other honest men."

"You are being less than honest now," Kasan said shrewdly. "What are your true reasons for refusing? Perhaps your objections might be overcome."

Gavin hesitated, knowing he risked infuriating his host, but he could not deny a request for honesty. "I accept that the ways of the East are what they are, but I can't ally myself with a kingdom where slavery and piracy are a way of life."

The sultan frowned, but didn't erupt in fury. "That is a very Western way of thinking. The British and Dutch are the world's greatest thieves and robbers, and your America has built its wealth on the backs of slaves."

"I don't approve of that, either, which is why I've always worked for myself rather than any government. To represent Maduri's interests to the world would violate my principles by saying that I condone slavery and piracy when there is profit for me."

"I admire principles, except when they interfere with what I want." Kasan smiled charmingly. "Where do your principles leave the woman?"

The knot in Gavin's stomach doubled in size. He'd wondered when the issue would arise; it wasn't as if Alex had appeared in his room by accident. "I beg your permission to buy the freedom of the English-woman Alexandra Warren," he said, praying the sultan would be reasonable. "I wish to return her to her family."

"She is not for sale, now or ever."

The response was what Gavin had feared most. "I shall pay generously."

"I am not interested in your gold, but your time, and that you refuse me."

Though Gavin had prepared other arguments, merchant instinct warned him that Kasan had dug in his heels and wouldn't listen. But how could he leave Alex Warren in slavery? For her to find hope, then have it snatched away, would make her captivity even more unbearable. "If you will not sell, will you barter?"

Surprised, then intrigued, the sultan asked, "What would you trade for her?"

Knowing that only a lavish offer had a chance of success, Gavin said, "I will trade my ship *Helena* for Mrs. Warren."

The other man whistled softly. "You desire her that much? I've never found a woman worth a tenth of that."

"I want her not for desire, but for honor's sake." Though it would hurt to lose the *Helena,* he could afford the loss, and build another, even better ship.

"Work for me and you can have the woman to do with as you will, but the only price I will accept is your service."

Gavin's jaw tightened as he realized he'd been cornered. He was more than ready to leave the East. Staying would frustrate the ambitions that had driven him for more than half his life. How much did he owe Alexandra Warren? He'd done his best to buy her freedom, offered the ship that was the pride of his fleet. Wasn't that enough?

He'd given her his word. And after last night, she was no longer a stranger.

He tried to think of a solution that would aid her without trapping him. He should never have let the sultan know he cared about her fate, but that had been impossible to conceal from the moment he'd seen her struggling against her captors. Now, because of his interest, she'd become a pawn in Kasan's game.

His gaze fell on the twelve-sided dice resting on the palm of the goddess of fortune. Inspiration struck. The odds were long, but if Kasan agreed, it might be possible to free Alex without pledging his future to Maduri. "Your Highness has a reputation as a great sportsman. Will you let me play the Lion Game over the woman's fate?"

Shocked, the sultan said, "You'd risk your life in the *Singa Mainam* for a slave? You are a brave, honorable fool, Captain."

"Not entirely. I won't attempt the Lion Game if it means certain death. Does it?"

"Death is possible, but hardly inevitable. While some of the tasks require warrior courage and skill, others test the mind, and two are activities in which men find great pleasure." Gorgeous and exotic in his flowing silks, Kasan paced along the elegant pointed archways that divided the terrace from the interior, his brow furrowed. "This would be a Lion Game unlike any other. Special rules must be devised."

Gavin folded his arms and leaned back against a pillar, wondering what he was getting into. "I don't even know the regular rules. You said five throws were made?"

The sultan nodded. "In a challenge for the

throne, you would have no choice but to accept each cast of the dice. However, one or two of the tasks would be unfair to ask a man not bred in the Islands, so I will allow you one refusal."

That seemed reasonable. "When a task involves competing with another man, who would my opponent be?"

Kasan's teeth flashed white against his black beard. "Me, of course. I will welcome the opportunity to battle an opponent willing to try to defeat me. Few Maduris would so dare."

"Would there be combat to the death?"

"No. I want you alive." The sultan obviously did not expect to lose.

"What constitutes winning? Completion and survival of the dangerous challenges, and defeating you in any that are direct competition?"

"Exactly." Kasan frowned. "A neutral judge is needed in case of dispute. I suggest Tuan Daksa, the head of the Maduri Buddhist temple, who is known for his wisdom and integrity."

Gavin wondered if that would give Kasan an edge before deciding to agree. He knew other Buddhist monks, and all had been fair-minded men who would make good judges. "I accept Tuan Daksa."

"If you win, the woman is yours to do with as you will. If you lose, you serve Maduri at my pleasure for the next twenty years."

The thought of giving up control of his life for so long made Gavin ill. "Five years only. Trying to plan too far into the future tempts fate." The sultan smiled like a leopard seeing prey. "Ten years. I will accept no less."

Ten years. Still a large chunk of his life, but he'd do no better. "Ten years, then. In return, whether I win or lose, Mrs. Warren is freed and you attempt to discover where her young daughter was taken after their capture."

Kasan shrugged. "Very well. I have no interest in her apart from the fact that your strange honor has tied you to her fate. Have we a bargain?"

For a moment Gavin contemplated the insanity of risking so much of his life to help someone he'd just met. But damnably, he could not turn away from a woman in need. His father had taught him that it was a man's duty to protect women, and that belief was as much a part of him as his heart and mind. Helena had laughingly called him her knight errant. "We do." He offered his hand. "I might win, you know."

Kasan's hard brown hand clasped his. "You will not, Captain." He gave his flashing, dangerous smile again. "But it's worth the risk of losing for the sake of such a grand game!"

# CHAPTER 6

It was hard to pace in an enclosure less than ten feet across. Nonetheless, Alex did her best during the hours Gavin Elliott was gone, trying to decide whether his prolonged absence was good or bad.

When he finally returned, she sped across the cage and clutched the bars, trying to interpret his expression. "What has happened?" When he hesitated, she said with a sinking heart, "The sultan won't let me be sold to you."

"Not exactly," Gavin admitted, "but he's giving me the chance to win your freedom by competing in a Maduri tradition called the Lion Game, *Singa Mainam*. A special twelve-sided die is cast five times, and I must attempt whatever feat is indicated. I'm allowed one refusal for something beyond my skills, so the odds of winning your freedom are rather good."

She stared, trying to absorb the information. "That is . . . bizarre. But then, my whole life has been bizarre ever since I was captured. What sort of tasks?"

"I'm not sure about all of them, but Kasan mentioned unarmed combat, swimming, diving, marksmanship, and chess." Gavin smiled a little. "One was called fighting the dragon. I haven't the faintest idea what that is."

"This sounds dangerous for you. Too dangerous."

"There are no duels to the death, so I imagine this Lion Game will be quite interesting, and no more dangerous than being a sailor."

Slavery had sharpened her ability to read people, and she recognized that Gavin was deliberately downplaying the dangers. Disturbed, she said, "It isn't right that you should risk yourself for my sake."

"I appreciate your concern, but this is the

way Kasan wants to do it. Neither you nor I have any choice in the matter."

Not true—Gavin could sail away at any time. Instead, he was choosing to stay and engage in some barbaric game to save her. "When does the contest begin?" she asked.

"Tomorrow morning. The sultan intends to make the event into a court festival. A Buddhist judge, crowds of courtiers, music, food, and drink." Gavin smiled. "Lions and Christians to amuse his people."

She shuddered. "I sincerely hope not."

"Actually, this is more like the labors of Hercules than a Roman arena, and Hercules survived quite well." Gavin tugged uncomfortably at his collar. "Do you mind if I remove my coat? It's a warm day."

"An understatement. Please, make yourself comfortable." She gestured to her sarong. "The native garments are so much more practical in this climate."

"It's a nuisance having to dress as a Western taipan all the time." He peeled off his dark tailored coat and loosened his collar with relief. "The best news is that I asked the sultan if he could trace Katie, and he's starting that immediately."

"Thank God! He's in a better position to

do that than I'll ever be." Alex folded onto a cushion, weak with relief.

Gavin crossed the room to stand in the breeze that wafted through the arches. "Do you need anything?"

"No, both Suryo and the palace slaves have been going out of their way to be helpful."

As a stronger gust passed through the room, she noted how his sweat-dampened shirt clung to his shoulders and torso, emphasizing the strength and fitness that were usually concealed. She couldn't ask for a better champion to fight for her freedom. Or a more handsome one. A woman would have to be dead not to notice how attractive Gavin Elliott was—but then, that part of her *was* dead. What mattered far more than his appearance were his kindness and his courage.

Turning from the window, he said, "I need to visit the *Helena* this afternoon to let my chief mate know what's happening."

She suppressed a stab of fear that he wouldn't return. "Can you spare a book for me?" she asked lightly. "Living in a cage is rather boring."

Recognizing what she wasn't saying, he said quietly, "You don't trust easily."

Her hand gripped a gilded bar as she remembered the days when trust had been natural. "I used to. I've . . . lost the habit."

He enclosed her hand in his. "It won't be much longer."

Warmth flowed from him to her, more emotional than physical. A little flustered, she said, "I'm beginning to believe that. You're a good influence. But . . ."

When her voice trailed away, he asked, "But what?"

"Even if the best happens—I'm freed, I find Katie unhurt, we return to England safely—I don't know how I can ever regain the life I knew. The only life I wanted." Despite the heat, she shivered. "If what happened to me becomes known, society will gasp with sympathetic horror, then fastidiously withdraw, afraid of being tainted. The shame of this will follow Katie her whole life."

"Your perfect mother—will she cast off you and her granddaughter?"

Alex thought of Catherine, whose arms were always open with welcome. "Of course not."

"Will your stepfather condemn you?"

She had to smile. "The colonel will have to be restrained from sailing here and personally administering justice to the pirates."

"Society begins with your family. If they accept you, the rest don't much matter." His hand tightened around hers. "Be grateful you have a loving, supportive family. Many people don't."

She realized that he'd said very little about his own relatives. "Do you have family, Gavin?"

"None that I know. My parents are dead. I have no brothers or sisters."

"I've got lots of family, so you can borrow some of mine," she said impulsively. "And you only have to take the nice ones, I promise."

"You're kind. Perhaps I shall do that when we reach London." He drew her hand through the bars and brushed a light, courtly kiss on her knuckles. "Everything will turn out all right for you, Alexandra. I feel it in my fey Scottish bones."

His confidence left her optimistic even after he left to go down to the harbor. The afternoon was long and boring, except when children peeped around the door and giggled. She tried to coax them in, not minding that she'd become an object of amusement to the children of the palace, but they were too shy to enter the room.

The bright eyes and cheerful faces reminded her of what Gavin had said about Katie's probable treatment in captivity. Even if she was never rescued, she might live a happy life here—she had a happy nature—but Alex wanted to be the one to guide and guard her daughter. No stranger, no matter how kindly, could possibly love Katie as much as her own mother.

Such dismal thoughts made her glad when Gavin returned. He had two books: a collection of Byron's poetry and Sir Walter Scott's *Ivanhoe.* "If these don't appeal, I can send for others."

"Bless you, Gavin!" She stroked the leather bindings greedily. "I expected a book of sea charts, and even that would have been a pleasure."

"I have too many books in my cabin. I'm glad you like these."

As he withdrew to change his clothes for another palace dinner, she opened *Ivanhoe.* On the flyleaf a bold, masculine hand had written: *To Helena on her 22nd birthday, with all my love—Gavin.*

Her throat tightened at the inscription. How generous of him to lend his wife's own book which he'd kept for all these years.

Opening the Byron, she found *Helena Elliott* in clear, delicate handwriting. What had Helena been like? Surely pretty and sweet, adoring her handsome young husband as much as he'd adored her. What a tragedy that she'd died so young.

Offering silent thanks to Helena for the use of the books, Alex began to read *Ivanhoe.* She hardly noticed Gavin's departure. After the light became too dim to read, she ate the rice, curry, and fruit Suryo brought. Then she wrapped the *ikat* coverlet around her and settled down behind the screen, the books resting by her pillow as symbols of the life that was almost within her grasp again.

For the first time in months, she was happy.

The glare of a torch awakened her. She sat up, blinking, and saw four armed palace guards standing outside her cage, one of them quietly undoing the triple locks with a set of keys. Frightened, she tried to remember enough Malay to ask what was happening, then stopped when the leader frowned and made a slashing gesture for silence.

Guessing they didn't want to wake Gavin, she held her tongue. If they meant to take her away, Gavin couldn't stop them, and it might be dangerous if he tried.

The door to the cage opened, and she was beckoned out. Expression stony, she obeyed. Outside the sun was rising, but the palace was dark as she was escorted through a maze of corridors. Why was she being moved? Not to be executed, since Kasan wanted Gavin's goodwill. Most likely she would be placed in a prison cell until after the Lion Game was finished.

Several levels lower and in a distant wing, the leader stopped to knock on a carved door. A slave opened it, revealing a tiny, richly dressed woman with gray hair and great dignity. A swift exchange of words followed before the head guard bowed and withdrew with his men. Before leaving, he caught Alex's glance and patted his kris significantly. She understood: he and his men would be outside, and she would be very, very sorry if she caused the old woman trouble.

As soon as the door closed, a flock of women of all ages swarmed into the room through the inner door. They chattered with curiosity as they surrounded her, patting her hair, stroking her pale skin, clucking over her bruises and rubbing salve on her gouged wrists. Small boned, graceful, and exquisitely dressed, they made Alex feel like a great clumsy ox, but it was a relief to be in the women's quarters rather than a dungeon.

The older woman said, *"Mandi."*

Alex understood—they wanted her to take a bath. Could they be preparing to set her free? The women were friendly, and she was being treated like a guest, not a slave. To be clean again . . . *"Ya, mandi,"* she said fervently.

Several of the younger women helped her bathe, supplying soap, water, and giggles in profusion. As her hair dried, Alex played a lighthearted game of peek a boo with a toddler. The women approved. Though Alex spoke little Malay and they spoke no English, the language of femininity was universal.

After she breakfasted, she was dressed in bright new garments that actually fit properly. In addition to a patterned batik sarong and *kebaya,* she was draped with a *selendang,* a sort of shawl. The women took great pleasure in dressing her and styling her hair with elaborate formality, as if she were a large foreign doll.

Alex's amusement ended when the head lady brought in what appeared to be handfuls of golden jewelry. Expression regretful, she straightened one golden chain out.

Manacles.

*"Ma'af."* Even as she apologized, the woman snapped the manacles around Alex's raw wrists. Ankle chains were handed to a young girl who knelt to fasten them. They were lovely, the links shaped and interwoven like jewelry, but they were still chains, the gold plate concealing a remorseless alloy. Heart sinking, Alex realized why she'd been brought to the women's quarters: because the prize in Kasan's damned game needed to look worth winning.

She was still a slave.

*    *    *

Gavin awoke thrumming with tension at the knowledge that this morning the Lion Game began. It would run for five days, with one die cast per day.

As he washed and shaved, he admitted privately that a small, mad part of him looked forward to the challenge—a merchant didn't become successful without enjoying competition. But the stakes in this game were too damned high. He hadn't told Alex the consequences for himself if he lost—she felt enough guilt about the risks he might face. With luck he'd win the game, they'd both leave Maduri, and she would never need to know that he'd risked ten years of his life.

After dressing in clothing that allowed him to move freely, he entered the main room. "Alex?"

No answer. He called her name again without response, then looked behind the screen. She was gone. As his pulse accelerated with shock, the door from the corridor open. He spun around, ready to do battle, but it was Suryo. "Do you know where Mrs. Warren is?"

"I have been in the guard room, and they say she was taken to the women's quarters," his steward replied. "No harm will come to her there."

"Why the devil did Kasan move her?"

"It is not for common men to guess the ways of kings," Suryo said dryly. "But I have gathered more information about the *Singa Mainam.* You are skilled in most of the tests: swimming, diving, chess, climbing, fighting with the kris or with bare hands. You should do well." He frowned. "Information about fighting the dragon, dancing the fire, and worshipping the goddess is less clear."

"The names sound like elaborate descriptions of something mundane," Gavin observed. "I hope I don't have to fight Kasan. Even though he says there will be no duels to the death, I suspect he's very dangerous with either dagger or bare hands."

Suryo looked amused. "I myself taught you the art of *pentjak* and how to use a kris. You will not lose."

"I wish I shared your confidence." Gavin checked his pocket watch. "Time to go. I trust you know where the Lion Garden is."

"Indeed. Follow me, Captain."

Their route took them through the palace and down a spiral staircase cut from living stone. At the bottom, two guards flanked a massive door. Gavin blinked as he stepped through into glaring sunlight. A roar of voices struck him.

As his eyes adjusted, he found himself in the bottom of a small natural amphitheater. The door they'd just exited was cut from a sheer stone cliff that towered behind him. The opposite side of the arena had been shaped into rows of seating, with a gate that led down to the city. The excited faces of hundreds of onlookers made him feel like a Roman gladiator.

A palace official approached and bowed, then led him and Suryo across the sun-baked arena to a pavilion on the north side. Under the high thatched roof was a pea-cock throne woven from rattan, plus three similar but smaller seats. All were set in a semicircle around a pedestal carved from shining obsidian. On top of the pedestal rested a twelve-sided die formed from aged ivory, and large as a child's fist.

When Gavin was escorted to the seat on the left, Suryo positioned himself behind, ready to advise or interpret as necessary. Tuan Daksa, a serene, elderly man in the robes of a Buddhist monk sat opposite. Gavin bowed courteously to the monk, then to the audience, wishing this business weren't so blasted public.

A slow rumble of drums gradually amplified until thunder echoed from the stone walls. A hush fell as men stood and looked toward the tunnel entrance.

First to emerge was Sheng Yu, chief minister of Maduri. Then two guards in elaborate ceremonial gear, followed by Sultan Kasan, regally garbed in silk and jewels, with a priceless ruby flashing in his turban. He was a westerner's fantasy of an eastern potentate—strong, rich, and powerful, a man above the laws of lesser men.

Gavin stiffened when he saw Alex among the sultan's entourage. Dressed in Maduri garments, she was beautiful and furious, glittering with golden chains as she crossed the arena with swinging strides.

Kasan reached the pavilion and claimed the throne while Alex was guided to the chair set between him and Gavin. She was the only woman in the arena, present to show what the contest was about. Quietly Gavin asked, "Are you all right?"

Her eyes narrowed. "Apart from being chained and treated like a silver race cup, I'm well." Despite her thinness, in her rich garments and elaborate hair she was a splendid, exotic prize that any man might wish to win. A goddess in golden chains. No wonder her eyes blazed with anger.

Kasan raised both hands for silence and began speaking Malay in a powerful voice that carried easily to every man in the arena. "We gather here to begin a *Singa Mainam* in which Tuan Gavin Elliott, Captain of Captains and Taipan of Elliott House, will attempt to win the freedom of the beautiful Iskandra, a high-born lady of England. He will risk his life for the sake of honor and the lady."

After an approving roar died down, the sultan shouted, "Let the Game begin!"

# CHAPTER 7

Thinking the ceremony rather flamboyant for a New England sailor, Gavin stepped up to the obsidian pedestal when Sheng Yu said, "Make your first cast, Captain."

The ivory dodecahedron was warm, like a living body. Gavin caged it between his hands and shook while he closed his eyes and imagined the result he wanted: escorting Alex Warren and her daughter from the *Helena* in London. When the image was so vivid he could hear the sea gulls, he opened his eyes and tossed the die onto the shining obsidian. It spun tipsily before settling into one position.

Sheng Yu examined the symbol that

came up. "The first task for Tuan Elliott is to climb the Cliff of Sorrows." There was an excited murmur.

Kasan gestured to the great cliff which made up the back wall of the arena. "You must climb that, plant your banner, and descend, Captain."

Gavin studied the cliff, which was nearly vertical and made of dark volcanic stone. "Why is it called the Cliff of Sorrows?"

"Twice invaders sought to attack the palace by scaling the cliff. Many men died." It was Sheng Yu who replied, and his expression implied that he wouldn't mind if Gavin suffered the same fate.

"If a banner is needed, I must send to my ship for the American flag."

"Take this." Face white, Alex unwound the narrow *selendang* which was draped from right shoulder to left hip, then offered it to him like a medieval lady giving her favor to her champion. "Be careful, Gavin."

He accepted the length of scarlet fabric, then bowed over her hand. "Don't worry, lass," he said softly. "I've spent a good part of my life scrambling through rigging on pitching schooners. Climbing is one thing I know."

She gave him a shaky smile, but her eyes were still worried. He took off his coat to free his arms, then wrapped the *selendang* several times around his waist like a sash. "Your Highness, I shall begin."

"Climb well, Captain," the sultan said. "I do not wish to see you die."

"I'll do my best to make this trial as boring as possible." Gavin crossed to the foot of the cliff, glad it would be in shade until midday. The full force of the sun beating on the stone would make the climb much harder. Having chosen a promising route, he began to climb, ignoring the watchers who would find it much more entertaining if he fell and broke his neck.

Rock climbing was slow, patient work that couldn't be rushed. The surface was irregular enough to allow climbing, but the crumbly volcanic rock made it necessary to test each hold before transferring his weight. While easier than ascending a mast during a gale, it required strength and total concentration.

A gamelan orchestra began playing, presumably to entertain the audience during his slow climb, but he never looked down to see. What mattered was the slide of bare hands and booted feet across the stone—searching, testing, shifting—when one misjudgment could mean his life. Once a lizard stuck its head from a crack and spat its tongue at his face. He was so startled he almost lost his grip. Luckily, the little beast disappeared back into its den without further challenge.

By the time he pulled himself over the top edge, he was panting, drenched with sweat, and every muscle in his body trembled with strain. The summit was a narrow volcanic ledge with a spectacular view of the island and the azure seas surrounding it, as well as ominous storm clouds in the distance. On the far side, the jumbled roofs of the palace were only a stone's throw away. He could see why the cliff had been attempted for an assault, and also why the attackers had failed.

Looking down into the arena, he picked out the forms of the sultan and Alexandra, who had moved from under the protection of the pavilion to watch. Unwinding the *selendang,* he raised his arm, letting the wind whip the scarlet banner. "For America and Alexandra!" he shouted to the sky.

As drums pounded below, he allowed a

moment to savor the triumph of achievement. Then he knotted the *selendang* around a stone pinnacle and began his descent. Because of fatigue and the danger that overconfidence would make him careless, this was the most dangerous part of the climb.

The descent took increasing concentration. He was so intent that he didn't notice that the sky had darkened until a fierce gust of wind struck when he was halfway down. Caught in the act of transferring his weight from one set of holds to another, he became unbalanced. A blast of rain slammed into him and he lost his grip. As he slid out of control down the rock face, shocked cries rose from the arena.

Instinctively he scrabbled at the cliff, clutching at a tuft of weeds that pulled loose, a scrawny shrub that broke, anything to slow his fall. A terrifying lifetime seemed to pass before the clawing fingers of his left hand caught a jutting knob of stone. The jolt of his full weight exploded painfully along his arm, but his grip held long enough to find a narrow ledge with one foot, then the other.

He clung there, panting, as rain hammered unmercifully. Despite a passionate desire to be on solid ground, he didn't resume his descent until he recovered his breath and composure. Finally, cautiously, he began working his way downward again.

The squall ended as abruptly as it began. By the time he reached bottom the sun was shining and his drenched garments were drying. Trying to look as casual as if he were returning from a stroll in the park, he crossed to the pavilion and bowed to the sultan. "Your Highness, I have conquered the Cliff of Sorrows, and raised my lady's banner."

"Well done!" Kasan's smile seemed genuine. "Until tomorrow's trial, Captain."

Gavin glanced at Alex. She gave him a warm, relieved smile, looking as tired as he felt. "Well done indeed, my lord captain." Her soft words made him understand why medieval knights had risked their lives to win a lady's favor.

Then his gaze fell upon the ivory die where it waited silently for the next day. Triumph faded at the knowledge that surely his next trials would be worse.

*    *    *

Alex was pleased to be returned to the cage in Gavin's rooms. He'd been delayed by men wanting to congratulate his success, so she was waiting when he entered the sitting room. For an instant his expression was unguarded, revealing weariness and anxiety. Then he saw her and his face lightened. "They brought you back! I'm glad, though the women's quarters were probably more comfortable."

Heart lifting at the sight of him, she reached through the bars, ignoring the clank of her chains against the gilded metal. "Thank God you're all right! I lost ten years of my life when you slipped."

He took her hands, and she felt a startling jolt of emotion tingle between them. Not wanting to examine that, she said quietly, "It's hard to believe that we've only just met. The circumstances have taken us so far beyond social pleasantries."

"I know. I feel the same." His deep voice was perilously close to a caress.

Uneasy, she released his hands and found blood on her palms. "You're injured!"

He inspected his hands as if surprised. "Only scrapes from the stone."

"They need to be cleaned. Infection can

flare quickly in this climate." She bit her lip. "As mistress of my household, I was always prepared for emergencies—salves, bandages, pills, and teas as needed. Now I have nothing to work with."

"I have some salve here, I believe. The longer I stay, the more Suryo moves up from the *Helena.*"

"If you bring a cloth and a basin of water, I'll clean the lacerations." Perhaps it was foolish to offer when it would be easier for him to tend himself, but she wanted to do something for him, no matter how small. Words weren't enough to express how she felt.

He brought a basin of water from the bedroom, along with folded rags and a small jar of basilicum ointment. Taking a cushion, he extended one hand through the bars. Gently she washed away grit and blood, then spread ointment on the raw skin. Faint, long-healed scars showed that his hands were those of a working man, but they were also strong, well shaped, and capable. Hands that could be trusted.

Gavin seemed to be dozing against the bars, but when she returned one hand and took the other, he murmured, "It's nice to be pampered."

"I suppose that usually the captain sees to others, and no one sees to him."

He shrugged. "Suryo takes good care of me."

Though his steward was a fine man, it sounded very lonely. Once again she felt profound regret that Gavin's wife had died. With his patience and warmth, he was obviously born to be a doting husband and father. He deserved a pure and loving wife. Instead, all he had at the moment was her, a battered and ruined slave. But at least she could do her best to ensure his hands didn't become inflamed.

She frowned when she noticed scraped areas along the side of his forehead and cheekbone. Rinsing a cloth, she reached through the bars to gently clean the abraded skin. His eyes opened, only inches from hers. Her heart accelerated at the intimacy of his nearness. It took a strong man to be so unguarded.

But what she felt wasn't attraction, *no*. Attraction was something that the old, pre-slavery Alexandra might feel. It had no place in her present or future. Breaking her gaze away, she finished cleaning his forehead and applied the ointment. "What you need, Captain, is a bath and a good night's sleep."

"So I can dream of tomorrow's test?" He grimaced. "I hope it's swimming or diving or chess. Those I could manage fairly well."

"You did splendidly today. You'll do as well tomorrow," she said, trying to sound confident.

He stood, moving stiffly. "Let's hope God wants you free, because I can use all the help I can get."

As he vanished into his bedroom, she thought that God was probably busy, and that was why He'd sent Gavin Elliott. She smiled, knowing the thought would have embarrassed the gallant captain if she'd said it aloud.

She picked up the book of Byron's poetry and leafed idly through the pages, pausing at *The Prisoner of Chillon.* The description of a man long-imprisoned, despairing as he watched his brothers die, was chilling. Byron had imagined well, until the end, when the prisoner said, *"My very chains and I grew friends . . ."* She could not imagine such resignation. Like the prisoner's brothers, she would have preferred death.

Yet she'd loved Byron's work as a girl, hiding away a slim volume of his poems because she suspected her mother might not approve. Now that she was a mother herself, she sympathized—Byron could be quite ribald—but she hadn't noticed that when she was young. The exotic settings had enthralled her. He created worlds of high romance, with dashing, dangerous heroes who did great deeds and loved great loves.

Tall, handsome, and brooding, Edmund Warren had been the very picture of a Byronic hero. She'd probably not have accepted his offer if he'd been fair-haired and average looking. Her taste in men must have gone back to her father, who'd been a very dashing cavalry officer. When she'd married, she hadn't known how to look beyond a face to a man's soul.

A pity that she hadn't fallen in love with a decent, kind, undashing man when she was still capable of love. Now the thought of a physical relationship caused her stomach to knot. She was too old, too scarred for romance. She'd squandered her chance. Not that her marriage had been a disaster, but it had been far less than she had hoped for. She had expected the deep, joyous love that bound her mother and stepfather. Instead, marriage had put her in a cage as surely as the gilded bars that held her now.

Chiding herself for an overactive imagination, she returned to *Ivanhoe.* Poetry made her think too much.

The next morning began much the same way, except this time Gavin wasn't surprised to see that Alex was gone. When he and Suryo reached the arena she was waiting in the shade of the pavilion, her glossy dark hair styled differently and wearing a new *selendang.* More relaxed than the day before, she gave him a private smile.

Gavin returned the smile before casting the die again. This time when it tumbled to a halt, Sheng Yu announced, "Fighting the dragon."

Gavin frowned. "What does that mean?"

"The dragon is a beast from Komodo Island, called the *ora* there," Kasan explained. "For centuries, they've been bred on Maduri for their fighting ability. You must enter the ring with the largest of my dragons and steal the jewel of the sea from around its neck, armed only with a kris."

Jewel of the sea? Wondering if this was a bad dream, Gavin said, "Bring on the dragon, Your Highness."

Tea was served while the dragon was summoned and a fenced enclosure about thirty feet in diameter was assembled in the middle of the arena. Drums announced the entry of the dragon, which was roped between four large men who struggled to control their thrashing charge.

Gavin almost spilled his tea when he saw the beast. It was a giant lizard, easily ten feet long and weighing more than he did. Ugly, too, with a dark, scarred hide that looked like woven metal, and a foot-long yellow tongue that darted out as the heavy head swung from side to side. A giant, irregular pearl hung around its neck from a leather thong. Gavin didn't envy the man who had tied it in place.

"I've heard of the *ora*," Alex said under her breath. "Don't let it bite you. I don't think it's actually poisonous, but the mouth is so filthy that any creature bitten dies of infection within days."

"I'll do my best to avoid bites," Gavin assured her. "Does the blasted beast breathe fire?"

She smiled without humor. "Not that I know of."

"I must be grateful for small blessings." Gavin rose and set aside his tea. Despite the heat, he kept his coat on. The good worsted wool might offer some protection.

The dragon wranglers got their charge into the enclosure, carefully coordinating the release of ropes so they could bolt for safety at the same time. One man was knocked down, and dragged hastily from the ring by his fellows before the dragon could grab him.

With all in readiness, Kasan presented Gavin with a kris in its scabbard. "Wield this well, Captain."

The wavy-bladed dagger and scabbard were beautifully wrought. More important, the blade was razor sharp. As Gavin belted the weapon around his waist, he asked, "What if I kill the dragon defending myself?"

"Don't," Kasan advised. "The *ora* is traditionally considered sacred. Killing one would bring great misfortune."

Wonderful. Once more, drums rumbled as he crossed to the fenced enclosure. The attendants opened a small gate, and Gavin entered, dagger in hand. The dragon waited, still as carved stone except for the cold glitter of its hooded eyes. It looked . . . hungry.

"You have the advantage over me, Sir Dragon," Gavin said. "I can't kill you, but I'll bet you don't feel the same way about me."

The forked yellow tongue flickered, and the beast gave a short, evil hiss that raised the hair on Gavin's neck. "If you hold still and let me cut off the pearl, this will go easier for both of us."

Moving with shattering suddenness, the dragon whipped its massive tail around, knocking Gavin to the ground. He caught a nightmare glimpse of long, curved teeth, and rolled away barely in time to save his throat from being ripped out.

Not daring to stop, he leaped to his feet and retreated, gasping to recover the breath that had been knocked from his lungs. "You're fast, but your aim needs improving. Thank God."

The dragon became immobile again. Gavin edged to his left in a way he hoped wouldn't look menacing. Reptiles tended to be less active than warm-blooded creatures. He'd seen men approach crocodiles slowly without provoking an attack, and with luck that would work here.

He was within a yard when the dragon exploded into action again, this time slashing with its vicious hooked claws. Gavin dodged back, but the dragon ripped through his right sleeve and pain blazed along his forearm. He hoped those wicked claws weren't as filthy as the teeth.

The dragon swung its head sideways and lunged at Gavin. Trapped against the fence, he saw no choice but to leap onto the beast's horny back. As it pitched and hissed furiously, he flattened himself on the long spine, clinging to the torso with his knees and locking his arms around the thick neck. Like riding a tiger, he was in a precarious position, but out of range of the lethal fangs.

After a couple of minutes of frenzy, the baffled dragon suddenly stopped, uncertain how to rid itself of its unwanted burden. Gavin took advantage of the moment to slice the thong with the kris and grab the pearl with his left hand. Then he jumped off backwards, staying out of the dragon's sight.

Panting, he flattened himself against the wall of the enclosure as he waited to see what, if anything, the beast would do. It hissed and clawed at the ground, but didn't turn to come after him.

Scarcely daring to breath, Gavin inched around the ring toward the gate. As it swung open, the dragon spotted him and lashed its massive tail again. Prepared this time, Gavin leaped away and let it whip underneath. Grabbing a gate post, he swung onto the top of the gate, then jumped down outside.

Breathing heavily, he sheathed the kris and crossed the arena to the sound of cheers. This show was much quicker and more dramatic than rock climbing had been. He reached the pavilion and bowed to the sultan, then offered the pearl in one hand and the scabbarded dagger in the other. "The jewel of the sea, Your Highness, and your splendid kris."

"Keep the kris, Captain. You have earned it." Taking the pearl, Kasan turned and offered it to Alex. "As this jewel of the sea has been fairly won for your lady."

She stared at the pearl, still on its thong, as if unsure what to do with it. Then she tucked it into the waist of her sarong and stepped forward, pulling off the *selendang*. "Your arm needs tending, Captain."

Not waiting for a reply, she began wrapping the length of cloth, blue this time, around his right arm. Gavin became aware of how much the gash hurt. It was messy, too. His coat and shirt would never be the same. Speaking so only she could hear, he said, "Too many more challenges and I'll be an invalid."

Though he'd meant it as a joke, she shuddered. "That's what I'm afraid of."

Wishing he could retract his comment, he said, "Actually, my wardrobe is suffering more than I am. This isn't serious."

Hearing that, Kasan said, "You didn't come to Maduri expecting a *Singa Mainam*. I shall have garments sent to your room."

"Once more Your Highness is gracious."

The sultan's eyes glinted wickedly. "Merely helping you accustom yourself to the Maduri way of life. You have done well so far, but three trials remain."

Gavin was all too aware that he was less than halfway through the Lion Game. He never should have accepted the cargo that had brought him to Maduri. If he'd refused, he'd be well on his way to England by now.

But he'd never have met Alex. As he watched her tie off the crude bandage, admiring the stubborn set of her jaw and the sparkle of her aqua eyes, he knew that the risks he was taking were worth it.

# CHAPTER 8

By the third morning of the Lion Game, Gavin was beginning to feel cautiously optimistic. The night before, he and Alex had spent a peaceful and oddly domestic evening, assuming one overlooked the bars between them. She'd started reading Scott's *Rob Roy* while he'd spent some time with his ledgers, then turned to calculating his odds for succeeding at the game.

The answer pleased him. He'd survived the climb and the dragon, and the need to clean and repair ship hulls at sea had made him proficient at swimming and diving. He was also a good shot and a better-than-average chess player.

While he was still unsure what some of the trials were, most should be doable, as the dragon had been. The most worrisome possibilities were fighting the sultan either unarmed or with a kris, which would be risky both physically and politically. With luck, neither of those combat trials would come up. If one did—well, he'd use the one refusal he'd been allotted.

"Tuan Elliott."

Sheng Yu formally handed Gavin the ivory die for his third cast. Gavin rolled the die in his hands, then cast it.

The top of the dodecahedron was un-nervingly blank. Then he realized that symbols were being covered after a task had been selected once. No point in fighting a dragon twice. He picked up the die and threw again.

Sheng Yu announced, "Dancing the fire."

It was another category where Suryo hadn't found clear information. Gavin asked, "What does that mean?"

"It is an ancient tradition of Maduri," Kasan explained. "You must walk across a bed of burning coals."

Gavin tensed. "You're joking."

"Not at all. This dance is *adat,* custom,

performed when a boy becomes a man. It's one of the easier *Singa Mainam* tests, actually. I'd hoped you'd receive a more difficult trial." The sultan gave one of his lazy, dangerous smiles.

"You've done this yourself?" Gavin asked.

"Of course, when I was thirteen."

Already slaves were laying a square of wood in front of the pavilion. Unnerved, Gavin withdrew to consult with Suryo and Alexandra. "Suryo, are you familiar with this fire dance?"

"Not quite like this, but something similar is done in Bali."

"Don't Indian holy men walk across fire?" Alex added. "An officer who had been in India told me he'd seen that."

"I've seen it myself," Gavin admitted. "But I suspect there's a trick of some sort. A pathway that is less hot, maybe." He stared at the blazing wood, his skin crawling.

"There is no trick," Suryo said. "Or rather, it is not a fraud. The dancer is in a—I think the word is 'trance.' Prayer and exaltation take the mind elsewhere, and the fire is crossed with no harm."

Gavin took a deep, unsteady breath. "At sea there is no greater danger than fire."

"Have you been caught in a shipboard fire?" Alex asked quietly.

He nodded, unable to speak. Early in his seafaring career a blaze had started in the cabin of a chief mate notorious for his drunkenness. Even after eighteen years, Gavin remembered the stench of burning human flesh. Three men, including the captain, had died, two others had been seriously injured.

Gavin was a very young second mate, but as the only surviving officer, command of the ship fell to him. After organizing a successful fight to put out the fire, he'd nursed the damaged ship back to Salem with his skeleton crew. Ironically, the incident had been good for his career—the next time he shipped out he was a chief mate—but he'd never overcome an almost paralyzing fear of fire.

Alex unobtrusively took his hand, pulling him out of the past. He squeezed her fingers hard, grateful for her perception.

Flames were beginning to die down in the arena, and attendants raked the coals into an even surface that glowed menacingly even in the tropical sun. Thinking that it should be possible to cross the embers so quickly that no harm would be done, Gavin bent to roll up his trouser legs. He wore a loosely belted tunic and trousers that the sultan had sent to his rooms the evening before, and the finely woven blue and silver cotton might burn if it came too close to the coals.

"The fire is ready," Sheng Yu announced. "Remove your boots, Captain."

Gavin froze. "I'm supposed to do this *barefoot*?"

The Maduris in the pavilion looked surprised. "Of course," the sultan replied. "That is the custom."

"No!" Gavin shuddered as he remembered the white of bones against charred flesh. "I invoke my right to refuse one trial."

Kasan looked startled, then pleased. "You are sure? Truly, fire walking is not difficult for a man who is relaxed and in control of his thoughts."

"I appreciate your encouragement, but no," Gavin said dryly.

"As you will. Cast the die again."

Tuan Daksa intervened. "A moment. It would be a pity to waste a good fire."

With his face calm but an impish glint in his black eyes, the elderly Buddhist monk left the pavilion and stepped onto the burning coals. Serenely he crossed, steps light and the hem of his robes floating in the rising heat.

As he watched, Gavin didn't know whether to laugh or grind his teeth. Maybe walking through fire really was easy for a Maduri—but the mere thought tied his stomach in knots. Knowing that his inability to fire walk removed his safety margin and might end up costing his freedom, he waited until Daksa returned, then cast the die for the third time, praying that something he could manage would turn up.

"The breath of life," Sheng Yu announced.

What the hell was *that*? Before Gavin could ask, the sultan said, "The drinking contest! One of the two *Singa Mainam* trials that are also pleasures."

"How does the contest work?" Gavin asked warily.

"You and I must match each other drink for drink. Whoever stays conscious and is able to walk the longest wins."

"This is a test of leadership?" he exclaimed, incredulous.

"A leader must lead, whether drinking or fighting." Kasan grinned. "Competing with *arak* or palm wine is more pleasurable than dueling with a kris."

"I'll grant you that." Thinking it would be a long day, Gavin added, "This contest is not fit for a lady to watch. Can Mrs. Warren be escorted back to my quarters?"

The sultan nodded and gave the orders. Alex wanted to protest. Absurdly, she felt as if Gavin was safer if she watched, but drinking sessions were long and boring at best and not particularly dangerous, so she left quietly with the guards. She hoped Gavin had a hard head even if he wasn't a heavy drinker.

They had just entered the palace tunnel when they were intercepted by Tuan Bhudy, a powerful Maduri merchant—and her most recent owner. Shorter than Alex but wide and muscular, he was a formidable figure steeped in wealth, privilege, and cruelty.

Alex stopped dead, bile rising in her throat. Memories of his abuse were so intense they might have been burned into her flesh. She would have bolted if her retreat wasn't blocked by two guards.

"Issskandra." Her Malay name hissed from Bhudy's mouth as his gaze traveled over her with insulting familiarity. "You look remarkably fine. Perhaps it was hasty of me to send you to market after that last incident."

"Your mistake was in buying me in the first place," she said tightly. "I will never be any man's property. If you'd kept me longer, I would have killed you."

"Such bold talk for a slave. You need to be taught a lesson, and it will be my pleasure to teach it." He squeezed her left breast, hard.

She almost cried out from the pain, and even worse, the memory of pain. Refusing to give him the pleasure of seeing her suffer, she looked to her guards. They watched uneasily, not wanting to interfere with a powerful man.

Groping for the right Malay words, she caught the gaze of Wira, leader of the guards. "Sultan Kasan will not want his *Singa Mainam* prize hurt."

Bhudy snarled rapid words at Wira. Fearing that he might convince them not to interfere while he molested her, Alex suddenly pivoted, whipping her golden chains at his head. She felt savage satisfaction as the chains smashed into his temple, sending him reeling. Then she kicked Bhudy between his legs with so much force her toes hurt. He shrieked and collapsed on the floor, writhing back and forth in agony as blood flowed from his head wound.

Instantly four daggers were drawn. Knowing a sudden move would cost her her life, Alex stood stone still. "I am the prize in the sultan's Lion Game," she reminded them again, trying to keep her voice steady. There was no point in describing how Bhudy had abused her; after all, he'd been her owner and could do with her as he willed.

Invoking the sultan saved her from being skewered. Wira detailed one man to help Bhudy and took the others with him through the palace to Gavin's rooms. Alex walked meekly with eyes downcast, shaken by the encounter and the possible consequences. Ironically, her best defense was the fact that now she was considered the sultan's property, and it was impertinent to molest anything belonging to the ruler.

Being locked in the cage again was a relief. Once she was alone she crumpled to the floor and wrapped her arms around her knees to control her trembling. She wanted desperately to cry, but didn't dare. If she started weeping, she might never stop. The encounter with Bhudy had destroyed the fragile sense of safety that had been growing since she'd met Gavin.

When a measure of composure had returned, she looked for her water pitcher. It sat on a table across the room, moved by a maid. Even if she were dying of thirst, she couldn't have reached it. Her lack of control over the most basic needs of life suddenly swamped her. *My very chains and I grew friends* . . . Dear God, no, every day the chains chafed harder, body and soul.

Her utter frustration exploded into rage and she began slashing her chains against the bars wildly, chipping gilt and causing a clamor that jangled from the walls. How could anyone endure slavery? What made men so vile that they believed they had the right to own another human life? Most bitter of all, how much longer could she survive without going mad?

Drawn by the cacophony, a slave girl appeared in the doorway, her eyes wide with alarm. She was no more than eleven or twelve—not much older than Katie.

Hating to see fear in the child's eyes, Alex stopped battering the bars and tried to compose her expression. "Please, water. *Tolong air putih.*"

Glad for a request she could accommodate, the girl darted away. Alex sank to the floor again, praying that Gavin was right and that within a matter of days she would be freed. The closer freedom seemed, the harder slavery became.

Despite her best attempts to control herself, by the time the slave girl brought water and rice Alex was weeping uncontrollably. But boredom eventually defeated anguish. Worn out by tears, Alex used precious water to pat her swollen eyes. Then she unpinned her hair, combed it loose, and settled down with *Rob Roy.* Returning to her native land was soothing even if only through a book. Reading also kept her from thinking too much about the progress of the trial.

The sun was setting when the door swung open and Gavin staggered in, half supported by Suryo. His fair hair was tousled like a halo and his tunic gapped open to reveal his chest. Alarmed, Alex rose. "What happened?"

"Haven't been . . . this drunk since I was fifteen," Gavin said in a slurred voice. "Shipmates took me to a tavern for my birthday. Amazing number of beers in Antwerp."

He zigzagged to the cage, catching a bar to keep himself from falling. Upright but swaying, he said with drunken precision, "Don't worry, I won't be sick. Already have been. Several times." He leaned against the bars, eyes drifting shut.

Tight with anxiety, Alex asked, "How did the competition turn out?"

Suryo answered when Gavin didn't. "The captain won, though it was close. They both have heads of solid stone."

"If Kasan had lasted one more round, he'd've won." Gavin slid slowly to the floor. Suryo tried to lift him. "Captain, your bed will be more comfortable."

Nothing. Gavin was dead to the world. "Bring a coverlet and pillow," Alex suggested. "Sleeping here won't make him feel any worse tomorrow than he will anyhow."

Suryo smiled. "Very true, puan."

Together they laid Gavin alongside the

cage so Alex could tend him if necessary. "Find yourself some dinner," she told Suryo. "You've had a long day, too."

"Do you need anything more?"

"Light a lamp before you leave, and I'll be fine."

After Suryo complied and left, Alex sat down by Gavin. She reached through the bars, careful not to clang the chains, and drew the front of his tunic closed. It was amusing to think how outrageous this situation would seem to an English lady. No longer a lady, now she pragmatically accepted a man not her husband sleeping here in dishabille because she didn't want her champion to wake alone and ill in his bedroom. It was hard to imagine that distant world where the rules of propriety mattered.

Caught up in her book again, she jumped when a gravelly voice asked, "Is it hard . . . being beautiful?"

Alex found Gavin watching her with hazy eyes. "I wouldn't know. How do you feel?"

"My head spins like being in the crow's nest on heavy seas, only worse. If I tried to move now it would be a disaster." His words were less slurred than earlier, though his face was chalky white under his tan. "Hate being so . . . so out of control. 'T's why I prefer to stay sober."

"How much did you drink?"

"Far too much. Do you know they store palm wine in great long pipes of bamboo? Startled me the first time my goblet needed refilling and a bloody great pipe swung over my shoulder like a cannon." He gave a faint smile. "The palm wine was young, but far from innocent. We ended by switching to *arak,* sort of a rice brandy, because the palm wine wasn't getting us drunk fast enough." He closed his eyes, then opened them again hastily. "Odd. This drinking contest was as serious as any other trial, but it still feels ridiculous."

She laid her hand on his forehead. He was a little warm, but not feverish.

"Your hand feels nice," he murmured.

"What did you talk about while drinking for so many hours?"

"We both recited poetry by the mile. Maduri sagas have a nice rhythm. After I ran out of English and Latin verses, I started on improper songs in five languages."

Latin? The captain had been well edu-cated. "Whatever it took, I'm glad you succeeded. I was worried because I didn't think you were much of a drinker."

"Neither did Kasan—he calls me a Puritan. But young sailors learn to drink. A hard head is part of the job." He ran a hand through his hair, tousling it even more. "Kasan's an int'resting fellow, but I don't think I could bear ten years of this."

"Why ten years? Is that how long he wanted you to work for him?"

Gavin's gaze shifted away. "You still haven't told me what it's like to be beautiful," he said, ignoring her question. "Do men make your life difficult?"

She thought of Bhudy, and tried not to shiver. "There are men who will make any woman's life difficult, and beauty has nothing to do with it. At my best I'm passably attractive, but now I'm bone thin and disreputable."

"No." He reached through the bars to take her hand. "You're one of the loveliest women I've ever met."

His intense gaze made her want to put the width of the cage between them. It was unfair to blame him for drunkenness when he'd incurred it on her behalf, but she didn't know if she could stand it if he made a crude advance. She needed him to be a gentleman, a man she could trust to keep himself at a distance. A friend.

Before she could decide whether or not to pull away, his eyes closed. She relaxed again. Despite the drink, he was behaving with a restraint that spoke well for his character. Though he still clasped her hand, his grip wasn't suggestive. Rather, he held her as if she was his anchor in a tossing sea, which was probably how he felt.

When the lamp began flickering, she gently disengaged her hand. Instead of making her bed behind the carved screen, she laid her coverlet and pillow next to Gavin. Even with bars between them it felt intimate, but also safe.

After the lamp finally sputtered out, she reached through the bars and took his hand again. This time she didn't know who was anchoring whom.

# CHAPTER 9

Gavin woke with his head pounding like the damned Maduri drums. Though he didn't open his eyes, he could sense sunlight in the room.

A hand was intertwined with his. Cautiously he opened his eyes and turned his head a fraction to the right. Alex lay sleeping only a few inches, and a set of gilded bars, away. She wore his shirt and an old sarong and her rich hair tumbled gloriously around her face, the dawn light striking auburn and gold highlights. What had she said the previous night? Something about being thin and disreputable. Perhaps that was how she saw herself, but she still had a loveliness that haunted him.

*In vino veritas.* Too much alcohol had washed away most of the mental barriers he'd erected between them. Even in the grip of a major hangover, he desired her intensely, but she also inspired a potent mixture of tenderness and respect. He hadn't reacted to a female this strongly since meeting Helena. Though the two women were nothing alike, they both had strength and wit and warmth.

He'd tried to deny his attraction, but perhaps it wasn't such a bad thing. Alex worried that captivity would cast a dark shadow over her life when she returned home, but if she had a presentable husband there would be little or no scandal.

He'd had vague plans of establishing himself in England, then looking around for a high-born wife who would gain him entry into the society he despised. He'd never intended a cold marriage of convenience, though. He cared about Alex, and in time that might deepen into love. Affection mattered more than pedigree.

But such thoughts were wildly premature. First they must escape Maduri. If he didn't win the Lion Game, he'd be waving her goodbye as she sailed away. Even if he was successful in the last two trials, Alex was in no shape to think about marriage. She needed to be free, needed to come to terms with what she'd suffered, before making a major decision about her future. She might well decide she wanted no part of Gavin, who'd be a reminder of the worst time of her life.

There was also the risk that she might never heal enough to risk putting herself in a man's power; if she failed to find her daughter, she might be scarred for life. He wasn't selfless enough to marry a woman who was emotionally crippled. He wanted a wife whose companionship he enjoyed. A wife like Helena. His throat tightened.

Muscles stiff, he cautiously stretched, stopping when a wave of nausea swept over him. It was going to be a long and difficult day.

Alex's lids drifted up, revealing her luminous aqua eyes. "Do you feel like death would be welcome?"

"Not quite that bad, but close." He inhaled slowly to steady his queasy stomach.

"Did I do or say anything appalling last night?"

"You were very well behaved for a man deep in his cups." She sat up, sliding her hand from his grasp to cover a yawn. "Will you be able to perform another ghastly feat this morning?"

"Mercifully, I don't have to. Kasan said it's traditional to skip a day after a drinking contest."

Alex laughed. "What a very civilized island Maduri is."

In pressing need of his chamber pot, he gritted his teeth and pulled himself upright with the help of the bars. Then he leaned against the cage until his vital organs steadied. "Why couldn't I throw the symbol for swimming?" he muttered. "I *like* swimming."

"Perhaps that will turn up tomorrow. You've thrown four of the possible feats, so the odds of casting something you want must be increasing."

The odds were still not wonderful, but he was in no mood to think about mathematics. He took comfort in the fact that Kasan must feel as ghastly as he did.

The door opened to admit Suryo, who

carried a breakfast tray. As Gavin shuddered, the other man said, "I have a drink here that will make you feel better. A moment while I give the lady her breakfast."

Gavin nodded and headed to his bedroom, weaving only a little. After he closed the door, Alex said, "Last night Captain Elliott said something about spending ten years here. Is he still considering the sultan's offer?"

Suryo passed a small jug of tea between the bars. "He meant the ten years he must stay if he loses the *Singa Mainam*."

Alex gasped. "He'd have to stay here that long?"

"He had not told you?" Suryo looked thoughtful. "Perhaps it is best that you know. Since the sultan would not release you, the captain proposed this challenge as a way to win your freedom. If he triumphs in the Lion Game, you can both leave. If he loses you will be released, but he is pledged to serve the sultan for the next ten years."

Alex shook her head, dazed. He'd never even hinted at the price he would pay if he lost. She'd thought this blasted game was only about her freedom. Instead, Gavin had put his own future on the line as well. Losing would cage him as surely as she was caged now. His bondage would be more luxurious and his abilities respected, but he'd still be trapped, no longer his own man.

It was the most gallant, stupid, generous, infuriating thing she'd ever heard.

Looking less disheveled, her crazed knight errant returned to the sitting room and silently drank Suryo's hangover remedy. Part of her wanted to ask why he'd kept his devil's bargain secret, but she knew the answer to that—he hadn't wanted her to bear the additional burden of knowing what her freedom might cost him.

He was right, too—the knowledge horrified her. Reluctantly she decided to honor his wishes. At this point nothing she did could make a difference to his future. All she could do was pray for his success, for both their sakes.

The fourth trial had arrived. Feeling almost himself after sleeping a good part of the previous day, Gavin shook the die, uttered a silent prayer, and rolled it onto the table.

Sheng Yu proclaimed, "Empty-hand *pent-jak silat.*"

"Splendid!" Kasan exclaimed. "I have hoped for this chance to test the fighting arts of Maduri against the European style."

Gavin's belly knotted. His most fervent wish had been to avoid physically fighting the sultan, and empty-hand combat was almost as dangerous as using daggers. If he hadn't used his one refusal already, he would invoke it right now.

Kasan expected to win easily because the fighting arts of the East were truly amazing, very different from anything practiced in the West. However, Gavin was also trained in *pentjak silat,* the Indies style of combat, which meant that both their lives were at risk. Knowing he had no choice, he asked, "What are the rules, Your Highness?"

"We must stay within a circle that will be laid out in the arena. Any empty-hand fighting technique is allowed except biting and eye-gouging. A fall is when the shoulders touch the ground, and best of three falls wins. Do you need to prepare, Captain?"

Since he wore loose Maduri garb, Gavin shook his head and moved to the side of the pavilion to remove his boots. Under his breath, he asked Suryo, "What do you know about Maduri fighting?"

"It's rather like the Javanese style, using hands and feet equally. He will not expect you to know *silat,* so surprise should give you at least one fall."

"No more than one—he's too intelligent not to catch on quickly." Gavin looked into the arena, where attendants were marking a circle with a material like powdered chalk. "If I fight seriously, one of us may die or be permanently crippled. If I don't do my best . . ." His mouth tightened.

"I have trained you in the controlling and disabling moves. Use them." Suryo's lips curved into something that was not at all a smile. "And remember my other lessons. It is best to avoid fighting, but if you must fight—enjoy it."

Doubting he would enjoy this, Gavin gave Alex a reassuring glance. She smiled back a little tremulously. "I know you'll do well, Gavin."

She'd be even more concerned if she understood this kind of fighting. *Pentjak silat* was nothing like the English gentlemen's sport of boxing. Brutal and lethally effective, it was rather like highly refined street fighting. Move in close and fast. Grapple, crush, and gouge. Do whatever necessary to survive, including kill.

He stepped into the arena and paced across the circle, absorbing the textures of earth, air, and light as he mentally prepared for the match. There might not be another Westerner in the world who knew as much about *pentjak silat* as he did. Bereft after Helena's death and desperate for distraction, he'd accepted Suryo's offer to teach him the Island form of fighting. The training had opened a whole new world that required skill, discipline, and a high tolerance for pain. Beyond that was a spiritual dimension which eventually helped pull him from his black depression.

Gavin hadn't known that many Asian cultures had secret warrior traditions, with the skills being passed from teacher to trusted disciples. He'd quickly recognized the honor in being chosen as Suryo's student. The two of them practiced everywhere they traveled, the tight quarters on shipboard being a particular challenge.

During the seasons Gavin spent in Macao, he'd met other martial arts practitioners through Suryo. He'd learned about different Asian schools of fighting, and how to ward off attacks of up to seven men at once. More than once that had proved useful.

As drums began pounding rhythmically, Gavin turned to face Kasan, who stood on the opposite side of the circle. They were well-matched physically, Gavin a little taller, the sultan broader, though in *silat* size wasn't important. The trick was to use the opponent's own strength against him. Suryo was three stone lighter than Gavin, but he could still throw his student into a wall with ease.

Breathing deeply, Gavin narrowed his focus down to the dangerous, arrogant man across the circle. This match he could not afford to lose.

Sheng Yu called, "Let the warriors engage!"

Kasan pressed his hands together in front of his chest in the ritual salutation at the beginning of a fight. Gavin copied the gesture awkwardly, as if it were unfamiliar to him.

The sultan moved forward with hands open and the smooth, flowing movements of a trained fighter. He'd probably been studying *pentjak* since he was a child.

Instead of taking a similar posture, Gavin took the stance of a Western boxer, hands fisted and body upright as he advanced. *Pentjak* adepts generally preferred to let the other man strike first because an attacker left himself open to a wide range of ferocious countermoves. Though it was risky to give Kasan that opportunity, Gavin feinted a jab at his opponent's midriff, hoping Kasan would react with overconfidence.

The sultan avoided the blow with contemptuous ease before closing in for a grappling hold that could be used to slam Gavin to the ground. For an instant they were locked together, and Gavin saw something dark and forbidden in his opponent's eyes.

"Today you become mine," Kasan growled. "You should have saved your refusal for this test, for I am a master of *pentjak silat.*"

"Don't underestimate Western fighting skill." Having anticipated the sultan's hold, Gavin broke away and dropped low to grab the back of the other man's knee, yanking him off balance while shoving hard into the ribs. Before the astonished sultan realized what was happening, he was flat on his back.

"First fall to Tuan Elliott!" Sheng Yu called as the crowd roared with surprise.

Kasan rolled to his feet, eyes glittering with anger. "You were right—I underestimated your skill, and your cunning. But not again."

"We are well matched, Your Highness." Gavin relaxed into a defensive posture, knowing the risks had just increased sharply. *Silat* relied on memory trained into the muscles—Suryo often said that a move practiced three thousand times became part of one's body—and most moves were meant to cripple or kill. Kasan had the same training. He wanted to win, and if he thought he was losing—well, Gavin dead was no more useless to him than Gavin gone to England.

While Gavin didn't want to injure the sultan, in the tension of battle he might unintentionally break the other man's back, drive splintered ribs into his lungs, or worse. With both of them fighting to the limit of their skill, anything could happen. Though Gavin's situation was rather worse: if he killed the sultan the Maduris would execute him on the spot, even if the death was accidental.

Kasan struck toward Gavin's throat. Gavin deflected the blow, but wasn't fast enough to avoid having his wrist caught and forced back violently. He broke free before any bones snapped and flowed into a grappling hold that immobilized Kasan, briefly.

Methodically they tested each other, alternating defensive evasions with assaults. To anyone unfamiliar with *pentjak,* it would have seemed like an intimate, graceful dance rather than a lethal struggle, with death only one misstep away.

As they engaged, parried, and slid apart, the sultan panted, "I've traced your woman's child. It was sold into the harem of the Rajah of Sukau on Java."

As a distraction it was first class. Barely thwarting a savage knee toward his groin, Gavin asked, "What do you know of the rajah?"

"He is said to be civilized. The child should be well treated."

Hoping to God that was true, Gavin shifted his glance to make it appear that he was going to lunge to the left. Instead of falling for the feint, Kasan countermoved and caught Gavin's left elbow in a lock. As he applied pressure, shattering pain washed through Gavin, swamping all thoughts but agony.

Feebly he tried to break the hold as he was forced downward, but he was unable to summon enough strength. He blacked out from the pain, regaining consciousness an instant later to find himself sprawled on the ground.

"Second throw to Sultan Kasan!"

From a polite distance, the sultan asked coolly, "Did I break the elbow?"

Gavin rose, trying to conceal his nausea. A cautious flex of his arm increased the pain, but at least the joint still worked. "It's fine."

Kasan gave his charming smile. "Good. I don't wish to delay the time it will take for you to join my service. Are you ready for the final throw?"

Gavin nodded, thinking he should have risked burning his feet off in the damned fire walk. The long, demanding bout was draining his energy, making it harder to keep his reactions under control. A wrong move could be disastrous.

Wanting to end the match, he watched for an opportunity to apply a hold that would control Kasan without seriously injuring him. Less concerned with causing damage, his opponent caught Gavin in a turning, twisting head hold that tilted him backward and could easily turn into a neck snap.

Where a man's head goes, his body will follow. Instead of resisting, Gavin relaxed into the hold, letting his weight fall heavily back into Kasan. For an instant Kasan was off balance as he shifted his stance to absorb the increasing weight.

Gavin used that moment to twist away and apply a risky nerve block to the other man's upper arm, knowing that if he failed he'd be vulnerable to anything Kasan wanted to try. Damnation! The nerves were protected by too much solid muscle. He jabbed his fingers again brutally. Kasan gasped with agony, his body going slack. It was a perfect control move—paralyzing the opponent with pain but not causing real injury. "Yield, Your Highness!"

The sultan swore in Malay, raging but unable to escape. Ruthlessly Gavin forced him downward until Kasan hit the ground and the fight was over.

The drums erupted cataclysmically. "Match to Tuan Elliott!" In the pavilion, Alex jumped to her feet with relief and excitement.

Gavin stepped back diplomatically and bowed to the sultan. "You fight better than any ruler has a right to, Your Highness."

"And you fight better than any Westerner has a right to." Icy with anger and frustration, Kasan got to his feet. "Pray to your gods that tomorrow's challenge is an easy one, Captain, for you will be granted no quarter."

That Gavin knew. He bowed to the onlookers, then returned to the pavilion.

"Where on earth did you learn to do that, Gavin?" Alex asked, awe in her face.

"From Suryo." He nodded at his friend, who was examining the throbbing elbow.

"I'll bind this now, Captain," Suryo said. "Though not broken, already there is swelling." He picked up a bandage and began wrapping the joint.

"The sultan said he's traced Katie, Alex,"

Gavin said quietly. "She was sold to the Rajah of Sukau, and should be quite safe."

Alex lit up, luminous with joy. "Thank God! And thank *you.*" She swiftly brushed a kiss on his cheek, then ducked back, blushing at her forwardness. She smelled like tropical blossoms.

As she was escorted away by guards, Gavin touched his face. Alex's lips seemed to have burned their imprint into his cheek. In her own way she was as dangerous as Kasan. The sultan merely threatened his freedom and life. Alex might have the power to reshape his soul.

# CHAPTER 10

That night, Alex paced through the slanted moonlight and shadows of her cage, fidgety as a puppy. Though she'd learned to move silently, without even a hint of jangling chains, Gavin eventually emerged from his bedroom. Fair hair rumpled and dressed in light-colored tunic and trousers, he looked like the ghost of some fabulous pagan god. "You couldn't sleep either?" he asked.

"No." She took a deep breath to keep the tremor from her voice. "I'm sorry to be such a burden. I feel ready to shatter into pieces from sheer nerves."

"You're not a burden. You're a remarkable woman. I suspect that if I were captive and you had to play a Lion Game to free me, you'd do it magnificently."

Exasperated by his offering her such an unearned compliment, she blurted out, "I know the terms of your bargain with Kasan. Dear God, Gavin, how could you pledge away ten years of your future for the sake of a woman you scarcely know? In the middle ages, men like you were called saints."

"I'm no saint, Alex," he said, taken aback. "It's just that . . . how could I live with myself if I abandoned a woman of my own people in slavery?"

"To me, that's sainthood. Or at least courage and honor above and beyond the call of duty." Her mouth twisted. "With all you've been through, have you wished that you hadn't passed the slave market when you did?"

He hesitated, too honest to lie. "It would have been easier if I hadn't seen you, but who says easy is better? Most things of value require effort."

"Losing control of your life can't be better."

"Even if I end up working for the sultan, my situation will be very different from yours. I'll have wealth, authority, and considerable freedom." He shrugged. "I might even be better off staying in the East. This could be God's way of keeping me away from London, where I may fracture my skull by banging it against walls."

"You expect trouble there?"

He ran stiff fingers through his hair in a rare gesture of uncertainty. "Not exactly trouble, but—I hate Britain as much as I love it. Going back is something I've longed for, and also a great piece of idiocy."

"If the walls are too hard, you can return to America. From what I've heard in your voice, your love for your adopted country isn't complicated at all."

His expression eased into a smile. "You're right. When I finish laying my English ghosts, I'll go home."

Thinking of all he'd done in the last days, she said, "I imagine you'll deal with those ghosts as capably as you deal with everything else."

"Ghosts are a little out of my usual line. Chests of tea, now, or typhoons—those I can manage very well."

His teasing tone dissolved the tension between them, leaving intimacy. She gazed up into his shadowed eyes, almost regretting that this rare, strange interval was nearly over. If all went well, in two days they'd be on the *Helena.* Surrounded by his crew, they'd resume their real lives as captain and lady, even though inside she'd changed irrevocably. There would be a safe emotional distance between them.

But there was no distance tonight. In the last days and nights she had learned the rhythm of his breath, the texture of his skin, the wryness of his humor. They had become comrades in a great and strange adventure, and she would never forget him, no matter what lay in her future. Her effect on him could never be as profound for he was a man who had lived many adventures, but perhaps the risks he'd taken for her sake would lay some of the sorrow he carried for his lost beloved.

Pulling her mind back to the mundane, she said, "I hope that your last trial is swimming, Gavin."

He laughed. "So do I. It would be a fitting end to the contest."

Any finale that had them both sailing safely away from Maduri was fine with her.

\*   \*   \*

Gavin's left arm still ached from the punishment suffered at *pentjak,* but otherwise he was well and as prepared for the last task as possible. Alex stood to his right, tense as a drumhead and heart-catchingly lovely in a new *kebaya* and sarong of shimmering patterned silk. Kasan looked sardonic but composed, having mastered his anger of the day before.

As Gavin scooped up the ivory dodecahedron for his last cast, Kasan remarked, "I shall rather miss the excitement when this is over, but Sheng Yu will be glad to have me return to the affairs of the kingdom."

"Personally, I've had quite enough excitement." Mentally uttering prayers, Gavin rattled the die in the cage of his hands one last time, and threw.

Sheng Yu peered at the symbol. "Worshipping the goddess."

Before Gavin could ask what it meant, Kasan said coolly, "Your luck holds, Captain. The gods have given you the test that is one of man's great pleasures."

Gavin frowned. "What does worshipping the goddess mean?"

"You must have sexual relations with your slave woman."

Gavin's first reaction was stunned disbelief. No, surely he couldn't have heard that correctly. But Alex was staring at him with horror that matched his. He was supposed to force her down and . . . ?

Stomach lurching, he said, "You can't be serious. This is appalling. Obscene. Against the laws of God and man."

"You mean that, don't you, my Puritan?" Kasan snorted. "Such naïveté. The laws of the *Singa Mainam* are more ancient than those of your Christian god. The leader of a tribe must be potent, able to breed sons and enrich the land with his fertility. That is why this test is part of the game. You must publicly fornicate or forfeit." His expression turned malicious. "Given the effort you have devoted to liberating the lady, I'd think you would welcome this opportunity."

By the primitive rules of male strength and conquest, Gavin had earned Alex, but hell and damnation! His grandfather had been a Scottish vicar, his mother a woman of unimpeachable virtue, and he'd been raised to live by higher standards. "If the test is for virility, summon a girl from one of the flower boats in the harbor." He'd rather risk disease than do this to Alex.

"It must be Mrs. Warren, or no one," Kasan said implacably.

Gavin appealed to the Buddhist priest. "Tuan Daksa, what is your ruling? Doing this would be a crime by the customs of my people."

The priest hesitated as he thought the situation through. "The entire *Singa Mainam* is about this woman. You have taken great risks on her behalf, your fates are bound together. For you she is the goddess, and the only possible choice."

Gavin understood the priest's reasoning, but this was not about reason. "If it must be her, I will forfeit."

"Gavin, no!" Alex's voice cut through the babble of voices. "Look at me."

Gavin steeled himself to do as she asked. Though her face was gray under the tan, she held his gaze fearlessly. "If this is the only way to win this damnable game, *do it.*"

He shook his head, haunted by every sermon he'd ever heard, every spoken and tacit lesson on gentlemanly behavior he'd ever absorbed. "I . . . I can't."

"Gavin," she said with harrowing precision, "there is nothing—*nothing*—that you can do to me that would be as bad as what has been done already."

The humiliation and pain she'd tried to suppress blazed in her eyes, confirming his worst fears about what she had endured during her months of slavery. He hadn't wanted to think of her being ravished as well as beaten, but he could no longer deny the knowledge. She had already survived the unspeakable. By her own will, she was choosing to be violated again as a price she was willing to pay for his freedom, just as he had risked much for hers. Alex's furious struggle against her captors had proved she was a kindred spirit, and was much of the reason he'd felt compelled to free her from slavery.

He hesitated, revolted at the thought of her making such a degrading sacrifice. If he was the saint she claimed, he would refuse, but bleakly he realized he wasn't that self-less. Despite what he'd told her earlier about the easy life he'd have if he stayed in Maduri, the prospect of working for Kasan was suffocating. He needed freedom as a falcon needed wind and an endless sky. Being tethered to another man's will would

lead him to batter against his bars as frantically as Alex had.

He moistened dry lips, and yielded to fear
and selfish desire. "Very well, I . . . I shall do
it. But not in public."

"That is part of the sport of it," Kasan
said with wicked amusement. "Performing
in front of a crowd is not for the faint of
heart."

Gavin was going to have to dishonor Alex
in front of hundreds of avid eyes? *No!*

"The captain and his lady are not of our
people," Tuan Daksa interjected. "There
must be witnesses, of course, but the trial
need not take place in the arena."

Kasan scowled. "If that is your judgment,
Tuan Daksa, so be it. How many witnesses
do you suggest?"

"Two. You, because you are sultan and
part of this game." The priest grimaced.
"And me, because I am the judge and cannot avoid it."

An audience of two was better than a full
arena, but was still too many for what
should be private. The thought of ravishing
a woman who had already suffered too
much at the hands of men turned Gavin's

stomach. He would never be able to look her in the eye again.

Alex said tautly, "Ten years of freedom are worth a few minutes of shame."

She was right, but her role was passive. He would have to act against all his principles, and wasn't sure he could. Trying to match her pragmatism, he asked, "Where will this trial be performed?"

"In a royal guest chamber," Kasan said. "Come."

Gavin's gaze fell on Alex's golden bonds. "Take the damned chains off."

"She is still a slave," Kasan pointed out.

Gavin looked at the priest, hoping for agreement, but the old man said only, "The ankle chains should be removed. The manacles later."

The head guard who carried the keys knelt to unlock the ankle chains. Alex shivered away from him, trying unsuccessfully to hide her distaste when he touched her slender ankles.

As they trooped through the palace, Gavin tried to imagine a way out, but there was none. Alex had cut through shock and revulsion to the heart of their situation: a few minutes of appalling wrongness, or years of him serving a decadent and capricious master while she carried the burden of his sacrifice. Together they must endure this final degradation in order to win their freedom.

The spacious bedchamber was pleasant but neutral. He was glad not to be in the rooms he and Alex had shared. "Enjoy the final test of your Lion Game, Captain." Kasan's voice was edged. "Make sure it is obvious that you mount her properly. Otherwise, I will be forced to join you in the bed to be sure."

The bastard. Gavin had a brief, violent image of breaking Kasan's neck and escaping from the palace with Alex, but they'd never make it through the city to his ship.

Kasan positioned himself on one side where he'd have a clear view. Expression conveying distaste, Tuan Daksa chose a stool on the other side of the room, as distant as possible. The atmosphere was as chilling as a courtroom.

Reminding himself how much was at stake, Gavin came up behind Alex and placed his hands on her shoulders. She flinched as if he'd hit her. Wishing he were anywhere but here, he said softly, "I'm sorry, Alex. This is all so . . . so cold. So wrong."

She visibly collected herself before turning to face him. "It will be over soon. Close your eyes and pretend I'm a jolly pleasure girl you've found at some port."

Knowing honesty was essential, he said, "There have never been any pleasure girls. Only Helena."

Her eyes widened incredulously. "No other woman ever?"

"Never." His smile was wry. "Aren't I a poor excuse for a sailor? I was raised to believe that physical intimacy belongs between man and wife, and spending many of my earlier years at sea reduced temptation." Though he'd seen his share of attractive women, admiration had always been detached, except with the one girl he'd made his wife.

She smiled wistfully. "Helena was even luckier than I realized."

Knowing he must begin, he steeled himself to draw her into his arms. Her tall frame was unyielding as carved wood. For all her common sense and mental toughness, this was as excruciatingly difficult for her as it was for him. No, surely more so.

Gently he stroked her back until she began to relax a little. What next?

"You have beautiful hair." He undid the combs that secured her elaborate coiffure and loosened the coiled locks with his fingers. The silky cascade created a veil of privacy over her face and released a teasing floral scent.

She was a powerfully attractive woman, and he'd desired her since the beginning. The pure line of her profile was poetry. She was his friend, a woman whose strength and character he respected.

And yet his body seemed frozen. On some deep level, he felt that he was betraying Helena. Knowing he must admit what would soon become obvious, he said haltingly, "I don't know if I can do this. I've never felt less . . . less amorous in my life."

Alex glanced up from under her hair, first worried, then sympathetic. Blessedly free of scorn. "We've both been married. Perhaps if we pretend we still are?"

He closed his eyes, trying to transmute Alex into memories of his wife when they'd been alone in the sanctuary of their cabin. When the image became clear, he cupped Alex's face in his hands and trailed gossamer kisses across her forehead and temples. Helena had liked that. Alex, he sensed, was doing her best not to bolt.

Under the floral perfume was an alluring female scent, and she felt undeniably female against him despite her thinness. Yet still he felt no desire. The wicked wrongness of what they were doing overwhelmed everything else.

While he was trying to decide what to do next, she shocked him by running a tentative hand down his torso. The manacles jangled as her palm settled on what he'd thought was frozen. Raw lust flamed through him, hazing his mind and judgment. Dear Lord, it had been so long since he'd been with a woman. . . .

"Progress at last," Kasan said acerbically.

The comment jarred Gavin back to reality, though his blood still throbbed hotly. Thanks to Alex's caress, he knew now that he could perform as required, but his only carnal experiences were worlds away from this travesty. Ironic that this would be simpler if he was accustomed to taking women for quick, selfish pleasure. "Is there anything I can do to make this easier for you, Alex?"

She hid her face against his shoulder. "I suppose . . . just be quick about it."

He took her hand and led her to the low bed. She stretched out on her back, long limbs trembling and the wrist chains draped over her waist like loathsome jewelry. He propped himself on one elbow beside her, shielding her from Kasan's view as much as he thought he could get away with. "Relax, Alexandra. Close your eyes and pretend it's the middle of the night and you're three-quarters asleep. Hardly aware that I'm here."

"My imagination may not be up to this," she said shakily. Her eyes closed and she began slow, deep breaths, but her face was sheened with perspiration.

As cautiously as if she were a nervous horse, he skimmed an open hand over her torso. Though he meant to stroke down to her waist, her breast molded to his palm and the softness was too enticing to leave. Letting his hand rest there, he leaned forward for a kiss, but she turned her head sharply so that his lips met her cheek. Had the men who'd assaulted her forced their mouths on hers, half suffocating her?

Since kissing was too intimate, he

brushed his lips lightly along the line of her jaw and down her throat. The wrapped neckline of the *kebaya* had fallen open to reveal tantalizing curves. He bit his lip to stop himself from kissing her breasts, guessing that also would be too much. "Are you all right?"

She gave a tight little nod that cracked his heart. Could any man have been so valiant about accepting a hated invasion of body and soul?

Reminding himself that she wanted this over quickly, he released her breast and stroked down her abdomen, avoiding the profane glitter of the chain. The thin silk of her sarong warmed luxuriously under his hand. For a man who'd hungered too long, she was a tantalizing banquet of female-ness.

She quivered as he approached the juncture of her thighs. Was that all distress, or was there an element of physical response?

Another decision to be made. Would it be more emotionally destructive to coax her body to respond, even if readiness meant there was less physical pain? He swore to himself. Mating was meant to be joyous sharing, not this tortured navigation through reefs of agonizing complications.

Since physical pain was guaranteed if she couldn't relax, he chose to try to induce a response. Maybe words would help. "In only a few minutes this will be over, Alex," he whispered. "Tomorrow we'll be free, sailing to Java to find your daughter. Then home to England and your family and your real life. If the winds are fair, we'll be in London in four months. Maduri will be only a fading memory, a half-forgotten dream."

Her tension eased as he painted his picture with words. Encouraged, he continued to talk, spinning stories about his ship, his far-flung business interests, sights he'd seen, how much the crew would enjoy having a little girl on board. He poured a river of positive words and images over her, all the while caressing her with increasing intimacy.

But under the flowing words, his control was fraying. Celibacy had been a way of life for years, but now he wanted to bury his face in her hair and hear ardent gasps when he pleased her. He wanted to sink into her with intoxicated kisses and laughter, lose himself in heedless passion rather than thinking, planning, worrying.

*Be quick about it.* He slid his hand under her sarong, gliding over shapely calf and knee until he touched intimate flesh. Instinctively she clamped her thighs together, then forced herself to relax. Her breathing was quick and shallow.

Exploring with exquisite care, he found heat and dewy moisture. This was genuine response, and he nourished it with all the skill he'd learned in his marriage bed. There was a subtle change in the tempo of her breathing and her hands began to open and close on the bedspread like the paws of a kneading kitten.

When he felt she was ready, he moved between her legs, supporting his weight above her. Remembering the sultan's order to make it clear that they actually consummated this obscene act, grimly he exposed himself as he opened the front of the loose trousers. Yet even the knowledge of being watched couldn't dampen his aching, dry-mouthed urgency. The feel of her legs bracketing his, the rich carnal scent of intimacy, incinerated doubts and conscience.

*Be quick about it.*

As soon as he pressed into her heated depths, control shattered and he drowned in searing femininity. It was the headiest of drugs, too long denied. Like a boy on his first attempt, he erupted without even moving, arching his back as he gasped, "Oh, Lord, my dearest love . . ."

He hung suspended in rapture and fulfillment—which splintered when Kasan said tartly, "Congratulations, Captain. Not an impressive performance, but adequate for this test. You have won the *Singa Mainam,* and the woman is yours, to do with as you will."

Panting and disoriented, Gavin moved himself off Alex, jerking her sarong over her again as he did. The deed was done, and now he was saturated with shame for having experienced stunning pleasure in such a corrupt act. "Alex?"

She didn't answer. Her hands were knotted and the bones of her face sharp as a woman dying of fever. He raised a hand, intending comfort, then dropped it as he saw silent tears pouring down her face.

They had won the Game—but dear God, at what price?

# CHAPTER 11

Alex gripped the coverlet, desperately trying to prevent wrenching sobs. That would be the final, unbearable humiliation. Gavin had been a sensitive, generous lover—and that had made the whole experience worse. She had been violated, and didn't even have the satisfaction of hating the man who had done it.

As Gavin moved from the bed, she opened her eyes and pushed herself to a sitting position. For an electric instant their gazes met before she wrenched her eyes away. He looked as if he'd been emotionally flayed to the bone. Bleakly she recognized that they were bound together by a joint degradation no one else could ever fully understand.

"I thought you fortunate to throw the goddess, Captain," the sultan said musingly, "but it wasn't good luck after all, was it? You will not sail away from Maduri unscathed."

Alex watched as the two men locked gazes. They were opposite sides of a coin—one fair, one dark; one rigidly controlled, the other gloating. The sultan was enjoying Gavin's distress, while Alex's anguish was as unimportant to him as if she were a mosquito buzzing about the room.

Though she couldn't hate Gavin, with Kasan hatred was easy. If she knew *pentjak silat,* she would kill him with her bare hands. Was this how her father and stepfather had felt fighting the French? No, her stepfather had always spoken of his French opponents with respect. In contrast, the sultan was despicable—a man who abused his power as easily and naturally as he breathed. She loathed him in a deep and very personal way.

There was so much leashed emotion in Gavin that she feared he'd explode into violence, but luckily his control held. It wouldn't do to anger a ruler who could have them executed on the spot if he wished. "Since all of your requirements have been met, Your Highness . . ." Gavin stepped into the hall and retrieved the manacle key from the head guard. Mutely Alex watched as he unlocked her chains, taking pains not to let his fingertips graze her skin.

He lifted the manacles away—and in one smooth, furious gesture hurled them through the open arches that led to the terrace. Glittering in the sun, they sailed over the railing and hit the ground with a discordant jangle. She rubbed her raw wrists, scarcely able to believe that she was finally free.

Voice eerily calm, Gavin said to the sultan, "It has been . . . interesting, Your Highness. I wish you well in finding the right man to act as your agent to the West."

"I found him," Kasan said dryly. "A pity you did not agree."

"A man held against his will can never be the right man," Gavin said with equal dryness. "But a word of advice. When you return to your list of possibilities, avoid the Englishman, Barton Pierce. He is not a man of honor. The Dutchman, Vandervelt, is a much better man. There are other good choices as well."

The sultan's eyes narrowed. "Can I believe what you say? You are not well disposed to me at the moment."

"That is up to you, Your Highness, but on my oath, I wish neither you nor Maduri ill. Pierce is a man who does ill." Gavin inclined his head. "With your permission, we will now take our leave."

Alex stood, desperate to depart, but Kasan frowned. "I'd thought to hold a farewell banquet for you tonight."

"Now that truly would defeat me." Gavin gave a smile that matched the sultan at his most charming. "I haven't the strength to endure more Maduri hospitality, Your Highness. I still haven't recovered from my last experience of *arak.*"

Kasan laughed, and the tense atmosphere eased. "Travel safely, Captain, and if you ever return to these waters, call on me again."

"Thank you. I shall remember that." Gavin glanced at Alex. "But now we must make a voyage to Sukau."

The thought of Katie strengthened Alex.

She straightened her weary body, holding herself like a soldier's daughter.

Kasan's gaze ran over her with insulting thoroughness. "Don't turn your back on your slave woman, Captain. She looks dangerous. What a pity it will be if you can't enjoy her as you deserve."

"Mrs. Warren belongs to no one but herself," Gavin said as he ushered her out the door. "She is, and always has been, a free woman."

For those words, she could almost love him.

Within an hour, they were on the *Helena.* The journey to the harbor was a blur to Alex as she focused every shred of control on leaving bondage with her head held high. Gavin and Suryo flanked her, stern-faced, almost as eager to leave as she was.

The *Helena* was a sleek, impeccably maintained ship that looked capable of outsailing anything on the high seas. As soon as their party climbed from the jolly boat to the deck, Gavin excused himself and began snapping orders to prepare for departure. Alex gathered that the tide was about to change, and if they didn't leave immediately they'd have to wait for hours.

"This way to your cabin, puan." In Suryo's compassionate gaze she saw that he knew what had happened, and would never speak of it.

Near the breaking point, she followed him below and along a narrow passage to the rear of the vessel. As he opened a door, he asked, "Do you need anything, my lady?"

"Just . . . to be alone."

"As you wish. When you want food or drink, ring for me."

Gratefully she recognized that she'd been granted permission to be private for as long as she needed. Hardly noticing her surroundings, she crossed the cabin and fell onto the neatly made bunk, wrapping herself around a pillow as she began to shake violently.

In the past months she'd wept and raged. She'd damned the pirates and the Islands, blessed the soft-voiced slave women whose compassion had kept her sane, imagined slow, violent deaths for her abusers, and yearned desperately to find Katie. Now her complex emotions defied analysis.

She *couldn't* hate Gavin—he'd risked his life for her simply because he felt it was the right thing to do. But how could she ever look him in the face again without remembering his body inside hers? Her silent screams still echoed in her head. Yet somehow she must master her emotions where he was concerned. Otherwise months of proximity on a small ship would be unbearable.

She remembered his expression when he'd pulled away from her, and buried her face in the pillow, shuddering. Though the encounter had been dreadful for her, she'd been inured by months of bullying and abuse with little hope that she'd ever escape. The damned Lion Game was merely the last, and least physically painful, instance of what she had endured. She would survive it as she'd survived everything else.

For him, though, their forced intimacy had been shattering because he'd had to violate his deepest principles. That was a terrible burden for a man so innately decent. She must forgive him so he could forgive himself.

As she made sense of what had happened, her shaking stilled and eventually she drifted into exhausted slumber. When she awoke, late afternoon sunshine slanted through the windows that ran across one end of the room. The steady roll of the ship and occasional snap of canvas overhead proclaimed that they were at sea.

She stood, grabbing the edge of a built-in cabinet as her stomach shifted uneasily. Taking stock of her surroundings, she realized this must be Gavin's own cabin. Spacious and well furnished, it included a wide bed and jewel-bright Chinese carpets on the polished oak floor. Desk and chairs were secured with discreet staples, and handsome teak storage cabinets had been built into the walls. Bookcases had also been built in, with bars to keep the volumes in place during stormy seas. It was a warm and welcoming place, cozy rather than sumptuous.

Though she didn't like displacing Gavin from his own quarters, she recognized that he wouldn't offer a lady in distress anything less than the ship's best. Still another gift she must accept graciously.

She crossed to a window, still a little queasy even though she'd always been a good sailor. Outside, the sea was molten gold in the sun. In the distance, a dark line of rugged land separated water from sky. Maduri or another island? No matter. It was behind her now.

With slow wonder, she absorbed the fact that she was truly *free.* Captivity and humiliation were behind her now.

Joy bubbled up from deep within. *Free.* For most of her life she'd taken liberty for granted, but never again. It was a gift beyond price, one she'd die rather than lose again. The knowledge gave her an insight into Gavin's adopted homeland, which had paid for its freedom with the blood of its sons.

Suddenly anxious to remove all traces of slavery, she rang for Suryo. When he appeared, she asked, "Could I have hot water to wash myself?"

"Of course." He and a sailor returned with canisters of hot water so quickly that it must have been ready and waiting. She'd expected to wash herself with a cloth and water in a basin, but Suryo pulled a tin hip bath from one of the cabinets.

"A hip bath!" she exclaimed. "I've never seen one on a ship."

"It can only be used when the sea is calm, like tonight," said Suryo. While the sailor poured water into the tub, Suryo left and returned with a tray of food and some folded garments which he left on the desk.

As soon as the men left, Alex stripped off her clothing and settled into the tub. She almost wept as the familiar tang of English lavender slid over her skin. Tropical flowers could be intoxicating, but lavender was the fragrance of her childhood, of dried blossoms scattered among her clothing and the lotion her mother made for dry hands in winter.

The hip bath had high sides to prevent spills as the ship rolled, and was large enough to accommodate Gavin. How many times had he sat naked exactly where she was now? Her flash of embarrassment at the thought was instantly followed by memories of greater intimacy. Harshly she scrubbed her skin with a rough cloth and sponge, as if rubbing herself raw could banish the taint of slavery and defilement.

The water was almost cool when she climbed from the tub and dried herself. Most of the bruises that had marred her skin when she was first brought to the palace had faded to ugly shades of yellow and green. Soon those exterior marks of brutality would be gone. As for the interior ones—well, she'd spent enough time on wailing and self-pity. It was time to reclaim her life.

Suryo had brought a long skirt and over-dress made of Indian print cotton in soft shades of blue. Though similar to Island garments, they were made to her size and the cut was Western. When she donned them, she felt more herself than she had since the pirates had attacked the *Amstel.*

Wanting to regain her sea legs, she drifted around the cabin as she nibbled on a piece of the bread Suryo had brought. This wasn't just Gavin's cabin; it had been de-signed for his wife. That's why there was a hip bath and a bed large enough for two and luxurious Chinese rugs. His love for Helena showed in every detail.

Her eye was caught by a small painting tucked between the bookcases and a stor-age cabinet. Moving closer, she discovered the portrait of a young blond woman wear-ing a gown of blue Chinese silk and a radiant smile. So this was Helena. Lovely and ethereal, she was a woman who loved, and knew she was loved in return.

Alex glanced involuntarily at the bed. Gavin and Helena had shared that bed. Quite possibly Helena Elliott had died there. Yet she felt no sad ghosts lingering. Ghosts were born of regrets, not happy marriages.

Reminding herself again that Gavin had chosen to put her in this cabin, she decided that her first goal must be to eliminate the horrible awkwardness between them. Otherwise, he might spend the whole voyage avoiding her and tormenting himself. That could not be allowed to happen, and she must be the one to make the first move.

The thought undermined her fragile composure, but the longer she delayed the harder it would become. She tied back her hair with a length of ribbon—Suryo had thought of everything—then left the cabin and headed up to the deck. The helmsman and officer of the watch were back on the quarterdeck. It was too dark to see detail, but she thought the officer was the young chief mate she'd been introduced to when she came on board. He ducked his head respectfully when he saw her.

She was about to approach and ask the captain's whereabouts when she spotted a familiar form at the ship's bow. Gavin's hands were braced on the railing, and his fair hair tumbled in the wind as he stared into the darkening sky, standing as still as carved marble.

Wiping suddenly damp palms on her skirt, she made her way forward. A yard from the railing, she hesitated, swamped with vivid, disquieting memories of his physical strength. She'd seen him climb a sheer cliff, battle a dragon, defeat a master of unarmed combat—and trap her with his weight and scent and powerful male body.

Her heart accelerated as irrational fear burned through her. Once it would never have occurred to her to fear a man. As a child, she'd feared nothing. Certainly not the men in her life.

She *hated* being afraid.

Her jaw set. Of all men on earth, Gavin was the last one she should fear. She moved forward to the railing before she could lose her nerve. He stiffened when he became aware of her presence. She half expected him to bolt, but he stayed. Someday, maybe she would find humor in their mutual skittishness, but not tonight.

She lifted her face into the clean, free wind. The rhythmic rise and fall of the bow soothed her jangled nerves and reminded her why she was here.

"I thank you from the bottom of my heart, Gavin. Don't blame yourself for what had to be done. You saved me and yourself. That's not a sin."

"Perhaps not. But it's certainly no virtue." After a long silence, he said, "We can be married in Batavia. There are Christian churches there."

"Marriage?" Her head snapped around and she stared at him, shocked out of her composure. "What are you talking about?"

"Having behaved like husband and wife, we must now make that a reality," he said with bone-dry precision.

She should have realized he'd think this way. He was a gentleman, he had compromised her, and he was doing the honorable thing by offering marriage. Why was she so disquieted by the thought?

Because she didn't want marriage ever again. Because she wasn't fit to be a decent man's wife. Least of all, Gavin's wife.

Burying her feelings for later pondering, she said, "Of all the generous things you've done, this is the most generous, but it isn't necessary. You have sacrificed quite enough for my sake. You certainly don't have to marry a stranger as well."

"We're hardly strangers anymore, Alexandra." His deep voice was cool and emotionless.

"There's no point in being bound for life by something that happened on the opposite side of the world from our homes. You don't want to marry me, I don't want to marry you or anyone, so the subject is closed."

He smiled faintly. "I can see why you were so bad at being submissive."

She colored. "Sorry, was I rude? Don't think I'm not appreciative, Gavin. I already owe you more than I can repay in one lifetime. There's no need to make my debt even greater."

"Marrying you wouldn't be a punishment, Alex. I think we could rub along tolerably well. But . . ." he hesitated, groping for words, "perhaps there is too much between us to ever be comfortable with each other."

"I'd like to be friends. Is that possible?"

She could feel a lessening of his tension. "I'd like that, too," he said. "It's a long voyage to England. Better to be relaxed than walking on eggshells."

"Agreed then—we shall be friends, and it will be as if the . . . the last event of the Lion Game never happened." Forgetting wouldn't be that simple, but agreeing to put the incident behind them was a start. "If you ever wish to marry again, find a sweet young bride who hasn't been tarnished by life."

"I did that once. I'll not destroy another innocent girl."

"Destroy?" She frowned, sensing he'd said more than he intended. "From everything I've seen and heard, Helena was a cherished and much loved wife. That's hardly destruction."

He hesitated before saying haltingly, "Helena's health was always frail. I worried that shipboard life might be too much for her, but she didn't want us to be separated, and neither did I. If I'd left her safe in Boston maybe she'd be alive today."

Her heart ached for him. Believing he'd cost his beloved wife her life must have created a bottomless well of guilt. No wonder he'd felt compelled to rescue a desperate slave woman. Wanting to assuage that deep grief, she said, "I saw the painting of Helena. You gave her years of happiness. Many women don't have that much in a lifetime."

"We were happy," he agreed, "but her physician in Boston had warned it would be dangerous for her to have a child. If I hadn't . . ." He stopped abruptly.

Knowing she was on very delicate ground, Alex said, "Didn't Helena want a baby desperately?"

He glanced at her, a silhouette against a starry night. "How did you know that?"

"I'm a woman. It's natural to want to have the child of the man you love." Or to have a child even if the marriage was less than loving, but that didn't need to be said. "Helena took her risks willingly. And now—well, she and Anna are together."

"I'd like to believe that," he said in a raw whisper.

"Believe it." Alex had never been surer of anything. "Remember how Achilles was given the choice of a short, glorious life or a long, dull one? He chose glory and died young, but his fame lives on. If Helena was always frail, you gave her a great gift by letting her choose love and adventure. We all die. At least she died where she wanted to be, doing what she wanted to do with the man she loved, and she will always live in your heart. You didn't destroy her, you fulfilled her."

Gavin exhaled roughly. "I hadn't thought of this from a woman's point of view."

She remembered that ethereal girl with the shimmering smile. Helena had been born to love, and she'd given herself willingly. She'd chosen well, too. Alex wished that Edmund had loved as deeply as Gavin, and been as true to his marriage vows.

She shivered a little, thinking the wind was getting cooler. "Your Scottish vicar grandfather deserves credit for instilling integrity and honesty, but you're not responsible for all the world's ills, Gavin."

"The captain of a ship *is* responsible for all that happens aboard. It's a hard habit to break, but . . . I'll try."

"Remember Helena happy. That was the truth of your marriage."

There was a long silence while the ship rose and fell, occasional sprays of water spattering them, until he said quietly,

"Thank you, Alexandra. Are you always so wise?"

She was glad she'd been able to help, but honesty compelled her to say, "When I think of Katie, I'm not wise at all. Do you think we'll find her?"

"It's hard to say. Kasan said she was sent to the harem of the Rajah of Sukau. If she's still there, we're in luck. Suryo investigated, and the rajah is elderly and well respected." Gavin glanced at her. "Rajah Fahad is also the father of Kasan's chief wife."

"You mean Katie might have been sent as a gift to Kasan's father-in-law?" Alex said, appalled.

"Probably. It suggests that Kasan is more involved with the pirates than he would admit publicly."

She swore under her breath. "The man is a monster. I wish you could have broken his neck."

"He certainly made our lives difficult, but as Oriental despots go, Kasan is relatively enlightened. There are lurid stories of his personal life, some of which are probably true, and his people don't have the rights that Englishmen or Americans do. Still, he doesn't usually slaughter his own people out of hand, and he doesn't tax them into starvation. Maduri is strong and independent and likely to stay that way."

She remembered the strange, tense bond between the men. "You admire him."

"Some," Gavin admitted. "But I surely don't want to work for him. He has too much power, and that makes him dangerous. Rather like my idea of a mad English duke."

Alex thought of the English dukes she knew, who were actually a civilized lot, but she was willing to grant Gavin his republican principles. Power could indeed corrupt. "As long as the Rajah of Sukau isn't cruel or mad. How long until we reach Java?"

"Three or four days, if the winds hold."

"Then what? How does one approach an Oriental despot and beg for a favor?"

"After we clear Sukau customs, I'll send Suryo to the palace with the fanciest gift on the *Helena.* I have a French clock that looks as if it were stolen from Versailles. Very impressive, and it should demonstrate we're rich enough to be worthy of the rajah's notice. Suryo will ask for an audience. Then we wait."

"I'm not good at waiting, but I suppose I'll manage." She closed her eyes and prayed. A miracle had brought her out of slavery. Now she needed another.

# CHAPTER 12

*Sukau on Java*

"His Most Gracious Majesty, the Rajah of Sukau will see you now." The chamberlain gestured for Gavin and Alex to come with him.

As they followed the chamberlain down a breezy passageway, Gavin studied his companion from the corner of his eye. Recurring seasickness had made her even thinner than on Maduri, and three days of waiting in Sukau harbor had her vibrating with tension. Yet her weight loss emphasized the elegance of her bones, and she glided through the palace with the grace and dignity of a queen.

During the passage from Maduri she'd

sewed industriously and now wore a European style gown. With her dark hair pinned
up, she looked every inch an English lady.
Very different from Alex in sarong and
gilded chains, which made it easier for him
to suppress the carnal thoughts that had
haunted him ever since their forced intercourse. Hot, vivid memories shamed him—
but he was unable to banish them from his
mind or his restless, haunting dreams.

He wrenched his mind away from that,
thinking it would be more appropriate to
pray they'd find Katie here. Failure would
crush Alex.

No, nothing could crush Alex. She'd continue her search until she succeeded or
died trying. She was worthy of her warrior
ancestors.

The chamberlain led them through a
small chamber with doors on each end.
They stepped through the second door into
an immense aviary. Gavin caught his breath
in amazement. The aviary had been designed as a woodland glade, with a stream
running across one corner. Waterfowl
splashed happily while brilliantly colored
parrots and songbirds squawked and fluttered from tree to tree. The French gift clock

stood on a mahogany pillar, a bird of paradise perched on top, preening its gaudy feathers.

The sight was so dazzling it took him a moment to focus on the elderly turbaned man who sat in a tall, lacquered throne in the center of the room. A canopy protected the chair. From its peak a drab bird sang a hauntingly beautiful song.

Certain the elderly man was Rajah Fahad, Gavin bowed deeply. "Your majesty, we are honored to be admitted to your presence."

The rajah made a dismissive gesture. In his hands he held a small white dove that was almost invisible against his white beard. "You interest me, Captain Elliott," he said in heavily accented but fluent English. "Your gift was magnificent. What magnificent favor do you want in return?"

The rajah's directness was surprising but welcome. "My companion, Mrs. Warren, is an English widow of high birth. While sailing from Sydney to London, her ship was attacked by pirates. She and her daughter were captured, and the child taken away from her."

The rajah turned his gaze to Alex. "The lady was enslaved?"

They'd discussed whether or not she should speak for herself. The fact that the rajah was acknowledging her presence gave Alex leave to plead directly. "Yes, Your Majesty. I was freed by the intervention of Captain Elliott, and now I seek my daughter. We were informed that she was sent to you as a gift."

She dropped to her knees and bent to touch her forehead to the marble floor in a Chinese kowtow of absolute submission. Looking up again, she said beseechingly, "Please, Your Majesty, if you can help me find her, you shall have my gratitude forever."

He studied her face, his bony fingers stroking the white feathers of the dove. "There are many children in my women's quarters. What does your daughter look like?"

"Katie is almost nine years old, with long blond hair and blue eyes like mine," Alex replied. "She was taken from me half a year ago."

The rajah gestured for her to stand and beckoned his chamberlain forward. After a low-voiced exchange, the chamberlain left.

Languidly Fahad raised the dove, which

took flight from his palm. On its breast was a scarlet circle the color of blood. "My sacred doves are said to be very rare. Do you have them in your country, Captain?"

"Not that I know of, Your Majesty." Gavin indicated the aviary. "Nor have I seen a sight to match this. Surely paradise can hold no greater beauty." A small bird landed on his shoulder and pecked on a gold-braided epaulet, pausing occasionally to regard Gavin with bright eyes.

Amused, Gavin fell into a discussion of birds and natural history with the rajah. Alex waited quietly, outwardly calm but hands knotted at her sides. A sacred dove approached and pecked at the hem of her gown. She flinched, startling the bird. Gavin worried that she might shatter during this last, excruciating wait. Or perhaps she might explode and shatter Sukau. Hell hath no fury like a frantic mother.

Behind them came the sound of an opening door. Gavin glanced back and saw that the chamberlain had returned with a heavily veiled woman and child. Gavin's heart sank when he saw the girl. She was about the right age, but surely that demure, submissive figure couldn't be the daughter of a woman like Alex.

Alerted by instinct, Alex whirled, her face lighting with joy. "Katie!"

*"Mama!"* Demureness vanished as the girl shrieked and raced across the aviary, startling birds into whirling clouds. As she ran, her veil and headdress fell away, revealing shining blond hair and an exquisite, miniature version of Alex's face.

They met in the middle of the aviary. Alex dropped to her knees to catch her daughter close, crying, "Katie, Katie, my love," as tears streamed down her face.

Gavin's throat tightened as he watched the reunion. His daughter Anna would be of similar age and coloring, but the thought didn't sting as it used to. In his mind was an image of Helena and Anna laughing together in a heavenly meadow, the child grown to the size she would be if she had lived. Alex's words the night they left Maduri had given him that peaceful vision.

Speaking through her tears to the rajah, Alex said, "The lost has been found, Your Majesty. I am penniless now, but if you will trust me, I shall send a ransom fit for a princess if you will let me take my daughter home to England."

"There is no need for that, Mrs. Warren. It is not right for mother to be separated from child. Go with my blessing."

As Gavin bowed and thanked the rajah, he thought with stunned disbelief that it couldn't be this easy. Granted, he'd sent a lavish present and the rajah had a reputation for fairness and decency, but could recovering Katie Warren really be so simple?

It was.

Alex accompanied her daughter and the veiled escort back to the women's quarters so Katie could collect her few possessions and say goodbye. She was bemused to hear Katie chattering in fluent Malay. From the hugs and flowing tears of the rajah's women, Katie had been a favorite, and clearly well treated. Gavin had been right that her daughter could have lived here happily. But, thank the Lord, that wasn't necessary.

As they left with their guide, Alex carried a bag of Katie's possessions in one hand while Katie clung to the other. Though Katie had chattered nonstop since their reunion, she fell silent after they left the women's quarters. Concerned, Alex said, "Are you all right, Katybird? It must be hard to leave the friends you made here."

Katie nodded. "I won't ever see them again, will I?"

Alex winced at the sadness in her daughter's voice. Less than a year ago she'd lost her Australian friends, too. "Probably not, sweetheart. Home is on the other side of the world."

"Can England be home when I've never been there?"

It was a good question. Alex thought before answering. "Home begins with family. When you meet your grandparents and cousins, England will begin to feel like home. You'll make new friends, and this time they can be friends for a lifetime."

"I'd like to have forever friends," Katie said wistfully.

Alex tightened their handclasp, vowing that her daughter would never have to suffer such drastic losses again. "It's hard to lose people you care about. I was terrified when the pirates took you away."

Her daughter looked suddenly older. "I

was frightened, too, Mama. I . . . I thought I'd never see you again."

How long had Katie lived in terror before being put into friendly hands? Swallowing the lump in her throat, Alex said, "That might have happened, if not for Captain Elliott."

"The man who was with you in the bird garden?"

"Yes, he's a sea captain. He found me on the island of Maduri and obtained my freedom." Which was all Katie ever needed to know about her mother's enslavement. "He'll take us on his ship all the way to England."

When they reentered the aviary, Alex gave Gavin a nod to say that all was well. He turned to the rajah, who now had a scarlet parrot on his shoulder. After more bows and flowery thanks and farewells, the foreigners took their leave.

As they walked through the palace, Alex introduced Gavin to her daughter. Katie said gravely, "Are you a Dutch sea captain?"

"No, I'm American," he replied with equal gravity.

"Good. I don't like Dutch sea captains."

The comment was another mark of the fear Katie had experienced in the pirate raid, because she had liked the *Amstel* captain well enough at the time. On the voyage home, Alex must draw her daughter into discussing what had happened. She was young; with luck she'd soon forget the worst parts.

A pity adults didn't forget so easily.

Katie loved their cabin. Excited by the drama of the day, she bounced around the room, admiring the books and furnishings. "This is ever so much nicer than the *Amstel.*"

"That's because Captain Elliott gave us his own cabin." Alex relaxed in a chair, her gaze following her daughter's movements around the cabin. She'd grown noticeably in the last months. She wasn't such a little girl anymore, but Alex was so happy that it was easy to swallow her regrets for the time together they'd lost.

Katie ran her fingertips over the leather bindings of a shelf of books. "The captain likes you."

Alex felt a flutter of nerves, as if Gavin had made an advance. The thought was both alarming and . . . gratifying. Reminding herself not to read too much into a child's casual comment, she said, "I'm very fond of him, too. He has been all that is kind." Wanting to forestall more comments about Gavin, she continued, "We'll start your lessons again tomorrow morning. I hope you've not forgotten everything you ever knew about French and numbers and globes."

Katie stared at her, appalled. "Lessons again so *soon*?"

Alex almost laughed at her daughter's dismay. "Well—perhaps we'll take a day or two of holiday. Don't look ill-used—you've always enjoyed your schooling."

"One can't admit that," Katie said, voice prim but eyes dancing. "Did you have lessons in the palace?"

"Yes, but not numbers or French or books. Yasmeen, who looked after me, taught me Malay. All of us girls had lessons in dancing and singing and how to behave like Island ladies." Gracefully Katie began the precise, delicate movements of a Sukaun dance. "I liked the dancing. They said I was good."

"I'm sure you were." Alex watched, impressed and a little uneasy at more proof of how adaptable children were. How many years would it have taken Katie to become a Sukaun girl, her English heritage almost forgotten? Hugging her daughter, she said, "I've missed you so much, Katybird. So terribly, terribly much."

"I missed you too, Mama," Katie whispered. "I told myself I must be brave and not cry, but sometimes I couldn't help it."

"Neither could I." Alex found tears in her eyes again, and didn't even bother to feel guilty over her lack of control.

Despite her joy, that night Alex was jerked from sleep by nightmares, as she was most nights. She awakened sweaty and gasping and nauseated. Though her mind knew she was free, that didn't stop panic from flooding every particle of her being. Fear of captivity. Fear of losing the world she knew.

Fear of rape.

Careful not to wake her sleeping daughter, she slid from the bed and went to one of the windows that overlooked the wake of the ship. Opening it brought her fresh air, and she'd found that watching the horizon helped control seasickness.

The night air and the horizon that divided the ocean from sky helped settle her churning stomach, while repeating fiercely that she was safe and free gradually slowed her hammering heart. Wearily she wondered how long the nightmares would last. She was only a week out of slavery. Surely time would diminish the night terrors.

Quietly she returned to the bed. Katie, at least, suffered no nightmares. The innocent curve of her cheek and the soft rhythm of her breath soothed Alex as nothing else on earth could have. She was so lucky. So incredibly lucky. So full of love she had no words to describe it. She brushed a kiss on Katie's forehead. "Rest well, my darling."

Then she lay back on her pillow and forced herself to relax until she drifted once more into restless sleep.

Despite nightmares, the next days were the happiest time Alex had known since she'd married and left her parents' home. As Gavin had promised, the crew enjoyed having a child on board, and Katie was the ship's pet. She and Gavin became particularly good friends, for he always listened to her with the attention he gave adults.

At first, Alex worried that Gavin would find it painful to be around a child the age of his lost daughter. Instead, she sensed that he found it healing. He and Katie had an easy relationship very different from the one Katie had had with her father. Though Edmund had loved his daughter, he'd never known quite what to do with a lively little girl.

After two days of holiday, Alex fulfilled her threat to resume teaching. Gavin's books and maps were good sources for reading and arithmetic and geography, and Katie ate her lessons up like a hungry puppy. She'd always been a good student, and her sojourn in another culture had increased her appetite for learning.

One daily assignment was for Katie to start a journal of her Indies experiences. Besides offering writing practice, the entries gave Alex the details of her daughter's life in captivity. ("Sukau has many ways of cooking rice. I like peanut sauce and *nasi goreng*.")

It was a relief to read confirmation that after the first wrenching shocks, Katie had settled down comfortably in her new world. There should be no future nightmares, other than the fear of losing her mother, which kept Katie close now. Alex didn't mind—they both needed that closeness. By the time they reached England, they should be capable of a more normal existence.

She was ready for that. Lord, was she ready!

# CHAPTER 13

As they anchored in the harbor of a small island to provision before crossing the wide
expanse of the Indian Ocean, Gavin saw
Alex and Katie hanging on the railing,
watching raptly as praus skimmed around
the *Helena* with islanders offering food and
other wares. He smiled at the sight. Alex
was like a girl herself these days. Though
still too thin from captivity and not yet in full
possession of her sea legs, there was a ra-
diance about her that was irresistible. Katie
had some of that same glowing quality.
When she grew up, she'd be a stunner.

As he approached Alex and her daughter,
a boatman held up a simple cloth doll

dressed in scraps of fabric. While Katie stared longingly, Alex bit her lip in frustration.

Realizing that Katie had no toys and Alex had no money, Gavin leaned over the railing and bargained with the boatman. They reached a price and Gavin tossed down a coin. The doll soared upward in return. Katie squealed at the prospect of it falling into the water, but Gavin leaned over the rail and snagged it in midair. "Here you are, Katie," he said as he presented it with a flourish. "A remembrance of the Islands."

"Oh, thank you, *thank you,* Captain Elliott!" She cradled the doll in her arms, her eyes shining.

"Thanks indeed, Captain," Alex said warmly. While she never asked anything for herself, she welcomed attempts to please her daughter.

Wanting more of that warmth, Gavin said, "We'll be here for a good part of the day while we top up the water supply and load fresh provisions. How about if I take you two ladies to a pretty little beach just north of here? We can take a luncheon basket and enjoy one last day on land before we set off across the ocean." And maybe Alex would be able to keep food down better on solid land.

His invitation was accepted with alacrity. While Alex took her daughter below to prepare, Gavin arranged for food and hired a prau from the island head man.

Because of the day's heat, Gavin went below to put on island clothing. It was odd to be living in a small mate's cabin after years of being a captain. He could stand in the middle and touch anything in the room, and his head just missed the ceiling when he stood straight. No matter; Alex and Katie needed the space and comfort of the captain's cabin more than he did. Meals in the cramped cuddy and charts and logs jammed in with his shirts were a minor inconvenience.

As practical as Gavin, Alex also dressed herself and her daughter in island clothing, with feet bare and straw hats to protect pale northern complexions. They left the ship in a holiday mood.

The prau was small enough that Gavin could easily handle the sails by himself, and he enjoyed its swallow-like maneuverability as they rounded one of the horns of the harbor to reach the cove. Protected on the land side by cliffs, it was a Northerner's dream of an island paradise, with transparent aquamarine waters lapped against a crescent of white sand. They had a lazy luncheon sprawled in the shade of rustling palm trees, chatting idly on topics of no importance.

In danger of falling asleep, Gavin said, "I feel like stretching my legs. Does anyone care to join me for a walk?"

"We'd love to." Alex and Katie got to their feet and the three of them began to walk along the water's edge, feet and ankles being splashed by incoming waves. Katie dashed ahead of the adults, playing with the waves and shrieking with laughter when the water caught her unexpectedly.

"Thank you for bringing us here," Alex said. "Today will provide a warm and lovely memory in cold English winters."

"I suspect that the English became such great explorers because they're always searching for a better climate. And finding it almost everywhere."

She laughed. "I expect you're right, but I, for one, will be delighted to spend the rest of my days in Britain. I look forward to being an eccentric little old lady with cats, who will bore my grandchildren with tales of my travels."

He studied her elegant profile. "I have trouble imagining you as old."

Her laughter faded. "Sometimes I feel ancient. But you were right that eventually Maduri would be only a half-forgotten dream. Already it seems a little unreal. As if everything happened to someone else." She shivered despite the warmth of the day.

Thinking of the shadows under her eyes even when she was laughing, he asked, "Are you having nightmares?"

"Sometimes," she admitted, "but they're not important. Most of the time I couldn't be happier. Grateful to be free, and to have my daughter back." She slanted him a glance. "What about you? Do nightmares haunt your sleep?"

"Sometimes. Nothing like you must experience." He glanced away from her, afraid that the hot rush of memories of their intimacy might show in his eyes. Most of the time he was able to keep desire locked tightly away, but it still flared up awkwardly at unexpected moments, leaving him frustrated and yearning. Wanting to change the subject, he continued, "I'm glad to have today to say goodbye to the Indies. Though England is beautiful in its own way, it's not like this."

"You seem to love the East deeply. Might you return some day?"

"Perhaps to visit, but not to live." He tried unsuccessfully to skip a flat shell across the water. "I've spent most of the last dozen years at my house in Macao, or living on a narrow slice of waterfront in Canton, or sailing among the islands. It's been exciting and demanding and rewarding, but I feel as if . . . as if this phase of my life is over. It's time for a change. There will be no shortage of challenges in England."

"You seem to regard England as a grim trial rather than a longed-for destination." She sidestepped an aggressive wave. "What draws you to a place that makes you uncomfortable?"

He hesitated, wondering how much to say. There was no need to mention the score he needed to settle with a man who'd tried to ruin him for no good reason, but she deserved to know the family reasons. "My father left England in disgrace. His family was infuriated when he 'married beneath him,' even though my mother's birth was perfectly respectable. He was disowned by his father."

"That's why you hate the English class system so much?"

"Yes, and there's also more to my father's story. He was in the navy, and after a disastrous battle with the French his superiors put the blame on him because he no longer had any family support. He barely escaped court martial. In recognition of past service, he was allowed to resign his commission, and we sailed for America."

"So the lure of the sea was bred into you," she said thoughtfully. "Did your father ever make peace with his family?"

"No. I look forward to arriving in London, walking into the family home, and announcing to my grandfather that I'm the black sheep's son."

She glanced at him, eyes worried under the shadow of the hat brim. "If you want to be accepted by your father's family, belligerence might not be the best way to do it."

"I have no desire to be accepted by a pack of intolerant bigots. I just want to show them that I exist. My grandfather's condemnation didn't destroy my father's life, and matters nothing to me." He smiled at the vision he'd held for years. "I look forward to planting myself in London as a rich, vulgar American, and explaining to anyone who's interested that I'm a bent twig of the tree of Elliott."

She laughed. "That's rather wicked of you. I should think the pleasures of revenge would soon grow old, though."

"Revenge is too strong a word—justice would be more accurate. But most of my reasons for settling in England are good, practical business ones. Elliott House needs a London office, and I have enough friends and rivals there to make the city interesting." Friends, rivals, and one genuine enemy.

Katie came racing back with her hands full of shells. "Look, Mama!"

"How pretty these shells are!" Alex knotted them into a corner of her sarong. "I suppose you're going to collect more?"

Laughter floating behind her, Katie ran off to do exactly that. Gazing on her daughter, Alex said softly, "I would be very saddened if my family disowned me. Did your father really shrug off his family's disapproval so easily?"

"To be honest, no," Gavin admitted. "There was a sadness in him after we left England. He never spoke of the past, except once when he told me that the navy charges against him were nonsense. A few years ago I hired someone to look into the battle that destroyed his career. The investigator confirmed that my father was not to blame—in fact, his actions probably prevented the disaster from being even worse. But truth doesn't much matter when the authorities want a scapegoat."

"How did your mother feel about being forced to leave her homeland?"

"She regretted leaving friends and family, but she had an adventurous spirit, and America appealed to her."

"You're obviously your mother's son." Alex hesitated. "You said they're both dead."

"My mother always sailed with my father—she said they'd been separated too often when he was in the navy." Gavin swallowed, not immune to the pain even now. "They were on their way home from the Caribbean when a hurricane drove the ship onto an offshore reef. There were . . . no survivors."

Alex touched his hand. "I'm so sorry, Gavin."

"The sea is a dangerous mistress. She gives, and she takes." The words were stoic, but he clasped her hand for a moment before releasing it.

Ahead of them, a wave knocked Katie from her feet and rolled her along the sloping sand. Though she didn't seem endangered, Alex caught up her skirts and skipped off to retrieve her daughter. Katie emerged from the water sputtering and totally soaked, but beaming. After pulling her above the water line, Alex enfolded Katie in a hug even though the embrace soaked her clothing.

Sunshine and sand shimmered around the pair, creating an image Gavin would never forget. Madonna and child. Unconditional love and youthful innocence. He was struck with a paralyzing burst of longing. He wanted to be part of that circle of love and acceptance. For too much of his life he'd been alone.

Building Elliott House had absorbed him—that and the desire to prove himself to the faceless family who'd cast off his father. He'd accomplished much through unrelenting hard work, but when he looked back at his life, it wasn't wealth and success that gave him satisfaction, but memories of Helena and the happiness they'd shared. He wanted that kind of happiness again.

He wanted Alex. He wanted her strength and loyalty, and Katie's sunny sweetness, and the chance of other children. He wanted to be part of a family. He had a mental image of Alex's parents—a bluff, hearty colonel stepfather, the loving mother whose only flaw was being too perfect. Half brothers and sister. A real family, bound by love and laughter and arguments. He wanted desperately to be one of them.

Giggling, Alex and Katie turned to walk toward him, arms around each other's waists. They were damp and draggled and so beautiful they made him ache. Trying not to notice the way Alex's damp garments clung to her lithe form, he met them with a smile. "Time we head back, before Katie is burned by the sun."

They ambled back to the prau, Katie collecting still more shells, while he reminded himself that Alex had not yet recovered from her months of captivity. Probably there would always be emotional scars. If he was to win her, he'd have to be patient, because making an advance too soon might drive her away forever.

Luckily, he was very good at patience.

Skin pinkened by the sun and tired from the day's adventure, Alex and Katie retired early that night. Katie fell asleep with the ease of childhood. Alex didn't, but tonight she didn't mind wakefulness.

Gavin was such good company. Every inch a man, he was so sure of himself that he could be comfortable with women. Though she guessed that he was still haunted by their forced intimacy, he wasn't allowing it to cripple him. Time healed, and the farther they sailed from Maduri, the more unreal the Lion Game seemed.

She had a swift vision of him laughing, his gray eyes as intimate as a kiss. The memory brought a stirring of desire, a feeling she'd thought was gone forever. Immediately she quashed it. She wasn't going to fall in love again, especially not with Gavin. If he decided to remarry, London had plenty of lovely young women for him to choose from.

She rolled onto her side, quelling that dis-

turbing image, but she couldn't fully suppress that unwelcome pulse of desire, and
no wonder—Gavin was the most attractive
man she'd ever met, and they knew each
other in ways most people never experienced. Unfortunately, desire was intertwined with fear and pain and hatred. With
suffocating weight and an unwanted invasion of her most intimate self. . . .

Her breathing quickened with anxiety,
and her stomach began to roil. Swearing
under her breath, she rose and opened a
window so she could breathe fresh sea air.

The full moon poured silver over the
waves, a primal image of peace and tranquility. Even if praus full of pirates showed
up, she'd feel safe with Gavin in charge of
the ship. He'd never have allowed the post-
storm laxness that had led to the capture of
the *Amstel.*

Feeling better, she said goodnight to the
moon and started to turn away. Then she
stopped.

A full moon.

How long had it been since her courses?
She tried to calculate, but it wasn't necessary. She knew in her bones why she'd

been ill so often, felt so fatigued and emotional. The horror of Maduri had reached out to snare her once more.

She was pregnant.

# CHAPTER 14

A storm was moving in, so Gavin went aloft to help take in most of the sails. When the work was done, he lingered in the rigging to enjoy the view and the pleasant burn of well-used muscles. At this height there was an exhilarating swing as the ship cut through the swells of the Indian Ocean. They'd seen no other sails for days. The world was reduced to wide sea and wider sky and the secure creak of the ship's timbers.

Seven bells struck. Eleven thirty in the morning, time to get his sextant and shoot the sun to check their position. They'd been making good time. If the winds held, they'd be in England by early summer.

He swung his way down to the deck, and found Katie watching with big eyes. "I didn't know that the captain went aloft," she said.

"The master of a ship doesn't have to, but he can if he wants to," Gavin explained. "I rather enjoy working the sails when I have the time."

Katie eyed the crisscrossed lines of the main rigging. "Can I learn how to do it?"

"No," Alex said as she joined her daughter. Her glance fell upon Gavin's casual, open-throated shirt and slid away. "It takes a great deal of strength to climb the rigging, doesn't it, Captain?"

"Yes, boys don't usually start working on shipboard until they're at least twelve. But I can show you how to shoot the sun with a sextant," he added when Katie looked disappointed.

Perking up, she asked her mother, "May I?"

"By all means—it's educational." Though Alex smiled at her daughter, her face was strained and there were dark smudges under her eyes.

Gavin had thought their picnic on the beach marked a breakthrough for Alex, but ever since that day she'd been getting thinner and quieter. Perhaps that was the effect of recurrent seasickness, or perhaps the closer they came to England, the more she worried about her reception. A deep sense of shame, even if it was undeserved, would make it hard to face family and friends.

On Maduri he might have asked her what was wrong and received a straight answer, but the closeness they'd shared was gone. He missed having Alex as a friend. It was also damned difficult to gently woo a woman who kept him at a distance despite the close quarters on the *Helena.*

Katie enjoyed her lesson on the sextant. "You'd make a fine sailor," he remarked after she correctly read the angle.

She smiled at the compliment but shook her head. "I like being on land, Captain Elliott. Days are too much alike on shipboard."

"Today will be different because we're sailing into a storm. Once the wind comes up and it starts to rain, you'll need to go below." Seeing worry in Alex's eyes, he added, "It's nothing the *Helena* can't weather easily."

"The ship will do well. I'm not so sure about my stomach."

She was right to be concerned—the storm would give her an uncomfortable night. "Try not to lie down—that usually increases the vertigo."

"Fresh air helps, too." She gave him a wry smile. "Don't worry about me. I've survived worse."

So she had, but that didn't mean he wouldn't worry about her.

Flashing lightning, pounding thunder, lashing rain. Alex's stomach hated the storm even more than the rest of her did. Though she'd spent enough time at sea to know the ship was in no danger, this was the worst weather she'd endured since the disastrous tempest that led to the capture of the *Amstel.* Even as she chatted and played games with Katie, her mind obsessively remembered that storm and its aftermath.

Since the galley fire had been extinguished for safety's sake, the evening meal was dry biscuits and cold tea. Bored and sleepy, Katie retired early. Alex tucked blankets and pillows tightly around her daughter to keep her secure in the bed, but she wasn't ready for sleep herself. Not only would lying down turn her nausea into full, roiling sickness, but she was drained by the effort of staying cheerful in front of Katie.

The hours passed slowly as she sat in Gavin's heavy chair, which was secured to the floor with bars to hold it steady against the ship's pitching. The drumming rain and howling wind were occasionally punctuated by the indignant squawking of poultry, whose cages had been taken below before the storm. She didn't blame them for complaining; she felt the same way.

Finally, in the hours past midnight, the storm began to abate. Craving fresh air, she pulled on the cloak she'd made out of ship's cloth and peered out the door. The silent passage lined with officer's cabins was empty, so she slipped out and climbed up to the deck. In the darkness, her navy cloak shielded her from the gaze of solicitous sailors who would tell her to return to her cabin.

Though the storm had diminished, enough savage energy remained to suit her mood. She scanned the deck. Usually members of the watch who weren't actively working gathered on the forecastle, but with rain still slashing across the deck, they'd taken shelter in the lee of the galley, so she was unlikely to be noticed if she passed on the windward side of the ship.

Hanging onto the railing, she made her way through the pelting rain to the privacy of the bow, occasionally getting splashed as water rolled over the deck. Everything loose had been secured or taken below like the chickens, and the ship carried only enough sail to keep it steady.

When she reached the bow, she braced both hands on the railing as the *Helena* slid into the troughs of waves, then rose triumphantly again. It was almost like riding a spirited horse, but on horseback, she always felt powerful and in control. Now she was a mere passenger, dependent on the skill of the *Helena*'s crew.

Underneath her was the ship's figure-head. Instead of the usual buxom female, the carving showed a blond, angelic woman modeled on the real Helena Elliott. A lady to respect and cherish and adore, not a bawdy tavern wench.

Despairingly Alex realized that she had neither the purity of the beloved wife nor the honest sensuality of the tavern wench. She was returning home a ruined woman, shamefully pregnant far too long after her husband had died. Without the traitorous testimony of her body, the missing months in the Indies could have been quietly ignored, with no one having to know what had happened to her. Now she would be revealed to the world as a slut or a victim. She wasn't sure which thought she hated more.

She studied the dark, churning waves, mesmerized by their angry grandeur. Would she even survive to return home? She'd been buoyantly healthy when carrying Katie, but now she was constantly unwell. How much of her illness was from the sea voyage, how much from the pregnancy, and how much her fear of the future? She was at the limit of her strength, tired every minute of every day, exhausted by the effort to be the mother Katie deserved.

If something happened to her, Gavin would ensure Katie's safe passage to Alex's parents. In fact, she'd written him a letter of instructions in case disaster befell her on the voyage. If? No, when. She was on the edge of disaster now, she could feel the darkness calling her. Though she knew she should turn away from the hypnotic swell of the waves, she couldn't. The sea was a siren that promised eternal peace below the fierce surging of the waves.

*No.* Someday she would go to her rest, but for now she must deal with the turbulence of life. She was about to move away when the bowsprit in front of her began to glow. After a startled moment, she realized that this must be St. Elmo's fire, the mysterious, inexplicable light that sometimes danced through a ship's rigging after storms. Though she'd heard of the phenomenon, she had never seen it. Fascinated, she stepped onto the middle rail to get a clearer look, clinging to lines with both hands as the luminescent bowsprit rose and fell against the dark, heaving sea.

She felt very small, a mote suspended above the waves, her problems meaning nothing against the immensity of the ocean. There was a seductive peace in the thought. . . .

Hard knuckles rapped on the door. "Captain, you'd better come topside."

Having only just dozed off after hours on deck, Gavin came awake with a curse before he opened the door to Benjamin Long. "What's wrong?"

"The ship is sailing fine, sir, but I've never seen so much sea fire. It's all through the rigging, and some of the men are skittish."

Gavin repressed a sigh. Sailors had their superstitions, and it wasn't wise to push them too far. "I'll be right up."

He pulled his damp oilskins on again. Even without a real emergency, it was appropriate for Benjamin to summon him. The two watches were headed by the chief mate and the second mate. As master, Gavin could come and go as he pleased, but he was always on call if needed. That included calming superstitious sailors, since the captain's authority was second only to God.

He caught his breath when he stepped onto the deck. With most of the sail reefed, the glowing masts and spars made a lattice of pale fire against the stormy sky. Phosphorescent globes drifted through the yards, some as small as a nut, others larger than a man's head. Though he enjoyed the sight, it was easy to see why superstitious seamen found the sea fire alarming.

He started by talking with the helmsman, who was aided by another sailor because of the heavy seas. Then he made his way to men huddled against the wall of the galley. It didn't matter much what he said; his presence steadied those who were nervous. He was glad there was no need to send anyone aloft. Climbing the rigging was inherently dangerous in this weather, and an anxious sailor faced with buzzing St. Elmo's fire ran the risk of a lethal accident.

He was about to join Benjamin on the quarterdeck when he spotted a dark figure floating above the bow, outlined against the shimmering fire of the bowsprit. For an instant his memory snapped back decades to the ship's carpenter who'd told him of the dark angel of death that appeared to doomed ships. Black wings fluttered as the angel beckoned them to ruin . . .

No, blast it, this was no mythical angel of death. It was as real as he was, perhaps an injured albatross taking refuge from the storm. He headed forward to investigate, swinging from one secure hold to the next as dark water periodically swept over the deck.

Dear God, it was a cloaked woman, and there was only one woman on the *Helena.* As the ship plunged into a trough, Alex swayed precariously. He dived forward and wrapped his arm around her waist, dragging her down to safety before she could pitch into the lethal sea. They crashed to the deck together.

Keeping one arm around her, he grabbed a stanchion with his other hand to anchor them. "Damnation, Alex, what the devil were you thinking?" he said furiously, his fear transmuted to rage. "If you meant to kill yourself, you should have done it when you were in slavery, not when you're safe!"

In the faint glow of the sea fire, her expression was confused. "I wasn't going to jump. I . . . I'd never do that to Katie."

He inhaled deeply, trying to slow his pounding heart. "You may not have meant suicide, but the waves can be hypnotic. When one is melancholy, it's all too easy to believe that the sea holds the answer to all one's problems." He knew that from personal experience.

She covered her face with her hands and began to shake with barely suppressed sobs. He pulled himself to a sitting position against the railing and drew her across his lap, holding stanchion and woman with equal firmness. "Alex, what's wrong? You've been haunted by your own ghost ever since we left the Indies. The worst is over now. Soon you'll be home safe among your family and friends."

She buried her face against his shoulder, her tears increasing. "The worst isn't over. I . . . I'm pregnant."

The news was a shock colder than the drenching rain. No wonder she'd been ill and miserable. "Then we'd better be married in Ceylon."

"Are you mad?" She raised her head, stunned. "I'm carrying the child of a rapist, and may God forgive me, I hate the fact of its existence."

Her bitter words were a slap in the face. "Is the thought of a child of mine so unbearable?"

"I doubt that it's yours," she said dully. "Probably it was fathered by Bhudy, my second owner."

How many times had the bastard raped her? Gavin cradled her close, wishing he could wipe the pain from her voice and her mind. "But it could be mine, couldn't it?"

"I . . . I suppose so." She pushed heavy wet hair from her face. "That's not as likely, though."

"But it might be. Marry me, Alex. If you

return to England as a wife, no one will question your condition."

"They'll know soon enough if I give birth to a half-Malay baby."

"If that happens—well, it's not the child's fault." His voice hardened. "And if I am your husband, I defy anyone to question you or the child's parentage."

A vast wave crashed over the bow, drenching them both. When it receded, he said, "This is a damn fool place to have a conversation. Come on."

He stood and hauled her to her feet, then started a slow progress to the nearest hatchway, one hand on the railing and his other arm around her waist. He still hadn't recovered from the terror of seeing her in danger, so it was a relief to get belowdecks.

Since Katie would be sleeping in the captain's cabin, he took Alex to his cabin, the one usually occupied by the chief mate. She was dull-eyed and shivering, so after lighting a tin lamp he stripped off her saturated cloak and wrapped a blanket around her shoulders. Then he sat her on the bunk, pulled brandy from a cupboard and poured for both of them. Leaning against the door because it was as far from her as the tiny room would permit, he said, "The subject under discussion was marriage."

She drank, coughed, and drank again. "You're a true knight errant, Gavin, and I appreciate your desire to rescue me once again. But marriage is for a lifetime. It's insane for you to tie yourself to me out of pity."

Though her stark honesty was impressive, it didn't change his mind. "Pity has little to do with it, Alexandra. We've been through much in a short time, and I've come to admire your strength and understanding. I care for you deeply. Is it impossible to imagine that you and I and Katie could make a family?" His glance went to her swaddled figure. "And this poor benighted baby as well."

Her eyes closed against more tears. "You tempt me too much, Gavin. I don't know if I'll ever be fit to be a wife again. Do . . . do you understand what I'm saying?"

He understood, but that didn't change his mind. Even if the child she carried wasn't his, he bore responsibility for Alex.

He also desired her, but not only for her body. He wanted to be with this damaged, indomitable woman by day as well as night.

He wanted them to weave a fabric of common experiences, of shared hopes and fears and laughter. He wanted them to be husband and wife till death did them part.

"After all you've been through, it's understandable that you're unwilling to share a man's bed," he said, choosing his words carefully. "But . . . time heals. Perhaps someday you'll feel differently. I'm a patient man. I'll wait for as long as necessary."

Her eyes opened, the aqua tone grayed by the dim light. "You're taking a big risk, Gavin. You might have to wait forever."

Would that exquisite, tainted pleasure he'd experienced in her body be the only physical intimacy they would ever know? He forced himself to accept the possibility. It would be an apt punishment for a dark deed. "Life and love and marriage are always risks, Alex. I want to take this risk with you."

Her gaze dropped to her brandy glass, and she turned it nervously in her hands before taking another sip. "If we were to marry, you'd be free to take a mistress, though I hope you'd be discreet about it."

He stared at her. "That's not my idea of marriage, Alexandra."

She raised her bleak gaze. "This wouldn't be a normal marriage. If . . . if I recover to the point where I can be a proper wife to you, that would be different. I would want you to be faithful, as I would always be faithful to you. But unless that happens, I can't bear to think of you celibate forever because of my weakness."

"The mistress isn't compulsory, is she?" he asked wryly, thinking he was too provincial for this much bluntness. "I doubt I could square that with my conscience."

She smiled faintly. "Not compulsory, but I can't marry you unless you'll accept the possibility that someday you'll want a woman who can be more than a . . . a companion and housekeeper. When that day comes, I don't want you to feel that you're committing an unforgivable sin."

How could it *not* be a sin to be married to Alex and sleeping with some unknown female? He'd be committing a crime against both of them, not to mention God. And yet, he reluctantly admitted to himself that his mind might change. He could live like a monk if necessary; he already had for years. He wasn't so sure that he could be a married monk, living with a beautiful, desirable woman he was pledged not to touch.

Yet at heart he didn't believe the worst would happen. Alex had already shown amazing resilience. Once she was home and secure and the emotional storms of a hated pregnancy were over, her wounds would begin to heal. They wouldn't disappear overnight, but as the two of them grew in fondness, she would want to please him, just as he wanted to please her. If she was willing to share a bed, even reluctantly, he was confident of his ability to help her bury the memories of horror with experiences of joy. Her nature was a passionate one, that he was sure of. Time, understanding, and caring could give them a satisfying marriage.

"Very well, you're granting me permission to keep a mistress, though you don't want to know about it. Do you have any other doubts that must be discussed?"

She ran stiff fingers through her wet hair. "Where would we live? England? America? The city? The country?"

"We can settle in England if you wish to stay near your family." He considered, then added, "Still, it's not inconceivable that someday it might seem best to return to America. If that happens—well, I suppose we'd argue it out like any other couple."

"If I'm ostracized as a fallen woman, I might welcome a move to America." She gave a sudden rueful smile. "Gavin, you've never even seen me at my best. I've been in a state of almost continuous desperation since we met. I might become a complete stranger if my life returns to normal."

"I doubt that stranger would be a woman I like less than the one sharing my brandy now. Many couples spend years together before they learn the depths of their partner's character. We're starting out at that deep level, Alexandra. Surely that must be a good thing. And if you're happy in the future, how can that not make me happy, too?"

Tears began to pool in her eyes. "You are so good, Gavin. What have I done to deserve you?"

"Does that mean you'll marry me?"

"I . . . I think it does. If Katie approves, and I think she will." Alex smiled unsteadily. "She adores you."

"Then we shall be married. Thank you, Alexandra." Gravely he lifted her hand for a kiss, thinking how different this marriage would be from his vague plans of finding himself an aristocratic wife in London. No matter. A good merchant needed to be flexible, and he was a very good merchant.

This marriage would be the greatest challenge of his life, but for better and worse, he and Alex belonged together.

# CHAPTER 15

*Colombo, Ceylon*

Katie frowned. "Mama, you're shaking."

"It's traditional to be nervous when getting married." Alex tried to keep her tone light. "I was when I married your father, too."

At that first wedding she'd been ready to bolt, sure she was making the worst mistake of her life. In retrospect it wasn't a disaster, but neither had it been the best possible choice. Today, inevitably, she wondered if she was making another mistake. Her life had spun out of control when the *Amstel* was attacked, and everything that had happened since had been under duress. In the normal course of life, she and Gavin were unlikely ever to have met.

And yet—he was right that they knew each other in ways most couples didn't before marrying. She had no doubt that he would be a good provider, a kind husband, and a loving father to Katie and the child yet to be born. After her first blink of surprise, Katie had agreed that he'd make a very nice stepfather.

But despite Gavin's considerable virtues, Alex knew she was marrying him out of fear and weakness. She wanted the security of arriving home under the protection of a powerful man, one her parents would like. Gavin and the colonel would get on famously. Now that she thought about it, they were alike in many ways. Gavin was more relaxed in his manner, but both men were kind, and utterly reliable.

The door opened and Jane Walker, chief wedding assistant, bustled in. After they agreed to marry, the *Helena* changed course for Ceylon. In Colombo, Gavin found lodgings for Alex and Katie in the home of Jane's mother, a British military widow who had decided to stay in the East. Eighteen-year-old Jane had a romantic heart, and happily volunteered her services when she learned that a guest was getting married.

"You look lovely, Mrs. Warren. You and the captain will make a handsome couple." Jane made a minute adjustment to the back of Alex's cream-colored gown. She and her mother were also seamstresses, and had been able to swiftly make up wedding finery for Alex and her daughter. Good clothes helped wavering confidence.

"It's time to leave for the church." Alex took Katie's hand. With Jane on her other side, she left the house for the short walk to the Anglican chapel. The tropical heat was oppressive, but at least the sun was shining. She hoped that was a good omen.

They reached the church precisely on time, as the clock began striking eleven. At the foot of the steps, Alex felt a moment of terrified paralysis. Taking a deep breath, she lifted her skirts so she wouldn't trip, and ascended the stairs. She was a widow and a mother, far too old for childish romantic dreams. Few women were as happy in marriage as her mother and the colonel; most must settle for less, as she had done.

With Edmund, she'd confused a love of

adventure with love for the man. This time she was marrying for reasons more of the head than the heart. At least now she was old enough and wise enough to realize what she was doing. She liked, trusted, and respected Gavin. The fact that she found him attractive was merely . . . a complication.

Yet when she saw him standing at the altar with Suryo and Benjamin Long, she felt deep regret. Gavin looked like a romantic hero, and he'd acted as one, too. She was the one who was too bruised and scarred for romance.

Chilled to the marrow, she walked down the aisle with Katie and Jane following. Gavin watched so intently that she wondered if he was having second thoughts. But no, there was no uncertainty in his smile when he took her cold hand.

Since there were so few people present, Katie and Jane stood beside her, as Suryo and Benjamin stood by Gavin. The elderly vicar nodded a greeting to the new arrivals, then said in a slow, sonorous voice, "Dearly beloved, we are gathered together . . ."

The ceremony was a blur of words, except when Gavin repeated, "With my body I thee worship." She must have flinched, because his hand tightened on hers as he slid the ring on her finger, his grave eyes reminding her of his promise to wait as long as necessary. She managed a smile to say that she trusted him. It amazed her that she could trust a man so much. But Gavin was not like other men.

The vicar said, "I pronounce that they be man and wife together."

After the final blessing, Gavin said softly, "Man and wife. I like the sound of that, Mrs. Elliott." He raised her left hand and pressed his lips over the wedding ring.

She was Mrs. Elliott now. The words struck her with more finality than the vicar's pronouncement.

As Jane Walker shed happy tears, Gavin knelt in front of Katie. "There is no ritual to join us as family, but I wanted a symbol of our new relationship." He drew a small box from his pocket and handed it over ceremoniously. "I am blessed to have you as a stepdaughter, Katie."

"And I am glad to have you for a stepfather, Captain," Katie said with equal formality. Opening the box, she gave a purely female gasp of appreciation at the sight of a beautifully made gold locket. Not too elaborate for a child, it was elegant enough to wear even when she grew up. "Thank you! Can I put it on, Mama?"

"Of course." Alex removed the locket from the box and fastened it around her daughter's neck. How thoughtful of Gavin to include Katie. Yes, she'd made the right decision. Now she owed it to him to try to become a true wife.

Even as the wedding breakfast drew to a close, Gavin still hadn't quite absorbed the fact that Alex had actually married him. She'd entered the church looking ready to bolt. A woman who'd fought captivity as furiously as Alex wouldn't have balked at leaving him at the altar if she decided marriage was a mistake. Thank God she hadn't.

As the party rose from the table, Suryo said, "Miss Katie, would you like to go see some elephants? If you wish, we can ride one."

"Yes, please." Katie smiled mischievously. "Mama and the captain must want to be alone." She hesitated. "Is it all right if I call you Captain instead of Papa?"

"Of course. May I sometimes call you Katybird, as your mother does?"

"I'd like that." Katie bounced from her seat, ready for an adventure.

Suryo said, "Perhaps Miss Walker would like to join us? She is surely a better guide to Colombo than I."

Jane agreed and the elephant seekers left, followed by Benjamin Long after a handshake for Gavin and a deep bow to Alex. Finally they were alone. Seeing wariness in Alex's expression, Gavin said, "I thought we might take a walk, too. We can practice answering to 'Captain and Mrs. Elliott'."

Alex's expression eased. "I doubt that you need the practice, but I do. And I'd like a chance to see a bit more of the town, since we're leaving tomorrow."

They left the quiet inn where they'd had the wedding breakfast, walking side by side without touching. Except for the night Alex had cried in his arms, she'd avoided physical contact with everyone but Katie. He supposed it was only to be expected.

As they strolled along the quiet street,

Gavin remarked, "Ceylon has a colorful history. India, Portugal, Holland, and England have all left their mark. A pity we don't have time to go to the highlands in the interior. It's cooler there, and very beautiful."

"It sounds as if you know Ceylon well."

"I have financial interests in several coffee plantations."

"Still more sources of wealth." She glanced down at her wedding ring. "I'm gaining so much more from this marriage than you are."

He frowned. "Never think that, Alexandra. We must enter marriage as full partners if we want to find mutual satisfaction."

Her mouth twisted. "Full partners. It's difficult to feel that way. I don't like being a . . . a taker, with so little to give."

"You give courage, strength, and honesty—pearls beyond price." And a rare, fierce beauty that hardship had only intensified, but he knew she would not believe that if he said so. He lightened his tone. "I expect you to be the sort of strong-minded wife who will keep me firmly in hand."

Her face lit in the truest smile she'd given all day. "I like the sound of that."

They came upon a street market brilliant

with scents and colors. Sari-clad women, laughing children, baskets of scarlet peppers and rose petals and cardamom. The street was crowded, so Alex drew closer and took his arm. Her clasp was feather soft on his forearm, yet even that slight pressure affected him with absurd intensity.

It was the first time she'd touched him voluntarily—an act of trust on her part, as rare and fragile as a hummingbird. He clamped down on his physical response to her nearness. He'd done it often since they met, and would have to do it countless times more. Perhaps restraint would grow easier in time. "I thought it would be pleasant today to relax and enjoy each other's company without a whole ship's crew within earshot. There's much I'd like to know about you. For example, after your mother remarried and you stopped following the drum, where did you live?"

"Mostly in Wales, where the colonel owns an estate in the most beautiful valley in Britain." A mischievous light showed in her eyes. "I just realized I'm going down in the world. My mother married a colonel, while I have settled for a mere captain."

He laughed, delighted at her teasing. "A

navy captain is the equivalent of an army colonel, isn't he? Though as a mere merchant, I've no proper rank even though Katie wants to call me 'Captain.' I suppose she got that from the way you call your stepfather 'the colonel.' "

"It comes from growing up in a military tradition," she explained. "A man's rank is such an important part of who he is. My father was a cavalry officer, my stepfather commanded an infantry regiment at Waterloo and he met my mother when she nursed him after he was wounded. The sound of drums shaped my whole childhood."

"Until you settled in the peaceful hills of Wales."

"With occasional visits to my great-grandfather, who lived on an island off Cornwall, and to London, so I wouldn't grow up a complete rustic. What about you? Where did you live before your family emigrated to America?"

"Mostly in Aberdeen, watching the North Sea. I suppose we'll need a house in London since I'll be working there, but I'd also like to find a country place by the water."

"I agree. London is delightful in small

doses, but escaping to the country is necessary for sanity."

"Were you happy in your first marriage?" He knew he probably shouldn't ask, but wanted to know the answer.

She sighed a little. "Edmund was somewhat older than I. Accustomed to being master of all around him. Sometimes that caused . . . tension. I don't think it occurred to him to wonder how a woman's mind worked. But he was very reliable and he took good care of Katie and me. When he died . . ." her voice faltered. "He was always so strong. I had trouble believing that a fever could take him so suddenly. It was as if the earth beneath my feet had suddenly cracked open."

So she'd had a solid marriage, but not a fairy-tale romance that Gavin would never be able to match. He was glad to know that, even as he acknowledged that Alex might feel it would be difficult to measure up to Helena. Knowing that must be addressed, he said slowly, "I think you know how much I loved Helena. But that doesn't make what is between you and me any less real, or less valuable."

"Were you full partners in your first marriage?"

He had to think about the answer. "You and she are so different that the words don't mean the same thing. Helena and I were young together, and we discovered life and marriage together. You and I—we bring each other our experiences. Our scars, our opinions, and I hope our compassion. We will be partners in a different way."

Her fingers tightened on his arm. "What an extraordinary man you are. I didn't know that couples ever discussed things like this."

"Not even your parents?"

"Certainly my mother and father didn't," she said slowly. "My father was a fine cavalryman, but not profound. My mother and the colonel must have these kinds of conversations, though, to be as close as they are. How strange that I never guessed that. Until now, it has been outside my experience. Already this marriage is an education."

"I hope we continue to teach each other throughout our marriage." Their walking had brought them to a small, lushly green park. Since there was no one else in sight, he said, "May I ask you something?"

"Of course."

"May I kiss you?"

She became still as a statue for the space of a dozen heartbeats. "I . . . I suppose that's little enough to ask on our wedding day."

Very carefully, she stepped up to him and raised her face for a kiss. Her lips were soft, a little anxious, brave. Warm, so irresistibly warm . . .

Forcing desire down, he made the kiss long but light, with no demand or invasion. Gradually she relaxed. He rested his hands on her waist, feeling her lithe strength through the cream-colored fabric of her gown.

Since she didn't seem to mind that, he slid his arms around her. Every muscle in her body tensed. He returned his hands to her waist, guessing that she didn't like feeling enfolded. Trapped.

With a last butterfly kiss along her elegant cheekbone, he ended the embrace before he forgot all his good intentions. "Thank you, Alexandra," he murmured.

"You're welcome." She touched her

mouth with her fingertips uncertainly. "That was . . . very nice."

A wedding kiss was a poor substitute for consummation—but it was a beginning.

# CHAPTER 16

Alex found Gavin to be a pleasant and un-demanding husband. Ever since boarding the ship, she and Katie had eaten with the officer's mess. Though they continued to do that for breakfast and the midday meal, now they had supper as a family in the captain's cabin.

Supper quickly evolved into spending the evening together, at least until Katie's bed-time. They would play simple card games, or Alex would read stories, which Gavin and Katie both enjoyed. Sometimes Gavin told Katie of his travels in what became informal lessons in geography.

Alex enjoyed his tales even more than her

daughter. Not only was Gavin a droll story-teller, but she learned more about him through his tales of long voyages, exotic destinations, successes and failures. She'd known he was a remarkable man, and his lighthearted, often self-deprecating anec-dotes only made her appreciate him more.

A new husband, barely a year after Ed-mund's death. She could never have imag-ined that. She tried not to think what her life might have been like if she'd met Gavin when she was eighteen, instead of Ed-mund, because she suspected that she would have fallen deeply into love with him—the forever kind of love that was now beyond her.

Even if they had met later, if the *Helena* had called at Sydney when Alex was look-ing for passage back to London, passionate love might have been possible. There would have been no slavery, no terrifying separa-tion from her daughter. Just a long voyage when two widowed but basically normal people could have slowly come to know and appreciate each other.

Instead she was scarred to the soul, and Gavin, despite his protests, had married her from pity, as someone might take in an injured cat or dog. Whenever she got to that point, she reminded herself that without disaster, they might never have become well acquainted. They could have spent twelve thousand miles addressing each other as Mrs. Warren and Captain Elliott, strangers from beginning to end. She and Katie would have been better off if they'd had that peaceful passage home—yet not knowing Gavin's character and compassion would have been a loss. She must simply accept what had happened, and do her best with it.

They crossed most of the Indian Ocean before seeing another set of sails. Gavin invited Alex and Katie up to the deck as the other ship neared its closest approach to their course. As it dipped a signal flag in greeting, he asked, "Can you tell what flag the ship is flying, Katie?"

She shaded her eyes with her hand. "Dutch?"

"Very good." He frowned as he studied the ship, which was close enough to see men moving about the quarterdeck. "My guess is that the ship was built in Portugal, with modifications made in the East over a number of years."

"You can read a ship like a book," Alex commented.

He grinned. "There often isn't much else to do out here."

"The ocean is very, very large, isn't it?" Katie said solemnly.

"It is indeed, Katybird," Gavin replied. "I know a New England ship owner who actually met one of his other ships in the Mediterranean, an event so rare that we're still talking about it. As you know, mostly we only see the sea."

"I saw on the chart that we're near a big island called Madagascar," Katie said. "Will we stop for fresh water and food?"

"No, Madagascar isn't safe for provisioning. Usually we stop at St. Helena, in the southern Atlantic. It would take longer, but we could stop in Cape Town instead. It has a lovely setting, as beautiful as Sydney." He glanced at Alex. "Would you like to visit Cape Town, or would you prefer not to take the time?"

She hesitated. "I'd rather not. You have tea and spices to sell, and I'm longing to get back to England to see my family." Luckily, they hadn't known when she intended to return, so they wouldn't be worrying yet. She wanted to be home before they did.

"Captain! Look at the Dutchman!" A shout rose from Benjamin Long, who was officer of the watch.

Alex looked also, and was surprised to see that square dark holes had appeared in a line below the gunwales. Surely not gun ports . . .

Light flashed raggedly from the ports and smoke rolled out. As thunder boomed across the water, Gavin shouted, *"Clear for action!"*

Moving with unbelievable speed, he scooped up Katie and grabbed Alex's arm to drag her to the nearby hatch. As he shoved her through and dropped after her, the *Helena* lurched under the impact of smashing cannonballs. Cracking, tearing sounds filled the air. Alex staggered and Gavin fell, protecting Katie from injury with his own body.

"Good God!" Alex gasped. Looking up through the hatch, she saw the top of the mizzenmast snap. Eerily slow, it fell toward the deck in a tangle of sails and cordage. "Why are they shooting?"

"That's no Dutch merchant," he said

grimly. "You and Katie stay in the cabin until it's safe. Keep away from the stern windows."

She felt the blood drain from her face. "Pirates?"

"Of some sort." His gaze caught hers, his eyes flint-gray. "The *Helena* will not be taken, Alex. I swear it." Then he was gone.

Alex caught Katie's hand and they raced down the passage to the cabin as feet pounded above and behind them. Another volley of cannonballs struck, shaking the ship again, and this time there was a scream from a wounded man.

"Don't worry, Mama, everything will be all right," Katie said earnestly. "The captain says we won't be taken."

Alex was not so optimistic—she suspected that Gavin had meant that the *Helena* would fight to the death rather than surrender. That was not the same as saying that they'd come through this engagement safely. Glad Katie didn't realize that, she said calmly, "Whoever attacked us is in for a surprise. Suryo said the *Helena* has more and larger guns than most ships its size, and it's very fast, too. We'll be out of danger in no time."

She opened the cabin door and ushered her daughter through, wishing she believed her own optimism. From what Gavin had said, she guessed the attacker was a pirate using a captured European ship and flying the Dutch flag until it was within cannon range of prosperous merchant vessels. If the *Helena* tried to outrun the pirates, they'd have to come about, all the time under the guns of the other ship.

The pirates were trying to dismast the *Helena* so she could be boarded, since there was no point in sinking a ship with its cargo. But if the *Helena* looked as if she might escape—well, the pirates would probably rather sink a ship than let it survive to bear witness to their crimes.

Cannon thundered, deafeningly close. Amazed, Alex realized that their own weapons were already firing back. She'd known that gun drills were held regularly, but that had seemed a matter of routine rather than because they might need to defend themselves from attack. In the Indies, pirate assaults usually involved stealth and hand-to-hand fighting. Yet through all of these peaceful weeks, Gavin had kept his ship and men ready, just in case.

Acrid smoke began to seep into the room from the guns. As their cannon fired again, she embraced Katie protectively and sank to the floor against the interior bulkhead, guessing it was the safest place. Trying to keep her tone light, she said, "You'll have no end of adventures to tell your cousins back in England. They'll be so impressed!"

Katie managed a smile, but she looked pale. "I'm glad the captain is in charge."

"So am I, darling. He's prepared for everything. That's why we were able to return fire so quickly." And he wouldn't be aiming for the rigging of the other ship—he could shoot to kill. Fiercely she hoped he'd succeed, and quickly.

Waiting seemed interminable as Alex cuddled Katie close and tried to keep fear at bay. Long, scarily quiet intervals were punctuated by horrendous noise and activity. Not knowing what was happening was the worst part.

Though she would prefer a fight to the death over captivity, how could she wish such a fate for her daughter? Yet if they were captured again, it was unlikely that Katie would fall into such kind hands as those in Sukau. The possibilities were so horrific that she forced herself to concentrate on the well-prepared crew and ship—and Gavin on the quarterdeck, in the line of fire.

She *hated* being helpless.

A bang on the door was followed precipitously by Suryo. "Puan, do you know anything of medicine? Men are injured and need care."

Alex's fear cleared instantly. "Bring the wounded into steerage and I'll take care of them there."

As he swung out of the cabin, Alex rose and opened the cabinet that held the ship's medicine chest. On a merchant ship the captain usually acted as physician and surgeon, and Gavin was well supplied. Barely able to lift the chest, she grabbed the handle on one end and dragged it across the floor toward the door. "Katie, stay here. Don't for any reason go above deck unless the captain or I say it's all right."

Following her down the passage, Katie said, "Let me help!"

For a moment Alex hesitated before remembering that she hadn't been much older when she'd helped her mother tend casualties from the Battle of Quartre-Bras as the soldiers staggered through the streets of Brussels. "Very well, but if it's too frightening or you feel ill, come back here. I don't want to have to worry about you."

Katie's jaw set pugnaciously. "I won't be scared." For an uncanny instant, Alex saw herself as a child. The nursing instinct ran strong in the women of her family.

They reached steerage and found two injured men already lying there. Alex opened the medicine chest and took swift inventory. Instruments, bandages, plasters, ointments, opium. "Katie, bring a pitcher of clear water and a glass. Offer water to the wounded men, then bring more for cleaning wounds."

The nearest man, an American who usually had an infectious smile for Katie, lay beside a barrel of lemons carried to prevent scurvy. The bright citrus scent clashed with the metallic odor of the blood pouring from lacerations made by splintered timber. As she knelt beside him, he gasped, "I'm not so bad, ma'am. Take a look at Ollie there."

Seeing that his condition wasn't critical, she moved to the other man, a Cockney. His lower leg had been smashed by a cannonball and would need amputation later.

But the bleeding must be stopped now, or he'd be dead in half an hour.

Calm descended over her as she remembered the field hospitals of the Peninsula, and the later years when she'd helped her mother nurse tenants on their estate. Alex was no surgeon, but she had plenty of nursing experience, wasn't afraid of blood, and had learned that common sense and basic care could do much to preserve life.

After applying a tourniquet to Ollie's shattered leg, she gave him a dose of opium and returned to the American, picking out jagged splinters and fabric scraps with painstaking care before cleaning and bandaging. When she was done, he lurched to his feet and limped off to rejoin his gun crew. She wanted to protest, but held her tongue. A merchant ship's crew was much smaller than that of a naval vessel. Every man was needed on the deck or at the guns.

Already two more walking wounded had appeared for a quick bandaging that would allow them to return to the battle raging overhead. Time blurred into cleaning wounds, pouring on raw whiskey, a favorite treatment of her mother's, and bandaging.

Luckily few men were grievously wounded, but there were many lesser injuries. Katie worked silently beside her, offering water, bringing bandages and instruments, and functioning as an extra pair of hands as needed. What a wonder she was.

Intent on her work, Alex blocked out smoke, fatigue, nausea, and painful cramping caused by kneeling for too long. She barely noticed when the guns stopped firing. Only that the stream of injured sailors slowed, and finally stopped.

She was bandaging her final patient when her shoulder was touched lightly. "Alex?"

She tied off the bandage before glancing up at Gavin. Though weary and smudged, he was intact. Lightheaded with fatigue, she asked, "It's over?"

"The pirate ship sank. No survivors." His eyes were the icy gray of a winter sea. "Madagascar used to be a notorious nest of pirates. A mixed Asian and European crew apparently decided to revive the tradition with a captured ship."

She nodded, not surprised that enterprising pirates would try the rich shipping lanes between India and Europe. "May they all rot in hell."

"My sentiments exactly."

If Alex hadn't known Gavin, his expression would have frightened her. Reminded that weak men did not build merchant empires, she asked, "How much damage has the *Helena* suffered?"

His expression eased. "We were lucky. Half the sails and lines must be replaced and two masts are damaged, but if we don't carry much sail in heavy weather, they'll make it to England." He scanned the steerage space, where four of the most severely injured men rested under the influence of opium. "No lives have been lost, either. I think two or three of the men would have died if you hadn't been able to treat their wounds quickly. Now . . . well, at least they have a chance. You've done an amazing job—you and Katie both." His smile made Katie beam.

Infection was always a danger, but these were strong men. She had hopes they'd survive. "Ollie's lower leg will have to be amputated." Wearily she got to her feet. "I've never done one, but I've seen it done. I . . . I'll do my best."

"You've done enough." He grimaced. "I've performed amputations a couple of times, so I'll do this one. They take a fair amount of brute strength, and you look done in. You've been working here for hours."

Now that her work was finished, she realized how weak and ill she felt. In fact, the cramping that had dogged her for hours was so acute that she pressed a hand to her belly to ease the pain. "I could use some rest."

She took a step, and found that her knees wouldn't support her. As she sagged to the floor, Gavin caught her. "You're bleeding!"

Just before she fainted, she saw the pool of blood on the floor.

She awoke slowly, rocked by the ship, feeling as gray and empty as an autumn husk. It was night, but a lamp burned somewhere to her left. Vaguely she recognized that she was in her own bed in the captain's cabin.

She turned her head a fraction to the left and found Gavin dozing in his heavy captain's chair a yard away, his face gray with exhaustion and his long legs stretched in front of him. She tried to speak but produced no sound. Moistening her lips, she managed a thin whisper. "Where is Katie?"

His eyes opened. "Sleeping in my cabin. Suryo is with her in case she has bad dreams, but she's been a real trooper." He poured a glass of water and raised Alex's head from the pillows so she could drink.

"Thank you." She took small sips until the glass was half empty, then shook her head that she'd had enough. As Gavin lowered her to the bed, she whispered, "I lost the baby, didn't I?"

He nodded. "Yes, along with a lot of blood. It's been over twenty-four hours since you collapsed."

"I suppose I should be glad, yet I feel so . . . so empty." She closed her eyes, trying unsuccessfully to keep tears from running down her cheeks. "Was it possible to tell who fathered it?"

"No. It was too early."

"I killed it with my hatred. Dear God, when will it all end?" She began to sob helplessly.

He took her hand, offering comfort through touch. "This wasn't truly a child, just the chance of a child. As ill as you've been, my guess is that you would have miscarried anyhow." After a heavy silence, he added, "Helena miscarried twice before she . . . she carried a child to term."

The child whose birth had killed Helena. Alex rolled over, pressing her cheek to his hand as she cried uncontrollably. She hated herself for her physical weakness, and for feeling both sorrow and relief at her body's loss. When she had no more tears left, she asked in a raw whisper, "What about you? You must be relieved that you won't have to raise a rapist's child."

"I don't know how I feel. This will be easier, yet I'm also . . . disappointed. I kept hoping the child would be mine. And if not—well, every baby is a new hope. This one would have been our child no matter who the father was." His free hand stroked her back comfortingly. "The worst was the hours when I was terrified of losing you. But you survived, Alexandra. You must be the strongest woman on God's earth."

"The reason for our marriage is gone," she said, infinitely weary. "It's not a real marriage yet—maybe there's a way to end it."

"Alex, don't." His hand tightened on hers. "Marriage is more than intimate relations and the lost chance of a child. Our marriage is real. There's no turning back."

She closed her eyes, shamed by the pain in his voice, too drained to talk rationally. She whispered, "Will you lie down and hold me?"

He released his breath in a long sigh. "I'd like that."

She inched back to the bulkhead, leaving as much room as possible. He was already in shirtsleeves and stockinged feet, so he lay down on top of the covers, careful not to jar her. Though he took up far more space than Katie, his warmth and strength were soothing. Taking his hand, she rested her head against his shoulder, and once more slept.

Her sleep was haunted by dreams of a child with dark almond eyes. As awareness slowly returned the next morning, she recognized that Gavin was right—her chronic unwellness had probably been a sign that the pregnancy was doomed from the start.

Yet if that possible child had been strong and healthy enough to be born, she would have learned to love it, forgetting the pain of its conception. As Gavin had said, every baby was a new hope. Now that hope was gone. No wonder her body mourned.

In the distance she heard four bells striking. Six o'clock in the morning. She opened her eyes, and found that Gavin was lying on his side with one arm around her. In relaxation his face was surprisingly youthful despite subtle marks of strain and fatigue. What a sore trial she'd been to him from the beginning.

She recognized how easy it would be to sink into melancholy after all the pain and loss she'd suffered, starting with Edmund's death. The night of St. Elmo's fire, when she'd been mesmerized by the depths of the sea, she'd come perilously close to giving up. Yet surrender was a coward's way. She was standing at a crossroads—and it was up to her to choose life. Katie deserved a healthy, loving mother, and Gavin deserved a wife who gave as much as she received.

She touched Gavin's jaw, feeling the prickle of whiskers though his fair coloring made them almost invisible. He had also suffered great losses in his life: his native land, his parents, his wife and child. Yet he survived with warmth and generosity in his soul, and he'd made a commitment to her and Katie that only death would end. She could do no less.

His eyes opened and he regarded her warily. "How are you feeling?"

"A little better. And tomorrow I'll be a little better yet." She took a deep breath. "I said a lot of nonsense last night. I'm sorry."

He relaxed visibly. "No need to apologize. The circumstances were extreme."

"How is Ollie?" she asked. "Have you done the amputation?"

Gavin made a face. "Yes. It's the sort of thing best done quickly. He came through the operation well. He's saying now that he always fancied becoming a cook because he'd get first choice of the food, and now he has a proper excuse."

"What courage," she said softly.

"The men are celebrating the fact that they defeated a larger ship with heavier guns." He toyed with the unkempt braid that trailed over her shoulder. "They're calling you St. Alexandra for your heroic labors."

She felt an unexpected smile. "Like my

mother was St. Catherine. The apple doesn't fall far from the tree, does it? Though my mother is far more saintly than I."

He smiled back. "Maybe you only thought that because she tried very hard to be good in front of her impressionable daughter, just like you are in front of Katie. I presume she was named for your mother?"

She nodded. "I can't wait for them to finally meet."

"It won't be long now, Alex. Only a few more weeks."

"A few more weeks." She linked her fingers through his and let her eyes drift shut. It was hard to imagine that normal life was so near.

Normal life. She craved it. Once she was safe in England, she would never, ever have another adventure.

# BOOK 11

# The Price of a Man's Life

# CHAPTER 17

*London, England, Summer 1834*

The Thames was a crowded highway after the vast tranquility of the oceans. Gavin enjoyed pointing out landmarks to his ladies. Alex was as eager as Katie to look at the Greenwich Observatory on a hill above the river, and as intrigued to learn that all the world's longitude was measured from the invisible meridian that ran through it.

Other sights were equally impressive, though Gavin made sure they were belowdecks when the *Helena* passed Gibbet Island, where the dry bones of four convicted pirates rattled in iron cages. Alex might have found grim satisfaction at seeing justice done, but it was no sight for a child.

The closer they came to the city, the more crowded the waters. By the time they reached the lock that would admit them to London Dock, the river was a raucous, noisy brawl of ships, large and small—one of the world's great trade centers going about its business at maximum speed and volume.

As Katie hung enthralled over the ship's railing, Gavin asked, "What is it like to see your homeland for the first time at the age of nine?"

Katie laughed, her cheeks pink with excitement. "It's wonderful! There's so much happening." Her glance went to her mother, who was quieter but just as excited. "Mama has told me so much about England that it already feels like home."

"You're lucky to arrive on a warm, sunny afternoon. If this was a gray, wet day in winter, you might wish yourself back in Sydney."

She shook her head. "I've had three summers in a row—in Sydney, in the Islands, and now here. I shall be ready for winter when it comes."

"What a wise young lady you are." He sometimes had trouble believing his amazing good fortune in acquiring this wonderful daughter as well as Alex. All this, and London—the goal he'd been working toward for half a lifetime. Though as captain he must look collected, underneath he was as tense as Katie and Alex. Worse, perhaps. He'd waited a long time to prepare himself. The scales must be balanced so he could finally move on.

Alex asked, "What is it like to be so close to the end of your sea captain days?"

He distilled his tangled feelings into a simple answer. "I'm ready for a life ashore, but I'll miss the sea."

"When we find that home by the ocean, you'll get a boat, of course." She smiled, tendrils of dark hair blowing enticingly around her face. "A nice little sloop that you can name the *Helena II*."

"Or the *Katybird*." He smiled back, thinking how much healthier she looked after the last long, blessedly uneventful leg of the voyage. Seasickness had ended with her miscarriage, and despite lingering weakness from blood loss, she began Katie's lessons again a mere three days after the pirate attack. The evening after that, she resumed reading aloud to him and Katie after supper. They'd gone through all of *Robinson Crusoe,* one of his favorite books. Never had it been more enjoyable than when she read the story in her rich, brandy-smooth voice.

He hoped she would continue reading aloud once they were ashore. It brought back warm memories of his childhood, when his father was at sea with the navy and his mother read to him in the evenings. And not always books her father, the vicar, would have approved of, even though they were living in the old man's house. There was a lot his grandfather didn't approve of, though he was kind in his own crusty way.

Katie gasped with amazement as the gates of the lock swung majestically open, permitting the *Helena* to sail into the basin at the center of the giant dock complex. "The London Docks are big as all Sydney!"

"Probably not that big, but large enough, and that's not counting the new St. Katharine's Dock west of here. Much of Britain's tobacco, alcohol, and wool come through the London Docks, as well as tea and spices and rice and a thousand other things." Gavin pointed out a great smoking chimney. "That's a kiln where unclaimed goods are burned after a year has passed. Everything except tea, which burns so fiercely it might set the warehouses ablaze. That's disposed of elsewhere."

"What a great waste," Alex commented.

"It would certainly be more sensible to have Customs auction the goods. The worst waste is the wines and spirits. There are acres and acres of bonded vaults under the docks, and if the duties and expenses aren't paid, the drink is just poured into the river."

"That must make the fish very happy." Alex's voice was demure but her eyes danced. In fact, all of her looked ready to dance now that she was finally home.

"Do you have a preference for any particular hotel, Alex?" he asked. "I've stayed in a couple that were good, but you may know a better one."

She looked surprised. "We don't need a hotel—we must stay at my Uncle Stephen's house."

"Without advance notice? What if your uncle is out of town?"

"His house is the family headquarters—we all stay with them when in London," she explained. "He should be in town now, and even if he isn't, he and Aunt Rosalind would be hurt if we didn't stay there."

"Very well—to your Uncle Stephen's we shall go." Anything to keep that glowing expression on Alex's face. Though she'd done her best to appear cheerful over the last months, he sensed that her smile concealed sadness and grief. The spirit healed more slowly than the body.

But today, she was truly happy. He wanted that to last.

"This is your uncle's house?" Gavin exchanged a stunned glance with Katie as their carriage pulled up in front of a vast, sprawling Grosvenor Square mansion.

Alex laughed. "He's only an uncle by marriage—my side of the family is poverty stricken by comparison. But he still welcomes me, even though I'm a mere connection."

When Gavin helped Alex from the carriage, she tumbled out like an impatient child before composing herself and taking his arm to walk to the house. Katie grasped her other hand as they climbed the broad steps. Liking that they were moving together as a family, Gavin wielded the huge knocker.

A haughty butler opened the door. His expression changed comically when he saw Alex. "Miss Amy?" He groped for her correct name. "I beg your pardon, Mrs. Warren."

With a smile, she swept Gavin and Katie inside a two-story-high atrium grand enough for a royal palace. "In person, Riggs. Are my aunt and uncle in residence?"

"Yes, and your parents also." Looking dazed, the butler trailed after the new arrivals. "But . . . but . . . we thought . . ."

Before Riggs could sputter out what he meant to say, a well-dressed woman appeared at the railing of the upper level and looked down at the newcomers. Her graceful posture turned rigid. Then she cried, "*Amy!* Dear God in heaven!"

She raced down the lavish double staircase at breakneck speed, her black gown streaming behind her.

"*Mama!*" Alex darted toward the other woman. They met in a wrenching hug at the foot of the stairs, both of them weeping.

This was the intimidating Catherine? Gavin stared, understanding why Alex had found her alarmingly perfect. Alex must have been born when her mother was in the schoolroom, because Catherine looked not much more than forty now. Only a scattering of silver strands in her dark hair and fine lines beside her eyes revealed her age. The resemblance between them was pronounced, though Alex was a little taller and her demeanor suggested a more active, forceful temperament. Catherine's face had a gentle, Madonna-like quality that must bring men to their knees.

Still crying, Alex stepped back and wiped her eyes. "Lord, I've missed you all so much." Her gaze went over her mother, and she caught her breath. "You're wearing mourning. Not . . . not the colonel or the children? Or Aunt Rosalind and Uncle Stephen and their children?"

Catherine laughed. "I've been wearing mourning for you and your daughter, Amy— sorry, Alexandra. I'm having trouble remembering what to call you." She produced a handkerchief and wiped eyes the same rare aqua shade as those of her daughter and granddaughter. "I've never been so happy about a mistake in my life!"

Alex's jaw dropped. "You thought we were dead? What did you hear?"

"Several months ago we received word through diplomatic channels that the *Amstel* was attacked in the Indies, and you both died."

"The attack was chaotic, but certainly no one could have seen us killed." Alex shook her head. "I'm so sorry. It never occurred to me that we'd be reported dead."

Gavin knew why—the *Amstel*'s captain and crew hadn't wanted to admit they'd abandoned a woman and child, so they'd reported deaths instead. Cowards.

"All that matters is that you're safely home." Catherine turned to Katie. "Surely this beautiful young lady is your daughter. Except for that wonderful blond hair, she looks just like you at that age." She knelt for a hug. "I'm your grandmother, Katie, and I am so happy to meet my oldest grandchild."

Kate hugged her with delight. "I've wanted to meet you my whole life, Grandmama."

Catherine stood, her quizzical glance going to Gavin. Seeing that, Alex said, "Mother, this is my husband, Captain Gavin Elliott."

Before she could finish her introduction, two men entered the hall from an unobtrusive door tucked under the sweeping staircase. Tall, distinguished, and in late forties or early fifties, they were clearly brothers. The man with more gray in his brown hair had shrewd eyes watching from a deceptively mild face. The younger brother was whipcord lean, with a commanding manner that would not accept fools gladly.

They swooped down on the returned prodigal and Alex disappeared into fervent embraces and incredulous cries of "Alex!" and "Dear God, we thought you were dead!"

Temporarily forgotten, Katie took Gavin's hand. At sea himself, he squeezed her hand comfortingly and wondered what the devil he'd got himself into.

Katie whispered, "Who are all these people?"

"Your mother's family, and they love her very much. As her daughter, they'll love you just as much." He was sure that would be the case; what normal person could not love Katie? He was less sure about how Alex's randomly acquired husband would be accepted into a close and obviously wealthy family.

Laughing and crying, Alex emerged from the men's embrace. "I'm sorry, I'm completely forgetting my manners. Mother, Colonel, Uncle Stephen, this is my husband, Captain Gavin Elliott. Gavin, my uncle, the Duke of Ashburton." She gestured to the older man. "And my parents, Lord and Lady Michael Kenyon."

Gavin choked. Her uncle was a bloody damned duke? And the "colonel," whom he'd vaguely imagined as a bluff, retired officer, was a knife-sharp duke's brother.

Though Lord Michael would be formidable under other circumstances, today he was fervently grateful, like a man who'd been relieved of a killing load. "Thank you for bringing Alex home to us, Captain," he said with a powerful handshake.

The duke also shook hands. "In the nick of time. Michael was on the verge of haring off to the Indies in search of Alex and Katie."

"I knew it would take more than pirates to sink Alex." Lord Michael put an arm around his stepdaughter's shoulders and squeezed her close. "But I'm relieved not to have to go looking for you. What the devil happened out there?"

Catherine intervened. "There is obviously much news to exchange, but we must give Alex and her family a chance to freshen up."

Ashburton summoned the butler and gave low-voiced orders. Alex hadn't been joking about her family assuming that everyone stayed in this great glittering pile. Gavin would have preferred the neutral privacy of a hotel, but this was a time to accept gracefully—no matter how much he might wish he was elsewhere.

Alex watched fondly as Catherine took Katie off to the nursery, both of them chattering like magpies. Her mother, her daughter. Something that had been incomplete was now whole.

By the time the housekeeper led her and Gavin upstairs, their baggage was waiting. Ashburton House ran like fine clockwork.

After the housekeeper withdrew, Alex sank onto the bed. "I feel as if I'm dreaming. When I was in Maduri, it was hard to imagine that I'd ever be home. Now, just as you said, it's becoming difficult to remember that Maduri wasn't a bad dream." She watched Gavin prowl restlessly around the room. "I owe you for this a thousand times over."

"Surely not so many as a thousand." Gavin paused at the window to study the luxuriant garden. "I didn't realize that I'd married into the cream of the British aristocracy."

Uneasily she recognized that she should have told him more about her family so he wouldn't have been caught off guard. "I'm just a connection by marriage, not a real Kenyon. Though the colonel's family has always treated me as one of them, my own relatives are not so elevated. Mostly gentry and soldiers."

"And I suppose my remarks about the English aristocracy didn't encourage you to volunteer more than was necessary." He examined a Renaissance Italian painting of a Madonna and child. "Your mother is as beautiful as you said."

"Have you fallen in love with her already?"

Hearing the edge in her voice, Gavin

caught her gaze. "Of course not. Mostly I was struck by your resemblance to her, and by her joy in having you safe."

Alex's gaze dropped. "I'm sorry, I shouldn't have said that. But when I was first presented, young men would politely call on me, and stay to worship at my mother's feet. Not that she was flirtatious—they simply couldn't resist her."

"So you put half a world between you." His voice softened. "It wasn't because Lady Michael is more beautiful, but because you were a girl and she was a woman, and young men are drawn to female mystery and experience. Now, you are both women, equally beautiful in your individual fashions."

"Really?" The idea was startling, but not unreasonable. Young girls who had just been presented were treated like porcelain dolls, and very boring it was, too. In contrast, her mother was not only beautiful and worldly, but too kind to humiliate an infatuated youth. No wonder those bright young men had been mesmerized by Catherine instead of her sometimes awkward daughter. "I was generally considered the second best-looking woman in Sydney, but I thought that was only because the settlement wasn't large, and my mother wasn't present."

"You will be much admired in London as well, I assure you." He returned to his pacing. "How do the Kenyons feel about admitting tradesmen into their ranks?"

Recognizing that he had reasons of his own to feel tense, she said, "The colonel has been involved in mining and manufacturing as long as I've known him, so I doubt that anyone will faint at the thought of having a merchant prince in the family. Uncle Stephen will probably be interested in investing if you have suitable projects." She hesitated. "Perhaps I should have told you more, but I don't think of my relatives as nobility. They're just—my family. I thought that when you met them, you'd like them and not be bothered by the titles."

"They seem like fine, caring people," he said with disquieting composure. "Don't worry, I feel like a gull whose feathers have been blown backwards, but I'll get over it. Titled relatives are not the worst of the problem." His gaze touched the wide canopied bed, then jumped away.

Alex flushed as she registered that they'd

been put together in the room that was always hers, and this time there were no bars separating them. "I . . . I can sleep on the floor. I got used to straw sleeping mats on Maduri."

His brows arched skeptically. "Maduri is a long way off, and we really need two adjoining rooms. That's common among aristocrats, I believe, and the house certainly appears to have the space."

"This family doesn't use separate rooms," she said wryly. "Kenyons mate for life, like swans."

"And you'd rather not have them wondering what's wrong between us," he said with uncomfortable perception. His gaze went to the bed again. "But I can't do this, Alexandra. You'd really better ask if the adjoining room is free."

Recognizing what lay under his quiet words was disturbing. Though she trusted him, he was made of flesh and blood, not marble. "I'll take care of it this afternoon."

She was so glad to be home—but why had she thought life would become easier? The complications had just begun.

# CHAPTER 18

Getting settled in Ashburton House took the rest of the afternoon. The bedroom adjoining Alex's was vacant, and Gavin's belongings were moved in without comment, though he was sure there would be speculation about what, if anything, it meant when newlyweds didn't want to sleep together. No matter—he could bear gossip more easily than sharing a room with Alex while having to keep his distance.

The two of them visited Katie in the schoolroom, where she was making friends with Alex's young half-sister and the Ashburtons' youngest daughter. Having been deprived of the company of other children for months, Katie was delighted to find girls near her own age, and obviously no longer needed to cling to her mother.

Suryo arrived an hour before dinner with the rest of their luggage, so Gavin was able to dress appropriately for dinner in a duke's house. Good—the more he blended into the background, the better.

By prearrangement, Alex came into his room when she was ready. He turned from the window where he'd been watching lengthening shadows, and caught his breath. Wearing a rose-colored gown and with her dark hair swept up stylishly, she was every inch a London lady. "You look splendid. The gown is one of your mother's?"

"Yes, and the jewelry is my aunt's. The gown is a bit short, but because I'm also too thin at the moment, the effect is presentable."

Rather more than presentable. He tried not to notice how low the gown was cut, or how artfully the borrowed pearl and ruby necklace drew attention to her creamy skin. Though she could use a few more pounds, her happiness made her achingly lovely. "I have trouble believing you were only the second best–looking woman in Sydney. The other residents must have needed spectacles."

Alex laughed. "If you ever saw the glorious Widow Ryan, you'd be amazed that anyone noticed me at all. Frederica was an exquisite little blond who had men swooning whenever she entered a room. The rest of us were much relieved when she married a wealthy English merchant and shook the dust of Australia from her dainty little feet."

"It sounds as if you didn't like her very much."

"She had a tongue like a wasp when she spoke to women or servants." Alex regarded him with mock severity. "I suspect the reason we're discussing the odious Frederica is because you're looking for excuses not to go downstairs, but it can't be put off any longer." She took his arm. "No need to be anxious. Tonight will be only family and a few close friends. You look remarkably fine, and I shall be much envied."

"I need to appear at my best as protection from your male relatives, since they will certainly dissect me over the port later," he said darkly.

"Of course they want to get to know you, but there won't be a dissection."

"Little do you know." His voice turned serious. "People will want to know what happened to you. How much do you want revealed?"

She sighed. "As little as possible. Pirates attacked, Katie and I were separated but not injured, you gallantly rescued us. Keep it as vague as possible. I suppose my parents must be told more, but I don't ever want them to know the whole story."

He nodded and together they left the room. As they descended the sweeping staircase, he was acutely aware of the light pressure of her hand on his forearm. If they had a normal marriage, he would kiss the delicate curve of her throat and find a way not to crumple her gown while he made them late for dinner.

Suppressing that thought with difficulty, he followed Alex's lead to the salon, where family and guests gathered before dining. He and Alex were instantly surrounded by her family and at least a dozen more people, all of whom seemed to have titles and a deep fondness for Alex. She risked bruising from all the hugs.

Quietly he retreated to stand by a wall and watch, thinking that he'd never seen such an expensive-looking group of people in his life, with the possible exception of a dinner with Chenqua, Canton's richest merchant.

Despite his wariness of the nobility, he had to admit that none of this lot seemed particularly dissolute. Many were around the age of the Kenyons, and they looked like men and women who took their responsibilities seriously. Tonight they rejoiced in the return of one of their own with a warmth that was endearing.

"You look like a natural philosopher studying the behavior of penguins." Lady Michael approached with two glasses of sherry, one of which she handed to him. "Will you write a scholarly paper about this strange tribe?"

He smiled. "I'm content to watch. I've been in stranger lands than this."

"But you were merely passing through before. This tribe you've married into, so you must come to terms with it." She took a small sip of her sherry. "A rather overwhelming prospect at the moment, I'm sure."

"I've often wanted to be part of a large family," he said wryly. "I should have remembered that a man must be careful what he wishes for, lest he get it."

"I hope you'll forgive what might look like rudeness. Many of the friendships in this room are measured in decades. Most of these people have known Alex since she was a child, and they—" Lady Michael's voice broke. "They mourned with us. They've earned the right to rejoice with us tonight. It isn't often one experiences a miracle, Captain Elliott."

Seeing tears in her eyes, he pulled out his neatly folded handkerchief and handed it over. "Since I'm your son-in-law now, perhaps you should call me Gavin."

"Thank you, Gavin." She blotted her eyes and managed a smile. "I've been crying on and off ever since I saw my daughter walk in the door. This is one of the happiest days of my life, and I'm behaving like a watering pot."

"Women are fortunate to have tears as a way of expressing deep emotion. Men are mostly restricted to shouting and hitting things." Wanting to bring back her smile, he asked, "Earlier I met your younger daughter,

Anne. She informed me that she's eleven. How old are your boys?"

"Nicholas is seventeen and Stephen is fourteen." She chuckled. "All my children are wonderful, but Alex and I have a special relationship. I was so young when she was born that we more or less grew up together."

It wasn't only Catherine Kenyon's beauty that drew men, Gavin decided, but her charm. "Alex said that only after becoming a mother herself did she realize how difficult it must have been for you to follow the drum when you were a mere girl."

"It was an . . . interesting time. Luckily I was too young to realize how little I knew. Ah, here is someone you must meet." Ashburton was approaching with a striking blond woman about Lady Michael's age on his arm. "Rosalind, this is Alex's husband, Captain Elliott. Gavin, the Duchess of Ashburton, your hostess."

He tried to conceal his surprise as he bowed over her hand. Duchesses should be stiff and haughty, not rounded and golden and smiling.

"I'm so pleased to meet you, Captain," the duchess said warmly. "We must hold a ball to celebrate Alexandra's return and your marriage. Next week, I think."

"So soon?" he asked, startled.

"Since the Season won't last much longer, there's no time to waste," she explained. "Do you have friends in London you'd like me to invite?"

He thought about the shrewd, blunt British traders he knew. "A few, but with one exception, they aren't respectable society people. Mostly merchants."

Instead of being put off, she laughed. "Excellent. Gatherings are so much more enjoyable when not everyone is respectable. When you have time, please make a list for me so they can be invited."

"Who is the one respectable friend?" Lady Michael asked.

"Lord Maxwell, heir to the Earl of Wrexham. I met him in the East." To Ashburton, he said, "May I use one of your footmen to deliver a message? I believe Maxwell should be in London now."

"You're welcome to send a footman, of course, but your friend is the Earl of Wrexham now," Ashburton replied. "His father died about six months ago."

Given the state of the old earl's health,

the news wasn't surprising. "I'm sorry to hear that. It's fortunate Maxwell returned from the East when he did, so they could have some time together." His friend's letters had made it clear that he and his father had become closer in the two years since his return to England. That meant more sorrow, but fewer regrets. "I'll have trouble remembering not to call him 'Maxwell.' "

The duke smiled. "When my son is called Lord Benfield, I sometimes still want to answer even though I haven't had that title for close to twenty years."

"Having one name for life is so much simpler."

"I can't deny it." Lady Michael and the duchess had moved away to greet a new arrival, so the duke added in a lower voice, "You're welcome to stay at Ashburton House as long as you like, but I imagine you'll want your own place. Perhaps I can help you locate a suitable house."

Gavin wondered if his unease was that obvious. "You're very kind, sir. I appreciate the welcome you've extended, but I do want us to have our own home. One not too far away, so Alex and Katie can visit easily."

Lord Michael joined them, a purposeful

expression on his face. Apparently the dissection wouldn't wait until it was time to pass the port.

"Captain, what happened to Alex?" Lord Michael asked without preamble. "It's not a subject for dinner conversation, but . . . I have to know."

Alex's stepfather had vivid green eyes, and there was torment in them. Given how much Gavin loved Katie after only a few months, he could imagine how Lord Michael felt after raising Alex from girlhood.

Glad he'd asked Alex how much she wanted to reveal, he said succinctly, "The *Amstel* was attacked by Island pirates at dawn immediately after a severe storm. Those crew members who weren't killed outright abandoned ship, leaving Alex and Katie to be captured and sold into slavery. They were separated immediately. Luckily, Katie was taken to the women's quarters of an Island rajah where she became a pampered pet."

"And Alex?" Lord Michael's voice was harsh.

"She was taken to another island. By pure chance, I was in Maduri when she was brought to the local slave market. As soon as I realized she was European, I offered to buy her, of course."

Not noticing that Gavin didn't say that he actually had bought her, Ashburton said, "Was this soon after she was captured, and you looked for Katie together?"

Wishing he could lie, Gavin said, "Unfortunately, I didn't find Alex until she had spent six months as a slave."

"How badly was she treated?" Lord Michael was white-lipped.

"That is for her to say when and if she chooses to." Trying to soften that, Gavin added, "She had . . . a difficult time, but was unbroken in either body or spirit. I've never known such an indomitable woman."

"Very like Catherine." Lord Michael stared down at his sherry glass, turning it restlessly. "Women are stronger than men. If they weren't, the race would have died out long ago. But no man wants to see the women he loves tested so severely."

There was a taut silence among the men until Ashburton said, "Yet Alexandra is now home, whole and safe. Tonight is a night for celebration."

"So it is." Lord Michael's face eased. "Captain, the worst thing about having children is letting them go. It would be so much more satisfactory if we could lock them in stone towers. Especially the daughters. You'll find out with Katie."

"At least I don't have to worry about that for a few years."

"Don't count on it—my younger girl and Stephen's daughter are even now giving Katie alarming ideas." Lord Michael smiled wryly. "I guarantee it."

With surprise, Gavin realized that he had already been accepted into the family—and that he could grow to like his formidable new father-in-law.

As the evening progressed, he realized that he liked the other guests as well. The surfeit of earls and countesses pained his democratic American soul, but he had to admit they were interesting people. Though they were living lives of wealth and privilege now, he suspected that most had weathered their share of trouble in the past, and in Gavin's experience, surviving adversity made people worth knowing.

Alex was blossoming like a new rose in this atmosphere, laughing and teasing with family and friends. He remembered what she'd said when he asked her to marry him:

that he'd never seen her at her best. Tonight he did, and she was dazzling. Beautiful, vibrant, a woman whose clever tongue was always tempered by kindness.

As he chatted with the countess on his left, who turned out to be a former schoolteacher, he thought about how damnable fate could be. He should never have married Alex. He'd done it with the best of intentions—pregnant and desperate, she had needed a husband to protect her from slander and despair. But if she'd miscarried earlier, there would have been no marriage. She would be reentering this glittering world as a beautiful widow who was free to love and marry a man of her own background. Instead, she was tied to him. He wondered when she would begin to resent that.

Across the table she laughed and rested her hand on the arm of another of her honorary uncles, a lock of dark hair falling forward to curl against her neck. Gavin swallowed and looked away.

He also was caught in an inappropriate marriage that should not have happened. Yet he could not bring himself to be sorry.

* * *

Hazy with champagne, Alex bid the last of the guests good night. It had been a marvelous evening of talk, food, talk, tea, and more talk. Returning to England during the Season had been a stroke of luck. Since a number of the colonel's friends sat in the House of Lords, they were in London until Parliament ended and she could see many of her favorite people at once. She was really home. *Home.*

Despite his misgivings, Gavin had made it through the evening with ease and apparent enjoyment. She wasn't surprised—anyone who could navigate Sultan Kasan's court could manage anything. He'd been well liked, too. Several of the women had made approving comments to her.

She was home—and it was time to take the next step in their marriage. After the last good night hugs, she took Gavin's arm and they headed up the wide staircase together. She asked, "You had a good time, I hope?"

"Yes, your family and friends are very pleasant, though I'm beginning to think that everyone in London is a peer or peeress." He steadied her arm as she stumbled at the top of the steps. "You shouldn't have let them ply you with so much champagne, though," he said with a smile. "It appears to have affected your navigational abilities."

She chuckled as they reached her bedroom door. "A little. No one forced me to drink, though. I had all that champagne deliberately."

She tugged him inside after her, then closed the door and turned the key in the lock with unsteady fingers. In the dim glow of the night light, he was as handsome as a young girl's dream of her future husband. Reminding herself that she'd been planning this all evening, she said in a voice that wasn't quite even, "I . . . I want us to be really married, Gavin."

His smile disappeared. "You're asking me to stay with you tonight?"

She nodded, her hands clenching and unclenching. "I want to put the fear behind me. That's why I drank more wine than usual. I'm floating and happy now. Perhaps that will make this first time easier."

"In my experience, drinking makes most things more difficult, not less." He hesitated, visibly torn. "Are you sure you want to do this tonight, at the end of such a tiring day?"

"I don't like being afraid, Gavin." She

pulled the pins from her hair so that it fell over her shoulders with bedroom intimacy. "As a soldier's daughter, I need to face fear head on. Once I'm past it, we can look forward instead of being chained by the past."

He closed the distance between them in one long step. "I hope you know what you're doing, my dearest wife, because I want you too much to be sensible." He brushed his hands into her hair and held her head gently as he bent in to a kiss.

She clung to him, a little dizzy from champagne. The first time he'd kissed her, after their wedding, she'd been on edge, anxious about what he might expect of her. She knew him better now. Trusted him, recognized his warm, firm, lips. *I can do this,* she thought to herself. *Such a simple thing to relax and let my husband make love to me. I can do this.*

She refused even to consider the possibility that she couldn't.

# CHAPTER 19

Though Alex had known Gavin was a patient man, she hadn't fully appreciated the advantages of that until tonight. Instead of rushing her to the bed, he kissed her by the door for long, luxurious minutes, his hands gliding over her body to create uncomplicated pleasure. If she'd been a cat, she would have purred.

Clever, clever hands . . . Dreamily she realized that he'd unfastened the fussy hooks and ties that secured her gown in back. With his encouragement, the rose-colored silk slid down her arms and over her hips before rustling to the floor.

He was so deft at unlacing that she

scarcely noticed what he was doing until her corset miraculously released its grip on her torso. She inhaled deeply, her unbound breasts tingling at their new freedom.

Despite his skilled touch, uneasiness penetrated her pleasant haze as he rubbed her back with only the thin fabric of her chemise separating his palms from her bare skin. When his hands moved below her waist, she involuntarily moved away.

Wanting to cover up her reaction, she tried to remove his coat. He shrugged his way out of the closely cut garment with some difficulty while she worked on the buttons of his waistcoat. He chuckled when her fumbling fingers tickled him. "You're dangerous, lass."

She liked the deepening of his Scottish accent as much as she liked the idea of being dangerous. She tickled him again.

Laughing, he peeled off her corset, then swung her into his arms to carry her the half-a-dozen steps to the canopied bed. Her head spun dizzily and she swallowed hard, hoping she hadn't had too much champagne.

The bed was sumptuously soft after a

year of Indies' pallets and firm shipboard mattresses. While she breathed deeply to steady her head, he removed her slippers. "What elegant feet you have."

"They're large, like my hands," she protested. "Not dainty and ladylike at all."

"They're fine and strong and shapely, like the rest of you." He massaged one silk-stockinged foot, then the other. Her toes curled with unexpected pleasure as he gently rubbed the arches.

Then he untied her ribbon garters. Anxiety spiked through her again at the feel of his hands at her knees. Instead of moving higher, he merely removed her stockings, then leaned over to kiss her throat. Though he didn't pin her down with his weight, she could feel the warmth radiating from his arched body.

He took her nipple in his mouth, kissing through the fine Indian muslin of her chemise. She gasped, startled by her dual reaction of excitement and alarm. Her pulse drummed in her head. Blood? Champagne?

Fear.

As his caresses became more intimate, she clamped down on her anxiety, reminding herself that this was what she wanted. The first time would be the worst. After that it would get easier, and soon the horrors of slavery would be buried so far in the past that she would never think of them again.

He was breathing heavily, his desire barely in check. A hard pressure throbbed against her thigh, and she sensed that the rational man she trusted was being eclipsed by fierce male urgency. Her own breath quickened with rising panic. He wouldn't hurt her, she knew that. Even in the humiliation of the Lion Game, he hadn't hurt her. She had endured that, she could endure this in the privacy of her own bed.

His hand was under her chemise, inexorable on the soft fabric of her drawers. Her breathing was so rapid that she was on the verge of blacking out because she couldn't inhale enough air into her lungs.

Relax. *Relax.* A few minutes more and it would be over, and never so difficult again.

Yet she whimpered with fear when his fingers slid to the apex of her thighs, stroking deep. Oh, God, he was inside her, invading her body. She bit her lip so hard she tasted the metallic tang of blood.

Then he was on top of her, his hard muscled body trapping her, violent manhood jabbing against her. *Her owner, violating her at will.* Panic erupted and she shoved him hysterically. "No! *No!*"

Her mind a red scream, she hammered at his face and shoulders as she struggled for enough breath to cry out for help. Abruptly she was free of the crushing weight, but a hard hand clamped over her mouth.

"Alex. *Alex!*" He gave her shoulder a rough shake. "It's over. *Over.*"

Reason began to penetrate her panic, and she managed to focus on his face. He was breathing heavily, his skin sheened with sweat.

"Will you promise not to scream if I take my hand away? I don't think either of us wants your family crashing in here because they think I'm murdering you."

It took several deep breaths for her to regain her wits enough to nod. He released her and swung from the bed, grabbing at a carved bedpost to steady himself. Shoulders shaking, he inhaled deeply, then crossed the room. The connecting door closed soundlessly behind him.

She was alone, safe—and shattered. Wrapping herself around a pillow, she fought to prevent uncontrollable sobs from escaping. She had wanted so much for this to work. He was right, she shouldn't have hazed her mind with champagne. Though at first it had helped her relax, when she had most needed to control herself she'd become a frantic, mindless beast.

As her heart slowed and her dizziness faded, she realized that she couldn't leave matters as they stood. He must be furious, and as shattered as she. Perhaps worse, since he'd had reason to believe that all was going well. Her responses could easily have been interpreted as enthusiasm right up until she'd gone berserk. She shuddered, wondering if she'd finally pushed him beyond his ability to understand and forgive.

Even if she had, she must apologize for what she'd done. She blew her nose and donned a warm wool robe and slippers borrowed from her aunt. Then she tied her hair back with a ribbon and crossed to the connecting door.

She wouldn't have been surprised if he'd locked it against her, but the knob turned silently in her hand. She entered quietly, not sure what she'd find. As in her room, a well-shielded night lamp on the bedside table cast just enough light to prevent stumbling over the furniture. The bed was flat and undisturbed.

A quick scan revealed that he was seated by the window, his white shirt faintly visible and his profile dark against the night as he gazed out over London. He was sprawled wearily in the massive chair, his long legs stretched in front of him. Though he must have heard her come in, he didn't turn or speak.

She took a deep breath. "You must be furious, and you have every right to be."

"I'm not angry." His voice was painfully cool and remote. "You tried your best. One can ask no more."

"Nonetheless, I'm deeply sorry for what happened. I . . . I thought I could do it."

"Don't apologize for being brave." A brief flare of light illuminated his still features as he drew on a cigar, the wispy smoke curling out the window. She'd never seen him smoke before.

"I wasn't brave—I was a fool. You were right—the champagne was a terrible mis-

take. It made everything worse." She moistened her dry lips. "Beyond mending, perhaps."

He sighed. "Most things can be mended,
though this one won't be easy."

Encouraged that he was willing to talk,
she asked, "Did I hurt you?"

"Not physically. Luckily you don't know
any *pentjak silat,* or I'd be dead."

But she'd certainly inflicted emotional
harm. Gavin couldn't be so sensitive to others without having deep feelings of his own.
"It wasn't you I was fighting."

"I know." He drew on the cigar again. "If
we are to have any chance of getting beyond this, I think I must understand a good
deal more of your mind and past."

At least he was still thinking of them as
"we," but she realized with despair that she
must tell him everything, revealing the full
depths of her degradation. Fists clenching,
she perched on the wooden chair by the
desk. "Ask whatever you wish. I'll answer
as best I can."

"Do you find me attractive?"

Surprised by the question, she said honestly, "I think you're the handsomest man
I've ever known."

"Thank you, but that's not the same thing as attraction. One can admire a Michelangelo statue and not want to bed it. One can be powerfully attracted to someone whose appearance is quite unremarkable."

She gnawed at her lip as she recognized the depth of his question. Thinking of the itchy, uncomfortable feelings he'd aroused in her even in Maduri, she replied, "I am attracted to you, but it's tangled up with everything else that has happened."

"So your natural responses are tempered by fear and revulsion."

He was depressingly right. "I . . . I'm afraid so."

"Understanding is a beginning." He tapped his cigar against the edge of an ashtray. "Forgive me for asking, but what was the intimate side of your marriage like? Did you enjoy, or merely endure?"

Glad the darkness concealed her heated face, she replied, "I was not a shy bride. I found Edmund very attractive, and was . . . impatient to marry him."

"So your marital relationship was good?"

She should have known Gavin wouldn't settle for the simple answer. "To be honest, I was a bit disappointed. Mother and the colonel are always restrained in public, but even after twenty years, one can feel a kind of humming between them. It's clear that they rejoice in every aspect of marriage. It was never quite that way with Edmund and me. But truly, I did enjoy my wifely duties, and I loved that I could please him. He said once how proud he was to have me as his wife. He was always affectionate and indulgent after we . . . had relations."

"A man will do almost anything for a woman who satisfies him well. It's the source of female power," Gavin responded. The only movement was the faint pale twist of smoke from his cigar. "Alexandra—what was done to you in slavery? I know it must be difficult to speak of, but I need to understand."

Her nails cut into her palms painfully. "It wasn't so bad at the beginning. The voyage to Maduri was short. If it had been longer, I might have been given to the crew. A widow is much less valuable than a pretty young virgin.

"In Maduri, I was bought by a merchant, Payaman. He was plump and middle-aged, and his special pleasure was collecting different sorts of women. He owned Chinese, Indians, Africans, a blond Circassian—all shapes and colors. He wasn't a bad fellow, really. He liked women and a comfortable life, and couldn't understand why I screamed and fought when he tried to bed me.

"His head lady tried to make me understand how fortunate I was. All I had to do was behave, and I'd have a life of luxury. Tuan Payaman would probably only sleep with me a few times until the novelty wore off. But I was frantic to go after Katie, and I fought him off every time he sent for me. Eventually he decided there was no point in having a European woman who wouldn't let him touch her, so he sold me to Bhudy."

"The one who might have fathered your child?"

She began shaking. "Unlike Payaman, Bhudy liked resistance. When I fought, he called his guards and . . . and they chained me down. I wasn't the first—there were brass hooks embedded in Bhudy's bedroom floor."

Gavin made a sharp, involuntary movement. "How often did that happen?"

"Whenever he got bored with compliant

women. But after a few months he also decided I wasn't worth the trouble." She stood and began pacing the room in agitation. "To teach me a lesson, he decided to sell me at public auction. He had me chained down again and raped me one last time. Then he . . . he let the guards have their way with me."

"Dear God." Harsh silence filled the room. "How did you survive without going mad?"

"I thought of Katie. Even more, I imagined the ways I would kill Bhudy if I could. May rats eat his liver, and his precious male organs rot and fall off." She reached the wall and pivoted, her hands clenched as she paced back and forth. "Payaman's head lady was right—I would have been much wiser to submit quietly to her lord. If I'd done that, I would never have been defiled by Bhudy and his horrible guards."

"If you hadn't fought, you'd have spent the rest of your life in Payaman's harem, and Katie would never have met her grandmother." His voice was very gentle. "You should have been born a man, Alexandra. You have a warrior heart."

"You're not the first to suggest I'd have

been better off as a man," she said, her bitterness overflowing. "Certainly I wasn't woman enough to keep Edmund from acquiring a mistress after Katie was born."

Gavin swore under his breath. "Any man who could be unfaithful to you was acting from his own weaknesses, not yours."

"Perhaps—I never knew why he did it. Maybe the fact that I was a mother meant I was no longer a woman worthy of desire," she said wearily. "At least he was discreet. His mistress was a pretty Irish girl who'd been transported for theft. She was our maid. When I found out and confronted him, he refused to discuss the matter, but he did move her into a small house on the other side of town so I never had to see her again. I was grateful for that."

"I'm surprised you can bear to be in the same room with a man."

"Luckily, I've known many men of the better kind." She couldn't imagine the colonel being unfaithful to her mother. Of course, her father had been willing to bed anything in skirts. At least Edmund wasn't like that. The thought was cold comfort. "Gavin, I need to understand you also. What was it like for you and your wife? How did you learn so much about women when your experience has been with only one?"

He rubbed at his temple as if memory was painful. "Helena and I were like clumsy young puppies—completely innocent but full of enthusiasm. We both wanted so much to please that we did. As for having limited experience—knowing one woman very well is a better education than knowing dozens in a purely physical way."

That was true; she'd known much about Edmund, and nothing about her rapists other than their brutish bodies. Grateful Gavin hadn't left in disgust when he learned the extent of her violation, she asked, "Now that you know the full story, what comes next?"

"There is no way to punish those who abused you—we must leave that to God. The best revenge is for you to surmount your experiences to live a full, happy life." He blew a slow trickle of smoke toward the window. "So we allow time to perform its magic. You're only a few months out of slavery, and you've only just returned to your homeland. When you invited me to stay with you earlier, my instincts said it was too early, but I wanted to believe otherwise, so I certainly share some of the blame for tonight's disaster." His voice was rueful. "It's easy to delude oneself where desire is involved, and I desire you greatly."

Darkness made it possible to say, "I'm glad to know that I don't disgust you. That you can still desire me despite the hell I'm putting you through."

"The greatest prizes are the hardest won."

"If difficulty creates worth, this should be a very valuable marriage." She tried to make her voice light, without much success. "More than time, we need for me to separate desire from anxiety. I . . . I don't know how to do that. But at least I have some idea where to start."

She didn't want to end the night with them so separated, so she made herself cross to where he sat. "Thank you, Gavin." She took his hand and pressed it to her cheek, hoping she could absorb his strength and compassion. "You give me hope."

His hand tensed noticeably, but he squeezed her fingers before gently disengaging. "For now, let us concentrate on living. Meeting each other's friends, finding a house, creating a life together. The rest will come."

She nodded agreement in the darkness. For now, that must be enough.

# CHAPTER 20

Eventually Gavin's weariness drove him to his bed, though not to sleep. He was haunted by visions of Alex being brutally ravished. How could any man do such things to a woman? Though he'd known his share of callous, violent men, he still found such behavior incomprehensible.

He was, to his shame, still painfully aroused. If Alex had been able to finish what they'd begun, perhaps the worst would be behind them. Now he wasn't sure he'd be able to bring himself to initiate physical intimacy again, since her rejection had been as harrowing emotionally as it was physically. It was up to her to make the next move when she was ready—if she ever was. Though he'd talked confidently, now that he knew the full scope of what she had endured, he recognized bleakly that she might never recover enough to be the joyful lover he longed for.

He reminded himself that despite their problems, they had the foundation of a good marriage: commitment, mutual desire, and the ability to talk honestly to each other. Enough to counterbalance what they didn't have.

For now, he could allay the pain of arousal, though he found no real satisfaction in doing so. But at least his whirling mind finally slowed enough to rest.

After a few restless hours of sleep, he rose early and dressed, then wrote a note to his friend Maxwell—no, blast it, Wrexham now—while keeping an ear tuned to the sounds of Alex rising and preparing for the day. When he judged that she was ready, he tapped at her door.

"Come in," she called.

He entered and found her wearing another fashionable gown, this one a soft, expensive blue that enhanced her fair skin.

She looked like a stylish London beauty—except for the shadows in her eyes which spoke of things no society matron could know. For an instant he was paralyzed by multiple images of Alex in slavery that obscured the woman she was now.

When he saw how warily she regarded him, he clamped down on his reaction to the past and gave her a light, husbandly kiss on the cheek. "Shall we go down to breakfast, my dear?"

Smile bright with relief at his casual manner, she took his arm. "I long for a huge English breakfast. The food on the *Helena* was good for a sailing ship, but still . . ."

"A long way from a decent breakfast," he agreed. They chatted easily as they went downstairs, united in an unspoken agreement to keep their problems private.

After Gavin gave his note to the butler for delivery, he and Alex entered the sunny breakfast parlor. The adults of the household, plus Katie, were helping themselves to a variety of foods set in warming dishes on the sideboard. More hugs all around. Gavin had never seen a British family so affectionate. Maybe the hugs would end when the Kenyons were used to having Alex back.

Gavin hoped not; he found that he quite enjoyed being hugged by Lady Michael, with her warm serenity, or the duchess, who radiated sunny, good-natured charm.

As Gavin and Alex settled down with the food they'd selected, Lord Michael asked, "Do you ride, Captain? Catherine and I are going out to the park after breakfast, and we thought it would be pleasant if you and Alex joined us."

"I know one end of a horse from the other and can generally stay on if the beast doesn't have strong opinions about where to go," Gavin said, thinking that if this was a test, he was going to fail. Sailing ships presented few opportunities for riding. "But I'm willing to try if Alex wants to go."

"The horses we bring to London are steady in temper," his father-in-law assured him. "Alex, have you forgotten how to ride?"

She grinned. "Wait and see."

Katie swallowed a mouthful of egg before proclaiming, "Mama was the best lady rider in Sydney. Everyone said so."

"I haven't been on a horse in—heavens, over a year! I doubt I've forgotten how to ride, but I'll have to borrow a habit." Alex ruffled her daughter's hair. "Katybird, you and I must find ourselves a dressmaker now that we're home. We can't borrow clothes from our kind relations forever."

"I thought the three of us could do that tomorrow morning." Lady Michael smiled at Gavin. "I'm sure you'll be glad to know that your presence is not required."

"I am relieved beyond measure," he said promptly.

The rest of the breakfast was like that—light teasing, discussion of plans for the day, welcoming the other two girls of the household when they came down, yawning. Gavin liked that the young ladies weren't relegated to the nursery for all their meals. The atmosphere was so relaxed that he half wondered if Ashburton was really a duke. The man seemed far too human. He could have been a New Englander whose greatest pleasure was in having his family around him.

The spacious stables where they met after changing into riding clothes were certainly ducal, and the horses were first rate even to Gavin's inexpert eye. Alex, splendid in a scarlet habit with military styling, quickly made friends with a handsome dark bay gelding. Gavin rather envied the horse for the way she murmured endearments to it. He settled for helping her into the sidesaddle, enjoying her scent and foaming skirts and the supple warmth of her waist. His own chestnut mount was mercifully placid.

For the short blocks to the park, Gavin rode beside Lady Michael and Alex with the colonel. He was bemused to find himself in the middle of the aristocratic life he'd always despised. Well, he was too stubborn a Yankee to change his mind about class merely because he'd married into a family he could actually like.

When they reached the park, which was quiet at this hour, Lord Michael said to Alex, "Do you think you can beat me to the far end of Rotten Row?"

"We'll see!" Alex and the bay tore off at a gallop, her stepfather a half stride behind and laughter floating behind them.

Gavin remarked, "Alex was born on a horse, right?"

Her mother chuckled. "Not quite, but she had her first riding lesson when she was about three, and of course Michael has spent half his life on horseback. I love seeing them like this—in some ways she's more like Michael than any of the other children even though they're not related by blood." She gave Gavin a sidelong glance as they entered the park at a more sedate pace. "You and Katie seem to get along well."

Hearing the unspoken question, he said, "When Alex and I agreed to marry, Katie and I were already friends so it was easy to become family." He smiled. "Plus, she has the making of a good navigator."

"I'm glad to hear that," his mother-in-law said, clearly not talking about navigation. Her gaze went to her husband and daughter, who were far down the path. "For a man who has lived a demanding, very masculine kind of life, I think a little girl can be rather magical."

"You must have been very grateful for that, Lady Michael."

"I was. By the way, you may call me Catherine if you like. I'm used to living in Wales, where life is rather less formal than London."

"Very well, Catherine." He studied her heart-shaped face, the elegance of her posture as she rode sidesaddle in perfect form.

"I must hope that Alex continues to take after her mother. If she does, I'll be a much envied man for decades to come."

"Flatterer," Catherine said with amusement. "And too modest about your riding abilities. You're a very competent horseman."

"As a boy I raced over the Scottish hills on my pony as if I were immortal," he admitted. "But I've not ridden regularly since going to sea."

"The skill will come back quickly." Catherine adjusted the veil of her dashing top hat. "How badly was Alexandra mistreated? Rape? Torture? Beatings?"

Shocked by the bald question, Gavin involuntarily tightened his grip on the reins, making the chestnut shy with confusion. "What makes you ask a thing like that?"

"Don't be a fool, Gavin." Catherine's aqua eyes were ice cool. "I'm her mother. Don't you think I can see how much she's hurting?"

Wishing he were somewhere else, he said, "Alex doesn't want to talk about what happened. Last night was the first time she's spoken even to me about what she suffered in slavery."

"The truth may appall me, but I won't be shocked." Her mouth tightened. "I spent a dozen years nursing in countries at war. I know how vile men can be, and how women are used when social rules break down. If you don't tell me the truth, my imagination will conjure up worse horrors than whatever happened."

Seeing her expression, he asked, "Have you been . . . ?" He stopped, knowing he had no right to ask.

"Raped? No, though it was a near thing more than once. I ask again, Captain Elliott—what happened to my daughter?"

"Rape, and more than once," he said bluntly. "No deliberate torture, but beatings because she would never surrender. No permanent physical injuries, but the emotional wounds are still raw."

"I see. Thank you for telling me." Catherine swallowed hard. "Don't you *dare* pity her. She would hate that more than anything."

That was good advice—the pride that had kept Alex from breaking would despise the condescension of pity. "I said earlier that I hoped Alex would be like you when she gets older. I now find the prospect terrifying. You're an alarmingly perceptive woman, Catherine."

"I've made mistakes, and learned from them." She glanced at him again. "Do you love my daughter, Gavin?"

He hesitated as he searched for the right words. "I was married before, and losing my wife and infant daughter left me so numb I thought I could never marry again. With Alex, everything is different. She inspires respect, desire, friendship, and a yearning to protect. I care for her deeply. That's a kind of love."

"Not the unequivocal answer I hoped for, but thank you for your honesty." Catherine's gaze was shrewd. "You'll do, Gavin. Alex was fortunate to find you."

"I'm benefiting as much as she is," he said with dry humor. "I've always wondered what it would be like to have a large family prying into my business. Obviously I'm going to find out."

Alex was happy to see that by the time she and the colonel had galloped off their high spirits, Gavin and her mother were well on their way to becoming friends. If her husband and parents hated each other, she'd be in a devil of a position.

As the party headed back to Ashburton House, she fell in beside Gavin. "That was wonderful. I've missed riding dreadfully."

"Is this a way of saying that we need to look for a house with decent stabling?"

"If we can afford it, yes," she replied. "You like riding too, don't you? You're doing rather well for a sailor."

"I do enjoy it, but I'm going to ache all over tomorrow."

As Gavin smiled at her, the sun emerged from behind the clouds and gilded him with light. The sheer physical beauty of his fair hair, tanned skin, and powerful shoulders sent a swift surge of desire burning through her.

It was gone in an instant, suffocated by her revulsion with sex. Yet for a few heartbeats, attraction had been uncontaminated by fear and anger.

It was a beginning.

After they stabled the horses and entered Ashburton House, the butler approached with a note for Gavin. He broke the seal. "Wrexham has invited us to dine with him and his wife today. Would you like to go,

Alex, or do you have other plans? I think you'd like them."

"Of course I want to meet your friends." She made a face. "I'll have to borrow still another dress from my mother. I'd forgotten how tiring it is to always be changing clothes. There is something to be said for a simple sarong and *kebaya.*"

"I'm beginning to suspect that requiring different costumes for different activities is how the upper classes fill their time," he agreed. "Like you and Katie, I'll need to add to my wardrobe. What I have was not made for London's society or weather."

Their gazes met with amused under-standing before she turned to climb the stairs. Who could have guessed that she would come to yearn for the clothing of the Indies? Those months had shaped her in good ways as well as bad.

But for now, she needed to borrow an-other gown.

As a ducal carriage took them to Wrex-ham House, Alex asked, "How do you know Lord Wrexham? And how did you overcome your distaste for his title?"

"I was doing my best to get drunk in a

rather low-class establishment in Calcutta. I must have been looking grim about it, because Maxwell invited himself to sit down." Gavin chuckled at the memory. "I thought Maxwell was his family name, or I might have said no. But he was good company, so when he asked what was wrong, I told him how Elliott House was on the verge of bankruptcy."

"How did that happen? The company is prospering now, isn't it?"

"After Helena died, I was fairly useless for months, and at the same time Elliott House hit a run of bad luck—a lost ship, legal persecution in a South American port, misjudgments about some large cargos. We were weakened but would have pulled through, until a British merchant decided to drive me out of business. Then Maxwell appeared. He rather liked the idea of becoming part owner of a trading company, so I sold him a quarter of Elliott House for enough money to weather my financial problems."

"He's done well from his investment?"

"We both have. He spent time in Macao and Canton and knows the business, so he's been useful here in London." Gavin grinned. "I think it appeals to him to continue active trading. Very antiaristocratic."

"No wonder you get along well." Alex's brows drew together. "The merchant who tried to drive you out of business—is that the man you told Sultan Kasan to avoid? Pierce, I think the name was?"

She was already as perceptive as her mother. "He's the one. Given the circumstances, I'm surprised you remembered that."

"It seemed so unlike you to go out of the way to criticize someone. I presume the fellow is quite dreadful."

"He is." Gavin hesitated, wondering how much to say. But Alex was part of his life now, and she should know, particularly since there was a chance she'd meet the man here in London. "Barton Pierce is the worst kind of villain—the sort who appears smooth and honest. He can be quite charming, but he's ruthless when he thinks his interests are threatened—and he is a man who feels easily threatened."

"What did he do that caused so much trouble?"

"He offered to buy a large amount of tea from me at a price that would keep the company going. The deal was done on a handshake, which made it easy for him to repudiate later. I was left with a lot of tea very late in the season with no chance of getting the price I needed."

"A nasty but effective tactic. Your word against his, and if you complained publicly, you'd look weak and foolish."

"Exactly. Later I investigated and found that he'd played similar tricks on other men, and destroyed at least one company that way." Gavin thought of his despair on the night he'd met Maxwell. He'd lost his family and was about to lose everything else. It would have been easy to throw his life away as well. "Pierce had no reason to ruin me—there was profit enough for both of us. I think he enjoys destruction."

"Appalling man. Where is he based—Macao?"

"The last I heard, he was planning to return to London so he could settle down and enjoy his fortune."

Alex's eyes narrowed. "Is there a connection between his returning to England and your deciding to move here?"

"There's a connection," he admitted, "but

I have no colorful plans for revenge. Merely a bit of . . . justice."

Alex bit her lip. "It isn't good to pick fights with snakes, Gavin. They are so much better at being venomous. What do you intend to do?"

"I really don't know. If I have the opportunity to act against Pierce in a lawful way, I'll take it, but I'm not about to challenge him to a duel." Gavin smiled. "That's another aristocratic custom I have no use for."

"Why do I find your declaration less than comforting?"

Because his wife was entirely too perceptive.

# CHAPTER 21

Before Alex could pursue the subject of Barton Pierce, they arrived at their destination. The situation disturbed her. Though she had faith in her husband's competence, unscrupulous men had an advantage when dealing with those who were honest. A merchant who crushed opponents for sport would be a dangerous adversary.

But that was a topic for later. As they were admitted to Wrexham House, a beaming dark-haired man emerged from the drawing room and took Gavin's hand in a hard clasp. "So you're really here! I never quite believed you'd make it to London."

"I ran out of excuses not to come." Gavin

returned the other man's handshake with equal fervor. "But I was sorry to hear about your father."

"I never would have guessed how much I'd miss the old devil. But his last years were good ones, and he died quietly in his sleep. We're all grateful for that. Now, please introduce me to your wife." Wrexham turned to Alex, and his brows rose. "Actually, we know each other already. Aren't you Miss Melbourne, Ashburton's niece?"

She offered her hand with a laugh. "I was a dozen years ago. We danced together several times, as I recall. You were dreadfully serious." He'd been stiff and rather intimidating, actually, the kind of rich young man she'd had no interest in marrying. She barely recognized him in this relaxed man with the warm smile.

"I was bored beyond belief, and plotting how to escape to see the world. Succeeding at that did wonders for my disposition."

Alex rummaged through her memory. "Don't you have a twin brother? I once mistook him for you. He was rather offended at the mistake, I think."

Wrexham laughed. "We hated being confused with each other then, but we've mended fences since. Please come and meet my wife."

As they entered the drawing room, a slender woman rose. To Alex's surprise, she was Chinese. No, Eurasian. As tall as Alex, Lady Wrexham was stunning, stylish, and as exotic as a tropical orchid. Laughing, she gave Gavin a hug. "Honorable Elliott! It has been far too long."

"Jin Kang, just look at you!" Gavin hugged her with the warmth of long friendship. "Or should I call you Mei-Lian?"

"Troth will do."

Alex was intrigued to hear that the other woman had a faint, charming Scottish accent rather like Gavin's. London seemed much more interesting than it had been a dozen years earlier.

Gavin said, "Troth, allow me to present my wife, Alexandra Elliott."

"I am pleased to meet you, Mrs. Elliott." Troth's calm face showed recognition of the fact that not everyone would approve of a Eurasian countess.

Thinking this was a woman she wanted to know better, Alex said, "I gather you know Gavin from Macao? I do hope you can tell me wicked stories about his past."

Troth's brown eyes danced. "I shall be delighted to do so."

The men looked at each other. "It was a grave error to get them together," Gavin said soberly.

"Disastrous," Wrexham said with equal gravity. "Let us hope that dinner will prevent them from plotting mischief."

The meal did delay plotting, as well as giving Alex the chance to learn more about the Chinese past the others shared. She liked discovering pieces of Gavin's history. The excellent food included rice and several Chinese dishes in addition to the usual English fare. The countess's graceful hand also showed elsewhere, in furnishings and arrangements that added a dash of elegant East to luxurious West.

As dinner ended, Gavin said, "I've never been fond of the custom of men lingering over the port, but Maxwell—sorry, Wrexham—and I have business to discuss. Will you ladies excuse us if we promise not to talk too long?"

"Of course." The countess rose and collected Alex with a glance. "Mrs. Elliott, would you by any chance like to meet my little boy?"

"How did you know the exact entertainment that would please me most?" Alex exclaimed as they left the room.

"I didn't. Selfishly, I wanted to visit him."

"What could be more natural? I have a nine-year-old daughter." She smiled. "I never knew how thoroughly one falls in love with one's child."

"How can a woman know before she becomes a mother?"

The women shared a glance of perfect understanding as they headed upstairs together. By the time they reached the nursery, they were on a first-name basis.

When they entered, a very small boy looked up from his toy blocks, then ran to his mother with open arms. "Mama!"

"Dominic, my darling!" Troth scooped the child up, making nonsense sounds as she cradled him. No, not nonsense, she was speaking Chinese. Alex couldn't understand a word, but the intonation was unmistakable.

After Troth and her son finished their

greeting, the countess asked, "Would you like to hold Dominic? My small viscount is very sociable."

"I'd love to." Alex took the warm little body into her arms.

He blinked up at her for a moment, then planted a smacking kiss on her chin. "Pretty."

Alex laughed as the boy latched onto her necklace. "I think he approves of me."

"He knows welcoming arms when he meets them."

There was a hint of the Orient around Dominic's eyes. Alex thought of the almond-eyed child she might have had, and had to blink back tears. "He's beautiful."

"Thank you." Troth hesitated. "I'm sorry— is something wrong?"

"I had a miscarriage on the voyage home. Seeing this little fellow makes me feel the loss." Alex detached her necklace from the child's fist and returned him to his mother.

"I'm so sorry," Troth said with compassion. "I also had one several months ago. The physician assures me there is no reason to suppose it will happen next time, but that does not cure the sadness for what might have been."

It was another strand of understanding in what Alex hoped was the beginning of a real friendship. Troth kissed her son and handed him to the indulgent nursemaid. As they left, Alex asked, "You're teaching Dominic Chinese?"

"Yes. With luck, he'll pick it up painlessly. If he goes to the East, it will come in handy." Troth hesitated, then said, "I also want my children to have some sense of Chinese culture."

"Of course. It would be a sad loss if they were raised in ignorance of such an important part of their heritage."

"I'm glad you understand. Not everyone does." Troth made a rueful face. "Particularly not the elderly Renbourne cousins and aunts. But they've become used to my ways. The old earl ordered them to accept me or else, and they didn't dare find out what 'or else' meant."

Alex laughed. "I'm sure you're bringing strong new blood into the Renbourne line, and about time. Many of these old families have been marrying each other for too many generations. My uncle was pleased to learn I'd married a Yankee, and disappointed when he found out Gavin is British by birth."

"Ah, but you can do no better than Gavin Elliott for a husband." Troth's smile was mischievous. "Shall we take tea in the conservatory while I tell you more about him? Though you may be disappointed. I worked for him as a translator on and off for years, and never saw a single example of wickedness or dishonesty."

"I'd be surprised if you had." They stepped into the conservatory, and Alex gasped. "How beautiful this is! Like a tropical garden."

"It was Kyle's gift to me when Dominic was born." Troth bent her head to inhale the perfume of a gorgeous pink-and-white lily. "We have a larger conservatory at Dornleigh, the Renbourne family seat, but this is special because one needs the beauty so much more in London. My sister-in-law is a great gardener, so we designed the conservatory together. Meriel can make anything grow."

Alex wandered down the curving path, touching flowers and leaves in wonder. Scattered among the greenery were small statues, both Chinese and European, and a fountain sang gently nearby. "What a wonderful piece of the East to find in London." And also a gift of love from a husband who truly understood his wife. The conservatory was a living testament to how people could build a bridge between very different worlds.

The path ended in a sizable area that was floored with warm Spanish tile. A small table and several chairs were set there so one could enjoy both the conservatory and the conventional garden on the other side of the glass. "Do you take meals here often?"

"Whenever Kyle and I dine alone together." Troth bent to scratch the head of a tabby cat that emerged from under a low palm to twine around her ankles. "Since you've lived in the East, you know how buildings blend indoors and outdoors. Kyle and I both liked that, so we've created a cold-climate version."

A footman appeared with a tea tray and left it on the table. Troth poured for them both as the cat tucked its paws and watched with sleepy interest. "Is Suryo Indarto still with your husband?"

"Yes, he's in London now."

"Excellent. I hope to see Tuan Suryo soon. We often worked together at Elliott House. When business was slow, I taught him Chinese. In return he taught me Malay and *pentjak silat.*"

Alex put down her tea cup in amazement. "You know Indies fighting?"

"A little. I'm surprised you know what it is."

"I've seen Gavin use *pentjak silat.* He's very, very good."

"Tuan Suryo must have taught him." Troth took a sip of tea. "I learned some moves and holds from Tuan Suryo, but I'm not an expert. My principal training is in *wing chun,* one of many forms of Chinese fighting. They say *wing chun* was developed by Buddhist nuns, and it is particularly well suited to females."

"A fighting art specially for women?" Alex leaned forward eagerly. "Can you teach me? Please?"

"You wish to learn?" The other woman looked startled. "It takes years of training. I began studying *wing chun* as a child and have practiced my whole life. It would take a very long time for you to master."

"I understand that I would never be an

adept, but can you teach me basic skills of self defense? A woman needs to be able to protect herself." Hearing the vehemence in her voice, Alex said more quietly, "I don't ever want to be helpless again."

"I see."

Troth's shrewd gaze saw far more than Alex had said, but the thought was not distressing. There had been an immediate sense of connection between them that was creating more honesty than was usual with new acquaintances. Was it because Alex had seen some of the world Troth had grown up in? Whatever the reason, she was glad.

"Eastern fighting arts are as much a matter of mind as body," the other woman said pensively. "They require thought, discipline, and reflection. Basic moves can be taught. The problem is that few women have the minds of warriors. One must have the will to fight as well as the knowledge."

Alex thought of her vain, furious struggles in slavery. "I can and will fight. What I want is to know how to fight *well.*"

Troth's mouth curved into a smile. "I warn you, even simple lessons can create many bruises."

"No matter. Can you give me a demonstration?"

"Now? We are not dressed for sparring." She indicated her stylish, full-sleeved gown disparagingly. "A tunic and loose trousers are best."

"Perhaps a very, very small lesson?" Alex wasn't sure herself why this was so important to her, only that she desperately wanted to learn. "If I ever need to defend myself, I'll probably be dressed much as I am now."

"True. Very well, if you wish it, and don't mind a hard floor." Troth stood and pushed the table and chairs to one side of the tiled space. As soon as her chair was relocated, the cat jumped into it, curling up to absorb the warmth left by her mistress.

Troth moved to the center of the open space and took a relaxed, balanced posture on the balls of her feet. "Attack me."

Feeling suddenly absurd, Alex moved forward to throw an uneasy fist at the other woman's shoulder. Troth caught her wrist effortlessly, twisting it just enough to make further advance painful. "Remember what I said about women not knowing how to fight? Try again as if you mean it."

"I don't want to hurt you."

"You won't. But remember that to be a warrior, you must *want* to do harm. Think of me as the worst enemy you ever had. Someone you hate."

Alex stepped back and stared at Troth while imagining Bhudy's vicious cruelty. The *bastard.* She stepped forward and swung her right fist hard at her target's jaw.

She was preparing to follow up with her left fist when she found herself on the floor. Troth had caught her with a firm, inexorable grip, tilting Alex off balance and forcing her down to the tile. For a slender woman, she was remarkably strong.

"Better." Troth offered her hand to help her opponent rise. "But are you sure you want to do this?"

"Yes!" Alex bounced to her feet, excitement buzzing through her. "I appreciate that you were careful with me, but you needn't worry that I'll break. Can you show me how you did that?"

Troth gave a long, slow smile. "I think, Alexandra, that we will have a most unusual friendship."

"I do hope so. Now . . . where did you

place your hands?" Alex didn't care how many bruises she acquired. What mattered was to be strong.

Never to be a victim again.

# CHAPTER 22

"The Earl's Blend tea is selling like a bonfire. It is going to make us very rich." Wrexham accompanied his comment with a sheet summarizing the last six months of income and expenses. "Or rather, even richer than we are already."

Gavin whistled at the figures. "Inventing that blend was the best day's work you ever did for Elliott House, Maxwell." He caught himself and shook his head in irritation. "Sorry, I'll get that right eventually. I keep thinking of Wrexham as your father."

"Perhaps you should call me Kyle—that name hasn't changed."

"Thank you. It might be easier to remember." Knowing how formal Englishmen were about using first names, Gavin felt honored. Setting aside the financial statement, he asked, "Is Barton Pierce in London?"

"He is indeed, and making quite a splash in the City. He found a beautiful blond widow in his travels, managed to buy a knighthood, and now Sir Barton and Lady Pierce are gaining a reputation for lavish entertainments. He's going to stand for Parliament. They say he's bribing some lord to put him in a safe seat, so at the next election he should become a Member of Parliament."

"Pierce an MP? Talking about setting a wolf to guard the sheep!"

Kyle poured them both more port. "According to my sources, Pierce's fortunes have suffered badly since the East India Company lost its trading monopoly in China. He's not bankrupt, but he's on thin ice."

"Interesting." Gavin sipped at his port. "Then justice should be easy to administer."

"I won't ask you not to extract your pound of flesh—Pierce behaved despicably, and deserves to have his sins catch up with him." Kyle frowned. "But do be careful. He's a chancy devil."

"I won't do anything drastic. At most, I'll give his shaky kingdom a push to encourage it to collapse of its own accord." Not wanting to discuss the subject further, Gavin stood. "Shall we see what mischief our wives are creating?"

"I'm almost afraid to find out." Kyle finished his port and got to his feet. "It's amusing, and somehow right, that you managed to find Alexandra Melbourne halfway around the world. She was different from the other young ladies of the Marriage Mart. More alive. More interested in the world. And of course, a real stunner."

Gavin grinned. "I've noticed."

The butler sent them to the conservatory to find their wives. As they wound their way through the leafy jungle, they heard Troth say, "No, not like that, like this. Use your opponent's strength against him."

"Ah, I see what you mean," Alex replied breathlessly. "Like *this.*"

Gavin and Kyle emerged into an open area in time to see Alex throw her hostess to the ground. Troth rolled effortlessly and sprang back to her feet in a flurry of skirts. "Well *done,* Alex! You have good instincts."

Gavin stared. "Good God. I must have drunk more port than I realized."

"The port is blameless." Kyle seemed remarkably calm about discovering his wife and a guest in unarmed combat. "Troth, my love, are you damaging our guest?"

Laughing, both women turned to the newcomers, disheveled and looking like mischievous schoolgirls. "The fault is mine," Alex said. "Once I learned that Troth knows an Eastern fighting art, I asked for lessons. I hope she'll give me more."

"It will be my pleasure." Troth smoothed down her rumpled skirts.

"I like the idea of having a female student. I learned *wing chun* from my old nurse, and it is only right that I pass the skills on to another woman."

"I trust that in the future you'll have your lessons in the studio with the mats?" Kyle picked a crushed blossom from the tiled floor. "It's safer for you both, not to mention easier on the conservatory plants."

"We forgot ourselves." Troth grinned, unabashed. "I will plan a more organized path of study, and we will exercise suitable care. But this was *fun.*"

Even though he knew that *wing chun* was more of a sparring art, not designed for pure lethalness like *pentjak silat,* it made Gavin nervous to think of his wife studying a warrior skill. But Alex looked so alive and happy as she hastily straightened her gown and hair. This was the way she was meant to be. If it took the risk of broken bones and worse for her to find her way back to happiness, so be it.

The next morning, the females living in Ashburton House left en masse for the planned visit to a dressmaker's salon, to be followed by stops at sundry other shops. While the principal business of the day was to order new clothing for Alex and Katie, Gavin presumed that Catherine and the duchess and their daughters would not come home empty-handed.

As Gavin was about to leave to spend the day organizing his new office, Ashburton called him into his study. "Since you'll be looking for a house, you might want to consider this one." He jotted down an address, and handed it over with a key. "It's a place I own not far from here. A decent address, and quite a pleasant property. The previous tenants had to leave London before the end of the Season, so it's empty now. If you're interested, take a look."

"Thank you, sir." Gavin pocketed the address and the key. "I'll stop by this afternoon." Sight unseen, he guessed that the house was of a quality that would be hard to find without this kind of family connection. He wasn't sure whether he felt grateful or overwhelmed. Some of both, but more grateful, he decided. He'd be glad to have a roof of his own over his head, even if it was owned by Alex's uncle.

Leaving the house, he traveled from the fashionable West End to the hardworking East End. The offices Kyle had leased in a dockland warehouse were well situated above a huge storage area, and had a fine view over the forest of masts in the basin.

After approving the offices, he went aboard the *Helena*. Benjamin Long was capably managing the dual tasks of ship repair from the pirate attack and unloading the *Helena*'s cargo. Suryo had already packed Gavin's personal belongings for the move ashore. He planned to stay on the ship until it left, then move either to Ashburton House or whatever new house was found.

Since his presence was unneeded, Gavin summoned a cab to take him to Ashburton's rental house. The back of his neck prickled when he saw that it was on Berkeley Square—the same location as his grandfather's home. Coincidence, or a sign? Was today a good day to make the family visit he'd planned for twenty years?

He debated the question during the long ride across London in heavy traffic. Still undecided, he dismissed the driver when he reached Berkeley Square. He'd walk back to Ashburton House from here.

The duke's house was spacious and well kept, and would do nicely if Alex liked it. Looking out a window, his gaze was drawn to his grandfather's house on the opposite side. Probably, the old devil had daily looked over the square's central garden. When he saw the statue of a hero on a horse, had he ever thought of the naval son he'd disowned, the grandson he'd never met, the daughter-in-law he'd scorned? Or had he long since dismissed them from his mind as unworthy of his attention?

Decision made, Gavin locked the duke's house and crossed the square. Seabourne House was substantial, its bland façade reeking of money and influence. As he climbed the steps, he told himself he was a fool to call without warning. His grandfather might not be in London, or if he was, he was probably out terrorizing servants at some club. He might even be dead, though he'd been hale enough a year earlier, the last time Gavin had received information. Even if by some wildly unlikely chance he was at home, he was unlikely to receive an unannounced stranger.

Nonetheless, Gavin rapped the door sharply with the dolphin-shaped knocker. Less than a minute passed before the door was opened by the stiff butler who seemed to be standard in London houses. The man scanned him and decided Gavin looked gentlemanly enough to be invited inside. "Good day, sir. Do you wish to leave a card?"

Gavin glanced around the vestibule. It was smaller than Ashburton House, but impressive enough. Handing over the card, he said, "I'd like to see Lord Seabourne."

The butler looked at the name, back to

Gavin's face, then ushered him into a drawing room. "I will see if his lordship is receiving."

The wait seemed interminable. Gavin fidgeted around the room, unable to sit. Though he'd planned this for years, he didn't know what he expected, or even what he wanted, other than to brandish a symbolic banner to honor his father. He certainly wouldn't be clasped to the bosom of the Elliotts. Nor did he want to be.

"You're Gavin Elliott?"

Gavin turned at the cold voice, and was disappointed to see a man younger than himself who appeared to have swallowed a hot poker. "So I am," he said, his accent at its most American. "I gather Seabourne refuses to see me."

"On the contrary." The young man's manner had all the arrogance of his class, but his cold gaze was intent. "I am Phillip Elliott, the seventh Earl of Seabourne. My grandfather died last winter."

The disappointment was crushing. Gavin had come too late. "My regrets on your loss." He studied the other man, intrigued by an undeniable family resemblance. Height, coloring, even the general cast of features, were similar enough that the two of them could pass for brothers. "I suppose you're my cousin."

Seabourne scowled. "What kind of rig are you trying to run? If you're some bastard Elliott relation, I have no interest in making your acquaintance."

"I'm no more a bastard than you." Gavin clamped down on anger. "My parents were lawfully married in the Church of Scotland by my other grandfather, though the old devil who died last winter refused to recognize my mother or the marriage. Since I'm settling in London I thought I'd call, but I see I've wasted my time."

Seabourne turned white. "Who was your father?"

"James Elliott, who married Anna Fraser in Aberdeen." Gavin's voice turned dry. "Captain the Honorable James Elliott of the king's navy, hero of Trafalgar, scapegoat for disaster after his family disowned him, and a successful American merchant. Don't worry, I'm no more enthralled to be related to you than vice versa. I'd hoped to meet the sixth earl so I could tell him what a damned fool he was, but I left it for too long."

He was donning his hat when Seabourne asked, "Do you have proof of your identity?"

"Of course. Certificate of birth, my parents' marriage lines, the usual documents." Gavin wondered at the younger man's reaction. "Though I think my face might be proof enough. Why does it matter? I want nothing from you."

Sounding as if the words were bitter in his mouth, his cousin replied, "Because if you're who you claim to be—you are the rightful Earl of Seabourne."

# CHAPTER 23

Gavin's jaw dropped. "Me, the earl? That's absurd! My father was a younger son."

"James was the second son." Phillip looked like thunder. "My father, Albert, was the third. The eldest, John, his son, and my own father all died before my grandfather."

If that was true, it explained his cousin's anger—the man thought he was about to be displaced. But if that was so, why did he bother to mention the subject to Gavin, who'd been happily ignorant of the family tree?

Probably because the truth had a way of coming out, and the younger man recognized that sweeping a senior cousin under the carpet would be risky if Gavin intended to stay in London. Gavin felt a certain reluctant admiration for his cousin's willingness to take the bull by the horns. "No need to look as if you'd like to strike me dead. I've no interest in your precious title, nor the fortune I presume goes with it. But how could you not know of my existence? My father occasionally communicated with the Elliott family lawyer. I was born well before we emigrated to America. It should have been known immediately if I was the legitimate heir."

"It was reported that you drowned with your parents. Either the report was wrong, or you're an imposter."

With an heir at hand in England, there would have been little incentive to check on Gavin's reported death. "I'm no imposter, but as I said, you needn't worry. Pretend I never called today."

Philip glared at him. "And live with you hanging over my head like the Sword of Damocles? How could I sleep nights knowing that at any moment you might decide to claim Seabourne? This must be settled. Where are you staying?"

"Ashburton    House    on    Grosvenour Square."

"My solicitor will call on you," Philip Elliott snapped. "Now leave. You are not welcome in this house until and unless you prove yourself the rightful owner."

Still dazed, Gavin swiftly found himself outside in Berkeley Square. Whatever he'd expected from visiting his father's family—it sure to God hadn't been *this.*

Serious shopping with a crowd of one's female relations was delightful but exhausting. By the time Alex returned to Ashburton House, she was ready for a nap. Not Katie; apparently tireless, she scampered up to the schoolroom with the other two girls, whom Alex had decided to call "the cousins," even though Anne was Katie's half-aunt and Maria was—a step-cousin once removed? Alex fell asleep on top of the bed while trying to puzzle out the relationship.

She woke when the connecting door between her room and her husband's opened. Sleepily she rolled over. "Gavin?"

"Sorry, I didn't mean to wake you."

Hearing an odd note in his voice, she sat

up, trying to see his expression in the lengthening shadows. What she saw worried her—his posture had an explosive tension unlike anything she'd seen during the Lion Game, or even when the *Helena* was fighting off pirates. "Gavin, what's wrong?"

He stayed by the door in the shadows. "Today I visited my grandfather's house. He died last winter."

"I'm sorry you never had a chance to meet him, but based on his behavior, he doesn't sound like much of a loss," she said bluntly. "Did his death upset you more than you expected?"

"Some, but I'm more bothered by the fact . . ." he drew a deep breath. "I found a cousin who tells me that I'm the Earl of Seabourne."

She caught her breath. "You're one of those Elliotts? Good God, I had no idea! Congratulations, my lord husband. What an unexpected honor."

He stared at her. "You think this is *good*?"

His expression shocked her to wakefulness as she recognized how badly she'd misjudged. An Englishman would be delighted at such news, but Gavin was genuinely appalled. "I'm sorry, I've been raised to think that inherited titles and fortunes may not be the measure of a man, but they're quite nice."

His mouth twisted. "And I've been raised to think them the work of the devil. I want no part of that damned title. I'll renounce it or refuse it or whatever it takes."

She hesitated. "That may not be possible."

"Why not? Is the prospect of being a countess irresistible?"

He thought her that shallow? She bit back a desire to snap at him. His patience with her fears and moods had certainly earned him patience in return. "I've lived without a title quite happily, and I don't crave one now. But the legalities are complex, I think. We should talk to Uncle Stephen. He's knowledgeable about such things."

"Very well." Gavin turned back into his room. "I'll see if he's available."

Not wanting to be shut out, she asked, "Would you like me to come with you?"

He hesitated. "That might be a good idea. You can translate British to American thinking for me."

"I'll try, but no promises." She slipped on

her shoes and made a half-hearted attempt to smooth her hair before accompanying Gavin to the duke's study. If there was bad news, she wanted to be there.

Ashburton glanced up from his desk when the door opened. "Yes, my love?" His expression changed when he saw who it was. "Sorry, at this time of day Rosalind is the only one likely to come in."

"I didn't mean to disturb you." Having had time to realize how the duke might view American revulsion to the aristocracy, Gavin started to retreat. "I've something to discuss, but that can be done at another time."

"No, come in, I'm studying a proposed trade bill and it's deadly boring. Did you like the house?"

It took Gavin a moment to realize what the duke was talking about. "Your house on Berkeley Square? It's very handsome. If Alex likes it, I'd be pleased to rent it."

"I know the house," Alex said, "and if it's available it would be a wonderful city home for the time being."

"Then it's yours." Ashburton studied Gavin shrewdly. "But that's not why you're here, is it? Sit down and tell me what's on your mind."

Gavin sat, Alex taking the chair next to him. "I'm told that I'm the Earl of Seabourne." Tersely he described his family situation and his visit to Seabourne House, ending with, "I want no part of this inheritance. How do I refuse it?"

Ashburton frowned. "You can't. There's a fair amount of case law on this subject, and it has always been held that the dignity of a peerage is fixed in the blood. I believe you could have disavowed the title if you'd been born in America, but since you were born in Britain, you really have no choice."

Gavin muttered an oath. "What about the estate? Can I refuse that?"

"It would depend on how the estate has been settled. Any property entailed to the heir—and probably most of it is—goes with the title. There may also be unentailed funds, but they would be only a minor part of the estate."

"It seems unfair that my cousin have everything he thought was his wrenched away from him."

"Primogeniture isn't about fairness," the duke observed. "It's about preserving property and power, and on the whole it has served Britain well. The system is hard on individuals, though. If your cousin is left in dire circumstances, you can choose to make a settlement on him, but it would have to come from your personal fortune, not the entailed property. Before you do anything rash, you need to discuss your situation with an expert in this area of law."

Grasping at straws, Gavin asked, "What if I don't produce the documents that prove my identity? Can I avoid inheriting that way?"

The duke sighed. "The cat is out of the bag, Captain. You look like an Elliott—I noticed myself and assumed you were a Seabourne connection, though I didn't guess how close the relationship is. If you'd never called at Seabourne House, changed your family name, and never talked about your parents, you could have avoided this, but now events have been set in motion that can't be stopped. Your father is well remembered, and you are revealed as your father's son: the seventh Earl of Seabourne."

"So even after all these years, my father's name is blackened?"

Surprisingly, the duke said, "For those familiar with his situation, there's general agreement that your father was ill-used by both the old earl and the navy. I knew him a little, and respected him greatly. The scandal over his marriage centered not on his choice of bride, but his father's reaction. Disowning a son who was a naval hero over a perfectly respectable marriage was considered disgraceful. Your grandfather had never been well liked, and this made him even more unpopular."

Feeling as if the world had turned upside down, Gavin said, "So it wasn't society that spurned them, only the old earl?"

"I'm sure that was bad enough from your father's point of view—such rifts can tear families apart."

The Elliotts certainly had been. "What was the reaction when my father was forced to resign from the navy?"

"As other men who'd been part of the engagement returned home and began to speak up, it was recognized that your father behaved like the good officer he was." Ashburton grimaced. "There's no chance that the Admiralty would ever admit they were wrong, but for what it's worth, your father's name is still respected."

"Do you think he knew that?"

"If he kept in touch with the Elliott solicitor, he must have. My guess is that if he lived in America, it was because he preferred it to England."

Gavin fell silent as he reevaluated the past. James Elliott had carried some bitterness about his treatment in England, but he'd genuinely loved the freedom of his life in America. Perhaps his silence had been less from pain than because he simply didn't want to think about the past anymore.

Perhaps it had been Gavin, not his parents, who had felt the deepest pain at leaving Britain.

Alex took his hand. "You don't have to understand it all right now, Gavin. Come upstairs and relax for a while before dinner."

"I appreciate your taking the time to explain this, sir." Feeling numb, Gavin got to his feet. "My reaction must seem laughable to you."

"There's a certain irony in this," the duke acknowledged. "But it's not laughable. I don't blame you for feeling oppressed by the weight of an inheritance you didn't expect and don't want."

Glad for Ashburton's understanding, Gavin left the study, Alex's hand still locked in his. Alex? No, the Countess of Seabourne. God help them both.

Worried by Gavin's bleak expression, Alex turned into him and slid her arms around his neck after they entered her room. "I'm so sorry. You look as if the sky has fallen in."

"It has." He buried his face in her hair, his arms tight around her. Tension burned through him like molten steel.

She pressed closer, wishing she could absorb his distress. For the first time since they'd met, he needed her. Though she didn't like seeing him so miserable, she liked knowing she could comfort her golden, utterly competent husband. "You have reason to hate your grandfather, and it must be painful to think of bearing his title," she said softly. "But if you wish to honor your parents, isn't becoming a good earl the best possible revenge on your dreadful grandfather?"

"I suppose you're right—the old devil

would surely loathe knowing that his heir is the child of the son he banished from his presence. The trouble is that I loathe it, too." After a long silence, he said, "It might be easiest to just leave Britain and never come back. Would you come with me, Alex?"

She clamped down on her distress at the thought. "Of course I'd come with you—I'm your wife. But leaving wouldn't allow the earldom to pass to your cousin unless you faked your own death, and that would cause all kinds of other problems. Leaving and ignoring your obligations as Seabourne would create a monstrous tangle, and the tenants and dependents of the estate would be the ones to suffer for it."

He sighed. "I suppose you're right. But the thought of taking you and Katie down to the *Helena* and sailing away is very appealing."

"You are who you are, Gavin. Being a peer doesn't make you any different."

He shook his head. "Who we are, how we see ourselves, has much to do with how others treat us. Act like the captain and you become a captain. If you're treated with awe, pretty soon you'll feel as if you deserve it. Look at Sultan Kasan—he'd be a much better man if he hadn't been treated like royalty his whole life."

"That's hard to argue with, but he's an extreme case." She hesitated, wondering what might help him come to terms with his unwanted inheritance. "I think you need to separate how you feel about the nobility from how you feel about your grandfather. Wrexham is your friend, and you seem to like Uncle Stephen. Being peers hasn't ruined them, and it needn't ruin you. And your grandfather—well, he's dead. He would have been dreadful even if he wasn't a peer, though power and money probably made him worse. But he's gone now, and nothing you do can change the past."

"Actually, the past has changed greatly in the last few hours, or at least how I see the past." His arms tightened further. "The way I saw the world appears to have been rather wrong-headed."

As a man who was usually in firm control of his life and mind, of course he found that upsetting. With no words strong enough to help, she turned her head and kissed him, wanting to say that she cared, and to give assurance that this would pass.

He responded with yearning intensity. They'd shared so few kisses. Enough, though, that now there was some familiarity. A sense of rightness. Tonight, a powerful undercurrent of emotions bound them, and the kiss deepened to open-mouthed carnality. She sensed the desire he usually suppressed, and instead of being alarmed, her own desire was stirred more deeply than she'd known in years.

They were pressed so close that she felt him hardening. An instant after she recognized that, he started to break away, remembering the barrier her fears had built between them.

But this embrace was about him, not her. She leaned into him so that he retreated until he was backed up against the door. Trailing her mouth from his ear to his throat, she slid her hand down his body to clasp the pulsing ridge of male flesh, feeling heat through the tight fabric of his trousers. He gasped, tension of the mind transformed to that of the body.

She kneaded him with a rhythm echoed by her eager mouth, her own desire spiraling upward as hot sensuality engulfed them. Wanting greater intimacy, she fumbled with the buttons that secured his trousers, loosening the garment so that she could reach inside and touch the silky heat of his bare flesh. He groaned roughly, thrusting against the pressure of her hand.

She teased him with wanton deliberation, building, then slowing, then building again until he spasmed against her, his arms crushing around her ribs as he gasped her name. Sandwiched between her and the wall, he gradually slackened after the violent release, clinging to her as if she were his lifeline.

His passion echoed through her like waves across the sea, leaving her panting for breath. She felt powerful, and profoundly glad that she'd been able to give him such intense satisfaction.

He rubbed his cheek against her hair. "You have a remarkable gift for distracting me," he said huskily.

She laughed, reveling in their intimacy, in the absurdity of their tangled bodies being supported by the door. "I shall try to improve on it."

"Please do." His embrace loosened and he pulled out a crisply folded square of handkerchief which he tucked into her hand. As she dried them both, his large hands drifted gently over her back and waist and hips. "At the moment I can't even remember why I dislike lords."

Cupping her breasts, he stroked the tips with his thumbs. At first the gentle pressure soothed their itchy tenderness. Gradually the effect reversed. Her breasts increased in sensitivity and a hot fluid ache formed deep inside her, as if she were melting. She was glad when he slid a hand down the front of her gown to the nexus of heat between her thighs. There, yes, that pressure was exactly what she needed. . . .

He was raising her skirt. She stiffened involuntarily. Damnation, *no,* not when this was going so well! She wanted to weep as icy tendrils of panic began to suffocate desire.

Uncannily sensitive to her reaction, he released his grip on her skirt and eased his hand back to where it had been, separated from vulnerable flesh by layers of skirts and petticoats. Her fear subsided and once more she relaxed, able to enjoy the erotic rhythm of his touch. Her legs separated to allow him to rub harder and deeper. Oh, yes. . . .

To her shock, her hips convulsed in a harsh involuntary rhythm. She ground into his hand as shudders of fierce satisfaction racked her. Startled and embarrassed, she bit the shoulder of his coat, her teeth sinking into the smooth wool as she swallowed the cry that threatened to burst from her throat.

The strange attack passed, leaving her so limp that she might have fallen without his support. "I'm sorry," she whispered, amazed at her uncontrolled reaction.

"For what? Feeling pleasure?" His cherishing hands smoothed over her. "We are husband and wife. Aren't we permitted to find delight in each other's bodies?"

She breathed deeply, trying to steady her nerves. "Was my reaction . . . normal?"

"Quite—it's the female equivalent of what men experience."

"I . . . I didn't know that was possible." Her world spun and reoriented. Though she had been shocked at losing control of her body, the result had been diabolically satisfying. She wanted to feel that again, this time knowing what might happen. "I always enjoyed marital relations, but this was . . . different. More intense."

"Women are more complicated than men, and may enjoy intimacy on many levels. That intensity is normal when a couple is well suited." Gavin's voice was matter-of-fact, but she could hear an undertone of deep male satisfaction that he had been the one to introduce her to fierce urgency and intoxicating release.

Alex had always thought of herself as an average, healthy woman who enjoyed her marriage bed. Edmund's kisses and eagerness to exercise his marital rights had made her feel attractive and desirable, and she'd liked the physical sensations when they were intimate. Yet until now, she hadn't known there was a whole physical dimension missing. For the first time she understood the mysterious smiles women sometimes gave when speaking of their husbands, and why a woman might choose to abandon respectability for a lover.

If she'd been more passionate with Edmund, might that have prevented him from straying? Had he turned to a convict housemaid because the girl had suited him better physically than his wife had? Perhaps this was the reason she'd searched for. He was still wrong to have betrayed his marriage vows, but now she understood better.

An ache in her throat, she hid her face against Gavin's shoulder as she mourned the lost opportunities of her first marriage. Misinterpreting, Gavin said quietly, "There's hope for us, my dear. And I am so very, very glad."

So was she. What they had just done together brought her closer than ever to Gavin. She had thought her ability to be a willing bed partner had been destroyed forever. Now his understanding and gentle lovemaking were building a new pathway to intimacy, one quite different from her previous experience.

A new path opened the future to new possibilities—perhaps even the chance that she might once more become a willing wife.

# CHAPTER 24

When Gavin woke early the next morning, he had to think twice to decide if he'd dreamed the strange events of the day before. No, he really had been told he was heir to an earldom, and that passionate interlude with Alex had been too vivid for a dream. The mere thought was enough to rouse him again.

With a softly muttered curse he swung from his bed, wishing that he and Alex were sharing it, and on the kind of terms where he could roll over to waken her with kisses and more. That would come, if he was patient. Though patience became progressively more difficult as their intimacy increased. It was easier to turn desire off entirely than to live with the knowledge that it might be satisfied.

Since it was too early for breakfast, he shaved and dressed, wondering if becoming an earl meant he'd have to hire a damned valet. Surely not.

He sat and began listing what the new office would need to run efficiently. He worked until a tap at the door was followed by a quiet maid carrying a tray with pots of tea and fresh hot scones. Ready for a break, he said, "I'll take my wife's tea to her."

The girl gave him a knowing smile and handed over the tray. Balancing it in one hand, he opened the connecting door. Alex rolled over as he entered, her eyes sleepy and her long dark braid falling alluringly over one muslin-clad shoulder. He paused a moment, weighing the restraint he'd have to exercise against the quiet pleasures of private talk, and closed the door behind him. "Ready for your morning tea?"

"Please." She dropped her eyes as she sat up against the pillows. The night before at dinner, she'd hardly looked at him. The

Ashburtons and Kenyons probably thought there had been a fight.

He gave her a light, unthreatening kiss on the cheek, then set the tray down and poured them both tea. Taking his cup, he sat on the end of the bed and leaned against one of the massive posts. "I'll have to send over some premium tea for the household," he said after a sip. "This isn't bad, but I have better."

She tasted hers. "I'll take your word for it. This seems quite nice to me."

The advantage of her keeping her gaze down was that he could admire her at leisure. He wondered if he'd ever tire of studying her strong profile, or the feminine curves that were gradually filling in. Probably not. "Now that we have a house, how long will you need to prepare it so we can move in?"

"You're eager to be under your own roof?"

"I'm afraid so. I like your family very much, but I don't want to stay at Ashburton House indefinitely."

"I know what you mean. I adore my mother and my aunt, but living here returns me to childhood." She broke her scone in half. "The Berkeley Square house is spacious. Shall we use one of the rooms for Eastern martial arts?"

"Of course. Suryo and I need a place to practice, so that would be convenient."

She washed a bite of scone down with tea. "Troth and I discussed teaching women techniques of self-defense. Not *wing chun,* which takes a lifetime of study, but some of the moves and ways of thinking that Troth is showing me. Just knowing that it's possible to fight back makes a difference."

So Alex was channeling the anger of her mistreatment into helping others. He wondered what the men of London would think of Alex teaching their wives and daughters to fight back. "I think that's an excellent idea. Knowing how to fight makes one stronger and more confident, and sometimes that's all that is needed to win a battle." He poured more tea. "Are you ever going to look at me again, or will we spend decades with your eyes cast modestly downward?"

"Sorry. I still haven't quite recovered from what happened yesterday." Cheeks flushed, she lifted her gaze. "My view of the world changed, just as yours did earlier in the day."

It confirmed his guess that while she'd enjoyed physical intimacy in her first marriage, there had been little passion. Her husband must have been a prig or a fool. "Passion does change the world. With the right partner, it's a great and precious gift."

She began crumbling her scone. "I can see that it would be."

He wondered how long it would be before she could see him as an object of passion. Despite her response to him, her fears were still a barrier. "I have a theory. Perhaps you can tell me if I'm right. I think that what frightens you most about intercourse is being trapped. Pinned down and held helpless by a male body."

Her gaze shot up and her color drained away. After a long silence, she said, "I think you're right. The mere thought terrifies me. There are other fears, but that is the worst."

"There are many positions for making love."

She opened her mouth, then closed it again, looking embarrassed but intrigued. "You're giving me ideas, Captain."

"I was hoping for that." He gave her a teasing smile. "I'm game for any experiments you wish to try."

Her gaze dropped to her mangled scone—but this time, her lips curved in a thoughtful smile.

Pleased that the new office was coming together so quickly, Gavin returned to Ashburton House in the late afternoon. As the butler admitted him, he found himself facing an attractive older woman who had just left a calling card.

Turning, she caught her breath, arrested. "You must be the new Earl of Seabourne?"

"I beg your pardon?" he said, unnerved.

"Sorry, I go too quickly." She offered her hand. "I'm Lady Jane Elliott Holland. Your aunt. Do you have a few minutes to spare for me?"

His aunt? Recognizing that she had the fair coloring and bone structure that seemed to be the Elliott look, he said, "Of course. Riggs, is there a drawing room where Lady Jane and I can talk?"

The butler ushered them into one of the smaller reception rooms and left with a promise to send refreshments. As they seated themselves, Gavin said, "Forgive me if I seem rude. I'm not yet accustomed to the idea of titles and relatives." He studied her strong face and silver-streaked hair. "Why do you assume that I am who I say I am?"

Studying him with equal interest, she said, "James was my favorite brother. I met you once, though you were too young to remember. I paid a secret call to your mother in Aberdeen, not letting my father know. Did James ever speak of me?"

A phrase suddenly formed in Gavin's memory. *Jane is the only decent one of the lot.* He blinked as other long-forgotten comments surfaced. "You were the only member of the Elliott family that my father liked, I think."

"I missed him after he left for America," she said wistfully. "We corresponded until he and your mother died. James was so proud of you. He wrote that you took to the sea like a dolphin—a true Elliott. The sea is in our blood, you know. The title Seabourne was granted to an ancestor who was an Elizabethan privateer."

"I never knew that," Gavin said, surprised that the family seafaring tradition was so old.

"He missed having you with him when you became a seaman in your own right, but he felt it best for you to gain experience under other captains. Knowing that, I suspected that you hadn't drowned with your parents. But I had no proof, and no one wanted to hear my doubts, least of all Philip."

"I could still be an imposter."

Lady Jane smiled and leaned forward to trace a faded, almost invisible scar on his forehead that stretched an inch or so below the hairline. "I was present when you acquired this. You were running after the vicarage cat and fell down on broken stones. This gash bled fearfully, but your mother took it very calmly. So did you, for that matter. You were always running headlong."

Another memory clicked into place, this time of him pressing a hand to his head while blood dripped through his small fingers. His mother saying, "You'll have a scar from this, laddie." And another woman who gave him sweets to make him smile after his head was bandaged. Feeling surprising warmth, he stood and hugged his aunt. "You were the one who gave me candied violets! The most amazing thing I'd ever eaten."

"You do remember!" She hugged back

with delight. "I can't wait for you to meet my children. A pity none are in London at the moment. My second son, James, is named for your father, and is a lieutenant in the navy."

"My family is growing by leaps and bounds," Gavin said rather dryly as he sat down. "And I haven't even started looking for Frasers from my mother's family."

"Since you married into the Kenyons and the Penroses, you're connected with half the British nobility."

Gavin blinked. "Penroses?"

"Lady Michael's family. They're very ancient—the Lairds of Skoal, a feudal island off Cornwall." She laughed. "You didn't know that either, I can see."

He'd never get this all straight. "I'm beginning to understand why people have social secretaries."

"If I can help you navigate the shoals of London society, let me know." Lady Jane hesitated. "May I offer some advice?"

"Please do," he said with even greater dryness. "Everyone else does."

Ignoring that, she said, "Apply for a writ of summons to take your seat in the House

of Lords right away. The sooner this is settled, the better for everyone."

"I've been told this is an honor I can't de-
cline," he said, wishing she'd tell him otherwise.

"You've been told correctly. You're Seabourne now."

"What if Philip fights my claim? He's the
one who has the most to lose."

"Yes, but he's not stupid. Once the evidence is in front of him, he'll accept it."

Since his cousin had brought the subject
up in the first place, Lady Jane might be
right. "Philip might accept the evidence, but
he'd be happy to have my head on a plat-
ter."

"He'll get over it. Luckily, it's been only six
months since he inherited, so he should ad-
just to being a commoner again without too
much trouble. Eventually he'll be glad, I
think. Like your father, he's very impatient
with protocol and the day-to-day business
of running a great estate."

So was Gavin, but it didn't look as if he
had much choice. Gavin Elliott, seventh Earl
of Seabourne. He still hated the idea—but
he was getting used to it.

The door opened, and the duchess

floated in. "Hello, Jane. Sorry to interrupt, but Riggs told me you were closeted in here with Gavin."

The women exchanged kisses. "I'm his aunt, Rosalind," Lady Jane said as she took her seat again. "Naturally I had to see how much he resembles my brother, and I've been encouraging him to make his claim to the title quickly."

The duchess looked thoughtful. " ' *'Twere well it were done quickly.'* If Gavin's cousin accepts the situation gracefully, the ball I'm giving for him and Alexandra can be an announcement of his new status."

"Excellent! If he's introduced here, there will be no question of his position."

Gavin felt as if he were adrift in a typhoon without sails or rudder as the women began an animated discussion of who should be invited and how the invitations should be worded. "I'm not needed here any longer, am I?"

"Not at all," the duchess said cheerfully. "Though you are allowed to invite other guests, of course. As I said before, make a list."

A wicked thought struck him. "Please invite Sir Barton and Lady Pierce." When the duchess lifted her brows with a faint suggestion of disapproval, he added, "I knew him in China. We weren't particularly friends, but it would be discourteous not to invite him." Pierce would loathe discovering that Gavin was an earl. It was the only pleasant thought he'd had in connection with this blasted inheritance.

In the office of the longtime Elliott lawyer, Albert Finn, Philip Elliott examined Gavin's birth certificate, parents' marriage lines, and the other documents offered as proof of identity. Included was an affidavit from Lady Jane Holland stating that she recognized her nephew's scar and was satisfied that he was who he claimed to be. Ashburton, Lord Michael, and the Ashburton lawyer were also present. All would be done properly.

Face set, Philip placed the documents neatly on the desk. "I accept your claim, my lord. I shall vacate the premises of Elliott House immediately."

*My lord.* It was the first time anyone had addressed Gavin that way, and the words weighed him down like manacles. "There is no need to rush. My wife and I have leased another house for the time being." He glanced at Albert Finn. "Lady Jane said that Hurley Manor is unentailed." After Finn agreed, Gavin continued, "I intend to settle the property on you."

As the duke and Lord Michael nodded with approval, Philip said, startled, "You're giving me Hurley? That's very generous of you."

Since the estate had an income of three thousand pounds a year, it was very generous indeed. Gavin stood and offered his hand. "I don't expect you're very fond of me, but we are family. Let us at least not be enemies."

"I can't blame you for being alive." Reluctantly Philip took the proffered hand. "But I wish you'd stayed far, far away."

Invitations to the Ashburtons' ball asked people to come and meet the new Lord and Lady Seabourne.

# CHAPTER 25

Alex glided backward, trying to remember exactly how to make the movement called "cloud arms." Hearing a small sound, she turned to see that her mother had entered the Ashburton ballroom and was waiting quietly by the door.

"Sorry to disturb you, but we're going to have to start decorating in here soon," Catherine said. "Are you performing an Eastern dance?"

"Not exactly." Alex gestured her mother to a chair and sprawled on a small, hard sofa that was set at right angles to it. One of the pleasures of wearing Eastern tunic and trousers was that a female could sprawl.

"Tai chi is a Chinese technique for relaxation. Troth—Lady Wrexham—has been teaching me. With Aunt Rosalind's ball tomorrow night, I thought it would be good to encourage calmness."

"The East captured your imagination while you were there?"

It was not a casual question. Alex reflected before answering. "My months in the Islands contained much that I would like to forget, yet there was power and beauty there. Troth is helping me to understand what is unique and special in the East."

"She's a remarkable young woman. I'm glad you've become friends." Catherine hesitated. "Alexandra, are you and Gavin having problems?"

The words sent a jolt through Alex. "Don't you like Gavin?"

"I like him very much, but you didn't answer my question. Is your marriage troubled?"

Alex fidgeted with the arm of the sofa, where the brocade was starting to fray. "What makes you think there's a problem?"

"Your inability to give me a straight answer, among other reasons." Catherine's voice softened. "I know you had a . . . a difficult time in the Indies. That sort of thing has to have repercussions later."

Her mother knew. Feeling betrayed, Alex said, "Gavin told you what happened?"

"No, but when I cornered him, he admitted that you'd suffered more than any woman wants for another woman. Especially not for her daughter." A tremor sounded in Catherine's voice and was swiftly controlled. "You've been a grown woman on the other side of the world for years, but this might be an occasion where maternal advice could be useful. It worries me that there seems to be so much distance between you and Gavin."

Alex flushed as she remembered the one time when there hadn't been any distance. Part of her craved another such encounter, but the intensity and lack of control had been frightening. Worse was knowing how much Gavin wanted more of that intimacy. Though he said nothing, she felt the pressure of his desire, and feared what might happen if passion was unleashed again. "There has been . . . awkwardness, but he's been very patient."

"That's a cool way of describing one's husband. Why did you marry him?"

Startled by the bluntness of the question, Alex answered with equal bluntness. "Because I was weak and desperate, and he was kind enough to offer the protection of his name. Not the best of reasons for marrying, perhaps, but we can't all be as lucky as you and the colonel."

Catherine's mouth twisted. "You think it was luck? A good marriage is earned through hard work, Alexandra, and that is even more true of physical intimacy. Though I didn't suffer what you did, I had ample reason to be grateful for Michael's patience and kindness. Trust your husband, my dear, even if doing so feels like stepping into the abyss. Trust is the bedrock of a good marriage—more than passion, even more than love."

"Did you trust my father that way?" Alex asked defensively.

Catherine hesitated as she sought for words that would not slander her first husband. "Though Colin had great courage and knew his duty, he was not well suited to marriage. Gavin is nothing like Colin. He is like Michael—the sort of man who will go to hell and back for the woman he loves, but you have to do your part, and that means taking risks. Risk your pride, risk your heart, risk your dreams. It's the best way for luck to find you."

Alex drew her knees up and wrapped her arms around them, feeling like the child she'd been when her mother had met the colonel amidst the tumult of pre-Waterloo Brussels. He'd been a major then, her father had been alive, and Alex had answered to the name Amy. How much had gone on behind the scenes that young Amy hadn't recognized? More than she wanted to know now—but enough that her mother could speak with authority on the challenges of marriage. "I'll try to do better. Gavin deserves more than I've given so far."

"You deserve more, too, my darling." Catherine rose and hugged her. "Whatever happened to you in slavery was horrible luck, or perhaps a great test of the spirit. It was not punishment for your sins. You were the most intrepid child I've ever known, and you'll have the courage to do what needs to be done, no matter how frightening it seems."

How nice that her mother had faith in her. If only Alex had equal faith in herself.

\* \* \*

Ashburton House hummed with anticipation of the ball that was about to begin. Early onlookers gathered in the square to watch the glittering guests who would soon be arriving, and the discordant sounds of tuning instruments floated up from the ballroom.

Resigned to his fate, Gavin stared morbidly at the well-tailored image in his mirror. "I look like a dashed penguin. Are you familiar with penguins, Hubble? They are birds that live in the far southern seas, and they look as if they're wearing a rather silly style of formal dress."

"I am familiar with the creatures, my lord." The duke's valet, who had been assigned to help the guest of honor, was imperturbable. "They look quite handsome in their avian way, just as you look very well in a gentleman's attire."

"My thanks for your efforts. I will try not to disgrace you."

Hubble inclined his head, then withdrew to see if Ashburton required further assistance. Wanting to see Alex, Gavin picked up a jewelry box and knocked on his wife's door to warn her of his entry.

She was staring into her own mirror. "Is it

too late for us to run away to America to avoid this ball?"

"I'm afraid so."

She turned from the mirror, and his breath went out of him as if he'd been struck by a swinging spar. Her fashionable blue silk gown opened over a white brocade under-skirt, with a close-fitting bodice that emphasized the magnificence of her figure, and décolletage that would make any man dizzy. Her dark hair was artfully swept up and decorated with delicate flowers from the Ashburton glasshouse. It was difficult to see her and remember the thin, desperate woman he'd met in Maduri.

Her gaze was equally approving. "You look very fine, Gavin. Every inch an earl, no matter how much you dislike the thought."

"And you look stunning."

She glanced away. "Stunning? Odd. I thought the 'S' associated with me stood for 'Slave' or 'Slut' or 'Scandal' or 'Shame', or some other mark of my ruinous past."

He should have realized how much her history would weigh on her tonight. At this ball she would face the society in which she'd been raised, knowing that what she had suffered would make people regard her with pity, distaste, or scorn if they knew.

"The 'S' stands for 'Seabourne'. No one need know any more than that." He gave into temptation and kissed her, keeping it light because this was not the time for anything more. Her lips were cool and her hands icy. "If anyone does learn what happened to you—be damned to them. You've done nothing to be ashamed of."

She gave him a shaky smile. "And woe betide anyone who rouses your protective instincts by being rude to me. Thank you, Gavin. It means a great deal that you know everything and can still look me in the eye."

He could spend the rest of the night looking into those splendidly honest, vulnerable aqua eyes. "Gratitude is mutual. We know so much about each other that marriage was the only solution."

She laughed at that. "Then the fates have been kind. I'm going up to the schoolroom to show my gown to the girls. Would you like to come along?"

"Yes, but first I want to give you these." He offered the jewelry box. "I bought the stones in Ceylon the day before we were married, and had them set here. A belated wedding present."

Alex gasped as she opened the box and saw the glittering sapphire necklace, earrings, and bracelet. "These are beautiful! I . . . I don't know what to say."

"If you dare say a word about being unworthy, I'll be strongly tempted to spank you." He lifted the necklace from the box. "Would you like to wear this tonight?"

"You know me too well." She smiled wryly as she unhooked the pearl collar that had been lent by her mother. "Please. They go beautifully with this gown."

"I chose them to go with your eyes, though no sapphire has quite that hint of green." He moved behind her to fasten the necklace, then rested his hands on the bare skin of her shoulders. "The rosebuds in your hair are exquisite, and so are you." He pressed his lips to her throat above the sparkling gemstones.

She shivered, and it was not from repulsion. "You have the gift of making a woman feel beautiful, Gavin."

"I only speak truth." He took her arm. "Now let's dazzle the girls before the hard part of the evening begins."

They climbed to the floor above, where the cousins were feasting on a selection of the same delicacies that would be served at the supper later. The girls abandoned their lobster patties and cheese tarts to admire their visitors. "You look like a fairy princess, Mama!" Katie exclaimed.

Alex laughed. "I'm glad you think so, but in ten years you'll out-shine me."

"Never!"

Anne Kenyon, Alex's young half-sister, said, "Since you're blond, you'll be even more fairy-like, Katie. Rather like Aunt Rosalind."

"But Mama was an actress, which is far more interesting than being a fairy princess," Lady Maria said firmly.

The girls began a spirited discussion on the relative merits of fairies, princesses, and actresses, so Alex kissed her daughter and they went down to the ball. Just before they stepped out into public, Alex stopped, rigid, as if again contemplating flight.

Gavin murmured, "Into the breach, my dear."

"Soldiers who are first to cross a breached wall invariably die."

He wished she hadn't taken him so literally. "I think you fear how you've changed more than you fear the other guests. Tonight will not be as bad as you think."

She moistened her lips with her tongue. "The colonel once told me that the events one most wants to avoid are never so bad as expected."

"Can he and I both be wrong?" he asked.

"Let's hope not." Head high, she entered the arena.

Luckily a reception line offered little opportunity to exchange more than bland pleasantries. People eyed Gavin with curiosity, occasionally making sympathetic comments about the loss of his grandfather. Some were interested in his politics, and one old viscount asked outright whether he was Tory or Whig. Gavin dodged the question, since an honest answer about his beliefs would send the fellow into an apoplexy.

Philip Elliott arrived early. Gavin said, "I'm glad you came tonight."

The younger man arched his brows. "One mustn't let the jackals see the blood."

The delicate irony suggested that Philip was past shock and into recovery. He'd survive. But it was a pity he hadn't been packed off into the navy or another useful profession when he was younger. He'd be a better man for some honest labor—which Gavin recognized as a very American thought. In Britain, being a gentleman was considered full-time employment.

Beside him, Alex had to deal with greetings from people who knew her family well, and many who had known her when she was a girl. She had buried all traces of her earlier anxieties and was the epitome of charm and graciousness. Her mother's daughter, and far more of a countess than he was an earl.

Gavin's most pleasant surprise was a rangy man of middle years with a satiric gleam in the eyes. "I'm Markland," he said with a faint American accent. "Welcome to the House of Lords—we need more radical colonials sitting there."

Gavin shook the man's hand. "How do you know that I'm a radical colonial?"

Markland chuckled. "My wife is twin sister to the wife of one of your father-in-law's cronies. At the highest levels, London is as small a town as Boston. You may have heard of me there under my real name, Jason Travers."

"Of course!" Gavin exclaimed. "You and I are in the same business. You're something of a legend in Boston shipping circles—the Yankee Earl."

"You may have that nickname with my blessing. I run my company from Liverpool and send my sons to Harvard College so they'll be corrupted by radical American ideas." Markland turned serious. "The reform movement is making progress here: Catholic Emancipation, ending the worst voting abuses, laws to keep children from being worked to death in factories. You'll be with us on such issues, I think?"

"Of course. Who could not be?"

"You'd be surprised how many men can't see past their own selfish noses. But step by step, democracy and compassion are making headway even here."

Gavin smiled. "You're actually making me look forward to the House of Lords. Perhaps I can contribute something useful there."

"You can. You will. And if you ever feel the need to talk with another American who's had his conflicts with the British establishment, feel free to call on me. You can curse about your dealings with the East India

Company, and I'll tell you about my time on the prison hulks in the Thames." Moving on to Alex, Markland said, "And why haven't you visited Kira and me yet, you wicked child?"

"Uncle Jason!" Alex went into the man's arms for an enthusiastic hug. "How wonderful to see you. Where is Aunt Kira?"

"A bit under the weather so she stayed home, but she gave me strict orders to invite you to a ladies' tea next week."

Gavin smiled wryly at still more proof that Alex was connected to most of the nobility of Britain by blood or long family friendships. At least two former suitors came by and greeted her warmly before introducing their wives. It was all very friendly—anticipation had been worse than reality.

The receiving line was nearing its end when Gavin turned to the next guest, and found himself face to face with Sir Barton Pierce. Tall and broad, Pierce had flourished in London, putting on weight along with self-importance. Holding out his hand, he said unctuously, "A pleasure to meet you, Lord Seabourne. I've been wanting to speak with you. . . ." Then he froze as he recognized who he was greeting.

Gavin shook the other man's hand with exaggerated politeness. "Glad you made it tonight, Pierce. Or do you prefer to be called Sir Barton?"

"How the devil did you get to be the Earl of Seabourne?" Pierce sputtered, shock and anger in his pale eyes.

"The usual way—the previous earl, my grandfather, died." Gavin was enjoying himself. "There was some doubt about my existence, but that's all sorted out now."

Recovering, Pierce said, "Now that you're a lord, you shouldn't be soiling your hands with trade. I'd be happy to buy Elliott House for a fair price."

Gavin laughed. "It's not for sale. There's another Yankee earl who has kept his shipping business, and I see no reason why I can't do the same." He turned to the woman at the other man's side. "Would this be Lady Pierce? I heard that you found yourself a beautiful wife in your travels, but rumor did her less than justice."

In this, he was honest. Lady Pierce was a petite, exquisitely lovely blond with a face and figure of classical perfection. She extended her hand with a practiced smile. "You are too kind. I gather that you are the reason we were invited to Ashburton House? I've always wished to meet the duke and duchess."

So she could fawn on them, no doubt. Under the lady's angelic exterior, Gavin sensed the avidness of large appetites. She and Barton Pierce shared ambition and greed, and had made one of the most ancient of marriage bargains—beauty for wealth.

As Gavin bowed over her hand, Alex said coolly, "Frederica, what a surprise."

Lady Pierce stiffened, as shocked as her husband had been when he identified Gavin. "Alexandra! A surprise indeed."

The two women exchanged patently false smiles. Gavin remembered Alex mentioning a wasp-tongued beauty named Frederica, and this had to be the woman.

"We are old acquaintances from Sydney, but haven't seen each other since Barton swept me off my feet and brought me back to England." Frederica Pierce's gaze slanted to Gavin. "How well you've done for yourself, my dear." Her voice managed to imply that it was a miracle that any man had wanted to marry Alex.

"Frederica was the most acclaimed

beauty in New South Wales," Alex explained to Gavin. "There was mass mourning when she married and left Sydney. I'd forgotten the name of your new husband. Much has happened since then."

Frederica Pierce's expression changed. "So I had heard. One of Barton's captains is recently arrived in London with the most remarkable tale. Were you really enslaved in the Indies and sold into the harem of a Borneo sultan for your weight in gold, my dear?"

Alex turned white. Gavin covered her shocked silence with a laugh. "Traveler's tales are always so much more dramatic than the truth. Perhaps you should let that story stand since it's so splendidly romantic." He placed a possessive hand at the small of Alex's back. "We've enjoyed meeting old friends again, but since our duties are done here, I'd like to claim a waltz with my wife. A pleasure to meet you, Lady Pierce." He bowed before leading Alex away.

The music had already begun, so Gavin swung Alex into waltz position as soon as they reached the dance floor. "I thought it best to get you away before murder was done."

Alex drew a shaky breath. "Of all the people in London to find out what happened to me! Frederica is a terrible woman. Though it's true that men mourned when she married and left the colony, the women heaved vast sighs of relief. She's the coldest, most selfish person I've ever known, and will cheerfully ruin me for spite."

"Her husband has connections to the East, but they're not very accurate. She doesn't know what really happened, and she won't."

"What if someone from the crew of the *Helena* got drunk in a dockside tavern and told the whole story?" Alex's face was starkly pale against her dark hair.

"Even if that happened, no one except Suryo and I know everything, and we aren't talking." His voice softened. "If the truth came out, would it matter? Frederica Pierce has no power to injure you. You have powerful, loyal friends and family—she is a spiteful nobody by comparison."

"And since I can't do anything about her, I might as well not worry." Alex forced herself to relax. "Since women always hate her, I suppose they won't take her tales seriously. Men tend to swallow everything she says, though."

"Not all men—believe me, any male with good sense will keep his distance. She has the lethal charm of a black widow spider." He grinned. "One must be glad that such perfect partners have found each other."

Alex's expression eased into a smile. "You have no need to administer further justice to Pierce. Frederica is punishment enough."

Not true, but at least Gavin wouldn't worry about harming innocent members of Pierce's family. There was nothing innocent about the lovely Frederica.

# CHAPTER 26

By the time they finished their waltz, Alex was in command of herself again, so they went their separate ways to mingle with other guests. Gavin was enjoying a country dance with his mother-in-law when he noticed that Pierce was talking with Philip, and there was a tension to the exchange that set off warning bells.

When the dance ended, he escorted Catherine back to Lord Michael. Even after almost twenty years, they still kept every second set for each other, which Gavin found endearingly romantic. Would he and Alex be like that in twenty years, or would they fail to create a deeper bond and slide into lonely isolation?

Not wanting to pursue that line of thinking, he concentrated on working his way across the crowded ballroom. By the time he reached his cousin, Pierce had moved on and Philip was staring at the dancers with a frown on his face. "I see you and Barton Pierce are acquainted," Gavin said casually. "He was startled to see me here, since we knew each other in the East."

"You have my sympathies," Philip said tartly. "If ever I've met an encroaching mushroom, it's him. Now that I'm not an earl, he's become damned rude. He probably oozed good nature to you."

"Hardly. We were never friends." An understatement. "Do you have business dealings with him? If so, I hope you held closely to your purse."

"Not closely enough." Philip hesitated. "I suppose I should mention this since in a way, you're affected. I promised to recommend him for the Seabourne seat in Parliament, and the district is old-fashioned enough that the earl's endorsement is a guarantee of election. He's most unhappy that I can no longer deliver what I promised."

And Pierce knew damned well that the

new earl would not follow through on such an agreement. Reading between the lines, Gavin said, "Did he express his gratitude in advance with gifts or loans, and now he demands repayment?"

"And if he did?" Philip was angry and defensive. "He's well qualified to be a Member of Parliament. I saw nothing wrong in endorsing him."

Gavin clamped down on his temper. "He presents himself well, but he's unscrupulous. Not a man I would choose to help run the country. If you owe him money, I'll lend you enough to repay him on better terms than whatever he offered you."

Philip's anger flared. "By what right do you tell me how to manage my affairs? You may be the head of the Elliott family, but you have no authority over me."

Realizing he was handling this badly, Gavin said, "I beg your pardon. Of course I have no authority over you. What I meant to convey is that Pierce can be difficult. If you need any assistance . . ."

"Very kind of you, cousin, but I have no need of your help, now or ever. By your leave." Philip stalked off like an angry cat.

Uneasily Gavin watched him go, and

hoped he hadn't just created an alliance between two men who hated him.

Cooling herself with a Chinese ivory fan,
Troth remarked, "You look much happier
now than when the ball began."

Alex smiled. "I was afraid I'd changed beyond redemption, and everyone would
know it in a glance. But while I'm a very different person from the girl who left London,
everyone has been so kind that it's hard to
remember why I was anxious."

"Perhaps you worry too much what people think. I found freedom when I followed
my husband's advice and stopped caring
about the opinions of others. Since I will
never be properly English, I can either
cower and hope not to offend, or scorn ill-
wishers as narrow-minded peasants." Troth
laughed. "So I do the latter, and find that
Kyle was right. I'm now considered a great
beauty and a great hostess, and all because I don't care. It's the most delicious of
ironies."

"I've always thought of myself as independent and a bit of a rebel, but perhaps
you're right," Alex said slowly. "I do worry
about what others think."

She'd been most free when she was an intrepid little girl in Spain, but growing to young ladyhood in more conventional circumstances had made her more cautious. She hadn't wanted to disgrace her mother or the colonel.

When she first emerged from the schoolroom, there had been embarrassing moments when she was too impetuous or too outspoken. Even though her parents were tolerant of her shortcomings, over time she clipped her own wings. She learned how far she could go to be considered spirited rather than wild. Usually she got the balance right, but not always.

One reason she'd chosen Edmund and Australia was to be free of the constant worry of setting a foot wrong. Instead she found a straight-laced society where she was constantly aware that she must not disgrace her husband. Even after she learned about his mistress, she'd done her best to be a worthy wife.

Yet despite all her attempts to be above reproach, on the voyage home she'd been ruined in social terms, through no fault of her own. It was time to stop wasting worry on matters outside her control. "You've given me some interesting thoughts to chew on. I shall try to care less about the opinion of the world."

"As a student of tai chi and *wing chun,* you are already well on your way to independent eccentricity," Troth said with a smile. "And the stronger one feels, the easier it is to ignore what others say."

Refusing to worry about the world's opinion should eliminate some of her fears, and eliminating fears lowered the barriers between her and her husband. She scanned the ballroom, finding him easily because of his height. He was talking with two older women who watched him, enraptured. He was so handsome that he took her breath away—and he was hers. She felt a surge of pure lust, followed by shock that she could react so strongly. Desire was definitely becoming separated from fear. . . .

"Alexandra?"

She turned to see another former suitor from her season in London, and a splendid sight he was in scarlet regimentals. "Mark! I see you're a major now. Well done! Do you know my friend, Lady Wrexham? Troth, Major Colwell is an old friend of mine."

Troth and Mark exchanged greetings, but

all his attention was for Alex. "Will you dance with me, Alexandra? I've waited a dozen years for another waltz."

"Of course." With a smile, she gave him her hand and they stepped onto the floor. Mark had matured well. Only a year older than she, he'd been a lanky, adoring ensign in that long-ago social season. Now he'd filled out and had the commanding presence of a seasoned officer. She'd been a little tempted when he offered marriage—it was flattering to be adored—but he'd been a mere boy compared to Edmund, and besides, his regiment was based in England. "It's so lovely to see you again. What have you been doing for all these years besides climbing the ranks? Have you married? Become a hero?"

"Neither of those. Your life has been far more adventurous. I was sorry to hear of your husband's death—and even sorrier to learn that you had remarried. I wish you'd waited until you returned to England so I would have had a chance." His voice roughened. "What wretched luck to lose you twice!"

Uncomfortable with his intensity, she said, "You can't lose what you never had.

It's been many years, and we've both changed."

"The years have only made you more beautiful. You have always been my ideal of feminine grace and charm. You still are." His voice became almost inaudible. "And I still love you."

He'd obviously spent years constructing a pedestal for a female who existed only in his romantic mind. "I'm honored by your regard, but I think you'll soon find that I don't match that ideal, Mark. I never did."

He smiled at her fondly. "And modest as well as beautiful."

Had he always been this moony? Yes, she decided, he had, but it had seemed more natural on a nineteen-year-old. "Have you met my husband yet? If not, let me introduce you."

His expression changed. "If you'd sent for me, I would have come to Sydney to escort you and your daughter home. I would have protected you from the horror of what happened in the Indies."

She felt a chill—Frederica Pierce was spreading her lies swiftly if Mark had already heard that calamity had befallen her in the East. Reminding herself that she didn't care, she said lightly, "Don't believe whatever odd stories you've heard. They're quite untrue."

"Weren't you forced to marry a merchant to save your name? If only you'd waited, Alexandra! I would have gladly given you my name, no matter how badly you've been defiled."

Caught between shock and irritation, she said coolly, "I wasn't 'forced' to marry a merchant—I had the incredible good fortune to find the best and bravest husband any woman could want. As to 'defilement' "—she made herself laugh—"you really shouldn't listen to rumors."

"I'm sorry," he said quickly. "Of course you are too honorable not to be loyal to your husband. But if only things could have been different!"

" 'If only' are the most useless words in the English language, Major Colwell." The music ended, so she summoned a smile. "It's good that you could come. I hope you're having a pleasant time. Now, if you'll excuse me . . ."

He held on to her hand. "Forgive me, Alexandra! I've offended you, and that's the last thing on earth I want."

Wondering if she would need a tugging match to escape, she was relieved when Gavin materialized beside her. "I believe the supper dance is ours, my dear?" He turned his gaze to the major. "I don't believe we've met, Major. I'm Seabourne. Are you another of my wife's old friends?"

For an instant Alex wondered if Mark would do something melodramatic, but he was too well bred for that. Accepting Gavin's hand, he said, "I'm Mark Colwell. As you surmised, Alexandra and I were . . . well acquainted before she went East." He looked as if he wanted to be disdainful, but it was hard not to be impressed by Gavin's calm presence. "London is the richer for her return."

"Indeed." Gavin took Alex's arm with a light, possessive gesture. "My dear, the most amazing rumors are circulating the ballroom. My favorite is that you were declared goddess of a primitive tribe in New Guinea."

She managed a laugh. "Is that what you heard, Mark? If only it were true! I've always longed to be a queen, but a goddess is even better." Far better than being a slave.

Mark flushed a little. "I'm sure you would

make a splendid queen. Good to meet you, Seabourne." He raised Alex's free hand and kissed it. "I trust we'll be seeing each other again soon, Alexandra."

After the major moved out of earshot, she said, "Thank you for rescuing me, Gavin. Mark has spent a dozen years turning me into a romantic ideal. Very tedious."

"Actually, I came over to rescue him." He steered her toward the supper room. "You looked ready to practice your *wing chun* on him."

"I wasn't there yet, but five more minutes and I might have been," she admitted. But she was still tense as they sat down to supper. It was one thing to say she didn't care what people thought of her, and quite another to make it reality.

"That went very well, I think." The Duchess of Ashburton gave a happy sigh as the last guests were packed off, rather earlier than at most balls, but the duchess was an expert at getting people out of the house when she was ready to retire.

"Indeed it did. Thank you so much, Aunt Rosalind." Alex hugged her aunt and uncle, then took Gavin's arm and climbed the steps to their rooms. As guests of honor, they had to stay till the end. Her parents had quietly slipped away an hour earlier.

She was very aware of the strength of his arm, of the quiet protection he'd given her all night even though he'd been as wary of this ball as she. Gavin hesitated when they reached her door, but she drew him inside with her. With the door closed, she went into his arms, wanting the warm comfort of a hug. "I'm glad that's over. We both survived. You were a great success, my lord."

"Allowances were made for me because of all the fine families I'm related to by marriage." He stroked her back, his touch both relaxing and reviving her. "You must be exhausted after so much dancing."

"I'm ready to sleep the clock around." She sighed, her pleasure fading. "I think Frederica Pierce spent the evening spreading her rumors. I'm trying not to care."

"Soon there will be so many contradictory stories they'll all seem false. In a week people will be saying you were chosen as the admiral of a Chinese pirate fleet."

"Better than the ugly truth." She buried her face in his shoulder, wondering if she dared suggest what she was thinking.

Gently he massaged her nape, loosening tight muscles. "Is something wrong?"

She thought of what her mother had said. *Risk your pride. Risk your heart. Risk your dreams.* "I'm trying to decide how to invite you to stay the night without making it seem as if . . . as if I'm inviting you for more than that."

"I think you just managed it." There was a smile in his voice. "There's an American pioneer custom called 'bundling.' Since travel was difficult, courting couples would spend the night in the same bed, but separated by a board or blankets."

"And these young couples behaved?" she asked, amazed.

"Usually. Not always. But we're adults. We can be as good as we want to be."

"How well you put that. Very well, let us bundle. Close, but not too close." Turning her back, she asked, "Can you undo the ties of this gown? I'm too tired to manage alone."

He did as she asked, his fingers deftly finding hidden tapes and hooks. How intimate and sensual to have a man help her disrobe at the end of a long day. And a little alarming, too. "I'll get ready for bed. By the time you join me, I'll probably be asleep."

He kissed the back of her neck. "And I'll be asleep five minutes later."

After he withdrew into his room, she hastily undressed and donned a nightgown of soft embroidered muslin, then brushed out her hair so she could braid it. She wanted to be in bed and giving a good imitation of slumber before he returned, since her desire to sleep with him was only slightly greater than her nervousness about doing so.

She'd barely slid under the covers and closed her eyes when he quietly returned. After turning out the lamp, he climbed into the bed, the mattress sagging under his weight. She tensed, then relaxed when she recognized that he was separated from her by a sheet and a blanket.

Rolling onto his side, he draped an arm over her waist. "Playing possum?"

So much for pretending she was asleep. "What does that mean?"

"Opossums live in the American South. Think of a rat the size of a cat."

She shuddered. "Must I? I loathe rats."

"Very well, think of a slow gray critter with

a long tail that can hang from tree branches. When an opossum feels threatened, he'll curl up and pretend he's dead, hoping the other beast will go away and look for a livelier meal."

She laughed out loud. "So I'm a pretend rat and you're a threat?"

"Apparently."

Hearing regret in his voice, she said, "You know it's not you, don't you?"

"Yes, I know." But there was still a trace of wistfulness in his voice.

She cuddled closer, enjoying his warmth and companionship. Muscles tired from dancing ached less in his presence, and the weight of his arm wasn't enough to cause distress. Because it was easier to talk in the dark, she said, "Half the fear is of being trapped. The other is of . . . of having my body invaded."

"That leaves quite a bit of sea room actually." His hand drifted up to her breast, cupping its fullness. Slowly he moved his palm in a circle, rubbing her nipple deliciously through the finely woven fabric.

"That feels nice," she murmured. "But I warn you, I'm too tired to respond."

"So am I." Lazily he continued to stroke her breasts, as if he was petting a cat.

She realized that she was less tired than she thought. His caresses were causing other body parts to feel surprisingly awake. She inched closer yet.

His hand moved lower, unerringly finding the place where heat was burning away all traces of fatigue. Her breathing changed as he brushed aside her nightgown so that his strong, knowing fingers could touch slick, heated flesh. A little lower . . . yes, *there.*

This time she recognized the building tension, the way sensations flooded her body. This time she didn't resist the furious urgency that dissolved thought and sent her thrusting against his hand as she gasped for breath. "Oh, my," she said weakly when she could speak. "And I thought I was tired before. Now I can't even move."

He chuckled, his hand becoming still as it came to rest on her most private parts. "Sleep well, my dear wife."

Much as she would have liked to roll over and fall asleep, she realized that he might not sleep so well. She slid her hand between the blankets, and found proof that he was far from restful. Her guess confirmed, she tugged up his nightshirt.

He said tensely, "You don't have to do this."

"I know." The garment out of the way, she wrapped her hand around that warm, silky length. "But I want to." She squeezed experimentally.

He gasped. "At this rate, little of your time will be required."

Propping herself up on one elbow, she concentrated on pleasing him as much as he'd pleased her. Interesting how that hard male organ didn't seem like a weapon when he was lying on his back, vulnerable to whatever she chose to do. This took trust on his part, just as she had to trust him when he touched her.

Her mother was right—trust was the bedrock of a good marriage. For her, the ability to trust a man had been shattered when she became a victim. An object, not a partner. Now trust was being rebuilt one small piece at a time. At least, thank God, she'd married a man worthy of it.

He climaxed with a long, harsh groan, one hand clenching her arm as he bucked against her hand. She loved that she could give him such intense satisfaction. This was more rewarding than lying on her back had ever been.

Deeply content, she relaxed back onto her pillow, one arm around him. "Is this being as good as we want to be?"

"Yes," he said huskily. "And you're very good indeed."

# CHAPTER 27

Alex gazed absently from the window of the breakfast room. The Berkeley Square house's garden was misty this morning, the summer blossoms having the hazy loveliness of a Chinese painting. She hardly noticed Gavin's arrival until he kissed her cheek. "Thinking deep thoughts?" he asked.

"Not really." She turned to him with a smile. "These last weeks have been like a dream. A year ago it seemed impossible that I'd ever see England again. Now I have Katie, a handsome home, a noble husband"—she laughed when he grimaced over that—"and my family nearby. I can't believe my luck."

"To a large extent, we make our luck. If you hadn't refused to believe your situation was hopeless, our paths would never have crossed."

He was right that her struggle for freedom had eventually put her in a place where she could become free. He was also too tactful to mention the price still being paid for her intransigence. If she'd been docile, she would be living peacefully with her first master, resigned to an alien but comfortable life in a tropical paradise. Fighting her fate had led her to Bhudy and rape, and scars which were still far from healed.

After their first night of sleeping together, she and Gavin had continued to share a bed. His warm, solid presence had banished the worst of her nightmares and they had enjoyed exploring each other's bodies—until the disastrous night when she'd been giddy with desire and all things had seemed possible.

She had pulled him to her, sure that this time it would be all right. Instead she panicked, every muscle in her body going rigid even though he'd supported his weight above her rather than crushing her into the mattress. She bit her lip until it bled, determined to endure as she had endured the Lion Game, but he was too perceptive not to notice her reaction. He'd rolled away, saying tautly that he would wait until she was ready. Then he'd left to spend the night in his own bed.

She'd been embarrassingly grateful for his understanding, but the episode had hurt them both, and they hadn't shared a bed since. Fear of failing again in such an intimate, emotionally fraught area was so intense that it was easier not even to try. Gavin had been even more upset than she. For a man who would cut off his hand rather than hurt a woman, it must be harrowing to feel that he was terrorizing his wife even though he knew intellectually that her reaction had nothing to do with him.

Still, they managed day-to-day life very well. They were friends, they trusted each other, and their lives were increasingly intertwined. In time, surely, the final barriers would fall. . . .

His voice interrupted her reverie. "What are you doing today?"

"After I take Katie to Ashburton House for her lessons, I'll join Troth for another *wing chun* lesson. She says I'm coming along very well. After lunch at Ashburton House, I'm going to Hatchard's with my mother and aunt. Are there any particular books you'd like me to pick up?"

"See if they have any American imports I might enjoy."

She nodded and crossed the room to pour them tea, wondering how to broach the subject on her mind. One thing she'd learned early was never to spring anything provocative on a man until he'd been fed, so she waited until they'd both finished eating before asking, "Is there any useful work I could do at your office? Now that the household is organized and Katie is busy with school and her cousins for most of the day, I have time on my hands. I don't want to spend it shopping and paying calls on people who don't interest me."

Most British husbands would have been aghast. Gavin merely looked thoughtful. "I could use another clerk, but the work is rather tedious. How much do you know about running an estate?"

"A fair amount. The colonel found estate business boring—he was much more interested in mines and manufacturing. Since Mama was busy having babies and taking care of the tenants, for several years I handled most of the routine business of Bryn Manor." She smiled reminiscently. "When I married, the colonel said he was losing not only a daughter, but a land agent."

"That's even better than I hoped." Gavin sat back in his chair, looking pleased. "Ever since the earldom descended on my hapless head, the Seabourne lawyer has been sending mountains of documents about the estate. I simply haven't enough time to do a thorough job while also establishing the new Elliott House office. It would be a blessing to have a knowledgeable person I trust to supervise estate business."

Alex frowned. "Do you think Finn is cheating you?"

"No, he seems honest and capable, but it's bad practice to accept all his recommendations merely because I'm too busy to study the issues more deeply. So far I've been following his suggestions and promising myself I'll do better when I have more time, but the situation has been troubling me. Shall I hand all the Seabourne business over to you?"

"Please do. Can I set up an office at Elliott House? That way if there is something you need to sign or make a decision about, you'll be right there. I can also learn more about the shipping business."

"Perfect! You need to have an understanding of Elliott House since, if anything happened to me, you'd be in charge."

Surprised, she said, "You would really leave your business in the control of a woman?"

"Who better? You're intelligent, trustworthy, and it's in your best interests to do the job well." He grinned. "Plus, it would make all the old mossbacks gnash their teeth. An irresistible prospect."

She laughed. "You're a Yankee rebel to the core, my dear."

"Thank you." They shared a warm glance.

"When can we visit the Seabourne family seat?" she asked. "You need to meet your people, see the condition of the property and the tenants' farms, and all the other tasks that can't be done long distance."

"Philip said he'd be out by Michaelmas. That's the end of September, isn't it?"

"September 29th. I look forward to seeing the estate. I love that it's by the sea, just as you wanted. Perhaps we can visit for a fortnight or so after Michaelmas."

"A good idea—Elliott House should be running smoothly by then. We can invite Katie's cousins to keep her company." He finished his tea and rose. "Shall we start the new schedule tomorrow morning?"

"The sooner, the better." She gave him a kiss. If she wasn't yet a true wife to her husband—well, she'd be a very good steward.

Hatchard's Bookshop teemed with fashionable people, some of whom were actually interested in books. As Alex entered with her mother and aunt, she said, "I'll see if they have any books on estate management. It wasn't hard to supervise Bryn Manor, but Seabourne is far larger."

"I see that you're really looking forward to this," Catherine observed.

"With all of you leaving for the country soon, I need something to keep me out of mischief." She smiled fondly at Catherine and Rosalind, thinking how fortunate she was to be part of a family where females were assumed to be capable creatures.

As they worked their way toward the rear of the store, Alex glanced down an aisle bounded by high bookshelves and saw Frederica Pierce. The other woman was accompanied by her maid, a slim black girl in a neat dove-gray gown who was trying to balance an armful of books. Alex was about to move on when Frederica dropped another volume in the girl's arms. The precarious pile collapsed and books crashed to the floor.

"I'm sorry, my lady." The maid knelt to collect the fallen volumes. Her soft voice had a lovely musical accent.

"Daisy, you stupid, stupid girl!" Frederica swatted at the maid with her reticule.

Alex wondered how long it would be before the young woman quit. Frederica's angelic face hid a vicious temper, and she'd always had trouble keeping servants in Sydney. Convict maids had run away from her household despite the consequences if they were caught.

"I'm sorry," Daisy said again, her eyes downcast. She stretched for a large volume and dropped it when she misjudged the weight.

"I don't know why I keep you around," Frederica snapped. "If you continue to be so clumsy, I'll have you sold back to the Carolinas and you can spend the rest of your life chopping cotton."

Alex froze, wondering if the situation could possibly be what it sounded like. She turned into the aisle. "Good day, Frederica. Do you need a hand?"

Frederica scowled when she recognized the newcomer. "My girl will manage." She prodded Daisy's leg with one dainty toe. "She's close to worthless, but she should be able to pick up books."

"The way you spoke to her made it sound as if she's a slave, but of course she can't be. Slavery has been illegal in Britain for years."

"Mind your own business, Alexandra. Daisy is American."

And slavery was still legal in the American South. Sick to her stomach, Alex knelt and began to help gather the fallen books. "Even if you were born in slavery, Daisy, you're a free woman now that you're in England."

The girl glanced up, her dark eyes terrified. About twenty, she was pretty and neatly dressed, her black hair pulled into a knot on her neck. Ducking her head, she scooped the last of the books into her arms and stood.

"How *dare* you interfere in my household!" Frederica said furiously. "You may be a countess now, but that gives you no right to tell me what to do."

Ignoring the other woman, Alex said, "If you wish to change your situation, Daisy, come to me at 42 Berkeley Square. No matter what your mistress says, you are as free as she is. I will find you a new position where you'll be paid and where you'll be able to leave if you don't like how you are treated."

"What makes you so interested in slave girls, Alexandra?" Frederica hissed. "Was it because you were a slave yourself in the Indies? Do you see yourself in a creature like her?"

Alex almost hit her. Only her mother's grip on her arm checked her temper. For a moment she hesitated. Until now, she and her family had kept silent about her experiences in the East, refusing to confirm or deny. But as Gavin said, none of it had been her fault, and in front of this girl it seemed cowardly to deny what had happened.

"Yes, Frederica, I was a slave," she said in a voice that carried to other customers who'd halted and were listening to the altercation. "A pity you've never been one—perhaps it would have broadened your understanding and compassion." She turned to Daisy again. "Will you come with me? I promise your situation will improve."

Daisy looked at her mistress, and froze as if she'd been struck. She glanced at Alex and shook her head, then dropped her gaze to the floor.

Having subdued Daisy, Frederica turned to glare at Alex with shocking malice. "You will pay for this."

Alex recoiled. Frederica had always been selfish and difficult, but now she looked almost deranged. Reminding herself that the other woman had no power to injure her, she repeated, "Remember, Daisy, 42 Berkeley Square, any time of day or night." Her voice dropped. "Please let me help you."

Daisy turned away. Frederica smiled triumphantly. "Now that you've admitted you were a slave, people can imagine what your life was like. Though you're far past your prime, there must have been some men desperate enough to buy you."

"What an unpleasant mind you have, Lady Pierce." The Duchess of Ashburton was the most easygoing of peeresses, but she'd once been an actress and she could pitch her voice to a note that would freeze glass. "I can't imagine that good society will welcome you in the future."

As Frederica turned white, the duchess pivoted on one heel, giving the cut direct, and walked away. Catherine gripped Alex's wrist and they followed Rosalind out into the street as a path opened up between silent customers.

Alex was shaking. When they reached the relative calm of Piccadilly, she said, "I'm sorry for embarrassing you both."

"I have never been more proud of you, my dear," her mother said quietly.

Rosalind added, "I've never liked that young woman. It doesn't reflect well on me, but I enjoyed demonstrating my opinion of her character." She smiled wickedly as she signaled for the Ashburton coach to pick them up. "In the future she will find that her social life is not what she would like."

"It will damage her social ambitions to be cut by the Duchess of Ashburton," Alex agreed. "But I failed to convince that poor girl to leave, and surely Frederica will punish her for everything that happened."

"Perhaps she will come to you later," Catherine suggested as she climbed into the coach. "I doubt that she knew she is legally free here. I'm sure Lady Pierce didn't tell her so. When she has time to think, she may very well run away from her mistress."

Alex hoped so, but she doubted that would happen. Neither of the older women could know how slavery broke one's will. Six months of bondage had nearly broken Alex; Daisy had probably been born a slave and treated as one her whole life. As the carriage rumbled through London, Alex closed her eyes and prayed the girl would have the courage to break free.

Then she thought about slavery. The fact that it was now illegal in several European countries was a start, but slavery was one of the most ancient scourges of humanity, and there was still much to be done. What could one lone woman do at long distance?

It was time Alex found out.

# CHAPTER 28

That evening Alex went in search of Suryo. Though they'd been living under the same roof since the *Helena* had sailed, she almost never saw him. She suspected that he could cross sand and leave no footprint.

Invited to come in when she tapped on his door, she entered. "Tuan Suryo, may I speak with you?"

He stood and gestured her toward the one chair in the simple, meticulously neat room. "Of course, my lady. How may I be of service?"

Sitting down, she said bluntly, "What is your opinion of slavery?"

A muscle jerked in his jaw. "I think it is an abomination."

She caught her breath, recognizing the note in his voice. "You have had personal experience?"

"I have. I do not speak of those years." After a pause, he added, "But it was the captain who freed me. I pledged myself to him that day."

Fascinated, she asked, "Isn't such a pledge a form of slavery?"

"I serve him of my own will. Never has he asked anything of me that was against honor or humanity."

Alex guessed that was a veiled warning to her that he would not do anything he thought was against Gavin's best interests. That was no problem; she would never ask him to. "Today I met a young female slave who has been brought here from America and is kept in bondage, not knowing she is free. I failed when I tried to get her to leave her mistress, but now I am wondering. I never expected to see a slave in England. Is slave trading still going on here in Britain?"

"Swift ships still sail from Africa to the Americas with illegal cargo. The Royal Navy tries to blockade such traffic." He shrugged.

"With limited success. Britain was the greatest slave trader in Europe, and there are still those who will risk the law in return for great profit."

She frowned as she thought. "You know the docklands and the sailors' taverns. In such places, might news of illegal slave dealing sometimes be heard?"

"There might be an occasional mention of a ship, a captain, a sailing date. But what can be done with such information? The navy will not listen to scraps of barroom boasting."

"Perhaps they will if it comes through the right hands." She leaned forward. "My step-father's family is connected to many of Britain's most influential men. As a woman, I could never gather information in sailors' taverns, but you could, and perhaps you might find others who would help. What do you think?"

"Some good might be done," he said slowly.

"Then you'll help?"

A light came into his eyes that she had never seen before. "It is work worth doing. But why do you discuss this with me rather than the captain? Do you intend to keep this secret from him?"

"Only for a little while. He carries many burdens now. I'd rather wait until I have some results to show him."

"As you wish, my lady."

She offered her hand. "Then let us work together for freedom."

He took her hand. "For freedom, my lady—and because justice is the best revenge."

Alex loved the Elliott House offices. Located on the top floor of the firm's warehouse, the area was scented with tea and spices, and high, arched windows overlooked the docks and river. The quiet, freshly painted rooms hummed with activity that sent ripples around the world. Obviously primed by Gavin, the four regular employees greeted her without so much as a blink. She was going to like working here.

The office Alex was assigned to already contained the Seabourne documents Gavin had received. He hadn't exaggerated the amount. Happily she settled down to the task of organizing and comprehending the complexities of the estate. At midday, Gavin came in with a basket of food the cook had packed that morning, and they discussed business over sandwiches and good English ale.

As she finished the last of her ham sandwich, she said, "This is great fun. I was born to be a land agent, I think."

"Better you than me." Gavin bit into an apple. "Do matters seem to be in order?"

"Yes, Finn does a good job. Philip became a bit giddy when he inherited and outspent the estate's income, but there seem to be no major problems. Next year there will be money for improvements."

"Are improvements required?"

"Improvements are *always* required on an estate. Drainage, better breeding stock, newly developed seeds and equipment, tenant and laborer housing. It is the nature of farmland."

"I leave it all in your capable hands." Gavin scanned several documents she'd set aside for his signature before lifting a pen to sign. "You're a godsend."

She returned to her work with a smile. It was wonderful to be useful.

*    *    *

As Alex finished her bedtime reading to Katie that evening, her daughter said, "Soon Anne and Maria will be off to the country. Does that mean I won't have to take more lessons?"

Alex laughed. "You know better than that. Miss Thompson, the Ashburton governess, has recommended a friend to me. I've talked to Miss Hailey and she's very nice, so she'll start as your governess next week."

Katie made a face. "I'd rather go into the office with you and learn about teas and spices and china. I want to be a trader like the captain."

Alex hid her smile. "If you want to be a trader, you'll need to know numbers and penmanship and geography and foreign languages."

Her daughter looked appalled. "You mean there's a reason for all those lessons?"

"There is indeed. Knowledge is power, Katybird." She kissed her daughter good night. "And a woman needs all the power she can get."

As she dowsed the lamp, her daughter was looking thoughtful. By the time Katie was grown, might women study at universities and run businesses as men did? No, not so soon, but surely some day. . . .

As she reached the bottom of the stairs, her butler, a footman promoted from Ashburton House, said, "My lady, there is a young person here to see you."

"At this hour of the evening, Bard?"

"A most unusual young person. She is in the small drawing room."

Curious, Alex entered the drawing room—and gasped to find Frederica Pierce's young black slave standing by the window. "I'm so glad that you've come, Daisy!"

She crossed the room and took the girl's hands. They were ice cold. Breaking away from everything she'd ever known must be terrifying. "Would you like some tea, and perhaps something to eat?"

"Oh, no, my lady." Daisy looked shocked at the suggestion of eating with her. She was neatly dressed in the same gray gown she'd worn the day before, and beside her was a small lumpy bundle of her possessions.

"I'll just order tea then. Please sit down." Alex took a seat. "Lady Pierce was a difficult mistress?"

Daisy sank into the opposite chair, one hand going to her bruised cheek. "Sir Barton bought me in Charleston. No one told me I was free here. Yesterday she beat me after we came back from Hatchard's. She said you lied, but I couldn't stop thinking about what you said. Is it true she can't send slave catchers after me?"

Alex swallowed, remembering beatings and how she'd feared pursuit if she tried to escape. "No slave catchers. Neither Lady Pierce nor her husband have the right to compel you to do anything ever again."

Daisy buried her face in trembling hands, her shoulders shaking. Though her lovely musical accent was of the American South, her demeanor and use of language were refined, like all good lady's maids. Sir Barton must have chosen her for her skill, and hoped that a young woman raised in slavery would be docile and never think to question her status. He'd been right, too.

Thank heaven Alex had been in the right place at the right time. "You're safe now, Daisy. Do you know what you'd like to do with your freedom, or is it too soon to decide? I'll help you find whatever you choose."

"You are too good, my lady." Daisy blotted her eyes with a handkerchief, then raised her head. "Please, can I work for you? I'm a good lady's maid, but if you don't need one, I can clean or work in the kitchen. I'll do anything, as long as I do it as a free woman."

"I do need a lady's maid." Alex had been meaning to hire one, so Daisy's arrival was perfect. What had her mother said was a good salary for the position? "You'll have a room of your own, bed and board, thirty pounds a year, plus clothes I no longer wear, which you can keep for yourself or sell as you choose. Does that seem acceptable?"

Daisy's eyes widened. "Thank you, my lady. I swear I'll be a good maid."

"I'm sure you will. By the way, what is your full name?"

"Daisy Adams, my lady."

"Do you prefer being Daisy, or Adams? Lady's maids are often called by their last names."

"I would like it if you call me Daisy, my lady." She looked as if no one had ever asked her preference about anything.

"Very well, Daisy it is." Alex studied her

face. "Is there anything special that you would like? Something you've always wanted but couldn't have?"

Daisy caught her breath. "Would it be possible . . . ? Could I learn to read and write?"

Startled, Alex said, "Of course. You were never taught?"

Daisy shook her head. "It's illegal to teach slaves to read."

Alex felt a wave of fury directed at a system that denied bright young minds like Daisy's the chance to learn. "I'm hiring a governess for my daughter. I'll ask her to teach you as well. Her references say that she loves teaching, so I'm sure she'll be happy to have another pupil."

"Thank you." Tears gleamed in Daisy's eyes. "You are so kind. I . . . I don't deserve this."

"Of course you do."

The butler entered with a tea tray. Alex said, "Bard, meet Miss Daisy Adams, my new lady's maid. Will you ask the housekeeper to prepare a room for her?"

Bard's brows lifted, but he'd been well trained at Ashburton House. "I shall take care of it directly, my lady."

After he withdrew, Alex poured them two cups of tea. "The room should be ready soon. If you'd like something to eat before you go to bed, the housekeeper will show you to the kitchen. I'm sure you've had an exhausting day."

Daisy nodded, her expression haunted. "May I ask something, my lady?"

"Of course. And you needn't call me 'my lady' all the time. 'Ma'am' will do."

"Were you really a slave, ma'am?"

"Indeed I was."

"And you aren't ashamed to admit it?"

Alex had been, but no longer. "The shame of slavery belongs to the owners, not the victims. In the sight of God, we are all equal. The day will come when that is also true in the sight of man."

Daisy looked as if she wanted to believe it, but didn't. Give her time.

Alex sipped her tea, thinking that her attempts to collect information about slave trafficking on the high seas might never produce results, but at least she'd helped one young woman to freedom.

# CHAPTER 29

Covering a yawn, Alex entered Gavin's office and placed several documents on the corner of his desk. "We seem to be the last ones in the office tonight. I thought my helping with the estate business would make you less busy. Instead, now we're both busy."

He grinned and pushed his chair back so he could stretch his legs. "I swear it won't be this way forever. I'm training Peter Spears to manage Elliott House. He has good experience, and by the end of the year he'll be handling everyday affairs. With you running the Seabourne estate, I'll be a man of leisure."

She laughed. "I'll believe that when I see it."

She drifted across the office to stand by the window that overlooked the London Dock. In the previous fortnight, she'd made her mark in ways large and small. His private office now sported a fine oriental carpet and a massive carved chair with lion feet, elegant Chinese paintings, and a vase of fresh cut flowers to brighten his desk. He hadn't realized how attractive an office could be.

He asked, "Do you mind that because I'm a merchant, we'll spend more time in London than most of your friends and family?"

"No, I like London, though I'll be ready for that country holiday after Michaelmas." She pivoted in a swift *wing chun* move, body and hands briefly poised for action. "But I miss Troth's lessons. Doing the exercises alone may be good practice and mental discipline, but it's not the same as working with a partner."

A pity that Gavin couldn't spar with her. Troth and her husband practiced *wing chun* together, but Gavin and Alex couldn't do anything that involved so much touching.

There was too much mutual awareness, too many barriers.

A flood of disturbing thoughts made him look away from the alluring sight of Alex silhouetted against the early evening sky. He still hadn't recovered from the searing failure that had left them both sleeping alone again. His mind understood that when she panicked, her reaction had nothing to do with him. But even for a man who prided himself on fair-minded detachment, that level of rejection hurt, especially since he had become optimistic about the intimate side of their marriage. No longer.

In some ways, it was easier to be celibate. He didn't have to wonder how she would feel if he kissed her, or worry that she was suppressing revulsion in a gallant attempt to be a good wife.

In other ways, celibacy was hell. The original haunting memories of coerced intimacy were now overlaid by happier ones of discovery and mutual pleasure. It was painful to look at her and not think about what might be—or might never be.

Yet he was happiest when she was nearby, which meant accepting, and hoping. He took a deep breath and began to read the documents she'd given him. "I'll take care of these so we can go home."

The first paper included her summary on why she thought the money must be spent now rather than later. Her judgment and arguments were good, so he signed. The same for the next two documents. So far, his grand inheritance was costing him more money than it was returning.

The last paper made him stop and reread. "Alex, I don't understand this. Why do you have shipping notes and so many question marks?"

"Sorry, I didn't mean to show you that yet. Suryo and I are collecting information about illegal slave trading. It's disgraceful how many of the ships involved in the trade are British. I've talked to Uncle Stephen, and he has agreed to give the Royal Navy anything that might help them intercept slave ships."

Frowning, Gavin got to his feet. "This is a very dangerous business to meddle with. Slave traders are ruthless—quite capable of violence to protect their profits."

"Suryo is merely listening for scraps of drunken gossip. Nothing to bring trouble down on us."

He caught her gaze, wanting to impress on her the seriousness of the situation. "Alex, you underestimate the explosive potential of such information. I wish you'd consulted me before embarking on this."

She pivoted from the window to stare at him. "It never occurred to me that you might object to fighting slavery in whatever small way I can. You didn't object to me helping Daisy."

"That's different. She is one person, not an abstraction." He gestured toward Alex's notes. "But these are very murky waters. You can't know what beasts may lurk below the surface."

Cheeks flushed, Alex said, "I'm willing to risk that."

"Brave of you," he retorted. "But what of Suryo? He is the one putting his life on the line in those taverns. How will you feel if he's killed for being too inquisitive?"

Her dismayed face showed she hadn't thought of that. "I'm sure he understands the dangers better than I. He also has other informants, so he's not alone."

"The more people involved, the more likely your secret network will be exposed," Gavin said with exasperation. "Informers are usually happy to take money from more than one source."

"Very well, there are risks, but isn't fighting slavery worth a risk? There is evil being done, and to ignore it is cowardly and despicable."

"Success can be bitter," he said grimly. "Did you know that slavers in danger of being overtaken will throw their captives overboard so the captain can't be charged with illegal trafficking? Hundreds of men die when that happens."

She gasped with horror. "All the more reason to destroy the slavers so they won't dare capture innocent people and sell them across the ocean!"

He bit back an urge to swear at her stubborn refusal to see reason. "I understand that this is personal to you, but . . ."

Before he could finish, she spat out, "How *dare* you think you can understand what it is like to be helpless! You are the master of control—you've never been helpless in your life. Do you 'understand' what it's like to be a woman and know you can't safely walk on a public street without fear of being assaulted and raped? Or what it is like to know you have absolutely no hope of escape, short of death?"

Her rage rocked him back. "You're right," he said quietly. "I can't fully understand no matter how much I try. I'll never know what it was like to be you."

Her eyes narrowed. "Perhaps I can demonstrate."

He hesitated before deciding that if she was this angry, he really must try harder to understand. "Please do."

She pointed to the lion-footed oak arm chair. "Sit!"

Gavin sat, wondering uneasily what she had in mind.

She pulled a handful of neatly folded handkerchiefs from the small drawer where they were stored, and used them to lash his wrists and ankles to the chair. Stepping back to survey her handiwork, she asked, "Does this give you some idea what it's like to be helpless?"

"It certainly does." He tugged at his bonds. With time he could probably work his way loose, but at the moment he was immobilized, unable to move his arms and legs, and anchored by the weight of the massive chair. It was not a comfortable feeling. "I've faced a dragon, but I've never been rendered helpless before a predatory lioness—which you're imitating rather well. You tie good knots."

"Suryo taught Katie and me on the voyage home."

If these were Suryo's knots, Gavin was well and truly trapped. He clamped down on an instinctive desire to struggle against his bonds. "Care to untie me now that you've proved your point?"

"Not yet." Her eyes glittered with edgy amusement. "That's part of being helpless—you can't just say that you've had enough and be free."

He watched her warily, wondering how far she'd push the game. He didn't think she'd physically injure him, but she was in a chancy mood. If that anger exploded out of control . . .

She leaned back against his desk and studied him critically. "Being tied to a chair barely scratches the surface of real helplessness. Imagine that you are thousands of miles away, in a strange country whose language you don't speak, presumed dead by everyone who loves you, treated as a *thing* by those who claim to own you." She picked up Sultan Kasan's jeweled kris, which Gavin used to open letters. "Then imagine your situation is *real,* not a mere exercise in attempted understanding."

He kept his eye on the weapon as she idly tested the blade. "Planning to punish me for the sins of all men?"

Some of the anger faded from her face. "I could never harm you, Gavin. But I must admit to a certain dark satisfaction in knowing you're uncertain what I am capable of." With a practiced snap of her wrist, she hurled the dagger across the room to stab into the door frame, hilt quivering. "Make no mistake, for the time being you are at my mercy."

He stared at the dagger. "Where the devil did you learn to do that?"

"I spent half my childhood in army camps. You'd be amazed what bored soldiers will teach a little girl. Did I ever mention that I'm an excellent shot? If I'd had a good repeating rifle, I could have driven off the Malay pirates myself."

His skin was beginning to crawl. Knowing that was her intention wasn't much comfort. "Now what? Will you ravish me to demonstrate what that's like? I don't think that could possibly be as devastating as what you've endured."

His words fell like a spark struck into tinder. Alex's anger, frustration, and the suppressed sexual tension pulsing between them blazed into furious life. For the first time, Gavin was in a position where she didn't have to trust his good will. The fact that he was trustworthy was beside the point—she had always been aware of his strength, and what he could do if he chose.

But now she had this beautiful man entirely at her mercy. The sense of power was heady and deeply erotic. "You think not? Then I will take it as a challenge to see if I can devastate you."

"Do your worst," he said, his gaze steady.

To find devastation, she must plumb the depths of passion and fear. She unfastened the hooks that attached her demure, high-necked bodice to her skirt, then removed the garment to reveal her quilted corset and embroidered shift. "Being a gentleman, you usually try not to stare at my breasts, though you don't always succeed. Now you can look all you like, but you can't touch unless I allow it."

She kicked off her shoes, then rested her

right foot on a chair and raised her petticoats to reveal her stocking and garter. "It's
too warm an evening for stockings."

The garter was white ribbon with a tiny
pink silk rose sewn on one side. She untied
the ribbon and let the silky strip slither to
the floor while she rubbed above her knee
to restore circulation. Knowing his gaze was
riveted to her leg made her feel deliciously
wanton. She peeled off the stocking with
sensual slowness, then repeated her performance with the other garter and stocking.

"You have lovely legs." Gavin's voice
sounded constricted.

"Thank you. My hair is rather nice, too."
She pulled out the pins and languidly shook
the dark waves over her shoulders. Then
she stripped a handful of petals from the
vase of flowers on his desk, and tossed
them over him in a fragrant shower. Petals
drifted down to settle on his shoulders and
lap. "I like you helpless. The knowledge that
I can do with you as I will is rather exciting."

"I'm finding it . . . educational."

Her corset hooked up the front. She unfastened the top hooks to release her
breasts from confinement, then swayed

across the room to Gavin. Desire radiated from him, along with profound uneasiness. She felt voluptuous and powerful.

"It's time to let you touch, but only what and when I allow." She braced her hands on his bound wrists and leaned forward. Her breasts spilled out in front of him, just out of his reach. She could feel the warmth of his breath on her bare skin as his hands clenched and unclenched on the chair arms.

She bent to trace the curve of his ear with her tongue. When he turned his head to kiss her she evaded his lips, preferring to trail her mouth over his warm, salt-tinged skin. This late in the day his face wore a faint bristle of blond whiskers, unseen but felt as a provocative, masculine texture.

Impatiently he rubbed the lacy edge of her shift away with his cheek, baring her left nipple. When his mouth closed over it, heat blazed through her. She caught her breath, feeling that she was St. Elmo's fire, ablaze in the night. Her other breast tingled with longing—and to satisfy that, she must take the initiative. The choice was hers. All the choices were hers.

When she shifted to present her other

breast, he murmured, "You are magnificent," before suckling as she desired.

Needing to return pleasure, she removed his cravat and unbuttoned his shirt so she could caress the warm, bare skin of his chest. Hard muscles tensed at her touch. She moved her hands in circles, rolling his nipples between thumbs and forefingers. They hardened instantly.

"Merciful heaven, Alex . . . !" He sucked in his breath, shivering all over. "It's hellish not to be able to touch you."

"While I can touch you anywhere I want." Pleased to see his control cracking, she removed her hands from under his shirt and began kneading his thighs, avoiding the hard ridge of male flesh that strained against his trousers. He twisted back and forth, pulling involuntarily against his bonds as if on the verge of jumping out of his skin.

She captured his mouth, falling into the kiss as if it would last forever. He responded greedily, his passion and hunger stirring her to fever heat. Blindly she unbuttoned his trousers and released him into her hand. She had to force herself not to bring him to swift culmination. She wasn't ready for this to end.

Climbing onto his lap, she slipped her legs under the high, lion-carved arms so that she straddled him with carnal abandon. Then she adjusted her skirts to cascade around them—and stiffened at the realization that her open-seam drawers meant they were pressed together with an intimacy just short of intercourse.

The throbbing of his blood echoed through her, fueling an urgency that swamped her momentary alarm. She rocked forward, the heated slickness of her most private parts gliding along the hard length of his arousal.

He broke the kiss, groaning a curse under his breath. "Untie the scarves, Iskandra, I promise I'll use my hands well."

"No." Giddily she ground into him. Iskandra was the feminine of Iskander, who had been Alexander the Conqueror. Now she was a conqueror, a woman warrior, and that knowledge released sensuality that had been too long frozen.

He thrust his hips upward, moving against her as much as he could manage while bound. "You will kill me with craving," he breathed.

She raised herself high enough to reach

down and take hold of him. Then she lowered herself onto that glorious masculine hardness, whimpering at how perfectly they fit together. This mating was right, searing away the shadows of their vile forced intercourse in Maduri.

She wrapped her arms around him and buried her face against his neck as she rolled her hips fiercely. The angle, the pressure and friction, were scorchingly intense, different from anything she'd ever known. She was on the verge of shattering—and then she did, crying out as she drowned in frantic waves of sensation.

Instinctively she tightened around him as her whole body went rigid. He gave a long, drawn-out groan as if his soul and body were being wrenched asunder.

Gulping for breath, she clung to him, a little dazed, feeling every heartbeat as the hammering gradually slowed. "I feel as if one of the devil storms of the Pacific has battered over me. And I've barely survived."

"You achieved your goal of achieving devastation," Gavin said unsteadily. "I wish I could hold you to protect you from the storm."

Face burning, she yanked the end of one

handkerchief to release his left wrist, then did the same for the right. His arms enfolded her in warmth and security. She rested her head on his shoulder, her face turned away from him as she gave thanks that he didn't hate her for her crazy, ugly behavior. "I feel ashamed. As if I've just suffered an attack of madness."

"Passion is a form of madness. In your case, driven by fury over all you've suffered." His embrace tightened. "I'm glad you chose this form of rage rather than using the knife on me."

She shuddered at the thought, but knew he was right about her rage. Some of that, she saw now, had been directed at him. Absurd, when she'd insisted he "worship the goddess" in her during the Lion Game. Yet a deep, primitive part of her had hated him for violating her, and her anger was all the more bitter because she knew she had no right to it. "It's true about the anger, but it was wrong for me to take it out on you. I found it very . . . disturbing."

"So did I, but I now have at least some inkling of what it is like to be helpless," he said thoughtfully. "You called me the master of control. Perhaps it's good that you smashed that control into splinters."

She groaned. "Perhaps, but I'm still sorry, Gavin. I don't much like myself at the moment."

"Hush, my dear Iskandra." He cradled the back of her head in one large hand, soothing her jangled nerves. "Though the experience was unsettling, you managed to accomplish what had been impossible before now."

Only then did she fully register that they'd finally consummated their marriage, though that was a tame term for such a mad, perverse coupling. Finally, irrevocably, they were husband and wife. The satisfaction of that banished most of her shamed regret. "I don't want to tie you up again, but I do like this chair. Sitting like this was . . . different. Exciting. I'd like to try it again."

He laughed, tousled and almost unbearably handsome. "I'll buy a whole set of these chairs so we can have them all over the house and office."

"Actually, there is a second chair like this at the house, but it's in a guest room." She smiled naughtily. "I'll have it moved into my bedroom."

His expression turned serious. "Could that become *our* bedroom?"

She hesitated while she studied the darker corners of her mind. "I believe it can. I feel as if a mental wall has come tumbling down. There may be a few loose stones lying around still, but the worst is over."

"I'm so glad. I enjoy sharing a bed with you. Having you near." He smiled. "And I'm also very glad that you decided to work in this office."

That brought her back to a sense of her surroundings. Evening had darkened to night, and they would be very late to dinner. She climbed off his lap with some difficulty. Straddling him was easier than untangling herself without tripping, but he steadied her with one hand.

As she knelt to release his ankles, she said, "This is all so absurd. Right here in your office!" She glanced out at the night sky again, glad there were no buildings placed so that people could look in.

He stood and stretched his limbs gingerly. "Passion is absurd, just as it can be mad. It is also one of the greatest joys we can receive." He took her hand and drew her to her feet, then bent into a kiss of deep tenderness.

She relaxed into him, unafraid. "I should never have accused you of not understanding," she whispered. "You understand more than any man I've ever known."

# CHAPTER 30

By the time they had straightened themselves to a semblance of respectability, it
was full dark. Gavin was glad for his lantern,
for he'd never seen the street so quiet as
when they left the warehouse to walk to a
livery stable on the nearby Ratcliff Highway,
where a Seabourne carriage waited to take
them home.

The privacy meant he could keep an arm
around Alex, though the way he felt tonight,
he might have anyhow. Despite the harrowing aspects of their sexual encounter, they
were both playful and giddy, scarcely able
to keep their hands off each other. He was
already looking forward to bedtime. At the

very least, he'd be able to hold her all night. And maybe they'd test if that wall in her mind really had come tumbling down. . . .

She slid her arm around his waist. "What are you chuckling about?"

He kissed her temple. "I am thinking wicked thoughts."

In the dim light, he saw her blushing. She looked adorably disheveled. He kissed her again, glad that he'd been right about the inherent passion of her nature. He looked forward to a lifetime of mutual exploration.

Several sailors emerged from an alley ahead with the unsteady gaits of men going back to their ship after drinking at a waterfront tavern. Gavin kept an eye on them, steering Alex closer to the buildings on their side of the street, but his caution was merely habit. Though the dangerous East End slums weren't far away, this area by the warehouses was quiet and patrolled regularly by constables from the new Metropolitan Police Force.

The sailors were opposite when the man in the lead suddenly swung around, a knife in his hand and his expression dangerously sober as he slashed at Gavin. "He's the one!"

Instinctively Gavin pushed Alex behind him while dodging the knife and the assault of another man. Dropping the lantern so he had both hands free, he grabbed his assailant's arm and wrenched it from its socket. The man was screaming with agony as Gavin hurled him against his fellows.

The ultimate test of *pentjak silat* was fighting one against many. Trained reflexes took over, and Gavin closed fast and hard with the next man, snapping his neck before he whirled and smashed a third attacker's leg with a brutal kick. Under his cool, lethal movements was rage that such an attack should be made when Alex was with him.

She shouted, "Gavin, behind you!"

He spun around, wishing he was carrying a kris or cane. Using his left hand to block the descending knife, he lunged into a grappling hold and threw his opponent into a brick wall. The man hit with an audible cracking of bone. Beyond, Alex backed against the wall as a wiry, weasel-faced man with a knife approached her. Gavin was about to spring to her aid when she kicked her attacker in the groin, then stamped on his knife hand when he fell to the street, howling with pain.

"Hey, there!" An authoritative shout was followed by the raucous clatter of a police rattle. The distinctive top-hatted silhouette of a constable appeared at the intersection ahead, his swaying lantern casting grotesque shadows.

"Peeler's coming!" Shouting the warning, one of the attackers bolted for the alley. Two others followed, both stumbling badly from their injuries. The constable pursued them, shouting orders to stop.

"Alex." Shaking with reaction, Gavin moved toward her, dimly aware that his left forearm was stinging. "Are you all right?"

She nodded unsteadily. "And you?"

"I'm fine." He wrapped his arms around her, feeling the fear there'd been no time for during the attack.

"I fought back," she whispered fiercely. "This time I fought back!"

"And did it very well." He hugged her closer, terrified by the thought of what might have happened.

The constable arrived, truncheon in hand and puffing from his futile chase. Bulky and powerful, he carried himself like a soldier. "You folks all right 'ere?"

"I think so," Gavin said.

"What 'appened, sir?"

"My office is above that warehouse," Gavin explained. "Usually my wife and I leave earlier, but we were . . . working late and lost track of the time. We were on our way to the livery stable when those drunken sailors suddenly attacked without warning."

The constable knelt by the two attackers who hadn't escaped. After a quick check, he said, "Both of 'em are dead." He gave Gavin a narrow-eyed glance. "You did that with your bare hands?"

Both dead? Gavin nodded, sickened by the knowledge that he'd killed without conscious thought. Though he'd used *pentjak* to defend himself in the past, never had the results been so deadly. "They had knives."

"So I see, but they don't smell of spirits. Odd for drunken sailors." The constable stood. "You'll need to come to the station for a report."

A pair of pale objects lay on the ground. Remembering that the leader had dropped them at the start of the fight, Gavin bent and scooped the objects up. As he stared down, chilled, the constable asked, "What've you got there?"

"Just a pair of dice. I suppose the fellows had been gambling somewhere." He dropped the dice in his pocket. "Might I delay my visit to your station until tomorrow morning? My wife has borne up bravely, but I'd like to get her home." He shot Alex a look, and she obliged by sagging as if on the verge of collapse.

When he started to put a supportive arm around her, she frowned and changed instantly from drooping to concern. "You're bleeding."

He looked down and saw that his left sleeve was saturated with blood. Alex efficiently rolled back his coat, then turned a handkerchief into a temporary bandage. He wondered if it was one of the ones she'd used earlier for unholy purposes. Digging out his card case, he handed a card to the constable. "I'm Seabourne."

The constable's brows arched as he glanced at the card. "The Yankee Earl. I've 'eard of you, my lord. I'm Constable Mayne, and this is my regular patch."

"A pleasure to meet you, Constable.

We're grateful you arrived when you did, or who knows what might have happened."

Mayne looked down at the bodies. "I doubt you were in much danger tonight," he said with unmistakable dryness. "But in the future you may want to be more careful where you walk."

"I intend to be." Gavin wrapped his arm around Alex's shoulders. "Would you mind escorting us to the livery stable? I'd feel safer with you."

"You can use your carriage for the ride to the station, but with two men dead, I must ask you to come tonight." Mayne was polite but implacable. " 'Twon't take long, my lord."

Gavin was tempted to wield his lordly status, but reminded himself he despised using rank in such a way. Besides, maybe it was best to get the official part of this incident over with as soon as possible.

He only wished the implications of the attack could be dismissed so quickly.

The police were courteous but very thorough. By the time Gavin and Alex finished answering questions and returned home, they were so tired they went straight to bed.

Together. He woke early the next morning to find himself wrapped around his wife, spoon fashion. It was a very married feeling, and had given him a better night's rest than he'd had in weeks.

Nuzzling through her hair, he kissed her neck and lazily caressed one full breast. It occurred to him that at least in the summer, it was warm enough to sleep without night gowns. He wondered if she would be willing to consider that. She'd been remarkably broad-minded the evening before. . . .

Alex woke and rolled to face him. Lightly she skimmed her hand over his shoulder and down his arm. "So last night really did happen."

"I'm afraid so."

"You weren't exaggerating about how deadly *pentjak silat* is. No wonder you worried when you and Kasan fought."

"I should have been more careful, but having you there . . ." A muscle jumped in his jaw. "I lost control."

She regarded him gravely. "Killing is not to be taken lightly, but I haven't much sympathy for murderous criminals." She rolled up the left sleeve of his nightshirt and checked the bandage she'd applied the previous night before they went to bed. "I didn't realize you have a tattoo."

"Which will have a neat little scar across it," he said, glad to change the subject. "I had a shipmate do this when I was young and foolish. Luckily, even at sixteen I had the sense not to be tattooed in a visible place."

She studied the picture, which was mostly covered by bandage. "What is it?"

"An American eagle." His mouth curved. "Branded a Yankee until I die."

"Not a bad choice." She leaned closer and kissed his throat, her hand running down his body. "Not a bad choice at all."

Passion blazed through him. Now that they were lovers, his body wanted to make up for his long celibacy. The same must be true for Alex, because she responded eagerly to his caresses. Her breath quickened and her legs separated, welcoming his touch.

He wanted to roll over and bury himself in her to obliterate the previous night's mayhem, but common sense intervened. "Do you still feel that mental wall is down?"

She hesitated. "I think so."

"That's not quite as definite as I'd like.

So . . ." Catching her around the waist, he rolled onto his back and pulled her on top of him.

"Oh!" She caught her breath with surprise. Then she said, "Oh," with a different intonation as she settled into the new position with her legs bracketing his. "I wonder if this will be rather like sitting on your lap."

"Find out." He should have thought of this earlier. He loved supporting the weight of her softly female body, loved being able to caress her delightfully curved backside, while she obviously liked not being trapped under his weight.

Deftly shifting their nightclothes out of the way, she sank onto him with a gasp of pleasure. As she began slowly rocking her hips, she said, "How civilized this is. The exact opposite of yesterday."

If the previous day had been educational but harrowing, this morning was gentle and deeply satisfying. They made love as fluidly as sea creatures bathed in the warmth of a tropical ocean. When Alex discovered she could control the pace of their lovemaking, she began to experiment with joyous delight.

Gentleness built into scalding desire and

ended with profound fulfillment. Even after both of them were spent and panting, he continued to hold her on top of him. "I'd like to wake up like this every morning for the rest of my life."

"I'm willing if you are." She kissed his throat, her lips soft against his pulse, her hair falling silkily over his face and shoulders. With wonder, he recognized that he was happier than he'd ever thought he could be again.

Perfect moments never lasted. Alex rolled onto her side, covering a yawn. "Let's get up before we fall asleep again. It was kind of the sergeant to send out for meat pies to sustain us through questioning, but it wasn't much of a dinner. I'm ready for a bath followed by a stevedore's breakfast."

"So am I." Gavin suspected that the meat pies had been police recognition of their status—and the sergeant's gratitude that they hadn't used that status to be difficult.

She swung from the bed, her expression turning serious. "I know the East End is supposed to be dangerous, but I'd always felt safe around the warehouse. Foolish of me. So close to the docks, I suppose thieves and drunken sailors are to be expected."

"There was nothing random about the attack on us. Or rather, on me."

She frowned as she pulled on a robe over her nightgown. "That's right—the man who attacked first said that you were 'the one.' Why do you think he said that?"

"Just a moment." Gavin stepped into his own bedroom to don his robe and collect the dice he'd found on the street. Returning to Alex, he dropped the dice into her hand. "These were thrown at me."

She gasped. "Maduri twelve-sided dice! But why?"

"My guess is that they were a cryptic calling card to be found by my dead body, with only the man who wanted me dead knowing the meaning."

"Would Sultan Kasan send men halfway around the world to kill you? If he'd wanted your death, he could have had you executed in Maduri."

"My thoughts exactly. It's probably someone else, but I don't know who." He retrieved the dice and studied the familiar symbols, which had led him to where he was today. "Perhaps Cousin Philip wanted to regain the title, or Barton Pierce has turned lethal with his resentment, or your possessive former suitor wanted to widow you again so he'd have another chance to win your favor."

Alex shuddered. "What a range of possibilities."

"Probably all of them wrong, with the truth something entirely different." He dropped the dice in his pocket, wishing he could turn this over to the police, but there was nothing solid to offer those sober, literal-minded gentlemen.

"Do you think I'm in danger also?"

He wanted to lie, but she was safer knowing the truth. "It's possible. They might not have wanted you left alive as a witness to murder." When she shivered, he said quietly, "I'm sorry, Alex. It never occurred to me that I might bring danger on you."

Her gaze was level. "On the contrary, I brought this on you. If not for rescuing me, you'd surely have left Maduri without making enemies."

"Perhaps. Whatever the reason for the attack, we need to take precautions. In the future I'll be armed, and I don't want you going anywhere alone."

After she nodded agreement, he girded himself for a suggestion she would not like. "I think it's best if you don't work at the office until this is settled."

Her cooperation vanished. "Will you stop going to the office?"

"No, though I guarantee I won't be working late."

"So you can risk your life, but I can't?" Her brows arched ironically. "If the warehouse district is unsafe for me, it is for you as well. More so, since you were the target of the attack."

He clamped down on his exasperation. "I don't want either of us taking unnecessary risks. I need to work at the office most days until Peter Spears is fully trained, but your estate work can easily be done at home, and this area is far safer. Hired thugs like those who attacked last night would stand out like camels in Mayfair."

Her eyes narrowed. "I won't be kept prisoner in my own home, Gavin, nor will I let my life be run by fear. If you can risk the East End, so can I."

"Damnation, Alex, I won't allow you"—he didn't realize he was shouting until the door opened and Daisy appeared with Alex's morning tea tray. Looking frightened, the girl stammered an apology and started to withdraw.

Gavin drew a deep breath. "It's all right to come in, Daisy. We were just having a discussion, but I'm sure my wife would rather have her tea." To Alex he said, "I'm sorry for losing my temper. We can discuss this after breakfast."

After she nodded, he withdrew to his own room, shaken by the way he'd exploded. His even temper was legendary among the men he worked with, but he was discovering that where Alex's safety was involved, he had a very short fuse. Last night he'd killed two men with his bare hands because she was threatened, and this morning the mere thought of her in danger had made common sense go out the window. He'd probably only strengthened her determination to put herself at risk.

When Alex's mother had asked if he loved her daughter, he hadn't known how to reply, but the weeks since they arrived in London had clarified his emotions. Because he'd thought his heart had died with Helena, he hadn't recognized that he was gradually falling in love with Alex. He wouldn't—couldn't—compare her with Helena; they were too different. But day by day, Alex had won him with her courage, her directness, her kindness, and her passion.

He loved his wife—and he couldn't bear the thought of losing her.

Alex stared blindly at her mirror, trembling a little. To think she'd believed life in England would be blessedly peaceful. In less than twenty-four hours she'd discovered an inner darkness she'd never suspected, come close to being murdered, and had her first fight with her husband. She hadn't realized how completely she'd come to rely on Gavin's steady temper and support. Having him angry with her was deeply disturbing.

"My lady, are you all right?" Daisy asked worriedly.

Alex wondered if the girl's experiences made her fear that Gavin might turn violent. Pulling herself together, she took a steaming cup of tea from the tray. "I'm fine. My husband and I merely had a minor disagreement."

Without further comment, the maid began to pick up the previous day's garments, which had been thrown over the sofa when

Alex returned from the police station too tired to ring for her maid. Daisy wore a simple but elegant dress that she'd sewn from a length of rose-colored linen Alex had given her. She had a natural sense of style that a professional dressmaker would envy. But she hadn't lost the anxiety that she'd had from the beginning. She usually looked on the verge of tears.

Alex asked, "Are you happy in this house, Daisy?"

The girl looked startled at the question. "Everyone has been most kind, my lady. I've never known such kindness."

And obviously she didn't know how to react to kindness. "How are the reading lessons going?"

Daisy's face lit with genuine pleasure. "Miss Hailey is a wonderful teacher. She says she's never had a student learn so fast. Yesterday I read a chapter of one of Miss Katie's books all by myself." She paused, then added conscientiously, "Miss Hailey helped with words I didn't know."

"I'm so glad," Alex said warmly. "My mother taught me to read. I remember her telling me that reading was the golden road to anywhere one wants to go."

"The golden road," Daisy repeated thoughtfully. "That's why slaves aren't allowed to read. Because the masters don't want them to learn to dream."

The quiet statement was chilling. Throat tight, Alex asked, "How did you bear slavery, Daisy? You're so bright and attractive—in a just world, you would have had so many more opportunities."

"Being attractive is no blessing for a slave girl, ma'am," the maid said bitterly. "Nor is intelligence. Because of that, Miss Amanda had me brought from the fields to the big house to train as a maid. Because she didn't like the way slaves talked, she made me learn to talk white, and whipped me when I made mistakes. As to being attractive—" She swallowed hard. "Miss Amanda's husband thought so. That's why she had me sold away from the plantation and my family."

"Oh, Daisy!" Alex stared at her, horrified. Her own experience of slavery gave her a visceral understanding of what the maid was saying—and not saying. "Slavery is *evil.* An affront to God and all that is best in mankind. I'm doing what I can to fight it, and will for the rest of my life."

"That's very good of you, ma'am." Daisy was polite, but her expression suggested that she thought Alex meant contributing a little money to the Anti-Slavery Society now and then.

A thought struck Alex. "Please don't discuss what I'm about to say because it's potentially dangerous, but I'm seeking information that might help the Royal Navy block illegal smuggling of slaves between Africa and the Americas. Do you know anyone who might have such information? Or who might be willing to listen and collect scraps and bits of conversation in sailors' taverns?"

"My lady, don't have anything to do with slavers!" Daisy gasped. "They're too dangerous."

Alex wondered what horrible experience had created such vehemence. "Yes, which is why they need to be stopped. Do you know anyone who might be able to help?"

Daisy's dark face grayed, as if some inner battle was taking place. After a long silence, she said reluctantly, "I might know someone. I would need to leave the house for several hours to find him."

"You have my permission to do so. And

thank you for the attempt." Alex finished her tea with satisfaction. Daisy's friend might open a whole new line of information, perhaps even imprison a slaver. That was worth a little risk.

# CHAPTER 31

Gavin loved the business of tea, which was why he found comfort in moving through his dimly lit warehouse. The previous night's attack had left him with the same restiveness he felt at sea, when he sensed a gathering storm but didn't know when or how it would strike.

The warehouse was a sanctuary of peace and order by comparison. He walked along quiet aisles between tall stacks of tea chests, occasionally touching one of the bright illustrations that had been painted on the chests by factory artists in China. One stack was delicate Young Hyson while the next was partially fermented Oolong, known in Chinese as the "black dragon." There was smoky Lapsang Souchong, sturdy Congou, popular Pekoe, and many more, each with its own character. He'd learned every step of the process from the planting of tea bushes by peasants through the harvesting, processing, and packing that allowed the blessed leaf to travel halfway around the world to soothe harried Westerners.

He paused at the huge section of Earl's Blend tea, which was mixed secretly in Canton with exact proportions of tea and bergamot peel to give a clean, fruity taste. He couldn't think of the tea without thinking of Kyle, who'd developed the blend. Gavin had been lucky the day a casual encounter began what turned into a rewarding personal and business relationship. A pity Kyle was at his country estate. It would be good to discuss the situation with him.

Kyle had chosen well when he leased this building. Like all the London Dock warehouses, it was built over the famous wine vaults which stretched for acres, but the structure was spacious and secure, and being located right on the dock simplified the transfer of goods from ships to storage. The warehouse was almost full now, chests of tea stacked almost to the ceiling. The stock would gradually diminish until early next summer, when new shipments would begin to arrive.

Though the company offices directly overhead had only a faint fragrance of tea, the scent was powerful in the warehouse. Too strong for some, but Gavin didn't mind. Tea had been very good to him. So had silk, spices, and porcelain. Each commodity had its section of the warehouse, but tea was the foundation of Elliott House.

After the London office was running smoothly under Peter Spears' management, Gavin would launch something new—an elegant teahouse where busy people could stop and sample different brews and have light meals in pleasant surroundings. After that was a success, he'd open more. A place where ladies would be comfortable. He had his eye on a couple of possible locations in the fashionable West End. The teahouses would be called, naturally, Elliott House.

"Hoping the tea will speak to you?"

Suryo's quiet voice pulled Gavin from his musings back to the present. Suryo's office was on this level, and was the ultimate goal of Gavin's warehouse wanderings. He turned to his friend. "I suppose so, but the tea isn't being very helpful. You've heard that my wife and I were attacked in the street outside?"

Suryo nodded. "And that *pentjak silat* came to your aid."

"If you hadn't trained me so well I'd be dead, and perhaps Alex as well." Gavin sighed. "But I didn't intend to kill two of them."

"You were protecting your wife. What man would do less?" Suryo's gaze became distant. "Killing a man with one's own hands is . . . disturbing. But they are no less dead when killed by cannon, as the *Helena* did to the pirates in the Indian Ocean."

As always, Suryo's calm sense helped put things in perspective. Gavin pulled the Maduri dice from his pocket and tossed them to his friend. "One of the attackers threw these at me. Any thoughts about who connected with Maduri wants me dead?"

Suryo caught the dice, expression grave. "Not Sultan Kasan, I think. The connection to Maduri might be important, or it might not. Though only you and I and your lady know the truth of what happened there, the fact that you visited Maduri and found her there is known. The dice could have been brought from the island by a member of the *Helena*'s crew and given to someone here, then used last night for misdirection." He handed the dice back. "There are many possible explanations."

Unfortunately true. Gavin considered the possibilities he'd suggested to Alex. Though he'd included her disappointed suitor, Major Colwell, hiring thugs seemed too complicated for a soldier. Colwell was the sort to try to force a duel. Philip Elliott was a more convincing prospect. He was clever enough, and still unreconciled to losing the Seabourne honors, but his disappointment didn't seem homicidal.

"I'd love to trace the murder attempt back to Barton Pierce, but I can't imagine a motive," Gavin said. "Though he's always disliked me, he's sane enough, and he certainly has no reason to kill me. I'm no threat to him, and I can't imagine him risking everything he's built to kill a man unnecessarily."

Suryo nodded agreement. "I shall listen in

the taverns to see if there are any whispers about the attackers who escaped."

"Thank you." That reminded Gavin of what Alex had mentioned. "By the way, I understand you've been recruited as Alex's chief investigator into illegal slaving. For God's sake, be careful."

"I am. You and your lady must be also."

"I'm taking precautions." From now on, he would always have his kris concealed on him, and when he went out he carried a swordstick. A pity he hadn't had either the night before. "Do you think your investigations might have anything to do with the attack?"

Suryo considered, then shook his head. "I'm sure no one knows what I am doing, or it would have been my life that was threatened."

Gavin nodded, having reached the same conclusion. "I've asked my wife not to come down here until the danger is past. She agreed to stay home today, but I foresee arguments ahead."

Suryo gave his rare smile. "She is a lady of rare independence."

And it was a mixed blessing.

*    *    *

Katie stared down at her embroidery. "Why must I learn to do needlework when I hate it, and you admit that you hate it, too?"

"Because doing things we hate is good discipline," Alex said, only half in jest. "Also, a woman needs to have some basic skill with a needle. It could be worse. It hasn't been that long since the lady of the house had to spin her own yarn and weave her own cloth. Some women still do."

"Could I shear the sheep?" Katie asked hopefully. "I like sheep."

Alex considered. "It takes a lot of strength to shear sheep, since they protest energetically. But next spring we can find some sheep that are being sheared and at least watch while it's done."

"Promise?"

"I promise." The colonel's estate had sheep. Going for the spring shearing would be an excuse to visit. Alex quite liked watching sheep herself.

Daisy entered the small sitting room, saw Katie, and started to withdraw. Noticing the maid's tense expression, Alex said, "Do you need to speak to me, Daisy?"

"Yes, ma'am, when you're free."

Alex said to her daughter, "Perhaps it's

time you checked the kitchen to see what's being baked?"

"Oh, yes!" Rescued from further embroidery, Katie bounced from the room after giving Daisy a grateful smile.

When Katie was safely away, Daisy said, "I found my friend. He knows things that can help you."

"Excellent! What does he say?"

Daisy stared at the floor. "He works in a tavern near the docks. Like me, he is American, a slave who escaped to Canada and then came here. He says he can name one of England's greatest slavers—a man who is respectable on the surface, but operates several slave ships. My friend wants to expose the devil for what he is, but who would listen to a poor black man?"

"I will listen, and I know men who will listen to me." Alex wondered if the "friend" was Daisy's sweetheart. Perhaps. The girl never talked about her private life, or the time she'd spent as Frederica Pierce's slave. Alex never pressed her. Daisy deserved, and needed, privacy.

"He says he'll meet you this evening." Daisy gave a quick darting glance. "Somewhere near the docks."

"So soon?" Alex echoed, surprised.

Daisy moistened her lips nervously. "He is frightened and might change his mind if too much time passes."

Alex could understand that, and she didn't want to lose a potentially valuable informant. On the other hand, after the previous night's attack she wasn't going to set foot in a waterfront tavern. "Will he meet Seabourne and me at Elliott House?"

Daisy hesitated. "I think he would go there. It is not far from where he works. But you must be alone. He will not talk to a white man."

"What about if I brought Suryo?" The Islander wasn't African, but he was also not white, and his quiet presence was unthreatening.

"Mr. Suryo?" Daisy looked dismayed. "No, only you, and only because you . . . you helped me." Her voice broke. "I will tell him to come early evening, after the office is closed, but before it is dark and the tavern gets busy."

Making a quick decision, Alex said, "Very well, if he will come to the Elliott House office at six-thirty this evening, I will be there alone." She would have the younger groom drive her there in the small carriage, with orders to pick her up again at the door an hour later. Gavin wouldn't like it, but he wouldn't know until later—they'd probably pass each other coming and going. It should be safe enough.

And if it wasn't—she would not be defenseless.

Gavin cleared all his employees from the offices and the warehouse a little early, so they could leave in groups. Though he knew he was being over-cautious, his instincts were itching. He'd alternated his day between planning security precautions and trying to imagine who might want to destroy him. The first question had been fairly straightforward, but the second still baffled him. All he could do was try to ensure that none of his family or employees became innocent victims of violence.

Yearning to talk to Alex, he rang for the butler and asked where she was as soon as he arrived home. Bard said, "Her ladyship has gone out, but she left you this note."

Gavin opened it, wondering why she was out of the house at this hour. *Dear Gavin—I shall be an hour or so late to dinner because*

*I must meet a man at the Elliott House offices. He claims to have important information about slaving. Don't worry, I'm not being the least bit reckless. I'll explain it all when I get home. Love, Iskandra.*

He swore with a sailor's fluency as his vague forebodings crystallized. Bard looked shocked, never having seen any signs of temper from him before. "Tell the cook that dinner will be delayed indefinitely," Gavin snapped. "I'm going to retrieve her ladyship."

He spun on his heel and headed back to the stables. Riding would be faster than driving a carriage at this hour, so he ordered a horse saddled. He'd been riding regularly, so he no longer worried about controlling his mount on crowded city streets.

By the time he finished the long ride from Mayfair to the East End, his temper was simmering on the edge of explosion. The street in front of the warehouse was quiet but not deserted as it would be later. He beckoned to a loitering boy who didn't look too larcenous. "Are you afraid of horses?"

"No, *sir!*" the boy said indignantly.

"Very good." Gavin handed over a half crown and the reins. "There's another half crown for you if you'll hold my horse for a few minutes."

"Yes, sir!"

"Thank you. I'll include a piece of advice for free. Don't ever get married."

Gavin tried the door to the warehouse, swearing when he found it unlocked. Why had he been fool enough to give Alex a key to the building?

Because she was his wife and he trusted her honesty. It was her judgment he had doubts about.

The staircase to the offices led up the left side of the building. He took the steps three at a time and strode into the offices, braced for an argument.

Dressed as demurely as a Quaker except for the Paisley shawl around her shoulders, Alex was quietly working at the junior clerk's desk, which had a clear view of the door. She glanced up at his entrance. "You're quick. I thought I'd be done before you could get here."

Her calm acceptance threatened to push his temper over the edge. "For heaven's sake, Alex, last night we were both nearly killed right outside on the street! What possessed you to come here alone?"

"I didn't come alone—the second groom drove me here and will pick me up again in just under an hour. And if trouble shows up . . ." Suddenly she was holding an elegant but businesslike pocket pistol. "I came prepared."

He blinked at the compact, two-barreled pistol, glad she knew guns well enough to automatically point it away from him. "At least you're showing common sense, but what is so important that you feel you have to do this?"

"A friend of Daisy's, a former slave, is coming in a few minutes. He says he can name one of Britain's leading slave runners. Wouldn't you take a risk to learn that?"

He hesitated. "I suppose I would. But if Katie did, would you stand by and not try to stop her?"

Alex was taken aback. "Of course not, but I'm not your child, Gavin. I'm your wife. I have the right to take a chance if the issue is important enough."

"For me, nothing is more important than your life," he said starkly.

Her expression softened. "No one could ask for a finer protector, Gavin. Ever since we've met, I've benefited from your strength and kindness and understanding. But at the moment, I need to act on my convictions more than I need protection. Perhaps Daisy's friend won't even come and I'll have wasted a trip, but I must do this." She glanced at a clock. "And you must leave right away. He'll be here any moment and Daisy says he won't talk in front of a white man. If you're still here, he might turn around and never come back. So please, *please,* leave before he arrives."

He hesitated, torn between his forebodings and Alex's plea.

"You understand so much, Gavin," she said softly. "Can't you understand this?"

He studied his tall, strong, composed wife. She'd worked hard to regain her courage and her belief in herself. Most women would willingly defer to his judgment and accept his protection—but she wasn't like most women, and that difference was what made her special.

Also maddening. "Very well, I'll leave and wait at the livery stable," he said reluctantly. "When your hour is up, the carriage and I will be back to take you home."

Her smile was radiant. "Thank you for understanding, Gavin."

"Just remember that I've lost one wife. I don't think I could bear to lose another." As he turned to go, he asked, "By the way, where did you get the pistol?"

"I borrowed it from Ashburton House. Now *go.*"

He obeyed, on the verge of turning back with every step. Outside he saw no sign of a black man. Maybe the fellow wouldn't come. But if he did, and his information was sound, Alex had the chance to make a real difference in the illegal slave trade. He prayed that would happen, and justify his present anxiety.

When he paid the boy another half crown for watching his horse, the lad said cheekily, "Your wife didn't listen?"

"Matters have been settled." He swung onto his horse and started down the street, knowing that Alex would surely be fine and he was worrying unnecessarily.

But he still felt goose-steps on his grave.

# CHAPTER 32

Daisy's friend was almost half an hour late. Hoping he hadn't seen Gavin and been frightened away, Alex continued to work and hope.

The footsteps were so quiet that she didn't realize someone was coming until the office door swung open. She glanced up—and realized with sick certainty that Gavin's fears had been justified when four men filed into the office, none of them an escaped slave. The first two were brutish, hard-bitten sailors. The third, a wiry man of the same type, was the attacker she'd kicked in the groin the night before.

The fourth was Sir Barton Pierce.

Though she'd met him only once, at the Ashburton ball, the fact that he was Gavin's enemy had emblazoned him on her mind. Under cover of her papers she lifted the pistol and concealed it in the folds of her shawl as she rose to greet her visitors.

"What an unexpected surprise. If you're looking for my husband, Sir Barton, he isn't here." She debated whether to say that Gavin and several servants would be arriving soon, then decided against it, since Pierce and his men might wait in ambush.

"I know he isn't. I saw him leave a few minutes ago." Pierce studied her critically. "You haven't half the looks of my Frederica, but I suppose all your fancy relatives made you worth marrying. They'll see that your husband doesn't marry again after his wife disappears, so he'll have no heir for his precious earldom."

She felt an icy chill. "I have no plans to disappear."

Pierce laughed as if this was a normal conversation. "You don't get a choice. Don't worry, you won't be hurt. Just come along quietly."

"There are always eyes watching in London." She glanced contemptuously at his villainous companions. "You and your men were seen coming in, and will be seen taking me out against my will."

"We didn't come in the front," Pierce said smugly. "I leased the warehouse next door under a false name. The buildings are connected, with only an old door nailed shut between the two spaces, so it was easy to get in here. No one saw us coming, and no one will see us going." His voice hardened. "Now get over here so we can gag you and tie your wrists, or I'll let my lads have some fun while they do it."

The wiry man growled, "I owe the bitch some rough handlin'." Though he was no taller than Alex, the viciousness in his gaze made her skin crawl. A pity she hadn't studied *pentjak silat* instead of *wing chun.* If she had, maybe she'd have broken his neck the evening before.

"Maybe later, Webb, there's no time for it now." Pierce glanced around the office. "Where is the cash kept? Be a pity to burn it up."

Burn? Alex realized that the scent of smoke was beginning to overpower the pervasive odor of tea. Pierce must have men setting fires in the warehouse below.

The business Gavin had worked so hard to establish here was going up in flames.

Her grip on the pistol tightened as she fought rising panic. She had two shots, but that wasn't enough against four men who were experienced fighters.

Get one of them out of the room. "There's a cashbox in Lord Seabourne's desk." She used the title deliberately and had the satisfaction of seeing Pierce scowl as he crossed the room to enter Gavin's office. Since she'd lied about the cashbox, he'd be busy looking for several minutes.

Webb crossed the room toward Alex. "Sly, Ned, give me a hand tyin' her up. The bitch fights dirty."

Three to one—her odds would not get any better. Alex raised the pistol and fired at Sly, who was closest. Seeing her weapon, he shouted and dodged to one side, grabbing at his arm with a curse when she pulled the trigger. The report was earnumbing in such close quarters.

One bullet left. She swung the pistol toward Webb and fired as he leaped at her. He gasped, a look of shock on his face. There was blood on his shirt and he swayed for a moment before lunging for her weapon.

He managed to grab the double barrel. Since the empty gun was useless to her, she let him have it. Darting around the desk and the wounded Webb, she raced for the door. If she could get to the stairs she had a chance. . . .

"Bitch!" Ned caught her arm and swung her around.

Before he could strike her, she jammed the heel of her hand into his throat, then twisted and kicked Sly, who was closing from the other side, blood streaming from his upper arm. Sly staggered as she smashed his knee, but he managed to stay on his feet and grab her other arm.

Pierce returned, drawn by the commotion. "Christ, can't you do anything right?" he roared at his men. "C'mon, the fires are spreading fast and we have to get out while the stairs are still safe. Take care of that damned woman!"

A blow smashed into the back of Alex's head. She had an instant to be glad that at least she would die fighting.

*Katie. Gavin.*

*Darkness . . .*

\*   \*   \*

Gavin paced around the livery stable yard while the younger Seabourne groom watched uneasily. Gavin had refrained from yelling at him since the groom had no reason not to obey Alex's orders, but a blind man would be aware of Gavin's displeasure.

He pulled out his watch. Only fifteen minutes until it was time to pick up Alex. "Is the curricle ready to go?"

"I'll check, my lord." Glad of an excuse to leave, the groom vanished into the back of the stable.

Fourteen minutes. Thirteen. Was it time to go? Not yet—the warehouse was only five minutes away, and Alex would not be happy if he frightened off her informant.

He tried to dismiss his increasing uneasiness. Maybe he was tense because of the heavy clouds that were rolling in, threatening the city with storms. Or perhaps it was because, as Alex had pointed out, he liked having everything under control, and this present situation wasn't.

Or maybe something really was wrong.

The boy who'd held Gavin's horse earlier stuck his head in the arch that led from the stable yard to the street. "Was that your warehouse you visited, mister?"

Gavin stared at him, his blood going cold. "Yes. Is something wrong?"

"It's on fire," the boy said cheerfully.

Gavin's forebodings blazed into a certainty of disaster. He swung into the saddle of his waiting horse, shouting, "Call the fire brigade!" to Fitzgerald, the stable's owner.

Recklessly he galloped down the Ratcliff Highway, then into the cross street that led toward the river. In the open air a column of smoke was visible to his right. As soon as he turned into the road that fronted the warehouses, he saw that the smoke was pouring from Elliott House. Praying Alex had made it outside safely, he raced toward the fire, not reining in until he risked trampling the onlookers drawn by disaster.

Abandoning his mount, he forced his way through the growing crowd. "My wife was in the building!" he shouted. "Has anyone seen her?"

A wizened man shook his head. "No one's gone in or out since you left."

No. *NO!* He stared at the flames, paralyzed by the horror of fire he'd had since the shipboard disaster when he was a young sailor.

But Alex was inside. Forcing the horror

down, he broke through the crowd that stayed a respectful distance from the fire, and sprinted toward the warehouse door. Since Alex had left it unlocked, he could be upstairs in seconds. Perhaps she was passed out on the floor. He could do this. He *had* to do this.

"Nay, lad." A huge stevedore tackled him, almost knocking him from his feet. "If she be in there, she's gone."

"God damn it, let me go!" Saturated with fear, Gavin fought to free himself of the stevedore's grip. "It's my *wife.* I have to get her."

The stevedore gave him a hard shake. "You're too late!"

Gavin was about to use a *pentjak* move when a thunderous crash shook the street. He whirled to see the warehouse roof collapsing. Flames and billows of smoke exploded upward with a hideous roar as the windows blew out, showering the street with hot glass and almost knocking Gavin and the stevedore down.

Gavin began to shake, refusing to accept what he was seeing. Alex couldn't be dead, she'd been perfectly healthy when he left her. She could easily have escaped in time.

"She must have jumped out a window on the river side before the building collapsed."

The stevedore eyed him pityingly. Not caring, Gavin worked his way through the crowd toward the end of this block of warehouses, where an alley led down to the river. His progress was blocked by the arrival of a fire engine. The London Fire Engine Establishment was funded by insurance companies, and its first priority was to prevent the flames from spreading to adjoining property.

The crew chief barked to his men as they pulled out the leather hose and connected to a fire plug. "This building and the one next door are gone, but there's time to save the rest of the block." Raising his voice, he shouted, "Free beer to anyone who helps with the pumping!"

A cheer went up, and within moments the pump handles were in place and volunteers were laboring to the rumbling chorus of "Beer-O! Beer-O!" The increased pressure blasted out a stream of water that created billows of hissing steam.

A second engine arrived as Gavin reached the alley that led to the river. Panting for breath, he cut down to the waterfront and looked along the river faces of the warehouses. Elliott House had partially collapsed, spilling fiery bricks over the loading dock and into the water. He gazed at the inferno his warehouse had become, bizarrely remembering that unclaimed tea wasn't destroyed in the Customs incinerator because it burned so fiercely that the official chimney had been set ablaze.

But Alex still could have escaped the building on this side before the fire got out of control. Perhaps she was looking for him at the livery stable. He returned to the scene of the firefighting, searching the crowd, checking the stable, asking again and again if anyone had seen her.

Not a trace.

As he returned from the stable, the threatened storm broke with a deafening barrage of thunder. The skies opened and rain poured onto the fire, far more effective than the three fire engines now on the scene. The first wave of volunteers had tired and gone off to enjoy their beer, so he began to pump, working until his back ached and his hands blistered, brusquely refusing offers to relieve him.

The thunderstorm passed but a cold,

steady rain continued, driving away most of the spectators. When the last flames hissed into extinction, a man touched Gavin's arm. "It's time to go home, my lord."

Gavin glanced back and saw a vaguely familiar face. With effort, he remembered the constable who had helped the night before. Only the night before? "I can't leave, Constable Mayne. My wife is inside. I . . . I . . . can't leave her."

"She's not there anymore, sir," was the quiet answer.

Trembling in every muscle, Gavin stared at the blackened ruins, no longer able to deny what had happened. "She's gone, and it's my fault," he said in a rasping whisper.

Because a person was presumed lost, members of the brigade began searching the ruins when the rain had cooled the rubble enough for safety. Gavin tried to volunteer, but the fire chief flatly refused. "You're not dressed nor trained for this, my lord. It would be worth my job to let you help."

So he waited through the rest of the endless night. Dawn was breaking in the east when the fire chief came to him. "We've found a body, sir."

"Let me see her." Gavin started toward the blackened shell of the building.

"No." The chief was blocking his way, and so was Constable Mayne. "There's . . . not much to see. Just enough to identify the remains as human. Your wife was a tall woman?"

The top of her head was level with his cheekbone. *Alex, damn you, why didn't you listen?* He drew a shuddering breath. "Yes, she is . . . was . . . tall."

Another member of the brigade approached with a blackened object. "We found this by the body. Was it your wife's?" He handed over a blackened metal object.

Gavin recognized the filthy, twisted remains of Alex's elegant pocket pistol. The heat had completely burned away the wooden grip, leaving only the warped double barrel. The last flicker of hope died. "Yes." His hand convulsively gripped the metal. "Yes, this was hers." *And may God have mercy on her indomitable soul.*

Gavin was barely aware when the Seabourne groom urged him into the curricle and drove home, Gavin's horse tethered behind. London was waking to sunny, rain-swept skies by the time they reached Berkeley Square. When Gavin stumbled wearily from the curricle, a maid scrubbing the steps looked up and gasped at the sight of him.

He found out why when he stepped inside and caught a glimpse of a gaunt-eyed stranger in the mirror. His clothes were still wet from the rain and bore charred spots from embers, he was smudged with soot, and he looked like . . . like a man who had just lost the woman he loved.

Bard approached soundlessly, looking less impeccable than usual. Apparently the bad news had reached the household. "What are your orders, Lord Seabourne?"

Gavin struggled to think of what must be done. "Send a footman to Ashburton House with word of her ladyship's d . . . death so her parents and the Ashburtons can be notified." Other people needed to know, but so many were out of London. He brushed that aside for later, too exhausted to think about it now.

The butler nodded gravely. "Shall I have a bath prepared for you?"

"I must talk to Miss Katie."

The butler looked ill, but not as ill as

Gavin felt as he climbed the steps to the nursery. Katie was breakfasting in the nursery with Miss Hailey when Gavin entered. Her swift smile faltered when she saw his condition. "Captain?" she said uneasily.

The sight of her small face, Alex in miniature with sunny blond hair, shattered his heart all over again. "Katie—" His voice broke and he stopped to compose himself. "There's . . . very bad news. A fire at the Elliott House warehouse. Your mother was working there, and . . . and she didn't escape in time."

"No," Katie cried as she slid from her chair, her aqua eyes huge. "No, Mama can't be dead, too. She *can't!*"

"I'm so sorry, Katie." If only he could have died in Alex's place, anything rather than have to tell her daughter what had happened.

Katie dissolved into wrenching sobs. He knelt and embraced her, fighting his own tears as he told her that she was safe and loved and would always have him, and that her mother had died heroically.

They stayed together until he felt a gentle hand on his shoulder. He looked up to see his aunt, Lady Jane Holland. "Mr. Suryo brought me the terrible news," she said softly. "You must rest, Gavin. Miss Hailey and I will take care of Katie."

Numbly he rose and let Katie go into Lady Jane's sheltering, maternal arms. Downstairs he avoided Alex's room with its excruciating memories of joy in favor of his own bland room. Heedless of his filthy clothes, he collapsed on the bed and slept with dreamless exhaustion.

When he awoke, it was evening again. He lay on his back staring blindly at the ceiling. After Helena's death he'd thought he could never feel such anguish again, but he was wrong. Apparently the ability to suffer never diminished.

He tried to order his thoughts for practical matters. Making the insurance claim, finding new offices, ensuring that his employees were taken care of.

What about the funeral? No decisions could be made before her parents arrived from Wales, which would be at least three or four days. Quite possibly they would want to take Alex's body home to rest among the peaceful Welsh hills.

He dreaded facing the Kenyons. He'd

pledged to take care of Alex, and he'd failed. As he swung his feet to the floor, he realized her parents might insist on taking Katie. Much as he wanted to keep her, he wasn't sure he had the legal right, and she might be happier with her grandparents and the young niece who was almost a sister.

He rubbed his forehead, smearing soot. A day earlier Alex had been alive. If he'd followed his instincts and refused to let her meet that stranger alone, she'd be alive still.

For the first time, he wondered what had happened. Neither the fire nor Alex's death were accidental. Had her visitor hoped for an easy robbery and ended by killing her because she resisted, then set the warehouse on fire to cover up his crime? Had the man had accomplices?

It was time to talk to the woman who had arranged that fatal meeting. He rang for a bath and asked that Daisy come speak with him. While he washed and made himself presentable, the house was searched from top to bottom.

Daisy Adams was gone.

Gavin was trying to make himself eat a late supper when Bard entered the room.

"There are two men here who say they must speak with you."

"I don't want to talk to anyone."

The butler said awkwardly, "They're from the Metropolitan Police, my lord."

Wondering if the police had information about the cause of the fire, he abandoned his supper. Waiting in the drawing room were a poker-faced Constable Mayne and a man who looked like a higher ranking police officer. The latter said, "I'm Superintendent Blake of the Metropolitan Police. You are Gavin Elliott, seventh Earl of Seabourne?"

"I am. Have you learned something more about how the fire started? I believe it was no accident."

He was about to tell about Alex's meeting when Blake caught his gaze. "My lord, it is my duty to charge you with the murder of your wife, Alexandra Elliott, the Countess of Seabourne."

# CHAPTER 33

Head throbbing with agony, Alex fell through nightmares of fire, pain, and nausea. Shimmering eastern seas faded into the cool northern skies of home, then dissolved into terror. She heard voices, but couldn't concentrate enough to understand the words. Coarse, profane men. A woman's soft but chilling tones. Blankets wrapped around her because she was shivering, clumsy attempts to spoon water or broth into her mouth, exclamations of disgust when she vomited bile.

Finally the world remained steady when she opened her eyes. She was lying on a cot with not quite enough blankets to cut the damp chill. A single candle revealed that she was in a stone vault. High above, strange masses of a gray, soft material like cotton wool hung from a shadowy brick ceiling. The silence was absolute, and the air thickly oppressive.

She rolled her head and saw that an archway separated her cell from a stone passage, but the exit was barred by a grid of shiny new iron bars that included a massive padlocked door. On the opposite side of the passage was an arch like the one into Alex's cell, only without bars and with several huge casks stacked inside.

She closed her eyes, trying to remember where she was and what had happened. When she was knocked unconscious by pirates, she had experienced violent headaches and nausea, but surely that was long over? She and Katie had returned safely to England.

*Gavin.* Memories of him slowly formed, including his anger because . . . ? Because she'd insisted on meeting a man about slave traders. She rubbed her head, trying to ease the ache. Four men had come, including Sir Barton Pierce, and she thought she had died, but apparently not, unless hell was a good deal colder than its reputation.

"Is our sleeping countess awake?" a dulcet voice cooed.

Alex turned her head on the cot and saw Frederica Pierce approaching with a lantern. She wore a blue velvet cloak that emphasized her angelic blond beauty, and was followed by a stolid man carrying a tray.

Alex sighed, hardly even surprised. Since Barton Pierce had been there when she was knocked out, it made sense for his wife to be here now. "Be careful, Frederica." Alex stopped, shocked by the raspy weakness of her voice. She swallowed and tried again. "You'll get that fine cloak filthy."

"It's worth it." A straight wooden chair stood outside the cell. Frederica sat down and carefully arranged the folds of her cloak while her attendant knelt by the iron bars and slid the tray of food into the cell. A narrow opening had been left at the bottom of the bars for precisely that purpose so the door needn't be opened to feed her.

At a disadvantage lying down, Alex managed to push herself to a sitting position. When her head stopped whirling, she swung her feet to the floor. The stones were cold and slightly sticky. "How long have I been here?"

"Four days. At first I feared that knock on the head might kill you, but you have the toughness of an Irish peasant." It was not a compliment.

Alex wrapped the blankets around her shivering body. "Why didn't you kill me outright? It would have been simpler than bringing me to this place." Unless they wanted to torture her. At the moment, she would believe anything.

"I have a much better plan than killing you, Alexandra." Frederica fixed Alex with a bright-eyed glance. "Barton was the one who arranged the ambush to get rid of you and your husband, but Seabourne fought well. We lost two good men that night."

Remembering that Gavin had believed Pierce had no motive for killing, Alex asked, "Why did your husband want us dead? He and Seabourne don't like each other, but that's a long way from murder."

"You think so? We have no shortage of reasons. To begin with, Barton 'lent' a substantial sum to your husband's cousin in order to get Seabourne sponsorship for a seat in Parliament. Since Philip Elliott lost the earldom, Barton may never recover all he gave to that worthless gamester."

"That's hardly my husband's fault," Alex pointed out. "Becoming an earl was a complete surprise to him."

"So he claims." Frederica's delicate features turned hard. "Barton was angered at the loss of his investment, but he has secured another lord's influence so he'll have his seat after the next election. Seabourne's unforgivable crime was telling Sultan Kasan not to use Barton as Maduri's exclusive Western agent. Do you have any idea how much that cost us? Tens of thousands of pounds a year! The news of your husband's viciousness reached Barton last week from his agent in Singapore. That was when Barton decided that Seabourne must be punished."

The news jolted Alex. To a man like Pierce, being denied a contract that would generate great wealth was indeed a motive for vengeance. Strange to think that Gavin's warning to a ruler half a world away could have such repercussions.

Interesting though it might be to learn the Pierces' motives, what mattered was now.

Bracing herself, she asked, "Is Seabourne dead?"

"Not yet. Barton intended another attack, this time with guns, but then I learned from Daisy about your passion for fighting slavery. She's fairly quick, for a slave. She realized you could be manipulated with your naïve idealism."

The young woman Alex had freed from slavery had betrayed her benefactors? "So Daisy was a spy."

Frederica nodded. "After you made that nasty scene at Hatchard's, I realized it was a perfect opportunity to place her near you. You'd be so proud of yourself for 'saving' that stupid slave that she would have the run of your household."

Alex remembered how Daisy had begged to be allowed to serve her, even if as a scullery maid. So much for gratitude. "Why did Daisy do it? Did you offer her a bonus for betrayal? I have trouble believing she's that devoted to you."

Frederica shrugged. "The slut was increasing when she left America. It was a great nuisance to have a pregnant maid, but Daisy is very good with hair and cosmetics, so I tolerated it. I even let her keep the baby as long as he caused no trouble. Since Daisy was reluctant to pretend she was an escaping slave, I had her child sent to Barton's country place. Daisy was obedient enough after that."

Alex gasped at the cold-blooded cruelty of it. What an impossible dilemma for a mother! No wonder Daisy had done what her first mistress had demanded—and no wonder she always looked distressed and couldn't meet Alex's gaze. "Having obeyed you so well, has Daisy been reunited with her child?"

"Yes, I sent her to the country as well. It seemed best she leave London after the role she played in trapping you and your husband. It wouldn't do to have the police question her—she might panic and let the truth slip." Frederica frowned. "I really can't have her back as a maid, but she cost Barton a huge amount. Perhaps it's best to sell her back in America. The child might bring a bit extra. He's quite a robust little beast."

Alex's empty stomach turned. She couldn't blame Daisy for following Frederica's orders, but if only the girl had revealed the truth to her new employers! Alex and Gavin could surely have found a way to retrieve the little boy so they'd both be free. But Daisy had no reason to trust in the goodwill of people she'd been sent to spy on, and now they were all in trouble.

Remembering that Gavin had also been "trapped," Alex asked, "Is Seabourne imprisoned in this place?"

"Much better than that." Frederica smiled with malicious satisfaction. "He's in the Tower of London awaiting trial for your murder."

Alex gasped. "How can that be when I'm not dead?"

"Divine intervention, I think." Frederica paused reflectively. "My husband and I make a wonderful team. Together we're stronger, cleverer, and luckier than either of us alone. Though Barton is shrewd and masculine and forceful, he lacks subtlety. I was the one who realized that kidnapping you would be a far better punishment for both of you. Since your husband couldn't remarry for at least seven years, he wouldn't be able to get himself an heir. Even better, your grand relatives would surely blame him for your disappearance and make him a pariah in London society. That is infinitely more satisfying than merely killing him."

To socially ambitious people like the Pierces, being ostracized probably did sound like a fate worse than death. Apparently it hadn't occurred to them that Gavin might have different values. "I fail to see where divine intervention comes in."

"That happened when you killed Barton's man, Webb."

Alex stared. "I killed someone?"

"You don't remember? You shot him in the chest. Because the fire they set was spreading so quickly, Barton and his men abandoned Webb, who was dying anyhow, and took you out instead. The fire burned so fiercely that afterward it was impossible to identify the remains." Frederica shrugged again. "Webb was about your height, and he was found with your pistol. Since they expected to find your body, that's what they saw. Honestly, I couldn't have planned this better myself. Such a lucky set of accidents."

*Folie à deux,* the madness of two. As Alex stared at Frederica's bright, demented eyes, she finally understood the meaning of the French phrase. Separately, Barton was vindictive but sane, while Frederica was spiteful and unbalanced but not murderous. Together, they urged each other into actions that neither would have considered alone.

She could easily imagine the two of them discussing their "enemies," magnifying their grievances until they convinced themselves murder was justified. With Frederica as his Lady Macbeth, Pierce had efficiently arranged this convoluted "punishment."

"Am I to spend the rest of my life here?" Alex surveyed the cold, gray stone. Something scuttled in the shadows.

"I was tempted, but it would be a great nuisance to have to bring food here forever. I have better uses for my servants' time. You'll stay through your husband's trial, and I shall come regularly to describe how badly he is faring. There's a very good case against him, and it's likely he'll hang."

Alex's heart sank. "There can't be any real evidence against Seabourne."

"There is plenty, but if he does manage to escape the hangman, Barton will have him shot. It will be assumed that one of your grief-stricken relatives decided to take revenge for the loss of your innocent life. Your stepfather, for example—there is already betting in the clubs that he might kill Seabourne." Frederica cocked her head to one side. "It's being whispered that there's something not quite fatherly in Lord Michael's affection for you. Did you marry a man who took you all the way to Australia to escape your stepfather's advances?"

Only the knowledge that fury would gratify the other woman saved Alex from trying to strike through the bars. "Pure nonsense—no man married to my mother would ever look elsewhere. My stepfather is naturally protective of his family, but he's also fair-minded and he likes Gavin. There will be no murder done."

"Probably you're right," Frederica said with regret. "But one can hope."

"What happens to me after the trial? A knife in the ribs and a drop in the river?"

Frederica smiled with bone-chilling malevolence. "Because you're so interested in the subject, one of Barton's ships will take you to the Barbary Coast, and you can spend the rest of your life studying slavery firsthand."

Horror paralyzed Alex. As she stared at Frederica's pale green eyes, she realized that the other woman had unerringly recognized Alex's greatest fear. Struggling to contain her panic at the thought of being returned to slavery, she said, "At least it will be warmer in North Africa than here."

Frederica's lips thinned. "Alexandra, you really are amazing. Such a pity you weren't born a man. If you had been, I'd have liked to bed you. You're nowhere near as appealing as a woman." Her gaze went to the candle burning in the corner of Alex's cell. "Shall I take that and see how you enjoy the darkness?"

Alex tried not to think of the creature she'd glimpsed in the shadows. "Naturally I'd prefer the light, but I can manage without." Wanting to turn Frederica's thoughts from the candle, she continued, "Where am I? I've never seen a place like this."

"You've never been in the London Docks' wine cellars?" Frederica asked with surprise. "There are four official Customs vaults, the largest covering a full twelve acres. They extend under the docks and nearby streets." She gestured toward the cotton wool-like substance hanging from the ceiling. "They say this fungus grows only here, where the temperature and damp are perfect for storing wine."

Wine vaults? She became aware that the oppressive atmosphere had a cloying, winy sweetness. "If I'm in a Customs' wine cellar, surely it's only a matter of time until someone comes by."

"No such luck, darling. This vault was built at the same time and is directly adjacent, but it's smaller and has always been in private hands. A few months ago Barton decided to expand into the wine trade, so he bought the vault and its contents. No one comes here but us. Barton didn't realize it would make such a splendid dungeon, but I saw the possibilities immediately."

Frederica rose and fastidiously shook the dust from the hem of her cloak. "I'll let you keep the candle and have one brought every day with your food. It would be quite unkind to leave you here in the dark. *Au revoir,* Alexandra. Look out for the rats."

Frederica and her man left, leaving Alex alone with the feeble light of the candle, which would never last until the next day. No longer needing to conceal her despair, Alex buried her aching head in her hands, shaking all over. Dear God, what had she done to be condemned over and over again to captivity?

As a child she'd been briefly kidnapped by her mother's ghastly cousin, and as an adult she'd been taken into slavery. Now it appeared that she was doomed to die in slavery in still another alien land, since there would be no Gavin to rescue her. One didn't have that much luck twice.

She'd kill herself before living in slavery again. It wouldn't be hard. . . .

*No.* Someday she might become that desperate, but for now she was alive and in England. If Frederica had been telling the truth—and there had been a ghastly plausibility to her words—Gavin would be on trial for his life. A case this scandalous would come to trial relatively soon, but it would still take several weeks. Time enough for Alex to find a way out of this damnable prison.

Which meant she had no time to waste on self-pity. Trying not to imagine her family's grief at her supposed death, she got to her feet. After a frightening spell of dizziness, she crossed the cell and picked up the tray of food. She'd need all her strength, and that meant eating.

After sitting down on her cot again, she found a lidded bowl full of thick vegetable soup. Though tepid, the flavor wasn't bad. With half a loaf of bread and a chunk of cheese, she had a substantial meal. There was also a pot of cooling tea. She drank it greedily, craving the stimulation.

She guessed the food might be from a laborers' tavern. If future meals were as good, she needn't worry about starvation.

Since her stomach was still queasy, she put the tray aside for later, hoping the food didn't attract rats.

*"Mrrowr?"*

Startled, Alex looked up as a tomcat squeezed between the bars of her cell. The large, tough-looking tabby fixed his gaze on the remaining food and meowed again.

"Come here, sweetheart." Smiling, Alex broke off a chunk of the cheese and set it on the floor. She should have realized that where there were rats, there would be cats.

The tabby wolfed down the treat and meowed for more. After a second piece, he allowed Alex to scratch his head. His fur was wonderfully soft, his lean body warm. "How about if I call you Captain Cat?"

He purred permission. "Very well, Captain, I'll be most pleased if you come by regularly and keep the rats away. In return, I'll share my food with you. Agreed?"

Captain Cat jumped on the cot, turned several times, and settled down to doze with his front paws tucked under him. Feeling better, Alex started a detailed survey of her surroundings. Wine-scented sawdust was scattered over the floor; the cell had contained casks until recently.

The sanitary arrangements consisted of a hole in one corner. She knelt and examined it cautiously. A stone had been chipped away, and there was enough empty space below to serve as a chamber pot indefinitely, though there would be a smell.

Next she studied the bars that kept her in the cell. They were new, solidly bolted together, and deeply seated in the stone. Impossible to breach.

She reached through the bars and examined the padlock. It was also new, and looked depressingly efficient. Perhaps a professional housebreaker might figure a way to pick the lock, but Alex doubted she could manage, especially since she lacked any pieces of metal small enough to fit into the keyhole. Probably only the Pierces had keys, so she wouldn't be able to charm a jailer into letting her out.

If only her guard had to open the door to hand over her meals! With *wing chun,* she'd have an excellent chance of bringing a man down since he wouldn't expect a woman to attack. But the cell had been arranged so the door needn't open until Alex was taken out and put on a ship for North Africa. She suppressed a shudder at the thought.

If the bars and lock were impregnable, that left the stone walls. She peered across the passageway and studied the construction of the wine storage rooms on the opposite side. She was on the end of the passage with storage areas stretching to the right as far as she could see. Each area was separated from the next by a solid masonry wall. Her side of the passage appeared identical.

She turned to the wall on her right and examined the damp, filthy wall by touch. The docks had been built at least thirty years earlier, and in a few places the mortar showed signs of crumbling.

What did she have that could be used as a tool? The crude, heavy soup spoon was her only choice. With the handle she scraped at a rough patch of mortar. A tiny fragment fell away. She felt a stir of excitement. It would take weeks to chip away the mortar around enough stones to make a hole large enough for her, but it could be done. Once she crawled into the next storage area, she'd be free to go to the main entrance and escape the next time someone entered.

Where to start? She decided on a spot near the front of the cell and at ground level. Anyone glancing in her cell would be unlikely to see her handiwork as long as she left the stones in place after the mortar was gone.

Face set, she began the long, slow business of escape.

# CHAPTER 34

Gavin's room in the Bloody Tower was more comfortable than the name implied. Though mostly cold stone and drafty enough to douse candles, there was a broad fireplace and carved Jacobean furniture, including a bed that was too short. He was standing at the window gazing blindly at the Tower yard when the door creaked open.

"It's always been your job to keep me out of trouble, not vice versa."

Gavin swung around. "Kyle! How did you hear about this so quickly?"

"Suryo. He had the sense to send a message as soon as you were arrested. Troth came to London with me, but won't call on you until tomorrow." Kyle gripped Gavin's hand in both of his. "She's badly upset about Alexandra's death," he said quietly. "How are you managing?"

Gavin closed his eyes for a moment. "Not well. I . . . I still can't quite believe that Alex is gone, much less that I'm supposed to have murdered her."

"Absurd, of course. What happened?"

"Don't you have any doubts about my innocence?"

"None at all." Kyle's gaze didn't waver. "I can't imagine you hurting a woman. Remember the female pirate when we were attacked in the Straits of Malacca? I would have shot her if it had been my head she was trying to slice off, but even in the middle of a battle you had the restraint to disarm her instead. A man who did that is not going to murder the woman he loves."

Gavin was painfully grateful for his friend's faith. His reaction to Kyle's assumption that he loved Alex was even more painful because of the bleak knowledge that he'd never told Alex he loved her. He'd barely realized it himself before she was gone. Words forever unsaid. "I suppose I should start thinking about why the prosecution is so convinced I committed murder."

"You need to do more than think about it—this case will come to trial with alarming speed. I've brought Sir Geoffrey Howard, the best counsel in London. He's waiting outside because I wanted to see you alone first. Shall I bring him in?"

Gavin realized he wasn't going to be allowed to wallow in despair any longer. "Please do."

What kind of hospitality should an accused murderer offer? He opened a bottle of sherry. His servants, universally aghast at his arrest, had stocked his prison well.

Sir Geoffrey Howard was a thin man with a deeply lined face and piercing eyes. "My lord Seabourne," he said formally when Kyle introduced him. "I'm glad to have the opportunity to consult with you on this matter."

Gavin guessed that the man's sedate exterior concealed an active, curious mind. "Credit goes to Lord Wrexham, who kept his wits, which I haven't. Thank you for coming."

Sir Geoffrey's eyes narrowed. "Do you have a history of disordered wits?"

"Not at all," Gavin said, startled. "It was merely an expression." He realized that the lawyer was already spinning a defense based on a disturbed mind. "Shall we sit down and discuss what case the Crown will try to make?"

"Please begin by telling me in your own words what happened on the fatal day."

Sherry in hand, the three men settled around the fire, which barely managed to take the chill off a damp, gray day. Gavin tersely described the events that led up to the fire and Alex's death while Sir Geoffrey donned a pair of half spectacles and took precise notes. He spoke little except for occasionally asking a question for clarification.

Gavin ended, "Is there anything there that would lead a jury to find me guilty?"

"A jury?" The lawyer frowned. "May I speak freely, my lord? There is much that needs to be discussed."

"Fire when ready."

"To begin with, you will be tried in the House of Lords, since they are your peers."

Gavin frowned at the idea of being tried by a group of mossbacked aristocrats. "I haven't yet been officially seated there. Can't I request a trial by jury in a regular court?"

Howard shook his head. "You have no choice in the matter. The case law on this subject is unequivocal."

Gavin swore under his breath. "Still another drawback to this damnable undemocratic system. What does it mean to be tried in the Lords?"

"On the plus side, you can speak in your own defense." Howard hesitated. "Also, the peers generally look after their own, especially if the evidence is not clear cut. The last time a peer was tried for murder was Lord Ferrers in 1760, and there was no question but that he shot his poor steward. However, if he'd been accused of killing a man in a duel, he would undoubtedly have been acquitted because many peers believe that an affair of honor is a gentleman's right."

"But I am not one of 'their own,'" Gavin pointed out. "I'm a stranger—a Scot and a Yankee and in trade, and I've only lived in

London for a couple of months. Apart from Wrexham, I have no friends among the peerage. Most of the other lords I've met are my wife's family or friends, and they may want to see me hang."

"You are not without friends," Kyle said. "Ashburton is scrupulously fair and he has a great deal of influence. If he believes you're innocent, others will also be inclined to give you the benefit of the doubt."

"You'll need it," the lawyer said dourly. "A major drawback of being tried in the House of Lords is that you can be convicted by a simple majority. In a king's court, the verdict would have to be unanimous."

That was not good news. "What kind of evidence does the prosecution have? Obviously there can be no eyewitnesses to an event that didn't happen."

"I am not privy to the Crown's case, but I believe much will be made of the facts that you and your wife were heard arguing vehemently, and that the evening before her death you killed two men with your bare hands."

"That was in self-defense!"

"Yes, but it makes you appear inclined to

violence. Also, there is evidence that the fire that destroyed your warehouse was arson, and you had quite recently taken substantial insurance coverage."

Gavin flinched as he saw the pattern forming. "So it will be claimed I was angry with my wife, killed her during an argument, then set fire to the warehouse to cover my crime and collect the insurance."

"Exactly. While there are no eyewitnesses, what you have described is very believable."

"But none of that happened!"

"It might be suggested that you didn't mean to kill her, but in the heat of argument you struck her, with tragic consequences. Manslaughter, not murder."

"I would never hit Alex!" Gavin bit off further protests, knowing it wasn't Sir Geoffrey he had to convince of his innocence. The manslaughter theory was frighteningly plausible. Would that gain him life in prison rather than the hangman?

Kyle intervened. "I'd like to know why a case was drummed up against Seabourne so quickly. On the face of it, the fire and death seemed accidental. To be arrested so quickly suggests that someone actively pursued charges against him."

"Very astute of you, Lord Wrexham. That is exactly what happened." Sir Geoffrey peered over his glasses. "Do you know Lord Wylver?"

Gavin exchanged a puzzled glance with Kyle. "I've never heard of the man. Do you know him?"

"He's a rather feckless viscount from East Anglia," Kyle replied. "Not someone I would have expected to involve himself in a criminal matter."

"Yet less than twenty-four hours after the fire, he presented himself at the headquarters of the Metropolitan Police with a file on you and your alleged crime," the lawyer said dryly. "He claims to be a connection of Lady Seabourne's first husband, which gives him an interest in seeing justice done. Are you sure you haven't made an enemy of the man, my lord?"

"I can't imagine how," Gavin replied. "A better question is whether Lord Wylver is acting on behalf of someone who is an enemy."

Kyle frowned. "Your cousin Philip was going to sponsor Barton Pierce for the Seabourne parliamentary district. That ended when you succeeded to the honors, but Pierce isn't the sort to give up. Might he have enlisted Wylver as a patron and used the connection again when he saw a way to make mischief over Lady Seabourne's death?"

"It's certainly possible." Gavin shook his head. "But I can't imagine what his motive might be. Encouraging murder charges seems extreme."

"You said that when Pierce learned you were Seabourne, he offered to buy Elliott House. He might think a capital murder charge would force you to sell."

"Far-fetched but not impossible," Gavin conceded. "Sir Geoffrey, I need to draw up a will leaving my business interests in trust for my stepdaughter." Katie was the closest thing he had to family. With a quarter interest in the business, Kyle could oversee Elliott House and insure that it didn't fall into Pierce's grasping hands.

"I shall have an associate draft a will for your approval, Lord Seabourne." The lawyer squared up his notes, signaling that the meeting was over. "The evidence against you seems largely circumstantial. Unless damning new evidence surfaces, I believe you have an excellent chance of acquittal."

Gavin hoped so. As they stood, he asked the lawyer, "What happened to Lord Ferrers, the last peer to be accused of murder?"

"He was hanged at Tyburn," Sir Geoffrey said. "But of course that case was quite different."

So much for the Lords taking care of their own. Despite his paralyzing grief, he wasn't going to die without a fight.

The candle had burned out. Relentlessly chipping at the mortar kept Alex from screaming and battering at the bars. She tried not to think of Katie. She was a cheerful, resilient little girl, but to have the horror of losing her mother followed by the arrest of her adored stepfather must be shattering.

Alex's only comfort was knowing that her daughter would not be neglected. Within days she would be in the care of her grandparents, and no one was more comforting than Catherine Kenyon. But there would be many tear-filled nights, and Alex ached for her daughter's grief.

A faint glow of light showed from the corridor. Swiftly, Alex retreated across the cell to sit on the cot, concealing her spoon under the blankets. She braced herself to see Frederica or Barton Pierce, but when the visitor appeared it was the same stoic guard from the day before, juggling a tray and a lantern.

"I'm so glad to see you!" she exclaimed. "It seems like forever since the candle burned out."

"Aye, it would." He hung the lantern on a hook, then pulled three candles from his pocket. "Knew one wouldn't last. These should make it through until tomorrow." He lit a candle from the lantern, then handed it and the spares through the bars.

"You are so kind. What is your name? I should know what to call you."

He hesitated before saying, "Jones."

She guessed it wasn't his real name, but at least it was a name. "Thank you, Mr. Jones." She pushed the previous day's tray under the bars.

He slid the new tray under, then scowled at the old one. "Where's the spoon?"

Alex thought quickly. "There was something scratching out there in the dark, so I threw the spoon at it."

Jones made a cursory survey of the passage and the opposite wine storage room. "Don't do it again, or you'll have to do without."

"I'll be more careful." It was easy to shudder. "With the light, I won't be so frightened." She sensed it would be a mistake to make a blatant attempt to win Jones over, but the gentle female glances and words that came naturally to her mother seemed to be effective.

She suddenly remembered that she had a little money in an inside pocket under her skirt. A quick check proved that no one had thought to rob her when she was unconscious, so she still had a folded bank note and a gold sovereign. Saving the note for possible future use, she drew out the coin. "Mr. Jones, I just realized I have this. Would you be able to buy a comb for me?" The sovereign glinted brightly in the lantern light.

He accepted without hesitation; paying for extra comforts in prison was an ancient custom. "Anything else you need, ma'am?"

She cast her gaze modestly downward.

"I'll need some clean rags in a few days." She gave him just long enough to become embarrassed before continuing, "Also, though it would be a great deal of extra work for you, if you could bring a bucket of water all the way back here every day, I'd be so grateful for the chance to wash."

"It's not that far from the main door, but a bucket won't fit between the bars," he pointed out as he deposited the sovereign in his pocket.

Too true. "A tin basin would fit where the food comes through. I could dip water into it from the bucket with my tea cup." She smiled bravely. "I have nothing but time."

The reminder of her captivity made him look uncomfortable. "I'll bring the water and rags, and maybe a towel and a bit of soap?"

"That would be wonderful. You're so kind, Mr. Jones." She smiled warmly.

The guard softened perceptibly. Touching his cap, he said, "See you tomorrow."

Collecting the old tray, he picked up his lantern and left. Thoughtfully Alex settled down on the cot with her food. She'd learned that the vault wasn't enormous, and she'd noticed a large key ring under his coat. When she was ready to leave, she'd be able to follow tracks in the dust and sawdust to the door, then wait for Mr. Jones to enter so she could escape. She hoped she wouldn't have to hurt him.

Once again her meal was soup, this time a thick potato and onion mixture. With the bread and cheese, it would feed her adequately for the next day. She estimated that the squat brown teapot held about six cups. She sipped it slowly so it would also last.

*"Mrrowr?"*

With feline genius for timing, Captain Cat appeared. She gave him his cheese. "You're doing a good job. I don't think any rats came too close, though there are little lizards and spiders."

She hadn't slept much in the menacing darkness, but now that she had light again she felt like resting. After eating about a third of her food, she set the tray down and curled up under the blankets. When she got the basin, she'd use it to cover the food. For now, she had to hope that the vermin kept their distance.

Captain Cat jumped up on the cot and turned several times to establish that he wanted a piece of space by her head. She was glad to cooperate. If she closed her eyes, maybe she could pretend that she was sleeping with Gavin. . . .

# CHAPTER 35

The moment Gavin had been dreading occurred the fifth morning after his arrest. When the door of his quarters opened, he stiffened at the sight of Lord and Lady Michael Kenyon. How does a man greet the parents of the wife he is charged with murdering?

Lord Michael had aged a decade since the last time they met. If he'd pulled out a pistol and aimed, Gavin wouldn't have been surprised. And he probably wouldn't have tried to avoid the bullet.

Catherine broke the tension by crossing the room and embracing him. "My dear Gavin. What a horrible, horrible business."

"I'm so sorry, Catherine. Sorry for everything." He hugged her hard, deeply grateful for her compassion. "How is Katie?"

"Devastated, but trying to be brave. Watching her breaks my heart." Catherine wiped her eyes with a gloved fist. "She's staying with us in Ashburton House. She wanted desperately to visit you today, but I thought it best not to bring her until we'd had a chance to speak with you. She said you didn't even say goodbye."

Gavin swallowed. "The policemen were impatient. Also . . . I didn't want her to see me taken away, accused of murdering her mother. Ever since, I've wondered if I did the right thing."

"Having children means one is always wondering if one does the right thing," Catherine said as she sat down.

"The same is true with wives. If I'd had more sense, Alex would be alive now."

"Sit down and tell us what happened. The note from Bard said very little." Lord Michael's expression was like flint.

For what seemed like the thousandth time, Gavin repeated the story. The Kenyons listened unemotionally, though their clasped hands tightened when Gavin described how Alex's body had been found. At the end Lord Michael said, "You couldn't have stopped her from doing what she wanted, Gavin. She always was headstrong. Like her mother." He gave his wife a ghost of a smile.

Catherine returned it despite the dark circles under her eyes. "Michael is right. Feeling as Alexandra did about slavery, nothing you said could have dissuaded her from doing what she could to stop it. If only . . ." Catherine bit her lip and looked away. There were a thousand "if onlys," and none of them could change the past.

Lord Michael said, "Has anyone investigated who might have entered the warehouse while you were at the livery stable?"

"An old man who lived across the street claims no one entered or left after me," Gavin admitted. "The barrister who is acting for me has hired Bow Street Runners to see what they can find, but so far no other witnesses have been located."

"Presumably the old man couldn't see the river side of the warehouse."

"True, but no one else seems to have, either. Half-a-dozen men could have entered that way for all we know. On the river side the warehouse had a pair of very large doors that could be opened to bring in merchandise, plus a regular door for use at other times," Gavin explained. "There was no sign of the lock being forced on the large doors. Since the smaller door vanished into the river when part of the building collapsed, it's impossible to prove anyone broke in that way."

"You mentioned evidence that the fire was arson?"

"Broken jugs of lamp oil were found throughout the ruins," Gavin replied. "Unfortunately they seem to have come from the Elliott House supply, so while the jugs prove the fire was set deliberately, there's no clue who did it. The witness doesn't think I was in the warehouse long enough to spread about gallons of oil, but he isn't sure." Gavin was grateful that nothing he'd said made the Kenyons seem suspicious of him.

"What is your theory?"

"I don't know," Gavin admitted. "The simplest explanation is that the maid, Daisy, had a criminal lover who thought this would be an easy way to rob a rich woman. But it wasn't likely that Alex would be at the office with money or jewels, and no one was seen going in through the unlocked door. If Daisy's lover only wanted to rob the warehouse, why not break in when no one was there? And why set a fire so quickly that there wasn't time to steal much? None of it makes sense."

"It will when the whole truth is known," Catherine commented. "But it's hard to find the truth when all you have is questions with no answers. I understand Daisy has disappeared?"

"Yes. She must have fled London immediately, or the Runners would have found some trace of her." Not only had she run, but she was well hidden. Or, possibly, dead, if this whole ghastly business was part of a larger conspiracy.

"Ashburton sends his regards," Lord Michael said. "He'd visit you himself, but feels it would be inappropriate when soon he'll be sitting as your judge."

Gavin nodded, understanding. Thinking Lord Michael might answer a question Sir Geoffrey and Kyle had been avoiding, he asked, "Do you have any idea how public opinion is running? If I'm widely assumed to be guilty, a number of peers will probably feel the same way."

"The gutter press has been railing against you, and Ashburton said at least one peer has been doing the same."

"Lord Wylver? I'm told he's the one who personally convinced the police I was guilty of what no one else thought was a murder, until he spoke up," Gavin said dryly. "He claims to be a connection of Edmund Warren's, but my aunt, Lady Jane Howard, is doubtful, and she knows the lineage of every aristocratic family in Britain. Wylver may just dislike me as a colonial upstart, unfit to pollute the hallowed halls of Westminster."

Or Wylver might be acting for someone else, but there was no proof of that. Though Sir Geoffrey and Kyle were pursuing every line of investigation either of them could think of, so far . . . nothing. And time was running out quickly.

Catherine got to her feet. "Shall I bring Katie before we take her to Wales?"

He hesitated. "Use your judgment. I want very much to see her, but not if a visit will be upsetting."

"She's more upset about not seeing you.

She's like . . ." Catherine's voice faltered. "Very like her mother, who always preferred truth and action to well-meaning attempts to protect her."

"Then please bring her to see me." Especially since it might be for the last time.

"Tomorrow then." Catherine hugged him again as she took her leave. "Have faith that justice will be done, Gavin."

"I hope you're right." As he escorted them to the door, he said, "It means a great deal to me that you don't think I'm guilty."

Lord Michael waited until Catherine had left, then said quietly, "If I did, you would be dead." Then he turned and walked away.

It was a day for visitors. News of the murder and subsequent arrest had reached those who'd left London for the summer, some of whom returned to complicate Gavin's life still further. Apparently anyone who presented himself at the Tower and appeared well bred could be admitted. Of course, it hadn't been that many years since a small fee allowed visitors to not only see the crown jewels, but even try on a crown.

In mid-afternoon Philip Elliott arrived,

looking uncomfortable. Gavin glanced up from the luncheon he was finishing. Not bothering to rise, he said dryly, "Come to chastise me for sullying the fair name of Seabourne, or are you hoping you won't actually have to vacate the Seabourne properties?"

The younger man flushed. "As your heir, I thought it right to call on you."

At least Philip had manners. "If you're curious, no, I didn't kill my wife, but I have no idea if the House of Lords will believe that. If I'm hanged, Seabourne will come to you unencumbered of debt, but my personal fortune will go elsewhere, so do try to handle your money more carefully."

Philip looked even more uncomfortable. "I'm not usually extravagant. After years of restraint I ran a little wild after I inherited. If . . . if I do become earl again, I'll be more prudent."

"I'm glad to hear that. The people dependent on the Seabourne estate will be also." A thought occurred to him. "If you need people to re-staff Seabourne House, the Berkeley Square servants are capable and honest." Hired by Alex.

"I'll remember that."

With no business to discuss and no real relationship, an awkward silence fell until Gavin said, "It was good of you to come. I do appreciate it, even if I'm not very hospitable."

"I can't say that I blame you. You're in a damnable position. Please believe that I'm not hoping for an innocent man to die merely to advance my station in the world." Philip paused with his hand on the door knob. "I'm very sorry about Lady Seabourne's death. She was a lovely woman."

His sympathy triggered one of the swift waves of anguish that struck Gavin many times a day. He nodded thanks and turned away, struggling to control himself. On some primal level, he couldn't really believe she was dead. Particularly at night, when he tried to sleep, she felt so close that he almost believed he could reach out and touch her.

Perhaps the spirits of the murdered really were restive, or perhaps sudden death had caught her by surprise and she wanted to stay close to him. He hoped the latter. He couldn't bear to think of her spirit as distressed and crying for vengeance.

The thought was painful, so he was not in a

good mood late in the afternoon when Major Mark Colwell stormed in wearing a travel-stained military uniform. Gavin glanced up from the business papers Suryo had brought the day before. Being noticeably foreign look-ing, Suryo hadn't been allowed to visit until he came with Kyle, yet a raging major with an unrequited passion for Alex was admitted easily. It was another thought that didn't im-prove his mood.

Colwell glowered at him from just inside the door. "You murdering *bastard.* I'll cheer when they hang you."

"Obviously it hasn't occurred to you that I might be innocent."

"They had enough evidence to arrest you. I pray the House of Lords doesn't give you the benefit of the doubt because you're an earl." Colwell's eyes burned with hatred. "You became a peer and no longer need Alexandra's family connections, so now you want some young girl with no children and a grand fortune. For that, you murdered the sweetest, most beautiful woman on earth!"

Any sympathy Gavin had for Colwell's grief evaporated. In a cold rage, he rose from the desk and stalked across the room toward his visitor. "You arrogant fool! You may have pined for your vision of Alex for years, but you didn't know the first thing about her. Do you have any idea how strong she was? How brave? How passionate? How stubborn? How idealistic?"

He stopped a yard short of the other man, his fists clenching as he struggled with a desire to knock sense into Colwell's thick head. In a quieter voice, he said, "She was my wife, Katie's mother, the daughter of Lord and Lady Michael Kenyon. Her death is our tragedy. It has nothing to do with you or your fantasies. Now get out."

Colwell turned white. "May you rot in hell." He spun on his heel and walked out.

A muscle jumping in his cheek, Gavin crossed the room to stare out the window. Probably Colwell was related to half the peerage and would now tell all his lordly relatives that Gavin was a murderer who must be punished.

What a damnable strange country this was, where Gavin's fate would be decided by a group of wealthy, arrogant men whose only qualification was an inherited title. There was no need for them to have intelligence, honesty, common sense, or good judgment. If Gavin escaped the gallows—

and he figured his odds were no better than even—he would leave England forever.

Without Alex or Katie, there was nothing to keep him here.

The sentry called, "Halt, who goes there?"

"The Keys!" replied the Chief Yeoman Warder.

"Whose keys?"

"Queen Elizabeth's keys."

"God preserve Queen Elizabeth!"

"Amen!" A chorus rumbled from the escort of four armed guards.

Gavin gazed into the darkness as he listened to the ceremony that took place every night at ten o'clock. The Virgin Queen had died in 1603, and over two centuries later her damned keys were still being carried around the Tower of London. Very British.

He spent a lot of time at the windows of his prison. Though his cell was spacious, his jailers polite, and his views splendid, he was still a captive. There were times when he felt like hurling himself against the bars like a caged bird desperate to escape. The experience was giving him a gut-deep understanding of what Alex had endured in slavery. Freedom was as natural and invisible as the air one breathed, until it was gone.

He was glad that his trial would begin soon. One way or another, it wouldn't be long until he left this place.

His anger from earlier in the day had long since dissolved into sadness. For one brief moment he'd had everything a man could want. Then it was gone before he had time to recognize joy.

*Rest well, Iskandra, wherever your spirit may be.*

# CHAPTER 36

Alex's captivity settled into a routine. Most of her days were spent relentlessly gouging at the mortar, with regular breaks where she stretched her muscles with *wing chun* exercises. Jones had given her a pencil stub, and every time he brought a meal she made a careful mark on the cell wall. She'd been here almost six weeks.

Being able to wash helped her morale considerably, and the food kept her and Captain Cat satisfied. The tomcat was a godsend in terms of her sanity. He still prowled the vaults in search of prey, and lately he'd taken to depositing dead rats outside the cell for her admiration. She could have done without the rats, but she enjoyed his company, and whenever she lay down he soon materialized to sleep beside her.

So far she hadn't needed any of the clean rags that Jones had provided. She had a strong suspicion that she was pregnant again. Unlike the disastrous pregnancy she'd endured on the voyage home, this time she felt fine, except for tiring easily. She'd felt like this when carrying Katie. God willing, she'd have another strong, healthy child. She refused to think about the possibility that she would be sent to the Barbary Coast. She would not bear and raise a child in slavery.

Her long hours of slowly grinding away the mortar gave her time to think about Gavin and their marriage. When they met, he'd been her savior and hero. She'd been profoundly grateful, and deeply aware that she was barely holding on to sanity.

After leaving Maduri she slowly regained her equilibrium, but she'd always felt that she was Gavin's charity case, protected because he was too much a gentleman to walk away in disgust. She'd been unable to think of them as equals, each giving and receiving. Perhaps a woman needed to be courted by an adoring man so that she entered marriage feeling the power of her femaleness.

She'd felt that with Edmund, and that sense of power had helped keep her from falling apart when he betrayed her. But there had been no courtship with Gavin—only a marriage born of his duty and her desperation.

No wonder she'd never really defined her feelings for her husband. She'd known she was grateful—dear Lord, she was grateful! She recognized his character and charm and how good he was with Katie, and as her fears slowly subsided she'd begun to feel a powerful attraction. But never had she asked herself if she loved him. Now, in the long silences of the vault, knowledge had emerged with vivid clarity.

She loved him as much as she admired him. She loved talking and laughing and being silent with him, loved that he accepted her as an equal like no other man she'd ever known. She also desired him to distraction. She had never fully appreciated how beautiful a man's body could be, or how profound sexual fulfillment created indissoluble emotional bonds. When she slept at night she dreamed she was safe in his arms, for with him she had found her soul and salvation.

Now she must free herself so she could free him.

She estimated that removing a dozen stones would make a hole large enough for her to escape. She couldn't remove the stones before she was ready to leave because that would leave a visible hole, so she dug out most of the mortar, stopping when the stone started to feel loose. Wadded shreds of rag pressed into the gaps concealed the empty spaces from a casual glance.

Slowly she was gouging away the outside perimeter of the group of stones she'd chosen. With luck, the whole section could be pushed out at once when the time came. She hoped so, but with only a blunt, bent spoon handle, the work was agonizingly slow.

Hearing sounds in the passage, she scrambled from her working position despite the protests of her strained muscles. Frederica Pierce was making one of her all too frequent visits; her lighter footsteps were distinct from Mr. Jones's. Amazing how well one learned one's surroundings when there was so little else to notice.

After straightening herself and brushing off sawdust, Alex lay on her cot as if she'd been napping. When Frederica appeared, she lazily sat up, covering a delicate yawn as if she was a lady of leisure. "Be careful where you step, Frederica. There may be dead rats."

The other woman gasped and jumped back, almost bumping into the guard. "Where?"

"A cat often leaves them about where you're standing." Alex watched with malicious satisfaction as Frederica squeaked and pulled her skirts tight.

There was indeed a dead rat. Without comment, Mr. Jones slid Alex's food into the cell, then put the rat into a sack he'd brought for the purpose. When the rat was gone from sight, Alex said, "I'm sure you have some bad news for me. Please feel free to reveal it. I'm in need of amusement."

Frederica gave her a poisonous glance. "Seabourne's trial begins tomorrow."

So soon? "I'm sure he'll be glad to have it over and be a free man again."

"The general public is convinced he's a murderer. I'm told most of the lords do, too. They can't wait to convict him for murdering his gentle lady wife. Obviously few of them know you personally."

Alex laughed. "Actually, many of them do know me, though I agree they're being sentimental if they think of me that way. Is there any other news?"

Frederica hesitated. Over the course of her visits, she'd gradually lost control of their interviews. Alex took pleasure in knowing that. "Daisy has vanished with her child. She took the boy and ran away from our country estate."

"Good for Daisy! Finally she is truly free."

Frederica's expression turned ugly. "Barton has charged her with theft so she can be arrested. She'll be found—a black girl with a baby won't get far without being noticed. As soon as we have her back, the slut goes to America."

Alex doubted that. Daisy was intelligent and determined enough to elude capture. She'd have to hide in London, the only city large enough for a black woman to disappear into, but she'd manage. Despite Daisy's treachery, Alex wished her well. The girl had been doing her best to save herself and her child. In similar circumstances, Alex might have behaved the same. "You do have the worst trouble with servants, Frederica. Perhaps you should treat them better."

"I have a French maid now. She is far superior to that stupid slave." With another scowl, Frederica turned and stalked away.

Alex's smile faded when she was alone. It was pleasant to bait Frederica, but it didn't alter the fact that she was still a prisoner. She waited until she heard the distant sound of the vault door closing. Then she returned to her work.

Time was running out.

In true British fashion, Gavin's trial would begin with a lengthy procession. "A pity the Westminster fire last year destroyed the usual chamber. This one barely holds two hundred fifty people," Sir Geoffrey murmured as he accompanied his client into the hall. "By the way, the Lord High Steward chosen to preside over your trial is Lord St. Aubyn."

The name meant nothing to Gavin. "Is that good or bad?"

Sir Geoffrey pursed his lips. "It's not bad. He is hard but fair. You could have done much worse."

As the lords filed into the long, high-ceilinged chamber, Gavin admired the flamboyant majesty of English ceremony. Dressed in flowing scarlet robes and wigs that erased individuality, the peers entered in order of precedence and seated themselves on the tiered benches. Dukes were in the first row, marquises next, then earls, with viscounts and barons at the top.

At the far end of the room sat an empty throne. King William would not attend; judging one of their own was for peers alone.

In front of the throne, the Lord High Steward took his seat upon the woolpack—literally a six foot–long bale of packed wool covered with scarlet cloth. Sir Geoffrey had explained earlier that the woolpack was recognition of how England's medieval wealth had been built on the wool trade. Gavin found it bizarre.

St. Aubyn, the chosen Lord High Steward, was about sixty, but fit and shrewd-eyed. While the King's Commission to hold the trial was read, Gavin studied the rows of seated lords. As a duke, Ashburton's robe rated gold lace and four bands of ermine on each side. Ashburton met Gavin's gaze and gave a faint nod of acknowledgment.

There were other familiar faces as well, mostly men he'd met at Ashburton House. The Duke of Candover and the Marquess of Wolverton, the Earls of Strathmore and Aberdare, and Lord Kimball, who was improbably both soldier and artist.

Kyle was so grave he was almost unrecognizable. His twin brother was nearby, looking uncannily similar and bearing a title from his wife's family that would have become extinct without a king's decree. Gavin had met Lord Grahame, who was a more relaxed version of Kyle. Hopefully he shared Kyle's belief in Gavin's innocence.

But most of the lords were strangers. Middle-aged or older, some had been ravaged by dissipation, others had the sleekness of men comfortable with their power. His judges, God help him. He wondered which was Lord Wylver, the man who had set the wheels of injustice in motion.

More documents were read, ending with the indictment. In the middle of a long passage, words jumped out. "The said Gavin, Earl of Seabourne, Viscount Handley, did feloniously, willfully, and of his malice aforethought wound his wife, Alexandra, Countess of Seabourne, and did destroy the building with fire and thereby caused the death of said Alexandra, Countess of Seabourne."

The words were like hammers, driving home that this horror was no nightmare—Gavin had not only lost his wife, but stood accused before the world of murdering her.

"Oyez, Oyez, Oyez! Lieutenant of the Tower of London, bring forth Gavin, Earl of Seabourne, your prisoner, to the bar, pursuant to the order of the House of Lords!"

Aware that every eye in the house was on him, Gavin walked to the accused's box flanked by the Deputy Governor of the Tower and the Gentleman Jailer, who carried a massive axe. Steeling himself, he bowed three times and knelt. He resented showing reverence for an institution he disliked, but Kyle had convinced him this would be a devil of a time to display his republican principles.

"Your lordship may rise," St. Aubyn said. His gray eyes sharply assessing, he made a lengthy statement about the nature of the charges and of the court.

When the Lord High Steward was finished, the Clerk of the Crown said, "How say you, Gavin, Earl of Seabourne, are you guilty of the felony and murder whereof you stand indicted, or not guilty?"

"Not guilty, my lords." Gavin spoke in a carrying voice, wanting every damned peer in the room to hear him.

The clerk asked, "Culprit, how will your lordship be tried?"

"By God and my peers." This required more gritting of teeth.

"God send your lordship a good deliverance."

The last was the only part Gavin could agree with.

The Crown opened its case, led by the Attorney General, William Oliver. An imposing man with a sonorous voice, he obviously relished the chance to prosecute such a splendid scandal.

Gavin stood stone-faced as witnesses were called. After being examined by the Attorney General and Sir Geoffrey, any lord present could ask questions to satisfy his own curiosity.

The first witnesses were two of Gavin's servants, testifying uncomfortably that they'd heard raised voices between master and mistress in the day or two before her death. Questions by Sir Geoffrey established that the servants had heard nothing threatening; the raised voices were notable only because they were so rare.

Constable Mayne then testified that he'd come on the scene immediately after Lord Seabourne had killed two men with his bare hands, one by breaking of the neck, the other by fracturing the skull. Murmurs came from the lords at the constable's graphic description. Some looked at Gavin as if he were a dangerous viper.

Sir Geoffrey rose and asked, "Constable Mayne, you say there were five attackers?" When that was confirmed, the counsel said, "So his lordship was fighting for his life against overwhelming odds. Was Lady Seabourne present?"

"Aye, sir, she was there, too."

"So his lordship was fighting for not only his own life, but that of his wife. Under such circumstances, any man would fight like a tiger." Sir Geoffrey waited for that to sink in. "In your opinion, did Lady Seabourne appear frightened of her husband?"

"Nay, sir, she looked at him as if he was the most wonderful man on earth."

The prosecutor objected that the constable's statement was mere opinion, but the words had been said. Perhaps they would influence the noble lords.

More witnesses were called to verify what had happened on the day of the fire. Jem Brown was the boy on the street who'd held Gavin's horse and later told him of the fire. The prosecutor elicited the information that his lordship had looked angry, and told Jem to "never get married."

Gavin winced internally; he didn't even remember making the remark. When cross-examined, Jem admitted that his lordship hadn't seemed crazy-angry, and his own old man said all the time that Jem should never marry.

After him, the elderly man who watched from his window all day testified that Gavin had gone into the warehouse for a time, and no one else had entered before the fire consumed the building. Sir Geoffrey elicited the information that the old man could see only the front, not the river side of the building, and that his lordship probably hadn't been inside long enough to spread lantern oil all around a large warehouse. Also, no smoke or flames had been visible until well after his lordship left.

By now it was late afternoon, so the session was adjourned until the next morning. As Gavin was taken away by his jailers, Sir Geoffrey paused to say, "If this is all the evidence they have, tomorrow I'll move to dismiss on the grounds they haven't proved their case."

That sounded good, but as Gavin again watched angry crowds outside his carriage, he didn't let his hopes get too high. Surely the prosecution was saving the worst for last—and believed that the worst would be enough to hang him.

Gavin's misgivings were fulfilled. The first prosecution witness called the next morning was a shifty-eyed man called Throup. He looked like a thief who was attempting to appear respectable.

After the preliminaries, Attorney General Oliver asked, "Have you ever met the prisoner, Lord Seabourne?"

"Yessir, the day Elliott House burned down."

Seeing his counsel's questioning glance,

Gavin shrugged to express his ignorance. The man could easily have been part of the crowd watching the fire.

Majestic as a great lion, Oliver asked the witness, "Will you tell us in your own words what happened that day?"

Throup stared at Gavin, his eyes burning with malevolence. "That fellow there asked me to help 'im at 'is warehouse. I waited outside the door on the dock till 'e unlocked it and let me in. 'e gave me ten quid to throw lamp oil around the warehouse, and half-a-dozen lucifers to set fires when I was done. He said to leave by the river door."

Gavin gasped at the blatant falsehood. "He's lying!"

"The prisoner must remain silent," the Lord High Steward warned. "Proceed, Mr. Throup."

"Did you find this request unusual?" the Attorney General inquired.

Throup shrugged. "Who knows why rich coves do what they do? Maybe he wanted the oil to polish the floors. Anyhow, 'e went off. I thought I heard a noise upstairs, but didn't think much of it. When I was done spreadin' the oil, I set it afire, a good long distance from the door so I'd 'ave time to get out. Then I thought I heard a cry, like a baby or a woman, from upstairs, so I went up to take a quick look."

When the witness paused, Oliver asked, "And what did you find, Mr. Throup?"

"A pretty woman with dark hair lyin' on the floor and bleedin' from a bullet in the belly."

The chamber filled with exclamations of shock. Gavin jerked upright, wondering if this could be true when the rest was lies. Had Alex really been shot?

"Was the woman dead or alive?"

"Alive, but only just. I bent over and asked 'er who shot 'er." Throup's gaze swung to Gavin again. "She told me it were 'er 'usband."

# CHAPTER 37

Hearing two pairs of footsteps, Alex quickly covered up the signs of her chipping and sat on the cot, flexing her cramped hands. Though wrapping rags around the spoon made it easier to handle, she still suffered shooting pains in her hand, wrist, and arm. If—when—she got out of here, she'd have an excuse not to do needlework ever again.

She'd been knotted with anxiety ever since Frederica had announced the start of the trial. That had been two days ago. It had seemed a good sign that Frederica hadn't returned, but as soon as she saw that the other woman was accompanied by her husband, her heart sank. Both of them were glowing with vicious satisfaction.

Determined not to show weakness, she said coolly, "Good day, Sir Barton. I trust you're well? I haven't seen you since that memorable day when I killed your henchman."

His expression hardly faltered. "It's a wonderful day—your contemptible husband has been sentenced to hang by the neck until dead."

Numb with shock, Alex struggled to breathe. She had never dreamed it would go this far. Who could believe Gavin a murderer?

"Only you can appreciate the delightful irony of this," Frederica said brightly. "To know that he will die for your murder—I can't even imagine how you must feel. Please tell me what it's like."

Alex ignored her to concentrate on Pierce, guessing that, like his wife, he wouldn't be able to resist boasting of his cleverness. "Who did you hire to perjure himself?"

"How clever you are—that's exactly what I did. I had to choose carefully, because testifying before the House of Lords must be frightening even if one is telling the truth. But I have the perfect man—Sly, whom you met at the warehouse. He was angered by the fact that you grazed his arm with a bullet, but he particularly resented your killing of his mate, Webb. Since Sly is a talented liar with considerable practice, he was able to tell a convincing tale to the noble lords."

Wishing her aim had been better, Alex asked, "What story did you invent?"

"That Seabourne paid Sly to spread lamp oil through the warehouse. After the fire was set, Sly heard you calling out piteously and went upstairs to find you bleeding from a mortal pistol wound." Pierce smiled with pleasure. "And with your dying breath, you accused your husband of the crime."

"Surely everyone couldn't have believed that," Alex said crisply. "Sly is such an obvious villain."

"Not everyone believed," Frederica agreed. "But enough did. Seabourne was declared guilty by a five-vote margin. It's said that everyone who knew him personally voted for acquittal, but Sly was really quite convincing, and there was indisputable evidence that Seabourne is a violent man."

"The fact that he isn't a true English gentleman made it easier to think him capable of murdering his gently born wife," Pierce added. "And few believed his testimony that he'd allowed you to stay in the warehouse alone to meet an escaped slave. No real man would do such a thing." Pierce smiled. "My cooperative patron, Lord Wylver, did a good job of spreading that thought among his fellows."

"Real men don't have to treat their wives like imbecilic children," Alex said, aching at the knowledge that the qualities that made Gavin special were being used against him. "Did the noble lords completely ignore the defense counsel case?"

"Sir Geoffrey Howard did his best," Pierce allowed. "He emphasized the lack of direct evidence and brought in witnesses like the stevedore who kept Seabourne from entering the burning warehouse in a suicidal attempt to rescue you. Was this the act of a man who wished to kill his wife? But nothing could overcome the fact that he murdered my two men, and with your dying breath you named him your murderer."

Frederica nodded solemnly. "Since he *is* a murderer, this is merely justice."

"Self-defense has never been considered murder." But Alex could see how the combination of circumstances—Gavin's adventurous life in foreign lands, his fighting skill, a plausible perjurer—had persuaded narrow-minded members of the House who had never been farther from home than Paris.

"The defense counsel's last hope was bringing your mother in to testify that she couldn't believe Seabourne killed you."

Alex's breath caught. "My mother was there?"

"Yes, and very touching she was," Pierce said. "Especially when she pleaded for Seabourne's life, saying that even if the noble lords judged him guilty, execution wouldn't bring you back."

Frederica picked up the story again. "When Seabourne was asked to speak in mitigation of his crime, all he would say was that as God was his witness, he had committed no crime. He wasn't the least bit conciliatory, and many of the more traditional peers took offense at his attitude. In a week he will pay for that outside Newgate

Prison. Usually hangings are early in the morning, but his will be at high noon, to show that British justice applies to the highest as well as the lowest."

Alex locked her hands together, chilled to the bone by the image of her mother pleading for Gavin's life. But though she was glad her family and friends hadn't believed Sly's lies, that was scant comfort when Gavin was condemned to death.

A week. Only a week.

"Enjoy your last days in England, Alexandra." Frederica gazed fondly at her husband. "Barton has promised that within two days of the execution you'll be on your way to the Barbary Coast, but not until I've described the hanging to you in detail. Barton has already booked rooms in the inn across the street from Newgate so we'll have a splendid view of Seabourne's death throes."

Pierce gazed back at his wife with equal fondness, his arm around her waist. In their own evil way, they loved each other.

"I'll see you again, Alexandra," Frederica said as she turned to go. She paused. "By the way, what do you do with yourself all day? It seems frightfully tedious."

Despite her feelings of suffocation, Alex made herself smile. "It's quite restful, really. Running an earl's estate is tiring. These last weeks I've relaxed and remembered books I've read, poems I've memorized. Since I've always loved to read, I have a well-furnished mind. Do you know how to read, Frederica?"

The other woman's mouth thinned. "I've more amusing things to do with my time. Come, Barton, I wish to go home." She caressed his face with sultry promise.

Alex was motionless for a long time after they left. A week, and she still had a long way to go. The wall was thick, and the handle of her bent, battered spoon was such a feeble tool. With a decent piece of forged iron, she'd have been out of here long ago.

No excuses. Trying to calm the pounding of her heart, she resumed working with grim concentration.

"It's a damnable crime!" Restlessly Kyle paced the bleak chamber in Newgate Prison where Gavin had been brought to spend his last night. This way the authorities wouldn't have to clear a path through the crowds to bring him from the Tower to the scaffold outside the prison.

"Crimes happen all the time," Gavin said. "The only thing unusual about this one is that I have money, and rich men are seldom victims of injustice."

Expression anguished, Kyle asked, "How can you be so calm?"

"Because the alternative is wailing and gnashing of teeth, which would be distressing all around. Have some of this excellent brandy."

Kyle accepted the brandy and sat down. There wasn't much to discuss except Gavin's impending execution, which was not an uplifting topic. Gavin had sorted out his business affairs and said most of his goodbyes. Only Kyle and Suryo were here tonight, and if possible he would throw Kyle out, since his friend was in an agony of frustration. Suryo was more restful company.

There was a knock at the door. Suryo opened it, and Ashburton and Lord Michael Kenyon entered. Their identical bleak expressions emphasized their blood bonds.

Gavin rose. "Have some brandy? It seems rather cold out."

"Please." Wearily Ashburton removed his cloak. "I had an audience with the king. William is not unsympathetic—as a navy man he has a fondness for all sailors—but he says it's the House of Lords' right to judge their own, and he can't intervene."

"That wasn't unexpected." Gavin poured brandy into two more snifters. In the grim gray depths of Newgate Prison, he was drinking the finest French brandy from crystal goblets. Did that make the prospect of death in the morning better or worse?

Lord Michael took a glass with murmured thanks before settling into a chair. He'd taken Catherine and Katie back to Wales, wanting them to be as far from the execution as possible. He swirled the brandy in his glass. "I've seen death in many forms. Mostly it's pointless, ugly, and a great waste. But I've never seen a death more wrong than this."

In a mood for honesty, Gavin said, "Really? I thought you had a reservation or two about my innocence."

"I did at first," Lord Michael admitted. "But not after that perjurer said Alex had been shot. With your Eastern fighting skills, it's at least conceivable that you might have accidentally hurt Alex in an argument, but it's unthinkable that you would shoot her. Throup's entire testimony collapsed then."

"A pity so many of the peers lacked your astuteness."

"Wrongful execution of the innocent is the best argument possible for ending executions," Ashburton said morosely. "I think I'll introduce a bill outlawing them."

"It will never pass," Kyle said. "The mob enjoys executions too much."

"The fact that it won't pass doesn't mean I shouldn't try." Ashburton the imperturbable looked downright angry.

"Alex was very much your niece," Gavin said with a faint smile. "More interested in justice than the tedious virtue of practicality."

There was another knock at the door. This time Gavin answered. A vicar stood there with a solemn expression and a Bible. "I am here to offer comfort to the condemned man."

Gavin sighed. It was bad enough to be hanged, but to be prayed over? "Thank you, but my conscience is clear so you can go home to your family." Politely he closed the door in the vicar's face. Turning to his visitors, he said, "This might be a good night to get rather drunk. Care to join me?"

Except for Suryo, who drank no alcohol, they did. As the night progressed, Gavin thought how fortunate he was to have four friends such as these men.

A pity he wouldn't have the chance to know them longer.

Bracing herself against her cot, Alex planted her feet against the section of wall she'd been trying to loosen, and pushed. Thinking that she felt some movement in the stone, she took a deep breath and pushed again. This had to work. She'd been scraping mortar frantically all week, and according to Frederica's most recent visit, Gavin would be hanged within a few hours. Though she had no clock to track time, she refused to think it might be too late.

The stone remained obdurate. Almost weeping with frustration, she pulled both legs back, then kicked her feet into the stone as hard as she could.

With startling suddenness, the section

crashed through into the next storage room. Giddy with relief, Alex scrambled to her feet, wincing a little. To the cat who watched with interest from the cot, she said, "I'll come back for you later, Captain. You can move in with us and become the tomcat terror of Mayfair."

After a quick scratch at his neck for luck, she inserted arms and head into the hole. By drawing her shoulders in, she managed to get the upper half of her body into the dark cell next door. Swearing as she heard fabric tear, she wiggled her hips through and folded down onto the stones and the sawdust-covered floor. If she'd been more pregnant it would have been impossible, but her body had not yet begun to change visibly.

Lighting the spare candle from the one inside her old cell, she swiftly followed the dusty footprints through the vault. Cross-passages stretched away at regular intervals, lined with arches into rooms that held six enormous casks each. Enough wine to make all London drunk, with the strange fluffy white growths everywhere.

The passage ended at a massive iron door. Holding the candle close, she investigated the lock, then looked to see if a spare key hung somewhere near. No luck.

She feared it would be several hours before Jones made his daily visit, but it was hard to judge. All she could do was wait, despite her agonizing awareness of the passage of time. She set the candle in a holder attached to the wall and began one of Troth's *tai chi* exercises. Calmness now would give her strength later.

Completing one form, she was about to start another when she heard a key grate into the lock. Instantly she blew out the candle and retreated into the shadows, hoping she could dart out the door without having to confront the guard.

It wasn't Mr. Jones. Frederica stepped through with a lantern, followed by her husband. "We really haven't time to stop here," Pierce grumbled. "We run the risk of missing the hanging."

"This will only take a moment, darling. I want to extract every morsel of suffering from that dreadful woman. Think how delightful it will be to tell her the sentence has been commuted, then return later to tell her the sordid details."

As Pierce laughed appreciatively, Alex bit

her lip at the sheer cruelty of Frederica's plan. The two of them together were wicked beyond her imagination.

Pierce swung the door shut and turned to lock it behind him. Alex's heart accelerated at the knowledge she would have to act immediately, because as soon as they reached the empty cell in the back they would know she had escaped.

Wishing she had Troth's *wing chun* skill, she leaped forward with a shout and snatched the key from Pierce's hand, then kicked him in the groin. Howling with agony, he staggered back into his wife, who shrieked and dropped the lantern. It smashed, plunging the scene into darkness.

Alex took advantage of the confusion to dart through the door, slamming it behind her. As she shoved the key into the lock, Pierce began trying to open it from the other side, gasping a stream of filthy curses. She pulled back on the knob with her full weight and hastily turned the key. The bolts slid into place with a well-oiled click.

Through the door, she said menacingly, "You'd better pray I stop the execution in time, or you will both die in unspeakable agony."

Hoping her threat would panic Frederica, she climbed the dimly lit stone steps, wondering where she would come out. When she opened the door at the top, she gasped and almost fell backward down the stairs, blinded by sunlight. She clung to the door a minute, eyes closed, until the first shock wore off.

Slowly she opened her eyes, squinting to block out some of the light. Her first glance was for the sun. It hadn't yet reached its zenith. At a guess, it was between eleven o'clock and eleven thirty. Not yet too late.

Then she studied her surroundings. She'd surfaced in a small building in the corner of a busy shipping yard. Wagons were being loaded and unloaded while horses stamped restively. On the back of the main building a sign read, *Pierce & Co.* This must be Pierce's headquarters on the Ratcliff Highway.

Trying to look as if she belonged, she closed the door and walked across the yard, keeping to the edge opposite the main building. A couple of men glanced at her but didn't ask her business. Even so, she breathed easier when she reached the street.

The livery stable Gavin used regularly was only two blocks away, so she turned left and ran. Despite the exercises she'd done in her cell, she was panting when she reached the stable. She went directly to the office on the left of the entrance.

Fitzgerald, the owner, looked up and turned dead white. "Holy Mother of God!" he gasped as he crossed himself.

"I'm not a ghost, Mr. Fitzgerald. If I was, I'm sure I'd be cleaner and better dressed. I was kidnapped and held prisoner near here." She gulped more breath. "The hanging—it hasn't happened yet, has it?"

Startled recognition showed in the stable owner's face. "Nay, but it won't be long now. Blessed Jesus, what can be done?"

"Would Seabourne still be at the Tower? Or on his way to Newgate?"

"He was to spend last night in the prison. 'Twas said friends might try to free him if he was brought to Newgate today in a carriage."

"Lend me your best horse and I'll ride there myself." She hesitated, knowing the distance wasn't great, but unsure of the route. "Can someone guide me?"

"I'll go myself." He stood. "But my only sidesaddle is broken, my lady."

"I can ride astride," she said impatiently. "But we must go *now*!"

And may God grant that she be in time.

# CHAPTER 38

"It's time, my lord," one of the two constables said respectfully.

"Very well." Gavin finished his tea, a cup of Elliott House's finest. Though he'd consumed a fair amount of brandy during the night, he'd avoided becoming drunk. Obliterating one's last hours seemed a waste.

Strange how hard it was to accept that death was imminent and unavoidable. Usually the end of life came by accident, or crept in with age and disease. There was something monstrously cold-blooded about an execution.

He stood and checked in the mirror that his appearance was presentable, then turned to his companions. Ashburton had left in the early hours to make a last desperate attempt to get the sentence commuted. The other three men looked ready to shatter into small pieces. In some ways this was harder for them than for him.

He shook Lord Michael's hand. "Take care of Katie."

"We will," the older man said gruffly. "She'll know the truth."

To Kyle, Gavin said, "Thanks for . . . everything."

Unable to speak, Kyle gave him a swift, hard hug, then turned away.

Taking Suryo's hand, Gavin said quietly, "You have been more to me than my own father."

"And you have been the son I never had." Suryo bowed over their joined hands. "May Allah guard your soul."

Gavin walked out of the room without looking back. His friends had been granted a place right by the scaffold. He wasn't sure if he was glad or sorry they would be present. There was comfort in knowing men who cared about him would be bearing witness—but it also increased the pain.

As they approached the Debtor's Door,

Gavin heard a rumbling chorus of voices chanting, "Seven, eight, nine . . ." The crowd was counting the tolling bells.

On the twelfth stroke of noon, Gavin and his escorts emerged from the building at the foot of the scaffold, where a line of constables was holding a small area open. In front of him was the largest crowd he'd ever seen. The roar that greeted his appearance rattled the windows. As he climbed the steps to the scaffold, he felt waves of barbarous excitement and sick curiosity beating against him.

Every window of every building in sight showed avid faces of people who'd paid a premium for a good view of the hanging. Thieves and workmen and drunken young bucks, fathers carrying children on their shoulders, enterprising peddlers who'd parked their carts against walls and were charging for the privilege of standing on them.

A constable raised his voice to say, "At one Tyburn hanging, the viewing stand collapsed and a dozen people were killed. The cove who was executed went off with a smile at the sight." Gavin understood the sentiment.

Gathered on the scaffold were the wardens of the Tower and Newgate, the executioner and his assistant, and a grim-faced Lord St. Aubyn. As Lord High Steward, he'd used his authority to suggest that the evidence was far from overwhelming, to no avail. Now he must preside over a sentence that troubled him.

The vicar was also present. "Will you pray with me, Lord Seabourne? For if not, I will surely pray for you."

This time Gavin nodded. What had seemed irrelevant the night before now appeared like a good idea. Two black cushions were produced, and he and the vicar knelt to recite the Lord's Prayer together. Though Gavin had long since lost the habit of churchgoing, his Scottish grandfather had taught him to live a principled life. Was that enough? He hoped so, because he'd always believed a man's acts mattered more than his words. If he hadn't lived well, last-minute repentance was not enough to save his soul.

When he stood again, Gavin recognized that the physical symptoms of fear were taking possession of his body. Pounding pulse, quickened breath, an explosive need for action—all the reactions that would be useful if he were in battle or fighting for his life. Now they only made it excruciatingly difficult to appear calm.

As his hands were tied behind his back, he hoped he would not disgrace himself. When death was all one had left, one wanted to do it well.

St. Aubyn said, "Do you have any last words, Lord Seabourne?"

Gavin had thought to remain silent, but found himself saying, "May God protect the innocent from injustice."

St. Aubyn nodded, his lips tight.

"The hood, my lord?"

Gavin almost refused the executioner's offer, not wanting to blot out his last view of the pale blue autumn sky with its drifting clouds. Then he saw the feverish, eager eyes watching him, and nodded for the hood. If panic contorted his face at the end, at least no one would see.

Despite its looseness, the hood felt suffocating as it cut off his sight. The first of his senses lost. Hearing remained, the hammering of his blood drowning out the blood lust of the crowd. He reached for the mental and emotional discipline he'd learned from

Suryo when he studied the fighting arts of the Islands. With detachment came a measure of peace. All men died; he'd cheated death more than once, and now his time had come. So be it.

The rope was prickly as the noose was fitted around his neck. He wondered if the vicars were right and soon he would be with Alexandra.

That was an outcome worth praying for.

Alex gasped with horror at the teeming crowd that extended out from Newgate. As they reined in their horses, Fitzgerald said, "It don't look good, my lady. You'll go faster afoot."

"Thanks for your help." She vaulted from her mount and began working her way through the crowd. "Please, I must get through!" she called over and over as a bell began to toll the noon hour.

Frantically she tried to force her way through packed bodies. A massive stevedore turned and growled, "What's your hurry?"

"I'm the woman Seabourne was convicted of murdering," she exclaimed. "Please, help me stop them from killing an innocent man!"

The stevedore snorted as he took in her shabby appearance. "You're Lady Seabourne? And I'm the King of England!"

She raised her hand and showed the expensive rings that the Pierces hadn't yet stolen. "Before God, I swear I'm Lady Seabourne. In the name of mercy, help me!"

His expression changed. Turning, he began to force his way toward the scaffold. "Make way, make way!" he boomed. " 'Tis a day for miracles."

She followed close behind him. Between jostling bodies and heads, she caught a quick glimpse of Gavin as his hands were tied behind him. He looked remote and beautiful, untouched by the raucous vulgarity of the crowd. She shouted in an attempt to get the attention of the men on the platform, but there was too much noise for a single voice to be heard.

The stevedore stopped. "I can't go no further, but mebbe you can go over the top if you're game."

Not sure what he meant, she said, "Anything! And thank you."

He grabbed her around the waist and tossed her forward onto the crowd, bellowing, "Help the lady before the damned government makes her a widow!"

Hands caught her and passed her forward in a crazy journey as men laughed and called, "Help the whore along!" Drunken men who thought this a game groped her, but she was getting closer, closer.

Dear God, the noose was going around Gavin's neck!

Her rough passage had her almost to the steps, and suddenly she was looking into the stunned faces of Kyle, Suryo, and her stepfather. "Stop this!" she screamed as she tumbled over the last of the crowd, crashing downward between a pair of startled constables.

"Merciful heaven!" Lord Michael plunged toward her while Kyle and Suryo pivoted and raced up the steps. But as the colonel pulled her into the space at the foot of the stairs she heard the sharp, unmistakably mechanical sound of the trap falling.

Motion slowed as the trap shuddered and fell away from Gavin's feet. The noose tightened with killing swiftness, choking the cry that threatened to rise from his throat.

Then someone cannoned into him, dragging him to one side. The noose was still choking but his feet were on the scaffold, preventing him from falling.

"Hang on!" It was Kyle's voice in his ear.

He tried to protest, unable to imagine the punishment his friend would suffer for interfering with an execution, but he had no breath, he was blacking out from lack of air.

Then the noose suddenly fell away and the hood was wrenched from his head. Dizzily he saw Suryo with a kris, fibers of the rope falling from the wavy edge. And Kyle, speaking as he moved behind Gavin to untie the bonds that held his wrists, but it was impossible to understand the words.

The officials on the platform were in turmoil, and the noise from the crowd had become a clamor that pounded like tidal waves. A tall, shabby woman with a disheveled dark braid falling between her shoulder blades was speaking to St. Aubyn, hands moving vehemently. Then she turned.

Alex. *Impossible. This was the hallucination of a dying man.*

"I'm really here." The hallucination smiled crookedly. "I owed you a rescue."

"Alex." He touched her, feeling solid flesh

beneath his hand. Did spirits feel real to other spirits? "No. You . . . you can't be."

"Believe it, my love." She stepped forward and embraced him, warm and shaking and feeling exactly like Alex. Breath ragged, he wrapped his arms around her and buried his face in her neck.

If this was hell, he wanted to stay forever.

By the time they reached 42 Berkeley Square, Alex was weaving from exhaustion. She'd acquired a variety of bruises in her passage through the crowd, but no matter. After St. Aubyn had ushered everyone into the relative quiet of the prison, she'd explained the plot and handed over the key to the wine vault. St. Aubyn had immediately sent constables to arrest the Pierces, assuring Gavin and Alex that this time, justice would truly be done.

The colonel, after a hug that threatened Alex's ribs, set off for Wales with the promise he'd have Katie and her mother in London within the week. Kyle, jubilant, left for Wrexham House to tell Troth the good news. He promised they'd call, but not until the next day. Gavin's heir, Philip, talked his way into the prison, and shook his cousin's hand with what looked like genuine pleasure. Then, blessedly, Suryo had taken charge of getting Gavin and Alex safely home in St. Aubyn's own carriage.

Throughout it all, Gavin said hardly a word. She guessed that he was still disoriented. What would it feel like to have accepted death, then be rudely jerked back to life? She shuddered when she thought how very, very close she'd come to failing.

Bard blanched when he opened the door and saw two people he thought dead on his doorstep. Alex said, "Suryo, will you please explain to everyone what happened?"

"With pleasure, my lady." Suryo's smile was white against his dark skin as he took Bard off to the servants' hall so everyone could hear the good news at once.

Since Gavin seemed uncertain what to do next, she took his hand and led him upstairs, saying, "All I want is peace and quiet and you."

When they reached the privacy of her room, he turned to her, shaking his head. "I'm still not quite sure you aren't a dying man's fantasy."

"Let me see if I can persuade you otherwise." She walked into his arms, wrapping herself around him. His hands began kneading her as if, piece by piece, he was confirming that she was real. "You'll just have to get used to having me around again, Gavin, because from now on I'm staying very, very close."

Her warm, dearly familiar body began to dissolve his emotional paralysis. "Alexandra." He breathed her name as he mentally tried to define a difference he sensed in her. A good difference. "If I live to be a hundred, nothing will ever match the joy of finding you alive."

"And I you," she whispered, her voice breaking. "It was so close. So terrifyingly close."

"You're a hero, Iskandra. The bravest, most indomitable woman in the world."

She grinned. "And also the most bedraggled. I'm glad I was allowed washing water, or I'd hate to think what my condition would be."

"It wouldn't matter. You're still the most beautiful woman in the world." He kissed her and slowly the warm essence of his wife began to thaw his frozen spirit.

The kiss deepened, and suddenly joy and wonder and passion blazed through his veins. Her response flared to meet his. Tripping each other with impatience, they moved to the bed. He fell backwards onto the mattress, pulling her down on top of him.

"No," she gasped. "Not this time."

For a moment he thought the last terrible weeks had created new fears, but instead of retreating, she locked her limbs around him and rolled over so he was on top of her, his weight pressing her into the mattress. "Today, Gavin, I'm afraid of nothing."

Urgently he tore at their clothing, clumsy with need. Her hips rose to meet his as they came fiercely together. The life he'd thought was over poured through him and into her, scalding and joyous. She cried out, and for an instant he felt their spirits become one. All that she was became part of him, enriching his existence.

They lay panting together for a long time, reluctant to separate. Finally he rolled onto his side, clasping her pliable body to him. She slipped one leg between his and rested her forehead against his cheek, twining them together.

"I've never felt so alive in my life. The very air seems to sing. And you, my dearest love, are magnificent beyond words." He kissed her forehead. "One of the things I regretted most was that I'd never said I loved you. I . . . I thought I'd lost the ability to love deeply, Alexandra. That's why it took so long to recognize."

She gazed at him through her dark lashes. "I had the same problem. I think it's because we did everything backwards. Disaster, marriage, and then love. It wasn't easy to get beyond everything that happened, but now. . . ." She traced the line of his jaw tenderly. "Finding you made everything in the Indies worthwhile."

He laughed. "I wouldn't have minded a boring courtship, but then I don't suppose I'd have fully realized how incredible a woman you are. You're whole now, aren't you? I can feel the difference."

He was right, she realized. The ragged pieces of her spirit had healed, and never again would fear rule her life. "More than whole, my love." She took his hand and placed it on her belly. "I'm quite certain that young Viscount Handley is here."

As he caught his breath, hope and concern in his eyes, she said quietly, "This time everything is going right."

"This time, and forever." He smiled with deep intimacy—her husband, her lover, her mate. "Don't you think we've earned the right to live happily ever after?"

# EPILOGUE

Usually the seating of a new peer in the House of Lords was a quiet matter, but never before had that august chamber received a man whom it had condemned to death. That fact made for an atmosphere that was . . . interesting.

Feeling a deep sense of unreality, Gavin entered the great hall with his two sponsors. He felt absurd in his formal robes of state—how many ermine had died for the glory of the Seabourne rank? Too many. And he'd never worn velvet before in his life.

In need of sanity, he glanced up at the small gallery to find Alex. She was seated between her daughter and mother, in the middle of a larger group of friends and relatives. Troth was there, and Lady Jane Holland, and the Duchess of Ashburton, looking very grand. The sight relaxed him, for in the last months they had become his friends, not merely women of rank and privilege.

Alex wore a necklace featuring the baroque pearl he'd taken from the neck of the Maduri dragon, and she touched it when he looked at her. The gesture was a private reminder that the dragons of the House of Lords paled in comparison to the ones he'd defeated in the past.

He smiled, briefly able to forget the gravity of the day. It had only been a month since the birth of their son, James Michael Elliott, and Alex's Madonna curves were softly luscious. She threw him a kiss, perhaps thinking of the night before, when she'd announced herself more than ready to resume her wifely duties. And she had, with enthusiasm and imagination. . . .

Wrenching his mind away from the intimacies of the night, he studied the seated rows of Britain's aristocracy. Today they were not his judges, but his peers. Many of them were

poker-faced in a way suggesting embarrassment—after all, they'd very nearly executed an innocent man, and in some cases
judgment must have been based on distaste
for his foreignness rather than the facts of
the case. Other expressions were more welcoming, particularly from those lords whose
consciences were clear where Gavin was
concerned.

Traditionally two sponsors of equal rank
introduced a new lord, so Gavin was flanked
by Kyle and his brother, Lord Grahame. It
was startling to see the twins together, iden-
tically dressed. Catching his glance, Kyle
winked. At least, Gavin thought it was Kyle.

First Kyle, then Dominic, gave brief, flattering introductions of the seventh Lord
Seabourne. At this point, Gavin was supposed to take an oath of allegiance to
Crown and country, then quietly sit down.
On some later date he would give his
maiden speech on an uncontroversial topic,
and anyone who spoke after him would offer compliments on the speech. All very or-
derly.

Yet when he stood, once again unreality
crashed in on him. How could a lad who'd
grown up barefoot in Aberdeen be about to

join the House of Lords? How could a blunt American sailor be putting down roots in England? His gaze went to his wife again. Most of all, how could a man who had thought himself incapable of loving again be so lucky as to find a woman like Alexandra?

With sharp insight, Gavin realized that before he could move into this amazing new life he'd chosen, he must turn this ceremony into a statement of who and what he was. Though in the future he would be a dutiful and well-behaved earl, today he would speak his heart.

"My noble lords, this is a most unexpected honor," he said in a voice honed on the open seas. "Having been born in Scotland and raised in America, my mind and heart were shaped by rebellion and republican ideals. I embraced the belief that all men are created equal in the sight of God, and I scorned the concept of a decadent aristocracy."

His gaze swept the chamber. "I was truly horrified to discover that I had inherited an earldom, and that it was as much a part of me as my blood and bone, impossible to disavow. Then this august body judged me, and condemned me to death."

Frowns appeared at his bad taste in bluntly referring to such an awkward matter. He didn't care. He lacked the flourishes of traditional orators who had been trained in rhetoric, and must rely on American directness.

"That was the day when I truly came to respect this chamber and the men seated here. Not for the mistaken verdict that came of my trial, but for the proof that even a peer of the realm is not above British justice. For the first time I recognized that what I love most in America is rooted in British custom and law, and I hope and pray these shared ideals will keep two great nations forever friends.

"British justice and love of freedom have joined with compassion to create a society that is a beacon for the world. It is Britain that has led the fight to end slavery, which is an abomination in the sight of God." His gaze went again to his wife. A lesser woman would be shocked at the way he was speaking out against tradition, but Alex nodded fierce approval.

"In the last decade, the Mother of Parliaments has created reforms to better the lot of men, women, and children throughout this great nation, and the work has only just begun. I hope to join here with other men of goodwill to help shape the Britain of the future—a land where justice, honor, and compassion will prevail."

Though traditionalists among the lords looked pained, the reformers nodded approval. Across the chamber the other American-born peer, Lord Markland, was openly grinning. Today Gavin had claimed his ground, and in the future he would work with men of like mind to build a better world. That was not a bad goal for a man's life.

Solemnly he took the oath of allegiance and became a member of the House of Lords for the rest of his natural life. The remainder of the short session passed quickly, and at the end a group of approving peers surrounded Gavin to shake his hand and welcome him to the House. The Duke of Ashburton said with a glint in his eyes, "Some of the noble lords are already regretting that you cheated the hangman."

Gavin laughed. "They'll regret it more before I'm done."

He was turning to Lord Markland when Alex appeared through an aisle that opened for her through the crowd. Clasping his hand, she said softly, "I am so proud of you, my love."

He gazed into her aqua eyes, forgetting his surroundings in his wonder at how they had found each other. "The greatest prizes are the hardest won," he murmured. Then, because he'd already broken plenty of rules today and might as well break another, he kissed her.

## Author's Note

The East Indies are the world's largest archipelago, with more than thirteen thousand islands sprawling across two million square kilometers of tropical seas. In the early nineteenth century, the cultural range reached from ancient, sophisticated societies to some of the most primitive tribes on earth. Almost seven hundred languages are still spoken in modern Indonesia. While Islam is the dominant religion of the islands, Bali has retained its Hindu traditions, there are pockets of Christianity, and ancient animistic customs are visible almost everywhere.

Given that rich diversity, I've taken the liberty of creating the fictional island of Maduri (not to be confused with the real island of Madura, which is adjacent to Java). The Lion Game is my own invention. Bali has a dance called the *Sanghyang Jaran* that is performed by young boys and involves dancing around and through fire while in a trance, but fire walking as a male rite of passage is also pure imagination on my part.

The Komodo dragon, largest reptile in the world, is real enough and can be extremely dangerous, but since the beasts are apt to spend hours sitting still without so much as a twitch, I devised a specially bred strain of them for fighting purposes.

The wine vaults under the docks were quite real, including the unique white fungus dripping from the roof and the cats who patrol to keep the rat population at bay.

To call the British legal system in the nineteenth century complex is an understatement of massive proportions, so it's not surprising that peers had their own form of justice, including practices different from the standard courts. The Lord Ferrers mentioned in the story was real, almost certainly mad, and hung at Tyburn in 1760 a mere four months after murdering his steward for no good reason. Other cases I've read of peerage trials indicate that usually the lords were disgracefully easy on their own, which is probably why being tried in the House of Lords was abolished in 1935.

And for those of you who are not cat people, they really do deposit dead rodents as a sign of affection for the humans who feed them.